MR MOJO RISIN

keep
your
mojo
risin!
scott

Library of Congress Catalogue-in-Publication Data available on request.

ISBN: 9798417420184

and sons go far away
to lose the fist
their father's hand
will always seem

Leonard Cohen

for all of us, the fathers and the sons

Bill
Scott
Michael
Caleb
Keegan
Wyatt
and
Benjamin

Author's Forward

Times like ours are difficult to navigate without an ethical compass, or worse, with one as moody and self-serving as mine. I loved to watch pro wrestling growing up. Every Saturday afternoon, I'd hunker down in front of the TV and watch epic battles between good and evil. Fifty's too many shades of gray. Our collective longing for simpler times made it inevitable we'd elect a president with a WrestleMania view of the world.

Because the story's set in the 1990s, anachronisms like payphones, video stores, and dial-up modems crop up from time to time. Things change. If you're too young to get the Thomas Brothers reference, ask your parents.

Cheezesteak's offer to help his partner with his wifey problem is meant tongue-in-cheek. Garbage disposals are fine for fingers and food scraps, but for a deserving ex-spouse, you need a wood chipper with enough "chew" for body disposal. Dismembering and partial freezing make clean-up easier.

Karl, the underappreciated and mostly forgotten Marx brother, once repeated a remark by Friedrich Hegel about important people and events appearing twice in history but suggested he neglected to mention the first time as tragedy and the second as farce. What if it happened a third time? If Watergate was a tragedy and Iran-Contra a farce, what would Karl think of a White House scheme to annex Jamaica?

Sometimes the chasm between fact and fiction's shallow and not very wide. The book's premise seemed more off-the-wall when I started than when I finished. Three presumed-dead rock stars have not reemerged as public figures and a Cleveland used car salesman wasn't elected president. If those were the smallest leaps of faith I asked you to take, you'd be getting off easy. Just close your eyes and take my hand.

Oh, and watch that first step.

Prologue

Morrison slept through most of the afternoon but woke in time to meet Alain Ronay for a late lunch at The Mazet. He ordered a *croque monsieur,* and they shared a bottle of white Bordeaux. Morrison barely touched his glass.

Ronay had dinner plans with director Agnès Varda and didn't eat. He sipped wine while Morrison recounted his trip with Pamela through Spain and North Africa -- shopping adventures in Marrakesh, shooting home movies at the Alhambra, a pilgrimage to the Prado to see Bosch's triptych, *The Garden of Earthly Delights.*

"We talked about the *Garden* when we were film students," Ronay reminded him. "You called it a 'deliciously ambiguous riddle.'"

"A picture in a book's one thing, but seeing it in person's an *entirely* different experience." Morrison rocked forward and rested his elbows on the table. "Remember the first panel where God presents Eve like a gift?"

Ronay nodded.

"In the early Renaissance, original sin was a euphemism for lust, but in the Christian creation myth, marriage wasn't invented until *after* Adam and Eve got kicked out of paradise."

"Or so I was taught in Parochial school. I remember Sister Magdalene mentioning something about Eve, a fork-tongued friend, and a misunderstanding involving stolen fruit."

"*Allegedly* stolen fruit."

Ronay smiled. He understood the subtext. Pamela was talking about getting married again, all the more surprising since, for the most part, they'd stopped living together. Their relationship was puzzling even for a lapsed Catholic and self-described "recovering

Frenchman" like Ronay. He started to say something, but the talk of original sin had reminded Morrison of a woman with a snake tattoo he met clubbing, and he launched into the story before Ronay had the chance.

"A few months before I left LA, I was spending a quiet evening at the Whisky with some friends." Ronay arched his eyebrows skeptically but didn't say anything. "We'd just grabbed a table when a stunning blonde sat down beside me. After small talk and a couple beers, we left for her place in Benedict Canyon."

"Not her Hollywood bungalow?"

"Poetic license," Morrison grinned. "Anyway, after we made love, she settled into a pile of pillows, cradled her perfect breasts in her hands, and asked, 'How do you like dem apples?'" He pantomimed the story in such exaggerated gestures, it looked like he was playing a drunken game of charades. Ronay laughed so loudly, he startled the couple at the next table and was still chuckling when the waiter brought Morrison's *croque monsieur*.

He hadn't eaten since lunch the day before and tore into the sandwich, scalding his tongue on the still-bubbling cheese. Morrison gulped down water and fanned his mouth with his hand, provoking another round of laughter. While he ate, they talked more about the *Garden* and vowed to buy an island where they could live communally with like-minded friends, rejecting marriage and practicing free love.

"We should call our republic *La Camaraderie des Amoureux*, the Fellowship of Lovers," Ronay suggested.

"Like Émile Armand, only plural."

Ronay raised his glass in a toast. "The more, the merrier." He glanced at his watch and realized it was almost time he left to meet Varda. After settling the bill, Morrison walked his friend to the Métro. Ronay turned and waved halfway down the stairs. Morrison waved back, neither realizing it was the last time they'd see each other for a very long while.

Morrison walked another couple blocks to the Pont de l'Archevêché and sat on a bench facing Notre Dame. He thought more about their fellowship of lovers and decided the motto should be, "Let the poets decide." Morrison rummaged through the shopping bag he'd been using as a tote and retrieved the leather-bound journal Pamela bought him in Casablanca. He flipped it open to the first page and jotted himself a note.

He sat thinking about his time in France until it was almost dark. One of the things he liked about Paris was he wasn't famous here. Except when he ran into other Americans, Morrison could go where he pleased without being recognized. Being a celebrity was less of a burden because he was less of a celebrity. He was finding the space to re-invent himself, but, as Ronay kept reminding him, the *enfant terrible* had to go.

If not gone, at least he was going. Morrison had shaved his beard and lost more than forty pounds. He still enjoyed an occasional beer or glass of wine but had given up the drunken binges and was writing again. In the eight weeks since getting back from Morocco, Morrison had filled three notebooks.

But living abroad hadn't bridged the growing distance from Pamela. As his stage persona receded, her drug use had spiraled out of control. On their trip to Marseilles, she picked up a kilo of the pink, Chinese heroin she jokingly called "cotton candy" for her drug-dealing lover Count Breteuil. She didn't tell Morrison the brick was in her bag until after they'd boarded their flight. Back in Paris, she partied with friends and burned through her "fee" in less than a week.

When it started to get dark, Morrison walked to the Rock n' Roll Circus, a nightclub on the Rue de Seine. His pace was brisk. The temperature was dropping, and he'd forgotten to bring a sweater.

He sat at the bar and nursed a beer for over an hour. It was early, and the place was mostly empty. The only people he recognized besides the bartenders were Le Chinois and Petit Robert. Both made a point of avoiding him. Two nights before, the three had gotten into an argument over Pamela's drug debt which ended with Morrison poking the diminutive Chinese dealer in the chest and *reminding* him their arrangement had changed. If Le Chinois fronted Pamela dope, he could talk with Breteuil and not him. He was out of the drug pimping business.

Morrison opened his journal and stared at the nearly blank page. Noisy and dark, the nightclub was a poor place for writing. He pulled a fifty-franc note from his pocket, tucked it under the half-empty beer, and headed downstairs to the bathroom.

As he reached for the handrail, he saw Petit Robert palming a baggie of white powder to a scruffy-looking kid in a tie-dye shirt. Morrison turned, backtracked to the bar, and took the shortcut through the kitchen to the Rue Mazarine. Down the adjacent alley, he found a quiet place behind some trashcans to pee.

Morrison was rebuttoning his jeans when he looked up and saw two men hurrying his direction. The hair on the back of his neck jumped to attention. He recognized the taller one from a meeting with his handler. The one he hadn't met looked like a movie gangster. They took up positions on either side of him with their backs to the wall, made no introductions, and didn't offer to shake hands. The American he hadn't met jerked his chin toward the club.

"A couple of Russians are looking for you inside. Two more staked out your place on Rue Beautreillis."

Morrison, failing to grasp the seriousness of the situation, was calculating the best way to get into his apartment to pack when two figures appeared on the opposite end of the alley. Backlit by a streetlamp, he couldn't see their faces clearly. They hesitated, apparently recognizing him. Before they could react, one of the Americans fired first, hitting the stockier Russian twice in the chest. He lurched forward and stumbled headfirst into a stack of produce crates.

"We're outta here now!" the taller spook shouted, and they ran down the alley toward the street. As they turned the corner onto Rue Mazarine, he stopped and, using the nightclub's wall for cover, pinned the surviving Russian down long enough for Morrison and the other agent to scramble into a dark sedan. When his partner revved the engine, he sprinted after them and dove headfirst through the open window into the back seat.

"*Go! Go! Go!*" he shouted. Tires squealing, they roared off along the Seine toward the Pont des Invalides. They were almost to Quai Voltaire when gunfire erupted from a chase car.

"*Get down!*" the driver screamed.

The agent behind him leaned out the window and fired back. Morrison stole a peek in the side view mirror as he slid down in his seat. He glimpsed muzzle flashes and a black Peugeot closing fast. A heartbeat later, the mirror exploded.

Morrison was at a London safe house when he read he'd been found dead in the bathtub of his Paris flat. Details were sketchy, but the cause of death was reported as "heart failure." He roughly folded the paper and tossed it onto the table, partially covering the remains of three breakfasts.

His freshly cut hair was tucked snugly into a baseball cap pulled down nearly to his eyebrows. Being shot at had convinced him of the importance of keeping a low profile. Even inside, he only took off the cap and sunglasses to sleep. The flight from Heathrow to Dulles was two hours away. Morrison finished his juice and wondered if there was enough time to shower.

It would be two and a half decades before anyone outside a small circle at the CIA knew what happened next.

1

Morrison bolted awake in the dark room, his heart jackhammering in his chest. His raspy breathing sounded like sobs. Maybe he was crying. He couldn't be sure.

The old Indian in the dream seemed so real, he was surprised he wasn't hovering beside the bed. Morrison probed every shadow until convinced nobody was there. As he reached for the water on the nightstand, he glanced at the clock.

"A little after four," he mumbled softly.

Morrison slipped on a pair of jeans and a baggy flannel shirt and tiptoed downstairs without turning on the lights. He'd lived alone for nearly a decade, but well-worn ways die hard. Since officially he was dead, it seemed appropriate to knock around the rambling Virginia farmhouse like a ghost.

The leaves on the scarlet maples and willow oaks along the fence line were beginning to turn. Daytime temperatures were warm, but things got chilly after the sun set. Not ambitious enough to haul firewood from the cord stacked against the garage, Morrison rolled newspapers into logs, lit them with a wooden match, and settled into the comfortable leather chair by the fireplace. Jaxx trotted in and curled up at his feet. Morrison reached down and scratched the red, husky-looking mutt behind the ear. Within minutes, a week of *The Washington Post* was burning merrily in the oversized stone hearth.

Morrison had been on edge even before the dream. It started with a call from Carver Hawkings, Latin America section chief when he was at Langley. Hawkings phoned after dinner as he was finishing the dishes. He still checked in from time to time to make sure Morrison hadn't fallen into "the long-suffering-artist abyss." It started as more or less a social chat, which was troubling in itself. Hawkings was the most purposeful man Morrison had ever met. It was almost a relief when the conversation turned serious.

"General McCullough called last month about somebody else in the program. I didn't give it much thought until he phoned again today and asked about another of your friends."

Morrison hesitated, processing the *"friends"* remark. "Why would McCullough come snooping around after all these years?" He didn't expect a real answer, just a chance to gauge Hawkings' response.

"I really couldn't say."

Morrison bit his lip. He didn't expect a career spook to give up secrets easily, but Hawkings would have known why or tasked somebody to find out. Either way, Morrison knew there was no point pursuing it further.

It was troubling Hawkings made a point of keeping him on a need-to-know basis after deciding he didn't need to know much. Before he said goodbye, Hawkings reminded him to watch his back the way he always did. Morrison tried to make sense of the call, but his efforts brought no more insight than his vision of the old Indian.

Jaxx, who had fallen asleep, whimpered softly.

He's having bad dreams too.

Morrison rocked forward and jabbed at the fire with the poker. "Watch your back, Cowboy," he mumbled. He'd heard that often enough around the Agency to know the difference between watching his back and looking back. When Morrison glanced over his shoulder, what he saw made him uneasy.

He stared at the fire, his thoughts wandering to a familiar game he often played in late-night vigils by the fireplace: wondering how life would have turned out if only he'd done things differently -- not that it really mattered now that she was dead. He slumped in his chair, unable to make peace with Pamela's memory any more than he'd been able to make peace with Pamela.

Whenever she stopped drinking, even for a day or two, he convinced himself this time was for good. Every relapse made believing the next time that much harder. The behavior became so ingrained, waiting became second nature.

Morrison poked at the fire again before heading to the kitchen. Jaxx stood and stretched and traipsed along behind him. As he was reaching for the light switch, somewhere down the street, a dog howled. Jaxx growled softly, his ears coming to attention. The howling set off the dog next door, then another and another, until every dog in the neighborhood was barking.

"Christ. It *is* catching. And now you've all got it." Morrison shuffled across the kitchen to the fridge for milk without turning on the lights.

He made himself hot chocolate and slid into his usual place at the chunky, oak table he and Pamela bought at an antique store in Chambersburg. When they couldn't agree on chairs, they hired a handyman to build a booth around it. Pamela fashioned throw pillows from gingham she found at a fabric store in Falls Church.

For the first ten years after Langley brought him in, Morrison worked in the Latin American Section monitoring Caribbean nationalist movements. The Agency would never again allow the region's modest democratic whims to run contrary to the interests of sugar, rum, coffee, bananas, gambling, cocaine, or prostitution. America's policy in the region could be summed up in three words: *no more Cubas.*

He obsessed over the work, but the daily routine wore on him. Nearly eight years after the Agency brought in Pamela, Morrison lobbied for school. After months of badgering, Hawkings finally relented.

Morrison wanted to teach college literature and enrolled at Georgetown in the graduate program. His studies focused on late nineteenth-century French writers: Collette, Artaud, Rabelais, and, of course, Rimbaud. He wore his hair short and hid behind sunglasses and a baseball cap. Aside from quarterly meetings with his faculty advisor, he kept to himself.

The isolation felt familiar. Morrison was used to being alone. Over the years, he and Pamela had become less and less a couple as their relationship transitioned from awkward to indifferent. At first, the little things stopped bothering him. Then he stopped caring about the big things too. One night, while he was working on his thesis, a paper on Rimbaud's poem "*Le Bateau ivre,*" she swallowed a fistful of sleeping pills.

Morrison found her unconscious on the bathroom floor, stuck his finger down her throat until she threw up, and dialed 9-1-1. As he carried her downstairs, he listened to her shallow breathing and reassured himself she was still alive. He laid her on the foyer rug, propped her feet on the landing, and sat beside her, helpless and afraid, waiting for the paramedics. The half-hour it took the ambulance to arrive was the longest thirty minutes of his life.

He squeezed her hand the whole ride to the hospital. Halfway there, Pamela opened her eyes and squeezed back. She was talking by the time they wheeled her into the ER and told the admitting nurse she had food poisoning. While orderlies helped Pamela to her room, the doctor pulled Morrison aside and asked if she'd been depressed. He thought about it for a moment and shook his head. Later, as he watched her sleeping, he realized he had no idea.

When she was discharged the next morning. Morrison called a cab from the payphone in the lobby. They waited outside in a light drizzle until the taxi arrived. He gave the driver their address and slumped against the seat. By the time they reached the state highway, he'd fallen asleep.

Morrison woke to the crunch of tires on the gravel driveway. He paid the cabbie and helped Pamela up the porch steps. She shuffled unsteadily inside, leaning against him for support.

As soon as the door closed, Pamela collapsed on the floor, promising between sobs to get help. She cried so hard, Morrison teased hours later after dinner, he thought about lining up animals two-by-two. He sat beside her, cradling her in his arms, and reassured her everything would be okay. Her eyes puffy and red, Pamela nodded. Too tired to climb the stairs to the bedroom, they slept on the couch most of the afternoon.

Morrison skipped classes and stayed home all weekend. After a couple days, his efforts felt forced. Going through the motions had overtaken genuine concern. Although he didn't see it at the time, she probably sensed that, too.

Before long, they slid back into old habits. They pretended nothing happened, quietly resettling into comfortable discomfort. Neither spoke about her *accident* again. They'd already stopped listening to each other. Finally, they stopped talking too.

Morrison studied the haggard reflection in the window glass. Had she sounded sincere about getting help or had he just quit caring? He still woke some nights, his face half-buried in the pillow, and reached across the bed knowing she was never going to be there.

After Pamela died, he stopped working on his dissertation. Nearly a decade later, he was alone in a dark house, holed up like a hermit with the discomforting memory of his dead wife and a mutt dog for company.

"What a long, strange trip it's been," he muttered quietly.

Jaxx wagged his tail and looked up expectantly. As he leaned over to scratch behind his ear, Morrison recalled the dream. A fragment floated up through gauzy layers of remembering. He closed his eyes, picturing the shaman's face, and wondered why he would summon him to Las Vegas.

Was the dream a wish or a fear?

That's what Alain Ronay would've asked. Morrison smiled. He hadn't thought of his old friend in years. People from that life seemed less real than the Indian. He was staring out the window when a chill rooted in the small of his back and crawled up his spine. He cocked his head to one side, his eyes chasing shadows through the dark.

No one there, he reminded himself. The dream and the colonel's call had spooked him more than he realized.

As he sipped his hot chocolate, motion detectors along the fence line triggered the security system. He jumped up, punched in the code to silence the alarm, and grabbed the Sig Sauer from the drawer by the phone. Morrison's heart pounded in his ears. His throat was dry, his breathing shallow. Maybe the colonel called so he knew where to find him. A single word ricocheted through his thoughts.

Assassin.

Four-Star General Abrams McCullough, the chairman of the Joint Chiefs, peeled back the foil on a fresh roll of Wint-O-Green Lifesavers, wedged one loose with his thumbnail, and flipped it into his mouth. As he ground it between his back teeth, the feral noise escaping his lips was close to a growl. The general found candy a poor substitute for the cigars he had flown in on the weekly shuttles from Guantanamo.

A barrel-chested bulldog of a man, he was accustomed to having things his way but was still subject to regulations against smoking in government buildings. Detectors in the Pentagon were so sensitive every time he thought about lighting up, emergency fire teams came running.

"Sweet Jesus," he groused. "What's the point of being the most powerful man in the world if I can't smoke a cigar in my own office?" When he spoke, you could hear the lilting Scottish brogue of his forefathers.

Colonel Hunley Timkins, the general's aide, barely looked up from the file he was reviewing on NATO training exercises. He was keeping a low profile. McCullough was in a foul mood.

"It's just not right," McCullough grumbled. "I can start wars, send a hundred-thousand men to their deaths, and rewrite the political map of the planet, but at my own desk, I can't even smoke 'em if I got 'em."

"It's a cold, cruel world," Timkins agreed, prudently neglecting to mention it was Congress's job to start wars.

McCullough directed his blistering stare at the humidor on his desk. "That Simms guy's out of the country, right?"

"Yes, sir," Timkins answered for the third time that morning. "The vice president left yesterday for a trade conference in Jakarta."

"Right," the general grunted, remembering he'd asked before. McCullough tried to recall if Jakarta was in Africa or South America. He plucked a cigar from the humidor and slid it back and forth under his nose. *Africa*, he decided. Jakarta sounded African. Either way, he found the vice president's troublesome notions of public service inconvenient and was glad to have the nosy do-gooder out of the way.

McCullough checked his watch. There was still nearly an hour before the president's briefing. He glanced at the open file on his desk and stared at a glossy eight-by-ten of the country's chief executive. McDannold was in his standard pose, hands on his hips, head back, huge smile. He looked like he was mugging for a toothpaste billboard.

"Can you believe that grinning idiot's president?" McCullough didn't notice his aide smirking as he dutifully nodded in agreement. Timkins knew what he meant. *Why the hell aren't I president?*

The future commander-in-chief vaulted into the public eye after stumbling into the wrong place at the right time. It was mid-spring, 1996, and McDannold was working as the sales manager at a used car lot in suburban Cleveland. One evening, after months of pestering, Betsy Callahan, the company number cruncher, reluctantly agreed to join him for drinks. Indifferent to his feeble attempts at getting into her panties, she left after a basket of wings and a Long Island Iced Tea and was snug in bed in time for *Letterman.*

McDannold stayed, guzzling scotch until the tables around him were stacked with chairs and the floors mopped. Two busboys carried him to his red Corvette, tipped themselves ten dollars each from his wallet, and wedged him inside. Too drunk to find his way home, he drove around aimlessly until he ran out of gas in front of an eight-story, black-glass building emblazoned with the Vulva Corporation's garish gold logo.

21

As he staggered inside looking for a place to pee, McDannold stepped over a gym sock wedged in the jam to keep the door open. The lock had been jimmied by Virgil Thibodeaux, the only member of the Nude Mice Army with any work experience, a brief but checkered career in breaking and entering. After relieving himself in a wicker wastebasket, McDannold retraced his steps to the exit. As he left the building, his heel caught on the sock, and he dragged it halfway to his car. When the door slammed shut behind him, Virgil and four other "soldiers" were trapped inside.

McDannold squeezed himself back into his Corvette and passed out, face-planting hard enough against the steering wheel to set off the alarm. When police responded to a noise complaint, they found the Nude Micers trying to bust out an office window with a desk chair. Suspects were taken into custody, and the accidental hero chauffeured home in a black-and-white. None of the subsequent news reports mentioned McDannold, who threw up twice in the backseat, pleaded with officers to "hit the lights and siren" the entire ride.

The next morning, a local radio station aired the Nude Micers pre-recorded cassette left in the night-drop. In the garbled manifesto, the self-proclaimed eco-terrorists ranted the break-in was to expose Vulva's complicity in "crimes against the environment."

At a hastily called press conference, the corporation's PR director denied allegations of wrongdoing. She repeatedly referenced the company's pioneering work protecting banana slug habitat and reminded the few reporters in attendance that Pax Vulva, the chairman of the board, was a longtime member of the Sierra Club.

Anthony "Fat Tony" Venetti, a New York City olive oil importer, cement contractor, and father of Anthony, Jr., another Nude Micer, hired the most expensive lawyers money could rent and sentences were plea-bargained down to a few hours of community service. As the dust was settling, a stringer for the *National Enquirer* discovered Virgil's father was Garland Thibodeaux, United States

Senator from Mississippi and late-night televangelist on the Jesus Broadcasting Network.

A CNN program director stumbled across the piece thumbing through the tabloid while waiting in line to buy dental floss, a six-pack of Diet Coke, and a rotisserie chicken. What started as a blurb in the *Enquirer* wound up a featured talking point on the morning show.

Other networks picked up the story. Fox News flashed cartoonish images of Virgil Thibodeaux's buzz-cut hair, scruffy goatee, and well-practiced snarl to TV screens across the country. They characterized the Nude Micers as "fiendish and diabolical" and lauded McDannold's quick thinking and decisive action. By dinnertime, Fox had proclaimed him "America's Vigilante Anti-Terrorist."

Not to be out scooped, CNN jumped back in with special correspondents Wolf Blitzer and Christiane Amanpour saturating the airways with field reports every ten minutes. By the following day, the story dominated coverage on every network. News crews flew to Cleveland from every corner of the globe and took turns interviewing each other, interrupting regularly scheduled programming.

During the weeklong media blitz, McDannold was featured on a *Sixty Minutes* segment and sat with Larry King two nights in a row before hitting the talk show circuit. He began with Arsenio and worked his way through Maury, Rikki, Geraldo before peaking with Oprah. Charming and vacuous, he was TV gold, as marketable as the second coming of the Hula Hoop.

With the financial support of Tarrant Rush, the billionaire Texas oilman, cattle rancher, and founder and CEO of the Jesus Broadcasting Network, a team of handlers coalesced around him, shaping his public image, and coaching him not to take policy positions on any issue. In his weekly editorial, a shill at the *Cleveland Plain Dealer* dubbed him "the prairie populist." The next day McDannold announced he was forming the Bullwinkle Party, choosing the name over the objections of his advisors, and mounting a third-party run for the White House.

With early polls pegging his support at less than four percent, few pundits took him seriously, but the national electorate, frustrated with politics as usual, quietly flocked to the fresh face from America's heartland. Dismissive of his surging popularity, the major party candidates, embroiled in a firestorm of personal attacks against each other, ignored him.

During the primaries, the eventual Republican nominee, South Carolina Senator Wallace Hartley, promised his administration would fight for the rights of all *real* Americans and ship any sodomite, wetback, or shanty Irishman to their ancestral homeland if they so much as jaywalked. But he saved his most passionate vitriol for those whose family trees traced their roots to the "Dark Continent."

At the national convention, Hartley declared it was "high time America elected a president willing to call a spade a spade" and suggested, "seeing how *those* people whine about how their forefathers were brought here against their will, they shouldn't mind being shipped back the same way."

For his running mate, he chose Mississippi Senator and cable televangelist Garland Thibodeaux. Their platform included making the Bible the primary public-school textbook, bombing America's enemies foreign and domestic back to the Stone Age, and repealing the amendments that abolished slavery and granted women the right to vote. Hartley also threw his unbridled support behind Thibodeaux's efforts to add former Vice President Spiro Agnew to Mount Rushmore.

Hartley proposed building a hundred-foot-high wall from Peace Arch State Park in Blaine, Washington to the West Quoddy Head lighthouse in Lubec, Maine to halt the flow of cheap prescription drugs from Canada. He threatened to station National Guardsmen shoulder-to-shoulder at the border with orders to "shoot first and ask questions never."

During a campaign speech in Climax, Minnesota, Hartley vowed to create a special task force to prosecute bootleg Viagra smugglers. "It's the patriotic duty of every American," he declared, "to pay full price for erections lasting four hours or more."

Hartley characterized Canadians, scathingly referred to as "Canuckleheads," as a mongrelized race of "Dudley Do-Nothings," promised an executive order requiring all Canadian bacon sold in the US be labeled "Liberty Bacon," and suggested the Democratic nominee, whose father played club hockey in Boston, was born in Toronto.

The campaign's anti-Canadian rhetoric was inflamed when an alleged plot to kidnap the Baldwin brothers by a Shania Twain-led terror cell was widely reported in pro-Hartley media outlets.

With his hawkish nose, sunken eyes, and long, asymmetrical face, the Republican candidate looked like a short, clean-shaven Abraham Lincoln. He wore lifts on the campaign trail and stood on his tiptoes for photographs. Negotiations for a televised debate broke down when the two sides couldn't agree on the height of the soapbox the diminutive Hartley could stand on.

The campaign platform of his Democratic counterpart, J. Wesley Woodward, the bookish two-term governor of Massachusetts, included a government-funded program to provide hyperbaric nap chambers for preschoolers and subsidized Zumba classes for every American over the age of twelve. Woodward proposed setting aside April as Zombie Apocalypse Awareness month and vowed to make Orville Redenbacher Day, July 16th, a national holiday. At a rally in Bucksnort, Tennessee, he told followers his administration would sponsor a bill requiring gun lobbyists undergo an extensive background check before they could buy a congressman.

Backed by a Hollywood coalition that included nearly the entire cast and crew of the soon-to-be-released movie *Men In Black*, Woodward told supporters if elected, he'd grant extraterrestrials resident alien status.

When challenged about proposed cuts to the defense budget, Woodward suggested bake sales as a funding alternative and promised to expand the cabinet to include an astrologer. On a campaign stop in Suqantum, New Hampshire, a town meeting was delayed for an hour while Duane Littlefoot, a Lakota medicine man and the party's vice-presidential candidate, cleansed the dais and podium with a smoldering bundle of sweetgrass and wild sage.

When he crisscrossed the country for campaign rallies, Hartley rarely used his opponent's name, instead referring to him as "that tofu-eating, Martian lover." He lampooned Woodward's proposed amnesty program for extraterrestrials, saying, "no God-fearing American would give little green cards to little green men." While stumping in California's Inyo County, he promised to revitalize the local economy by reopening Manzanar, the World War II Japanese internment camp, as a processing center for off-planet relocations.

Hartley was invited by ICE officers to use the arrest of an illegal alien as a photo op during a campaign swing through southern California. Armed with assault rifles, a swarm of agents kicked in the door and stormed a beachfront Malibu home where celebrity chef Wolfgang Puck was catering a fundraiser for Habitats for Hipsters, a group providing low-cost housing for people too cool to get jobs. After identifying and detaining the terrified server, an aspiring actor from Ottawa, Kansas, agents realized he wasn't actually Canadian.

Undeterred by the mix-up, Hartley stormed off-script that evening in Tarzana, whipping a crowd of supporters into a frenzy with a diatribe peppered with racial epithets. He called the DNC chairman the n-word and snarled Disneyland's *It's a Small World* ride needed "a good, ethnic cleansing."

The Democratic nominee was equally combative, calling his opponent a "blood-thirsty warmonger" and the recent red-state spike in cow mutilations (with graphic, hourly updates on Fox News) "a saber-rattling attempt to undermine intergalactic relations." On the campaign trail, he regularly referred to Hartley as "that pipsqueak" and his army of youthful campaign workers with shaved heads and swastika tattoos as "brown shirts" and likened his opponent's rabid campaign rallies to lynch mobs.

Attacks by the Republican and Democratic nominees were vicious, personal, and relentless, but their antics did not play well in Peoria or Pawtucket, Pascagoula, Pocatello, Pahrump, Parsippany, or any of the nation's thirteen Palmyras. Even voters in Petticoat Junction soured on the tactic.

The Hartley-Thibodeaux ticket did generate a small but devoted following among white inmates at the Pelican Bay Supermax, and Littlefoot swung at least one vote to the Democratic side of the ledger when he was stumping in Pyote, Texas and mistakenly passed out a mescal button instead of a campaign button.

A week before the election, Hartley and Woodward were arrested along with a busload of Taiwanese businessmen and a dozen blonde hookers during a Clark County, Nevada vice raid. Every news outlet in the country carried photographs of the candidates being led off in handcuffs and gorilla suits. Newspapers ran the story under banner headlines like "The King Kong Bust." Photographs depicting more sexually explicit situations appeared in the tabloids.

Flanked by his spouse and their three adult children, Woodward made a tearful public apology on the front steps of the couple's Beacon Hill home. His wife Bethany stood stoically beside her husband, staring at her shoes. She made no attempt to comfort him when he fell to his knees and sobbed uncontrollably.

The Republican nominee's wife was a no-show for his spectacularly brief press conference. Hartley bristled when a *New York Times* reporter asked a question and threatened "to hunt down the peckerwood who took those pictures and nail his ass to a tree." As he stormed out, the packed room of reporters agreed he was hot enough to fry the egg on his face.

Neither campaign recovered. McDannold won in a landslide.

McCullough set aside the president's photo and leafed through the file until he came to the notes from his chat with CIA Deputy Director Hawkings. Results for the current test subject, James "Jimi"

Hendrix, were impressive, but he consistently demonstrated a lax attitude toward military protocols. The general agreed with the assessment of Hendrix's platoon sergeant during his thirteen-month stint in the army: he would never measure up to the standards required of a soldier.

McCullough had decided to bring in the other two as a contingency plan. Since one was an admiral's son and the other had faithfully fulfilled his Army commitment, he figured Morrison and Presley would have a more patriotic grasp of the situation. He tossed the file into his briefcase and snapped it shut.

"An intelligence briefing," McCullough grumbled, uncomfortable mixing the president and intelligence in the same thought. "Delivering technology to that bozo's an act of lunacy."

"Yes, sir, it is," Timkins reminded him, "but it's also our job."

McCullough grumbled something under his breath and glanced at his watch. "Well, we better get going. I'm as ready as I'll ever be."

Timkins buzzed the front desk and told the driver to bring the Lincoln around. McCullough plucked two cigars from the humidor and slid them into his pocket. There weren't any damn smoke detectors in his Town Car.

Morrison scooted across the floor on his stomach, rotated his body as he sat up, and slid backward under the table until his spine pressed against the wall. He maneuvered into the corner and folded his knees against his chest. His arm brushed against the booth, and the coolness of the wood startled him. He took a deep breath and reminded himself to stay calm.

He had no idea who was out there or what they might want. There were lots of questions under the kitchen table but no answers. A security monitor was bolted to the underside of the cabinet next to the sink. Morrison collected his courage, rocked forward on all fours, and crept to the edge of the booth.

The screen showed a schematic of the property. Motion detectors plotted the steady but erratic progress of a blinking dot approaching the front door. Jaxx ambled over and licked his face. The two were at eye level.

"Probably the old Indian," he whispered, glad for the dog's company.

Had Langley sent someone to tidy up loose ends? They'd already killed him once. How hard would it be to kill him again? The more he puzzled over it, the less plausible that seemed. The Agency installed the security system and would have built in a back door. Even if they hadn't, it seemed unlikely anybody they sent would be clumsy enough to trip an alarm.

The route plotted by the dots looked almost random. Maybe a white-tailed deer had wandered onto the property. As the intruder came into range of the night vision cameras, Morrison stood for a closer look. Everything appeared in shades of green. He couldn't make out many details, but his guest was clearly human.

His face inches from the screen, Morrison tried to squint the figure into focus. He looked to be in his late fifties. He was wearing jeans, a baggy, tunic-style shirt, and Birkenstock sandals with no socks. His shoulder-length hair was parted down the middle and pulled back in a ponytail. A backpack was slung over one shoulder.

Morrison grabbed extra magazines from the drawer and stashed them in his pocket, his attention flitting back and forth between the monitor and the Sig. The gun's weight felt comforting. He pulled back the slide to chamber a round and sighted the silhouette on the TV down the barrel.

"What do you think, Jaxx? We going to have to shoot this one?" The dog cocked his head to one side but didn't answer. His guest appeared unarmed, but with his loose-fitting shirt, it was hard to tell. He had soft, hound-dog eyes and didn't look very sinister. Morrison set the gun down long enough to finish his hot chocolate.

The porch cameras clicked on as his visitor tripped over a tangle of cottonwood roots and stumbled forward, pin-wheeling his arms before crashing face-first into a pile of leaves. He picked himself up and looked around, trying to get his bearings. His wide-eyed expression suggested more wonder than pain or embarrassment. If he was a spook or a burglar, he was doing a good job disguising his skills. He raked the leaves from his hair with his fingers and started toward the house, stumbling again when the motion detectors switched on the porch lights.

Morrison thumbed the safety off and then on again and tucked the Sig into the back of his waistband. Shooting somebody for showing up without an invitation was beyond inhospitable. It was downright rude. As he walked through the living room, he heard footsteps on the porch. He undid the locks and pulled open the door before his guest had a chance to knock.

The man on his welcome mat brushed back a lock of white hair and stuck out his hand. "Mr. Morrison, I presume."

As Morrison offered his in return, his jaw dropped. The color drained from his cheeks. The man shaking his hand was Elvis Presley.

2

Morrison reached behind his back and squeezed the grip but left the Sig snuggled in his waistband. He slipped his finger inside the trigger guard and surveyed the heavily wooded yard. Half-crouching in a shooter's stance, he motioned Elvis inside with a quick jerk of his head.

"It's okay," Presley said softly. "I came alone."

Morrison's shoulders slumped. "Please, come in." He tried to sound confident but stole a glance over his shoulder as Elvis stepped inside.

Jaxx, usually suspicious of strangers, jumped around excitedly until Elvis knelt and patted him on the head. Morrison led them to the kitchen but stopped in the doorway, staring out the window. Wrestling with the urge to close the curtains, he flipped the switch, flooding the room with light.

"Please, sit down." As he nodded toward the booth, an uninvited thought came to him: he'd read somewhere most important decisions were made at the kitchen table, though he had no idea what he and Elvis had to talk about, much less decide.

"You're Elvis Presley?" he stammered.

"Yes," Elvis answered with the slightest trace of a drawl. "I guess I am."

"I mean, you're *him*."

Elvis smiled. "I'm right here. You don't need to talk about me in the third person. You make me sound mythic."

"You *are* mythic. You're the King."

Elvis took off his backpack and slid into the booth. "Well, if I was, I abdicated a long time ago."

"You're *Elvis Presley*," Morrison repeated, this time more a statement than a question.

"And you're Jim Morrison."

Elvis's words hit him with surprising force. Morrison hadn't realized how much he thought of his rock-and-roll self in the third person as well. He glanced up and caught his reflection in the window glass. The face staring back looked tired and a little sad.

"Jim Morrison," he mumbled as if his name was a kind of puzzle. He considered it for a moment before pushing the thought aside and settling into host duties. "Can I get you something? You hungry? Thirsty?"

Elvis rooted through his backpack for a box of herbal tea and handed it to Morrison. "This would be fine."

Morrison lit the burner under the kettle. While the water warmed, he set the teapot on the table, rinsed his cup, and grabbed a second mug from the cupboard. He'd decided to switch to tea so his guest would feel more at home, though Elvis didn't seem the least bit uncomfortable. Morrison, however, remained ill at ease.

When the kettle whistled, Elvis, who'd been quietly munching seaweed crackers from his backpack, added bags to the teapot. Morrison poured in hot water and left it on the table to steep. After the tea had had a chance to brew, Elvis wrapped the handle in a dishtowel and filled their mugs. Morrison stared suspiciously at the steaming cup as if it held a dangerous narcotic.

"Can I borrow your phone?"

Looking puzzled, Morrison nodded.

Elvis pulled a battered laptop from his backpack, unraveled several feet of phone cord, and jacked it into the wall. There was the distinctive crackle and hum of the modem connecting as he huddled over the keyboard, typing furiously. Jaxx hopped up on the bench and snuggled his head in Elvis's lap. After quietly watching for several minutes, Morrison's curiosity overwhelmed his reluctance to interrupt him.

"So, you just *happened* to be in the neighborhood?"

"No," Elvis answered without looking up. "But I guess you're wondering what brought me to this particular neck of the woods."

"Well, I'm not sure where you came from, but I'm guessing *here* was out of your way."

Elvis scratched absentmindedly behind the dog's ear. "The CIA recruited you and me as part of a courier network. We toured extensively. It was the perfect cover."

Network. Morrison stared intently at his tea. He was thinking about the colonel's reference to *somebody else* in the program.

Elvis pushed his laptop aside. "Then one day, it started to unravel. You were one of the first loose threads. A sleeper, a deep-cover Soviet agent, stumbled on the ring." He spoke matter-of-factly, no hurt or anger in his voice, no sinister undertones, no drama.

"A sleeper?"

Elvis nodded. "Ed Sullivan."

Morrison's face scrunched into a fist. "The guy who freaked when I sang *higher* on national television was a Soviet agent?"

Elvis nodded again. "The same Ed Sullivan, who insisted on waist-up camera angles of my gyrating hips. Politics and censorship make for strange bedfellows."

As Morrison poured more tea, he wondered how many rock-and-roll couriers it took to make a network. The question troubled him, but Elvis's manner made asking seem intrusive. Instead, he sat quietly, his thoughts wandering to an evening more than two and a half decades ago.

"My last night in Paris, a couple Agency guys met me in a dark alley and told me I was a number one hit with a Russian kill squad."

"Number one with a bullet?"

"Several bullets, actually." Morrison held up his hands, palms forward, index fingers erect, the others curled back, the tips of his thumbs touching to form the bottom of a box. He closed his left eye like a director lining up a shot.

"Cold-war morality play, nighttime Paris, exterior street scene. Two sinister-looking sedans, American agents in a Renault and a KGB hitman in a Peugeot blast away at each other in a chase sequence down the Champs-Élysées. They run red lights and trade paint with a motorcycle cop who radios for backup. In an instant, half of Paris's finest are in pursuit.

"They're almost to the Arc de Triomphe when traffic slows. The Renault turns down a narrow side street, careening off other cars like billiard cushions. In a frantic attempt to escape, the driver jumps the curb and races along the sidewalk. Terrified pedestrians scatter like bowling pins, diving out of harm's way at the last possible moment. Spilled stands of fruits and vegetables, overturned bakery carts, and tangled knots of café tables and chairs lie strewn in their wake. Zoom to a basket of baguettes exploding in a hail of bullets, showering an elderly man in a black beret with bread shrapnel.

"In a mad dash down an alley, the Peugeot gets wedged between the wall and a delivery truck. The Renault disappears around the corner, stops long enough for our hero and his accomplice to jump out and disappear down a Métro stairway, and then speeds out of sight." Morrison folded his hands, one over the other, on the table. "Fade to black."

Elvis applauded quietly. "Followed by your death and subsequent resurrection."

Morrison nodded. "Sounds romantic, right?"

"Kinda."

"Well, it was scary as hell. Except for Pamela, you're the only person I've ever told that story."

"That's not surprising. Word getting around would pretty much defeat the purpose."

Morrison glanced again at his reflection in the window glass. "Leaving behind the rock-and-roll lifestyle was hard, especially at first. Being isolated at Langley didn't help. Everyone in my section was gung-ho ex-military or a whiz-kid analyst. There was nobody to talk to, but who would understand better than the King?"

Elvis shrugged. "If you hung on any longer, you'd have wound up fat, fringed, and strung out in Vegas doing two shows a night." His eyes twinkled with mischief. "Besides, my records sell better than ever now. Who knew dying could be such a great career move?"

Morrison smiled, picturing himself strutting across a stage in glitter and spandex. "Now that the KGB's history, maybe we can be public figures again."

"Maybe, but there's work to be done first." Elvis was studying his laptop. It might have been a holdover from his Langley days, but Morrison couldn't bring himself to wonder out loud what those important things might be.

"So, how did you get here?"

"On a Moped," Elvis answered as if it should have been obvious.

Morrison grinned. The image of Presley riding a motor scooter struck him as comical. He noticed for the first time the sweat-creased layers of dirt on his neck and face and realized his arrival on the front porch had been a determined pilgrimage.

"No, I meant *how* did you know where to find me?" He was thinking again about the colonel's call.

"Cosmo."

Morrison rocked back in his chair, wondering who Cosmo might be.

Elvis typed something on his keyboard before looking up. "He says it's critically important we get to Vegas."

Morrison surprised himself and warmed to the idea immediately. Excited by the prospect of a cross-country road trip, he jumped up and rubbed his hands together. "Well, I guess I'd better pack." He kept the dream to himself. The whole Vegas-as-the-destination was probably a weird coincidence. Things were strange enough without throwing gasoline on that fire.

Elvis cocked his head to one side as if listening to a voice only he could hear. There was the faintest suggestion of a smile in the corners of his mouth. "We're meeting somebody," he said softly. "We need to hurry."

Abrams McCullough stood beside the oversized bookcase in the president's study and ran his finger along a shelf of leather-bound books. They were classics to the casual observer, but the general knew better: they were props, cozy bits of set decor for McDannold's carefully scripted fireside chats.

"I doubt he reads anything but the Sunday comics," McCullough grumbled.

Too preoccupied to hear him, McDannold spooned another mouthful of Cherry Garcia out of the container. Dressed in pajamas and a navy robe, he was watching Wile E. Coyote strap an Acme rocket to his back and light the fuse. It roared into the sky and disappeared. An instant later, an explosion flashed in the distance, and a mushroom cloud sprouted on the horizon line. McDannold bounced up and down on the couch, the epaulets on his robe flailing wildly. He pointed at the TV and hooted until tears rolled down his cheeks.

When the program broke for a commercial, McDannold stared blankly at the screen. With a what-can-you-do shrug, he set down the pint of Ben & Jerry's, scooped out a glob of ice cream with an Oreo, and stuffed the whole thing in his mouth, grinning like a five-year-old on a sugar rush.

Maybe identifying the president with the hamburger clown wasn't an act of confusion. Maybe voters were having a moment of clarity.

McDannold wiped his chin with his sleeve and half turned McCullough's direction. For one horrifying moment, he was afraid the president was going to offer *him* a cookie scoop of Cherry Garcia.

"Where the hell's Verduci?" McCullough growled. They were waiting for retired Marine Lieutenant Colonel and White House Chief of Staff Carmine Verduci. Before McDannold could answer, he stumbled in.

"Sorry, I'm late," Verduci mumbled, slurring the words. "I had to finish something."

A bottle of scotch would be my guess.

McCullough pointed to the couch, and Verduci plopped down next to the president. The general grabbed the remote and switched off the TV. McDannold stared glumly at the empty screen.

"I'll tell you how it ends," McCullough muttered. "The roadrunner outwits that *damn* coyote again." Confident he had as much of their focus as he could reasonably expect, the general cleared his throat. Like switching off the TV, it was one of the tricks he used to get their attention.

"Gentlemen, we need to reach a consensus on some new military technology while we can still seize the element of surprise." McCullough lowered his voice to a conspiratorial whisper. "We suspect the Russians and Red Chinese are moving along similar lines."

Military intelligence suggested nothing of the kind. McCullough made that part up, playing on the president's paranoid gullibility. "We need to move quickly," he added after a theatrical pause.

"Right," McDannold moaned, another cookie clenched in his fist. "My ice cream's melting."

The general took a deep breath and exhaled slowly, struggling to maintain his composure. "Gentlemen, as you're aware, we've put considerable effort into developing the ultimate camouflage, invisibility." McCullough furrowed his brow, trying to impress the moon-faced idiots in front of him with the importance of what he was about to say. "Initially, we were working with a mimetic polymer molded into body armor. Tiny plates, each embedded with a microprocessor, mimic shifting backgrounds, reflecting their surroundings like smart mirrors."

McDannold raised his hand. McCullough scowled. "Mr. President, do you need to go to the little boy's room?"

"No. I was gonna ask something."

McCullough folded his stubby arms across his chest. "I'll finish before taking any questions."

The president glanced at Verduci for support. When none was forthcoming, he lowered his hand and retreated to his corner of the couch.

"The chameleon effect works best in settings with irregular backgrounds like forests and grasslands when subjects are stationary. In urban areas, where backgrounds are more linear, subjects appear as lumpy but identifiably human shapes." McCullough coughed into his fist. "During the desert testing phase, some subjects complained the suits were uncomfortable."

The general glanced at his notes. If suggesting the suits were mobile was an exaggeration, calling them uncomfortable was an outright lie. The suits were prohibitively heavy, nearly half a man's weight. Three soldiers were hospitalized for heatstroke after their zippers jammed in Death Valley. Increasingly reticent test subjects started calling the bulky prototypes *crockpots* and characterized the program as a crockpot idea.

The president's attention flitted back and forth between the blank TV and his half-eaten ice cream. He looked inconsolable. Verduci was staring longingly at a bottle of scotch on the bar, but McCullough was not the sort to be deterred by lesser men.

"We'll continue to develop the mimetic technology in plastic paint for field artillery and armored units, but we've made a breakthrough along an entirely different line of research."

McCullough cleared his throat again. The president looked like he was falling asleep. The general was worried McDannold would doze off before he got to the good part. "We've taken the concept to a new level, as you will see or, as might be more appropriate with invisibility, you *won't* see."

He sounded giddy. McCullough walked across the room and opened the door to the adjoining suite. "Colonel Timkins, would you and the men come in, please?"

McCullough liked showing off and particularly enjoyed having a bird colonel tote and fetch for him. Timkins came in first, tall and erect, walking with pronounced military stiffness.

"General," he said curtly as he stopped at attention and snapped off a crisp salute. Following close behind was a pale, translucent figure carrying a Fender Stratocaster and a small amp. The president and Verduci stared right through him, the books and bookcase clearly visible through his wispy outline.

The president pointed with childlike amazement. "It's Casper the Friendly Ghost," he squealed.

Verduci sat up straighter on the sofa. "General, that's the most amazing thing I ever saw."

"The most amazing thing you *barely* saw," McCullough said, correcting him. Then, he nodded Timkins direction, and a completely invisible Jimi Hendrix picked up the guitar, jacked it into the amp, and ripped into a thunderous cover of "The Star-Spangled Banner."

Nasty, brutish, and short. If Hobbes's characterization of life in *Leviathan* included "round," he would have described Bobby Ray Darling perfectly. The mobster scowled as the cab lurched a few feet closer to LaGuardia. Being stuck in traffic with the half-wit Joey Cozzaglio had soured his already habitually surly disposition.

Bobby Ray rolled the window halfway down, compromising between the smells inside the cab, stale cigarette smoke, Joey, and the driver, and the smells outside the cab, ten million New Yorkers in the dog days of September.

"Why ain't everybody home watching the Yankees?" he growled. Joey tugged anxiously at the brim of his Mets cap and retreated deeper into the upholstery. Bobby Ray glanced at the driver, who jabbered something that might as well have been Martian. He closed his eyes, pictured Joey and the cabbie's chalk outlines on the sidewalk, and immediately felt better.

Darling worked for the Venetti brothers, Anthony and Santino. Anthony, AKA Fat Tony, ran most of the day-to-day operations, but the old man, Don Bruno, was still head of the family. When Tony called and told him to pick up tickets for Las Vegas, he didn't have to ask twice. A trip out west would be a nice break from working collections and scaring the bejesus out of scabs for the Teamsters.

Bobby Ray regarded Fat Tony calling him personally a gesture of respect until the mob boss *suggested* his cousin Joey "tag along and learn some stuff." Bobby Ray was skeptical. Joey's learning curve was flatter than a Famous Ray's pizza.

Being stuck in a confined space with Bobby Ray made Joey nervous. The more agitated he got, the more he ran his mouth. Joey had steadily unraveled since getting picked up at the basement apartment he shared with his mother and three cats. That took some doing since he wasn't wrapped all that tightly in the first place. As the airport trip dragged on, he'd droned on about various inane subjects, including the pluses and minuses of different brands of kitty litter.

Forty-five minutes into a twenty-minute ride, Bobby Ray had suffered through enough of Joey's verbal incontinence to rethink his decision to toss him out of the plane over Kansas or Iowa. He was leaning toward shooting him *before* they got to LaGuardia. By the time they exited the 495, he was trying to decide where would be the best place in Flushing Bay to dump the body.

Grand Central Parkway was bumper-to-bumper. Bobby Ray stared out the window, replaying Tony's instructions in his head: fly to the coast, take care of the business in LA, and be in Vegas by Tuesday. Bored and anxious, he rummaged through his carry-on until he found the flask of Smirnoff he packed for the trip. He twisted off the cap and took a drink as Joey launched into another monologue.

"The other day..."

Bobby Ray shook a chubby fist in his face. "This better not be another cat story," he snarled, his face as red as a baboon's ass. Joey slumped in the seat and buried his face in his hands. Bobby Ray stared at the back of his skull and pictured a gaping hole made by a large caliber bullet.

Probably not the best idea, he conceded grudgingly. Sicilians were funny about family, even family as irritating as Joey. Tony had asked him to make an effort to get along with his cousin, which almost certainly meant not shooting him. If the Don's nephew had an *accident,* Bobby Ray would have a lot of explaining to do.

As he tipped the flask to his lips, Bobby Ray briefly considered more temperate approaches like stuffing him in the trunk. In his pathological need to run his mouth, it never occurred to Joey he could sit quietly and limit his responses to spastic head shakes indicating "yes" and "no." Likewise, it hadn't occurred to him, it might not be a good idea to irritate a guy with a volcanic temper in a confined space, especially if the guy was armed and dangerous.

"S-S-So, what's Vegas like?" Joey asked, hoping the alcohol had dulled Bobby Ray's bad humor.

As he considered the question, Bobby Ray realized if he talked more, Joey could talk less and helped himself to more vodka. "Beneath the glitzy tourist stuff, Vegas is still a grab-em-by-the-balls, winner-gets-the-lion's-share free-for-all." He poked Joey's bony chest with his index finger. "But here's the thing: no matter how much there is to go around, somebody's *always* squeezing something outta somebody. Usually money."

Joey swallowed hard. His Adam's apple, roughly the size and shape of a ping pong ball, bobbed up and down. "No kidding?"

"God's truth." Bobby Ray held up his hand, palm forward as if taking an oath. "The difference is now there're rules. Sure, they get bent, but there're *still* rules."

Joey offered a tentative grin. "I know exactly what you m-m-mean."

"You don't know nothing from nothing," Bobby Ray growled. "In the old days, I'd fly to Vegas, take care of business, play a little blackjack, and be home in time for baked ziti at Rao's." Bobby Ray glanced in the rearview and locked eyes with the driver. The cabbie looked away and jabbered something incomprehensible.

I shoulda spent the extra money on a limo. At least then, I'd be stuck in traffic with a working air conditioner and a driver who spoke English.

Bobby Ray grunted as he half-turned to face Joey. "Vegas ain't the wide-open town it used to be, but the more things change, the more they stay the same. It's the way of the world."

"That's why Fat Tony n-n-needs guys like us."

Bobby Ray shuddered at the thought he and Joey might be alike in any way. He fortified himself with more vodka and glanced at a window display of back-to-school clothes.

They'll be putting up decorations soon.

The push for Christmas shopping started earlier every year. Over the holidays, Bobby Ray moonlighted as a department store Santa. He found something arousing about having rosy-cheeked cherubs climb on his lap for candy bribes. Thanks to his growing reputation as a pervert, *Uncle* Bobby's lap was off-limits at eight department stores and all family get-togethers. But there were plenty of stores less thorough in their background checks. The only drawback to the Santa job was a cold that lasted from Thanksgiving through the Orange Bowl, a nagging consequence of getting sneezed on by snot-nosed kids.

Even during the most hectic time of year, Bobby Ray found it surprisingly easy to reconcile his schedules. Besides giving him a chance to meet new people and break their knees, flexible hours was one of the great things about being a gangster. On rare occasions when his regular job intruded on the bucolic tranquility of pawing six-year-olds, Bobby Ray found time to slip off and squeeze a deadbeat borrower or, on special occasions, to whack somebody. Once, he put six slugs in a business associate suspected of ratting to the feds during a lunch break. He monitored the police band on the cab ride back, listening for an APB for an armed-and-dangerous Santa. Bobby Ray arrived with enough time to devour another employee's roast pork and broccoli rabe hero from the break room fridge.

As he tucked the flask back in his duffle, his hand brushed against the butt of his gun. Bobby Ray felt a tingle in his crotch.

"The meek may inherit the rest of the earth," he grumbled, "but they're not getting New York, and they're sure as hell not getting Las Vegas."

3

Morrison couldn't remember coming upstairs any more than he remembered agreeing to go to Vegas.

But I must have because here I am packing.

He scrounged a nylon gym bag from the back of the closet, tossed it on the bed, and packed in a manic blur: three pairs of jeans, a dozen of his favorite shirts, flannel pajama bottoms, toiletries, the Sig from his waistband, a second P229 from his nightstand, four magazines, and two boxes of ammunition. Morrison added half a drawer of socks in high, arcing shots from an imaginary three-point line and yanked the zipper closed. He slipped on a pair of well-worn Nikes, double-knotted the laces, and hurried downstairs, taking the steps two at a time.

"You need anything?" Elvis looked up from the computer long enough to shake his head. "Well then, let's get going."

Morrison grabbed a sack of dog food and headed to the attached garage. He opened the door, listing to balance the bag over his shoulder, and reached inside for the wall remote. As the lights came on and the door rolled up, he debated which car to take. With barely enough room for himself and some groceries, the MG would make for a cramped four or five-day drive to Las Vegas. The other car, a limo he picked up at a DEA auction, had not seen much open road since Pamela died. He drove it just often enough to keep the battery charged.

"We should take this one," Morrison suggested, nodding toward the stretch Lincoln. As Elvis opened the passenger door, Jaxx jumped in and over the seat and curled up in the back. Morrison stowed the bags in the trunk, walked around to the driver's side, and slid behind the wheel.

"Great car for a road trip." Elvis balanced the computer on his lap and traced his fingertip around a .38 slug cratered in the dashboard.

Morrison shrugged, trying to look casual. "The previous owner, a drug dealer named Toussaint Chardonnay, got caught shortchanging his mob partners. Apparently, they found his revised profit-sharing plan unacceptable. A backpacker stumbled across his body in a wooded area in upstate New Hampshire."

In telling the story, Morrison left out several important details like how the tinted windows were bulletproof and the door panels reinforced with ballistic steel, hoping those features wouldn't come in handy. In turn, Elvis neglected to mention he was the backpacker who found Chardonnay.

Morrison twisted the key in the ignition. The engine coughed and wheezed but caught on the first try. He shifted the car into reverse and backed down the driveway, gravel crunching under the tires. Morrison flipped down the visor and punched the button on the remote. The garage door rolled shut. At the gate, he noticed an orange Vespa propped against the mailbox.

"What about your Moped?"

"It's not mine," Elvis answered curtly, not feeling the need to explain further.

As they drove away, Morrison realized he hadn't locked the door between the kitchen and garage. He glanced in the mirror and gently goosed the gas pedal. As the house disappeared in the rearview, he felt twinges of sadness and relief.

"Head to Washington," Elvis told him. "We're meeting somebody by the White House."

"Return to Sender" was playing on the radio. If Elvis recognized it, it didn't show. A chauffeur's cap, a tongue-in-cheek gift from Pamela, was on the dash by the steering wheel. Morrison slipped it on and checked himself in the mirror. He watched to see if anyone was following them and got off and right back on the freeway several times to make sure. Elvis didn't seem the least bit curious about his behavior. It was thirty minutes before either of them spoke.

"I'm guessing you don't get out much."

Morrison shook his head. "Not since Pamela died." He stared at the river of taillights in front of them, deciding where to begin. "Our last couple of years together, she was using more and more. One night, I found her unconscious on the bathroom floor. When we got home from the hospital, she said she'd work at getting better but nothing changed. Her doctor got her into a private clinic. She snuck out with a junkie from her therapy group and scored some heroin. Police found her in an alley with the needle still in her arm."

"I'm sorry," Elvis said softly, "but it sounds like she was more serious about dying than she was about getting better." For several minutes they rode in silence, not awkward or uncomfortable, just respectful.

Finally, Morrison spoke. "There's something I've been wanting to ask. You said we were part of a network."

Elvis angled his shoulders so he was facing him. "You want to know if there were others?"

Morrison nodded.

Elvis mulled over the question before saying anything. "Rock-and-Roll's a hard way to go. The sixties was Pamela's cause of death as much as drugs. People die, sometimes by happy coincidence, sometimes with the Agency's knowledge and consent. The lucky ones, like you and me, just faded away." Elvis sat up straighter in his seat. "Unless we're going by way of Baltimore, you need to merge to the right."

Morrison flipped on the blinker and checked the rearview mirror before changing lanes. It was early, and the volume of traffic surprised him. He settled back in his seat and wondered about Cosmo, the mysterious figure who had prompted their equally mysterious cross country trip.

"So, what's Cosmo's story? Is he with the Agency?"

"No," Elvis chuckled. "He's from Rome."

"Like the pope?"

"No. Rome, Georgia."

That revelation and time spent in the Peach State as a boy failed to inspire faith in their mission. "So, Cosmo's the Grand Dragon of the KKK?" he joked, trying to sound casual.

"Not likely. He's a mostly black cat."

"A cat? Like a really cool cat?"

"No, like paws and whiskers."

Before he could sort out what to ask next, he heard snoring and realized Elvis had fallen asleep. Morrison exhaled slowly, wondering what he'd gotten himself into. Besieged by second thoughts about Elvis's middle-aged children's crusade, it felt like a sumo wrestler in golf spikes was standing on his chest. He fought the urge to turn the car around, squeezing the steering wheel so tightly his fingers turned white. Suddenly, more than anything, maybe more than everything, he wanted to be home, safe and warm in bed.

But Morrison didn't jump the median and drive home, and he didn't pull off the freeway and refuse to drive another inch until he got good answers. Instead, he stole a sideways glance at Elvis. An unexpected sense of calm enveloped him, and the voices in his head fell silent.

The driver behind them honked as the limo drifted into his lane. Morrison glanced at the speedometer and realized they were only going forty-five. He accelerated to the speed limit and set the cruise control. Twenty minutes later, when they were close enough to see the silhouette of the Washington Monument, he steadied the wheel with his knees, leaned over, and woke up Elvis.

As soon as Jimi finished playing "The Star-Spangled Banner," McCullough turned to face the president and his chief of staff.

"D-D-Did I just see what I didn't see?" Verduci stammered.

McCullough grinned. "Yes, gentlemen, we have achieved invisibility."

"Can I be invisible too?" The president's voice was high-pitched and squeaky with excitement. McCullough suspected he was scheming how to sneak into the secretary pool's ladies' room. The general gave him a disapproving glance and cleared his throat.

"The first test subject is standard government issue: male, Caucasian, mid-twenties, mild mother fixation, masturbates regularly, takes medication for a persistent acne problem, and is balding prematurely. He's smoked marijuana recreationally since his junior year in high school. We have upped both the quantity and quality of his consumption with only modest results."

McCullough pointed at the translucent figure standing next to Colonel Timkins. "Mr. President, Casper the Friendly Ghost is as invisible as we can make him."

Verduci raised his hand, waiting until McCullough nodded his permission before speaking. "His *consumption*?"

"Yes, of marijuana. You can put your hand down, Carmine. I'm getting to that part."

McCullough gestured toward the guitar suspended in the air and flipped through his file notes. "The second subject is an African-American male, mid-fifties, musician." The guitar floated a few feet forward and ripped through the opening riff of "Purple Haze." McCullough scowled in what he calculated was Jimi's direction.

"The subject's on loan from the CIA. He's been living at the Agency's Maui compound for the last twenty-five years, part of their retired agent protection program. He plays guitar and regularly smokes OG Kush, a particularly potent strain originally developed for enhanced interrogations."

The general glanced up from the file. "We borrowed the subject when early results suggested his profile matched revised test parameters. As you can see, or should I say, can't see, he was a breakthrough." McCullough turned to his aide. "Would you gentlemen please excuse yourselves so we can finish our meeting?"

As Colonel Timkins trooped Hendrix and the almost invisible man to the adjoining suite, McCullough raised his hand, stilling

Verduci and McDannold until they were out of earshot. He walked deliberately to the bookcase, turned, and drew himself up to his full five-foot, seven-inch height.

"The technology's only effective in a narrow range of subjects. On one end are NASA engineers who floss daily, support public television, and eat a diet high in soluble fiber. The effect on them is negligible. Even treated with near-lethal doses, they're only fuzzy around the edges. But we can make Rastafarians who play video games, listen to reggae, and chain-smoke marijuana completely invisible."

McCullough faced severely limited options if invisibility required a middle-aged musical virtuoso who could play guitar with his teeth, but after graphing results against test subject profiles, Lawless Childs, the young Ph.D. in charge of the project, had suggested the Rastafarian angle. The general enthusiastically jumped all-in.

The president stared blankly McCullough's direction, unable to draw any meaningful conclusions. He picked up a spoon and poked glumly at his ice cream that had melted into a soft, slurry sludge.

"What's the bottom line here, Mac?" He asked, making an effort to sound presidential.

McCullough clenched his jaw, trying not to cringe. He hated it when McDannold called him Mac. Standing rigidly at attention, he pretended to consider the answer he'd been rehearsing for two days.

"What we're talking about here is an invisibility gap. If we lose this race to the Russians or Red Chinese, everything we hold dear will be lost. The life, liberty, and happiness of every God-fearing man, woman, and child in America is in our hands." McCullough held out his cupped palms for dramatic effect.

Timkins should have stayed and hummed "The Battle Hymn of the Republic." There wouldn't be a dry eye in the house.

"In a word, gentlemen, we need Rastafarians. Lots and lots of Rastafarians."

McDannold stared at his spoon with grim determination. With extensive help from Verduci, he'd finally figured out how to operate the remote for the White House's satellite TV. That, and his feeble attempts at humping secretaries, comprised the width and breadth of his vision as chief executive.

"We need to install a government in Jamaica friendly to our way of thinking." McCullough paused, giving his words a chance to sink in. The president was squirming like a snail sprinkled with rock salt. He wasn't aware "we" had a way of thinking and now, all of a sudden, it seemed damned important somebody else had it too.

McCullough lowered his chin and stared at him with premeditated sternness. "That will require military intervention." The president looked visibly relieved he didn't need to come up with a solution. That was one of the convenient things about being president. Everybody told him what to do. It was a lot like being married.

"You should plan this, Mac. You know I don't like getting bogged down in details." He grinned his toothpaste-billboard smile again. McCullough tried not to wince.

Christ. You could tile a swimming pool with that smile.

He clasped his hands together in a practiced gesture of restraint. "The situation will require boots on the ground. Given the extreme sensitivity of the mission, it's critical we involve as few people as possible in the chain of command. Colonel Verduci, with your considerable military experience, you should, in the interest of national security, personally plan and command the operation. What do you think, Colonel? You up for it?"

Verduci jumped to his feet, snapped to attention, and gave the general an exaggerated salute. "Yes, sir. You can count on me."

McCullough grinned. "I knew we could."

Verduci was a puffed-up, little man susceptible to flattery, and McCullough wanted as much plausible deniability as he could muster. Jamaica was looking more and more like a win-win scenario. While there was a remote possibility the dimwitted President and his chief of staff would succeed and add a formidable new weapon to the US arsenal, it was more likely they would bumble into disaster and create an opening for McCullough in the next election. McCullough strutted to the bar, savoring the heady prospect of being the only unanimously elected president since George Washington. He poured three cognacs and handed McDannold and Verduci each a glass.

Verduci tossed his down as if it was a tequila shot, his face contorting like he'd swallowed napalm. As he coughed into his fist and curled up over his knees, McCullough clapped him firmly between the shoulder blades.

The president stared fretfully at his drink. What he really wanted was more Cherry Garcia. "Jamaicans. Aren't they the guys with the brightly-colored knit caps?" he asked, tugging on the general's sleeve.

"Yes, Mr. President."

"Maybe we could make the hats part of their uniforms."

"Right." Verduci's face was pinched and red from coughing. "We could call them the Rainbow Berets."

McCullough bit his lip. "Let's not get caught up designing uniforms for guys you can't see."

"Oh, right." Verduci stared self-consciously at his shoes.

McCullough poured himself another cognac and sniffed it thoughtfully before raising his glass in a toast. "Here's to a well-trained, well-equipped, well-disciplined, elite fighting force for truth, justice, and the American way."

Nobody noticed McCullough neglected to mention "well-medicated" and influenced by his lilting Scottish brogue, it sounded like he said elite fighting "farce." The irony was lost on the president, who hooted and clapped wildly like a six-year-old with a new toy.

Since nobody was watching, not that they would have seen him if they were, Jimi decided it was checkout time and slipped out with two women from housekeeping. He wanted to bring the guitar, but a Fender Stratocaster floating down the corridors of power would attract unwanted attention.

Jimi had mixed feelings about playing the White House. He'd always imagined a command performance for the president would be more inspiring. McDannold was even fuzzier in person than he was on TV. Jimi hoped it was the dope.

He stood on the White House lawn and turned his face to the night sky. Only a handful of the brightest stars were visible beneath the canopy of floodlights. Jimi tucked his hands in his pockets and walked down the driveway toward the gate and Pennsylvania Avenue. He was troubled McCullough referred to him as "disposable" in briefings, and worse yet, made it sound like a character asset.

"Just because he can't see me, doesn't mean he should talk about me like I'm not here," he grumbled under his breath.

Hendrix had been poked, prodded, and probably pap smeared by every whiz-bang gizmo in the lab. The dope was righteous, but there was more to life than music and getting stoned. He had no idea what that might be but had heard it often enough to wonder if it was true. Gospel or not, he knew he could get by without doing amazing pet tricks for the Pentagon. It was high time, he'd decided, they found themselves another Guinea pig.

He knew all about McCullough's plans for Jamaica. Being invisible had allowed him to eavesdrop conversations when people didn't realize he was listening. The question was, what to do with the information? Whatever he came up with, he needed to do it soon. McCullough didn't strike him as the sort who took disappointment well. The general would send the cavalry when he realized Jimi was AWOL. He suspected that meant SEAL Team 13.

Hendrix strolled through the gate when it opened for a Black Expedition with tinted windows and government plates. He stopped at a newsstand a few blocks down the street, grabbed a Snickers bar, and wolfed it down in two bites. The grizzled, old guy behind the counter glanced up from his *Racing Form*. When he didn't see anyone waiting, he went back to a chart of workout splits.

Jimi stashed three more candy bars in his jacket and walked to the corner. While waiting for the light to change, he dug his pipe from the other pocket, packed a bowl of military-grade dope from the pouch around his neck, and fired it with his trusty Bic. He was mulling over what to do next when a stretch limo pulled up beside him. A man with long white hair in a ponytail popped out of the passenger side. Something about him seemed familiar. Before Jimi could decide what, he opened the rear door and made a sweeping gesture toward the back seat.

"We're headed to Las Vegas. Wanna ride?"

Jimi was still getting used to people *not* being able to see him, and here was somebody who apparently could. He bent over, hands on his knees, to look at the driver, a scruffy looking fellow about his age in a chauffeur's hat. His eyes were darting back and forth like he was trying to figure out who the white-haired guy was talking to.

Jimi found his confusion comforting. "Nice wheels."

"Thanks," the driver answered, not sure where the disembodied voice had come from. Jimi was still sorting things out when it dawned on him who the man in the ponytail was.

"Well, I'll be damned. If it isn't the artiste formerly known as Mr. Blue-Suede Shoes himself."

He was grinning ear-to-ear as he slid through the open door and into the back seat.

4

The moon dangled low in the sky, nearly bright enough to drive with the headlights off. Morrison pressed his palms against the steering wheel and flexed the fingers of one hand and then the other. It was a little after ten. He'd worked his way south and west all day and into the night, skirting large cities, driving back roads, and checking the rearview for *them*. He had no idea who *they* might be any more than he knew why he was driving to Vegas.

Elvis was riding shotgun, huddled over his laptop, typing furiously. He hadn't looked up in more than an hour. Jimi was in the back, or so Morrison assumed from the sag in the upholstery, with Jaxx curled up beside him. When he heard Hendrix's lighter, Morrison glanced over his shoulder, but all he saw was the dog.

"Gotta keep smoking," Jimi chuckled. "If I don't, you can see me." Morrison cracked his window. It seemed as good a reason as any. Jimi exhaled a ribbon of smoke and offered him the pipe.

Morrison shook his head. "Thanks. I'm good."

Chauffeur duties had fallen to him by default. Elvis was busy chatting with Cosmo. Invisibility and cannabis consumption made Jimi driving a risky proposition. It looked like Morrison was in the driver's seat for the duration. Another hour at the wheel, and he'd be asking Jaxx to pull a shift. He checked the dashboard clock and set the car on cruise control.

Hendrix had given them a thumbnail sketch of his MIA years and the invisibility project but hadn't asked a single question about Las Vegas. Morrison briefly recounted his mad dash down the Champs-Élysées, escape into the Métro, and subsequent death and resurrection. He left details about Langley and Georgetown vague and skipped over Pamela entirely. Elvis remained as enigmatic as ever.

For the first few hours, the radio played an uninterrupted cycle of Doors, Hendrix, and Elvis songs. Like being stuck in a *Twilight Zone* episode, no matter how many times Morrison spun through the stations, the playlist was always the same.

When they stopped to stretch their legs and give Jaxx a chance to pee, Jimi was looking over Morrison's shoulder as he rummaged through the trunk when he spotted a distinctively shaped black case under an old blanket. Inside was a twelve-string Martin inlaid with mother-of-pearl, a Christmas gift from Pamela a few months before she died. Since finding the guitar, Jimi had entertained them, mostly with improvised jazz riffs.

Like much about their trip, Morrison found the discovery bewildering. Despite clear evidence to the contrary, he remained convinced the guitar was home in an upstairs closet. Jimi played a short progression and adjusted the tuning.

"Getting yourself together for an unplugged reunion tour?" Morrison joked.

"Doubtful. I never enjoyed life on the road. I'd be perfectly happy to settle down somewhere."

"Like Maui?"

"Actually, it looks like I'm headed to Vegas. Didn't you always want to grow old strutting your stuff in rhinestone jumpsuits?"

Morrison glanced at Elvis and shook his head. "I'm pretty sure the whole point of my old life was to die young."

Jimi played a jazzy version of the *Light My Fire* intro. "Better sold out than burned out, right? Back from the dead would be the ultimate encore performance." He flicked his lighter, raised it almost to the roof, and waved it back and forth.

"Maybe we should keep a low profile until we figure out who's looking for us," Morrison suggested.

Elvis looked up from his laptop for the first time in nearly a hundred miles. "Men make plans, and God laughs. It's a Chinese proverb Cosmo likes to quote."

"Does *he* have a plan?"

Elvis grinned. "Always. But he hardly ever shares."

"The journey, not the destination, right?" Jimi's fingers danced across the fretwork, improvising progressions as he played. "Follow the Yellow Brick Road. Follow the Yellow Brick Road," he sang softly.

"Somewhere out there," Morrison said, waving at the inky darkness, "the Emerald City awaits us."

"And Dorothy," Elvis added, "and the great and powerful Oz."

Morrison drummed his fingers against the steering wheel. The drive and lateness of the hour weighed on him. "We're almost out of gas. I'm going to look for a place to pull over and get some rest."

There was a soft hum as Jimi's window slid open. "Where are we anyway?"

"Down a country road in Virginia." Morrison sighed. "At least I *think* we're still in Virginia." He felt the mist before he saw it. The air suddenly turned wet and cold, and the hair on his arms jumped to attention. As they crested a small hill, the world outside disappeared into a dense fog.

Morrison leaned forward until his forehead nearly touched the windshield. Ghostly images flickered and danced in the murky darkness. He could barely make out the silhouettes of houses and street lamps. Jaxx sat up and panted excitedly. Morrison slowed to read a small sign scrawled with *Last Chance Gas, Shiftly* in hand-painted letters.

Beneath that, somebody should have added *Welcome to Munchkinland.*

After boarding, Flight 360 sat on the runway for more than two hours. By the time the pilot got tower clearance, like most of his fellow travelers, Bobby Ray's disposition had turned surly. Fearing a passenger insurrection, flight attendants tried to defuse the situation with free drinks as soon as the plane was airborne.

Bobby Ray and Joey were in the cheap seats toward the back of the plane. Don Bruno always flew the family economy. Joey was wedged in the middle next to a beefy dockworker from the Bronx.

Somewhere over middle America, Bobby Ray made the transition from mildly toasted to sloppy drunk. He leaned into the aisle and waved his empty glass at the stewardess. He couldn't remember her name and had had too much to drink to read her name badge. Their relationship showed no prospect of moving past the chitchat stage. She had adeptly deflected his clumsy advances.

The attendant was six or seven rows behind them, talking with a baby-faced guy in wire-rim glasses nursing a cola-colored drink. Apparently, he said something clever, and they both laughed.

Bobby Ray leaned into the aisle again and shook his glass like a small animal he had by the throat. "Not to intrude on your moment, but could I get another drink, *please*?"

The flight attendant looked up, raked her hair back with her fingers, and nodded. Baby-Face said something too softly for Bobby Ray to hear and rolled his eyes in exaggerated disbelief. She covered her mouth to hide a giggle and retreated to the service galley for another round.

Bobby Ray yawned, sleepy from the long flight, the late hour, and the steady stream of vodka tonics. "Christ, no wonder I'm tired. Look how late it is." He shoved his watch in Joey's face until it nearly touched his nose. "Course, I'm still on New York time."

Joey, who was working on his third beer, stared cross-eyed at the watch. "N-N-New York time?" It hadn't occurred to him there was any other kind.

"Yeah, *New York* time," Bobby Ray snarled as the flight attendant arrived with another round. To save herself a trip, she brought him two cocktails and another beer for Joey. She cringed when the gangster brushed against her hand as he snatched the drinks from the tray.

Bobby Ray watched her hasty retreat up the aisle, simmering in an alcohol-tinged rage. He drained the first drink in one long, steady gulp, wadded up the napkin, and dropped it into the empty glass. He turned and glared at Joey, who was stuffing trash into an air-sickness bag.

"Jeez," he muttered, beginning to slur his words. "You *ever* been on a plane before?"

Joey looked up and blinked twice. "N-N-No. But I rode a bus to Atlantic City once."

Bobby Ray tore open a bag of peanuts with his teeth and emptied them into his mouth. "Really, all the way to Jersey?" he grumbled, spewing half-chewed nuts. "We got ourselves a regular jet-setter here." Joey stared glumly at the seatback.

Halfway through his second drink, Bobby Ray closed his eyes and started snoring loudly enough to pop wing rivets. None of the other passengers considered waking him, least of all Joey.

Bobby Ray lived in Brooklyn with Nympha, his widowed aunt, who'd raised him even before his father's death. When he was four, his old man was found floating face down in the East River after trying to weasel out of a loan-sharking indictment. Don Bruno took a hard line on people turning state's evidence.

His coarse hair was prematurely salt-and-pepper gray, but regular applications of Grecian Formula kept it an unnatural jet black. His nose was disproportionately large and slightly hawkish. With his nasal voice and tendency to whine, people regularly assumed he was Jewish. Given his anti-Semitic prejudices, that was enough to drive him straight up a wall.

But Bobby Ray was only half Sicilian. His father was a US serviceman stationed on Hokkaido after World War II, and his mother a Japanese national. Bobby Ray's uncle Primo, one of the Venetti's capos, never disclosed the family secret. The ruse worked because Bobby Ray didn't look half-Japanese, an ethnic group the don held in particularly low regard.

Somewhere over the Rockies, the plane hit a patch of turbulence so violent passengers were bounced around the cabin like popcorn in a microwave. Startled awake, Bobby Ray got up to go to the bathroom. As he staggered down the aisle, he glanced over his shoulder at the flight attendant, who was helping an elderly woman retrieve her carry-on from the overhead compartment.

"Bitch," he griped under his breath. On the way to his seat, he clipped Baby-Face in the back of the head with his elbow. As Bobby Ray was wedging his portly body into place, the flight attendant delivered two more drinks before scurrying away.

"Get me to California," he muttered, slurring the words. "After I take care of family business, I'm gonna hook up with a couple tight-assed rollerbladers."

Joey was angled sideways between his oversized bookends, picking absentmindedly at a hangnail. "Do you think we'll see any movie stars?"

Bobby Ray ignored him, emptied a vodka tonic, and jacked his headphones into the armrest. He slipped them over his ears and turned the volume loud enough to drown out anything Joey might say. Elvis was belting out, "Viva Las Vegas."

Bobby Ray popped the catch on his seatbelt and slumped down in his seat. His head bobbing up and down with the music, he drifted off to sleep, thirty-something-thousand feet up, hurtling along at six hundred miles per hour like flotsam in the jet stream.

As flickering images of Shiftly slowly emerged from the haze, Morrison eased off the gas pedal, and the limo slowed to a crawl. Ramshackle houses with swaybacked roofs lined both sides of the street. Several had cardboard duct-taped over broken windows. Tire swings dangled from leafless trees, and stained laundry hung from rope clotheslines like tattered flags. There was a derelict car on cinder blocks in almost every yard.

A sad-eyed dog, his ribs showing through his flanks, was curled up on a porch. He watched as they drove past but didn't bark. At the end of the block was a small church where the rituals of town life – baptisms, marriages, funerals, and the weekly services that bound them together were performed. Like everything else, the church needed a good scrubbing and a new coat of paint.

Elvis rolled his window down and pointed at a gas station as it emerged from the fog and darkness. "Looks like they're open."

The office lights were on, and Morrison could see someone sitting at the counter. He pulled in and parked next to the rusty, side-by-side pumps on the only island. The gangly teenage boy hurrying their direction looked like he'd been interrupted playing dress-up in daddy's closet. The sleeves on his baggy coveralls were folded nearly to the elbows. An unrolled pant cuff dragged on the pavement. Even with his bowlegged gait, the inseams along his thighs chafed against each other as he walked. He bent down, rested his hands on his knees, and peered in the window.

"Fill 'er up?"

"Please." Morrison climbed out of the car and rubbed his palms together. The night felt cold and wet against his skin. The boy walked the hose to the back of the limo, unscrewed the cap, and inserted the nozzle. He wiped his hands on a rag and started the pump.

Elvis slid out the passenger side, motioning for Jaxx to follow. The dog stretched and trotted over to a bush by the payphone. The driver's side rear door opened by itself. If the kid pumping gas noticed, it didn't show. He flipped up the windshield wipers, soaped the front window, and wiped it with a squeegee, methodically repeating the process all the way around the car.

"Nice dog," the boy said, tugging on the brim of his cap.

"Jaxx."

"Does he hunt?"

Morrison shook his head. "No. But he chases rabbits in the yard sometimes."

"Well, that's something." He tilted back the brim of his cap and scratched his forehead. "Been kinda slow tonight. I guess most folks aren't in enough of a hurry to drive in this soup." He raised his hand and made a sweeping gesture for effect.

"Actually, it's mostly clear until just outside of town." The boy seemed bewildered by the thought of a world beyond Shiftly.

"I'm Hershel."

"Jim." As they shook hands, Morrison was thinking Hershel's uniform, like his name, was probably a hand-me-down.

"Want some coffee? Just made a fresh pot."

Morrison shook his head. "No thanks, but I wouldn't mind using your restroom."

"Inside." The boy jerked his thumb toward the office. "The door's not locked."

Morrison was pleasantly surprised to find the bathroom clean, with a new roll of toilet paper and the strong scent of Pine-sol. A tree-shaped room freshener hung from a hook over the sink. As he washed and dried his hands, Morrison puzzled over the town and open service station that appeared just when they needed gas. An even bigger surprise was waiting outside: Shiftly had awakened.

Morrison walked to the car, struggling to sort out the scene. A large group had coalesced around Elvis. Freckle-faced kids with straw-colored hair and sunburned noses made up the innermost ring, then teenagers and women with babies, and finally working men in overalls. Elvis was smiling and shaking hands, softly repeating "thank you" over and over again.

Hershel wiped his hands on the rag, closed the hood, and shuffled around to the back of the car. A broad-shouldered man was loading freshly-baked pies, jugs of cider, and a basket of apples into the trunk. The two men looked enough alike to be kin.

"Water and oil are fine," Hershel told Morrison, barely glancing in his direction. "The right rear was a little low, so I put in some air."

Morrison nodded appreciatively but was staring at the broad-shouldered man cradling a ham in his thickly calloused hand. He peeled back the wax paper wrapping and used his pocket knife to slice off a thin sliver and offered it to Morrison on the tip of the blade. The meat was dense with a deep, smoky flavor. He rewrapped the ham, slid it into a white cotton bag, and pulled the drawstring closed. After snuggling it between the pies, he grabbed two Mason jars of shimmering, incandescent liquid from the knapsack at his feet.

"Raisin Jack for your trip." He winked slyly as he nestled the jars alongside the ham. With a tug on the frayed brim of his John Deere cap, he turned and ambled over to join the group congregated around Elvis.

Morrison paid Hershel with a credit card and slid behind the wheel as Elvis climbed in beside him. Jaxx jumped into the back seat, and the door slammed magically shut behind him. Again, if anybody noticed, it didn't show. Elvis's hair had worked loose from his ponytail and radiated out in a fuzzy, white corona. He looked like an Old Testament prophet back from a chat with God.

"Where did these people come from?"

"With nothing but the clothes on our backs," Elvis mumbled cryptically.

Morrison, sensing the futility of pursuing things further, started the engine and eased the car through the crowd. He saw the same dreamy passion in their eyes he saw in Elvis's. As the limo rolled onto the street, Morrison watched in the rearview as the people of Shiftly waved goodbye and disappeared, melting into the fog.

5

Morrison pointed the car toward a horizon line that was deeply-bruised shades of purple and gray. A light wind out of the east piled brooding thunderheads the texture of old Brillo pads along the edges of the sky. If sunrise in the Blue Ridge Mountains looked like the beginning of the world, this looked pretty close to the end.

The night before, they stayed in a small town outside Nashville. The motel TV was broken, but Jimi boosted a portable and an adapter from the appliance store across the street. Plugged into the cigarette lighter, Jimi spent the morning consuming copious amounts of dope while he and Jaxx watched a *Jeopardy* marathon. Morrison had started to worry the mutt was developing a debilitating fondness for game shows and secondhand smoke.

Elvis huddled over the keyboard, his face scrunched in concentration, alternating between studying the screen and typing furiously. At breakfast, when Morrison asked about the avatar jitterbugging across the screen, Elvis explained Cosmo's icon was a burning bush. Morrison thought it looked more like a ball of green yarn with unruly red and orange hair. He might have wondered more about Elvis's sanity if the Shiftly experience hadn't made him question his own.

Spurred by the distance from Washington and a growing anxiousness to get where they were going, Morrison had switched from state roads to interstates, but the miles across Middle America passed slowly. When Jimi took a TV break, Morrison turned on the radio. Programming had drifted seamlessly from a medley of the trio's greatest hits to farm reports and country music. After an hour of twangy songs about women who loved cheating men who drank hard and argued with their fists, Morrison found a baseball game. Between innings, national advertisers hawked beer and cars. The local ads sounded like Chicago or maybe St. Louis.

The relentlessly unchanging landscape of Oklahoma was littered with oil pumps and occasional clusters of dilapidated single wides. It looked like a giant child had emptied his sandbox of all but a few broken toys and gone home. Except for bathroom breaks, to fill the tank, or retrieve food from the trunk, Morrison spent the entire day behind the wheel.

In Broken Arrow, they got gas and carry out fried chicken. Jimi lobbied for Taco Bell, but since he was driving, Morrison effectively had veto power. He wasn't sure they could survive the night after a dinner that included refried beans.

In a small park up the block from KFC, they stretched their legs and spread out the fast-food feast on a concrete table. Morrison barely had enough energy to chew much less to worry about anybody noticing Jimi's plate empty on its own. While Elvis munched seaweed crackers, Jaxx raced back and forth, rousting pigeons. When he sensed everyone had nearly finished, he trotted back to the table for food scraps and a bowl of water.

Morrison popped the last bite of biscuit into his mouth and stared at the limo, mustering the strength to drag himself over and climb inside. The miles were wearing on him, but the urge to be closer to Las Vegas was stronger than the one to find someplace to rest. They were all the way to Amarillo before Morrison pulled off the interstate and angled toward the Days Inn's black and yellow sunburst sign.

"Make sure to get a room with a working TV," Jimi reminded him as they pulled into the parking lot.

After two days on the road, Morrison didn't have the energy to watch himself, but Jimi and Elvis were unmanageable without one. Elvis had explained God talked to him through TVs. Since He didn't seem particular about program content, Elvis and Jimi never squabbled over what to watch.

Morrison parked the limo on the far side of the office, so the desk clerk wouldn't have a clear view of the car. As he walked inside, he was greeted by a sullen teenager who barely looked up from *Wheel of Fortune.*

"Need a room. Two beds." While the clerk ran his credit card, Morrison signed the register "Mr. Mojo Risin."

The boy plucked a key from a cubbyhole and slid it across the counter. "Room's on the far side." He glanced over his shoulder at the TV when the audience reacted to a middle-aged woman with frizzy hair and cat-eye glasses solving the puzzle. "Extra towels are in the closet."

"Thanks." The boy waved in acknowledgment, his attention evenly divided between Vanna White and a bag of potato chips.

Morrison pulled the car around and parked in front of the room. A woman was smoking a cigarette in the doorway next to theirs. As Morrison and Elvis were climbing out of the limo, she slammed the door and went back to fighting with her husband.

Morrison handed Elvis the room key and took Jaxx for a walk. His bag was on the far bed when they got back. Judging by the sag in the comforter, Jimi was stretched out on the one closest to the door. Elvis had arranged the extra pillows and blankets on the floor in front of the TV. He was chatting with Cosmo. Through the wall, Morrison could hear the woman screaming over her husband's pleas to calm down.

"Ain't love grand?" asked the indentation on Jimi's bed. Morrison shrugged, not remembering either way.

Morrison resisted the urge to crawl under the covers and took a long, hot shower. He interlaced his fingers behind the showerhead and lowered his chin until the water beat against his neck. As it sheeted across his face, he experienced a brief epiphany about why Christians had made water part of their ritual of renewal.

After toweling off, he slipped into pajama pants, stretched out on the bed, and immediately fell asleep. Morrison slept soundly, without dreaming about Dorothy, the Wizard, or the old Indian.

Hands on his hips, chin aimed belt high, Verduci's personal assistant, Jaysen Rush, fired a pouty scowl in his direction. "But you *promised*."

"I know, I promised, but affairs of state take precedence." Hunched over the paperwork strewn across his desk, Verduci glanced at his watch. McDannold had summoned him, and he didn't want to keep the president waiting.

Jaysen's father bankrolled McDannold's election campaign early and often. He leveraged his contributions into a White House position for his son, hoping the experience would "butch him up." That Jaysen, in his seventh year of undergraduate studies at Georgetown, looked like a young, white Lena Horne didn't hurt.

Tarrant Rush owned the Jesus Broadcasting Network, a half-million-acre cattle ranch, most of the state's privately held oil fields, and a luxury box at Texas Stadium. Last fourth of July, Jaysen strutted around his father's annual whole-steer barbecue in a Versace gown and red-soled stilettos. Surrounded by his drag-queen entourage, he bragged to the lieutenant governor that his shoe collection would make Imelda Marcos green with envy.

The old man believed his son's antics were calculated to ruffle his feathers. The strategy appeared to be working. Whenever they were together, Tarrant certainly looked ruffled.

Fuming quietly, Jaysen raked his hair back with his nails. Verduci could feel his prickly stare on the back of his neck. The over-the-top theatrics were camp, but he knew better than to say so when his aide was mid-tirade, even a mostly mute one. Verduci turned and squared his shoulders, determined to hold his ground. He stood on his tiptoes and gave his intern a patronizing smile and a fatherly peck on the cheek.

"Champagne's in the fridge," he said, hoping to placate him. "Play a video game. I won't be long."

Jaysen gasped in exaggerated disbelief, flopped on the sofa, and planted his heels on the coffee table without kicking off his shoes. Verduci, struggling not to overreact, clenched his teeth tightly enough to dimple his cheeks. Jaysen grinned wickedly, sensing he'd successfully pushed his buttons.

"Ruskin, the Commerce Secretary, was indicted this morning."

"I heard."

"We play Indictment Bingo at my fraternity. A brainiac frat brother thought it up during Watergate. Each square's somebody in the administration, like the president and his cabinet."

"And the chief of staff?"

"Absolutely. You're the center square on two of my cards."

"How many do you have?"

"Five's the limit. Cards are a thousand dollars apiece. The carryover pot's huge. There hasn't been a winner since Reagan was in office." He glanced at Verduci, who was staring vacantly into space. "Things were probably different when you were in school." Verduci couldn't recall his Naval Academy years clearly. That period, like most of his life since junior high, was a drunken blur.

Jaysen flicked his hand, shooing him dismissively. "Well, I guess you'd better scurry along then."

Verduci leaned over, gave his pouting intern another peck on the cheek, and hurried down the hallway to the president's suite. McDannold was in the theater room, wearing Spiderman pajamas, staring morosely at the blank TV. An empty pint of ice cream was on the table next to a crumpled package of Oreos. The president drained his scotch and handed Verduci the remote.

"Phyllis and I had a fight over the TV. I think she broke the damned thing."

Verduci tried to look supportive. He couldn't stand the First Lady, who never missed an opportunity to be petty or vindictive and took particular pleasure in tormenting McDannold and his chief of staff. Jaysen called her "the Wicked Witch of the West Wing."

"It's all right, Mr. President. The batteries are in backwards again." Verduci flipped them over, snapped the cover into place, and pointed the remote at the screen. The TV immediately filled with an enormous image of Wile E. Coyote chasing the Roadrunner in rocket-powered roller skates.

McDannold looked visibly relieved. Verduci was one of the few men in Washington he trusted. His mastery of the TV remote made him virtually indispensable. Besides, his preference for young men meant he was about the only guy in Washington not sleeping with his wife.

Besides me, McDannold thought sourly. He pushed the empty ice cream carton across the table. Looking at it after he'd eaten all the Cherry Garcia was depressing.

If George Washington was the president who couldn't tell a lie, and Richard Nixon the president who couldn't tell the truth, then Ronald McDannold was the president who couldn't tell the difference. An astute columnist with the *Miami Herald* summed up his public service legacy as "a lack of substance abuse." In the two days since meeting with McCullough, McDannold had obsessed over Jamaica and invisibility.

"Carmine, you ever been to Jamaica?"

"No, Mr. President." Verduci didn't know precisely where Jamaica was but was almost positive you had to cross an ocean to get there. Since he got seasick watching *Love Boat* reruns, that was a terrifying prospect. A hotel reservation was as close as they got to Hawaii, but when Jaysen planned a surprise forty-something birthday party in Waikiki, Verduci was so traumatized by the thought of flying over the Pacific, he was bedridden for days. He walked to the bar and poured himself four fingers of scotch, his hands shaking so badly, he spilled nearly as much as he got in the glass.

"So, what's Jamaica like?" Verduci's lack of firsthand knowledge had not deterred the president's line of inquiry. He gulped down half his drink, hoping to settle his nerves.

"A bunch of poor people in a shithole country, I guess." He drained his glass and poured himself another. "We could promise better schools, more police, lower taxes -- the same chicken-in-every-pot gibberish we trot out for voters here."

"And cable TV," McDannold reminded him. That morning he'd suggested free cable as part of a win-their-hearts-and-minds campaign.

"Right, Mr. President, and cable TV." That made Verduci more comfortable. Cable TV was something he knew about.

McDannold's face scrunched into a fist like it did whenever he tried figuring something out. "But we wouldn't actually do those things, right?"

"Of course not. They're like campaign promises. We're just telling 'em what they wanna hear."

"Not even cable TV?" McDannold looked distraught.

Verduci took another sip of scotch. "We could pipe in Cuban stations from Miami so they can watch telenovelas and Looney Tunes in Spanish."

"Hearts and minds," the president said, grinning his approval. "I could help plan the mission."

Verduci winced. He hated it when McDannold took the commander-in-chief thing literally. The president sensed his dissatisfaction and started backpedaling. "Of course, you'd be in charge, being an Academy man and all."

"We'll talk about it when I get back."

"You're going somewhere?"

"Vegas," Verduci reminded him. "Family business. But by this time next week, we'll have whipped up one helluva plan to take Jamaica."

The president, titillated by the brash words of a guy who graduated last in his class from Annapolis, rubbed his hands together. "Up for a little world conquest?" McDannold grinned his toothpaste-billboard smile. They played Risk, the perfect game for delusional megalomaniacs, almost every night. "I'm blue," the president nearly shouted, giddy with enthusiasm. McDannold was *always* blue and *always* went first – he called it "presidential

69

privilege." As he dealt out countries, Verduci glanced at his watch. He was thinking about Jaysen.

I hope the champagne's made that little fairy less snitty.

The president massed troops in Afghanistan and attacked China and then Mongolia. He always started in Central Asia. The chief of staff drained his scotch and wondered how badly he should slaughter him tonight.

It was late by the time Morrison and company slid into Las Vegas like a bull moose through a boa constrictor. Elvis was asleep in the passenger seat, his chin down, his hands folded over the laptop. The air conditioning was running full blast, but the rear windows were cracked to vent the sticky, sweet smoke from Jimi's pipe.

Morrison glanced at a sheet of stationery beside him on the seat. Elvis handed it to him as they were checking out that morning. On it was a phone number from Cosmo for when they got to Vegas.

As they cruised along the outskirts of the city, Morrison kept an eye out for gas stations. He pulled into the fast lane and accelerated past a lumbering motorhome. Strapped to the side was a banner that read *Viking Club* in blocky, purple letters edged in gold, and below that, *Duluth, Minnesota*. One of the corners had come loose and was flapping in the wind. The driver, an elderly man wearing a horned helmet, waved as the limo rolled past. Morrison waved back.

They were humming along about sixty-five when two guys in buzz-cuts and dirty, white T-shirts cruised by in a red Pontiac with the top down. A honey blonde was in the back seat.

"Clever disguise," said a disembodied voice behind him. Morrison was wearing the chauffeur's hat and wasn't sure if Jimi meant him or the kids in the Trans Am.

Morrison stole a sideways glance their direction. He'd halfway convinced himself every late-model American car was being driven by somebody from the Agency. Another hour of driving and he'd be looking suspiciously at import drivers as well. Morrison heard the rasping sound of Jimi's Bic as he fired another bowl.

"You gotta bad altitude. You gotta fly high above the radar." Jimi's voice was pinched and tight. He was trying to talk without exhaling.

"Thanks, but no thanks."

"You sure? The smoking lamp's lit, and the doctor's in." Morrison cracked his window and gently goosed the accelerator.

"Pretty girl." Jimi's voice was dreamier and more subdued this time.

As they pulled alongside the ragtop, Morrison stole another peek at the girl. She wasn't just pretty -- she was stunning. As the Trans Am surged ahead, she turned and looked their direction. Something flickered across her face, something he couldn't read -- sadness or maybe fear.

Jimi coughed into his fist. "Keep your mind on the road, or I'm gonna have to drive." Hendrix's fingers danced across the fretwork in a familiar riff. "Better move over, Rover, and let Jimi take over."

Morrison held up three fingers, his thumb clamping his pinkie across his palm as if taking an oath. "No, Scout's honor, I'm good."

Maybe it was nervous exhaustion, but Morrison couldn't stop thinking about the kids in the Firebird. Something about the threesome had grabbed his attention and wouldn't let go. The driver changed lanes, crossed in front of them, and slowed, cruising at the edge of the limo's headlights. The scrawny arm dangling out the passenger window was heavily tattooed in a motif that favored iron crosses and swastikas. The two guys looked like skinheads on a bad hair day.

Morrison sighed. *Jimi's right. I got a bad altitude.*

At the last exit before the Strip, he saw a gas station sign, banked to the right, and trailed the Pontiac down the exit. The convertible rolled through the stop sign as the limo ground to a halt. Morrison waited while seven or eight cars and a yellow U-Haul cleared the intersection. The engine groaned and wheezed as he gingerly nursed the limo into traffic.

Strip malls with nail salons, pawnshops, video stores, and fast-food joints lined both sides of the street. A Mobil station was on the near corner next to a McDonald's. The bay doors were closed, and only the office lights were on. The woman sitting inside was smoking a cigarette. A wiry guy with a scruffy ponytail was hosing down the concrete around the pumps.

Half a block down the street, the red convertible was parked in front of a Circle K. The girl, who waited in the car, was checking her makeup in the rearview mirror. Inside, the driver, a stubby guy with a bad complexion and wispy goatee, was fishing through the beef jerky jar on the counter while his friend grabbed beer from the cooler. Two police cruisers were parked side-by-side across the lot. One had backed in so the officers could chat while their partners fetched coffee and doughnuts.

As Morrison was driving past the Circle K, the limo coughed and sputtered and the check engine light started flashing. He turned into a residential neighborhood at the next intersection, hoping to find a quiet cul-de-sac where he could collect himself and come up with a plan.

Belching billowing wads of blue-black smoke, the limo limped a couple more blocks before Morrison pulled over to the curb and parked. He knew enough about cars to suspect the head gasket was fried. Worn out from the trip and unsettled by childhood ghosts from the morning's drive through New Mexico, he leaned forward and rested his chin on the steering wheel.

They were parked in front of a two-story, white house easily ten years older than the ranch-style homes that made up the rest of the neighborhood. It had a green-gravel yard with a short, circular driveway that looped through stands of prickly pear and yucca.

Jimi's voice floated up from somewhere in the back seat. "Isn't this something?"

Not sure if he heard sarcasm or wonder, Morrison grunted in agreement. He could see what Jimi meant either way. The house had been remodeled to look like a country church. The big double doors in front were propped open. Through them, Morrison could see five or six rows of pews and a pulpit. One of the dormers had been reconfigured to look like a steeple.

A hand-painted sign over the doors read *Reverend Elvis's Chapel d'Love*.

6

Morrison draped himself over the steering wheel, rested his forehead in the crook of his arm, and twisted the key in the ignition. The engine hiccupped and coughed but didn't start. After several failed attempts, he straightened up and looked around. If they stayed in the car much longer, a suspicious neighbor was going to call the police. The last thing they needed was cops poking around asking questions.

Reverend Elvis's Chapel d'Love. Morrison read and reread the sign.

Jimi played something on the guitar. It sounded early sixties Motown, maybe "My Girl," but Morrison wasn't sure. Hendrix was having fun at his expense. It was The Dixie Cups.

"I'm going to see if they have a phone we can use."

"And a room with a TV," Jimi reminded him. He sounded like his throat had been abraded with sandpaper.

Elvis opened his eyes and looked around. His window slid open with a soft hum. He mouthed the words on the sign as he read but didn't appear to attach any personal significance to the name.

"Oh, good. We're here." Morrison figured Elvis, who'd been asleep the last hundred miles, meant Las Vegas and was surprised when he opened the glove box and pushed the trunk release. "I'll get the bags."

"How about you guys wait here a minute?" Morrison asked, hopefully. "I'll check if they have a vacancy." He hoped that would hold Elvis long enough for him to call a cab or tow truck. Morrison shouldered open the door and fumbled through his wallet until he found his AAA card. As he was reassuring himself Jimi's door was still closed, he saw the dog staring expectantly in his direction.

"Come on, boy. Ready to stretch your legs?"

Jaxx barked, jumped over the seat, and bounded out of the car. After stopping to mark a scraggly bush, he caught Morrison halfway to the front steps. They were almost to the porch when an older gentleman with bushy sideburns and a black pompadour walked out in a sequined jumpsuit, gold-framed sunglasses, and a cleric's collar. Morrison rightly assumed he was Reverend Elvis. He grinned warmly and shook Morrison's hand with giddy enthusiasm.

"Howdy, son. I'm Digby. It's good to finally meet you." He stood for a moment appraising Morrison, then glanced over his shoulder at the car. "About time you boys showed up."

Morrison eyed him suspiciously as he extricated himself from the surprisingly firm handshake and caught a glimpse of his confused expression in Digby's sunglasses. He looked like he was trapped in a bad movie, unable to recall his lines.

"Do you have a phone we could use?" Reverend Elvis patted him on the shoulder and smiled without answering. He didn't seem the least bit surprised to see them.

"Well, hello there." Digby bent over and scratched Jaxx behind the ear. The dog wagged his tail and gave him a big, sloppy kiss. "Sparkle said you were coming."

Morrison looked like he'd missed another cue. "Sparkle?"

"My daughter. Oh, I almost forgot." He leaned closer and lowered his voice. "She told me to apologize if you showed before she got back. She ran out to pick up something for dinner. You know how she is. Figured you'd be hungry after the long drive and all."

"K-know how she is?" Morrison stammered. "I think you have us mixed up with somebody else."

Digby chuckled. "I reckon not. The postman delivered the letter this afternoon. Brought it Special D." He curled his lip in an exaggerated Elvis tribute and threw in a hip swivel, but the effect was lost on Morrison.

Jimi, who'd followed him up the sidewalk, leaned over, and whispered, "Might have helped if he'd hummed it."

Morrison clenched his teeth, trying not to appear startled. "The letter?" he asked, struggling to stay focused.

"When she read it, she was so excited."

"You don't understand. My friends and I, I mean my friend and I, were driving to …" Morrison's brow furrowed. "You got a letter that said we were coming?"

"Yes, from some fella named Cosmo. We've been expecting you."

Morrison stood frozen in place, dumbfounded. Behind him, Elvis trudged up the sidewalk. "Would you like some help with those?" Digby asked.

Elvis, his boyish features still fuzzy with sleep, set the bags on the sidewalk so they could shake hands. They each grabbed a bag and started up the porch steps with Jaxx trailing behind them.

"He certainly works in mysterious ways," Jimi teased.

"Beyond mysterious," Morrison mumbled. "This is too weird for words."

As they headed inside, Morrison realized how much, with his bushy eyebrows and the comically animated way he spoke, Digby reminded him of the wizard from *The Wizard of Oz*.

But he was in for an even bigger surprise. He hadn't met Dorothy yet.

Bobby Ray Darling stared out the cabin window as Southwest Flight 1193 banked left and swung around for the final approach. His expression was dark and brooding, utterly indifferent to Las Vegas that glittered at his feet like a gaudy piece of costume jewelry. Beside him, Joey Cozzaglio picked absentmindedly at an M&M-sized pimple on his Adam's apple. He'd finished his third Budweiser and was cruising the clear, blue skies on autopilot.

Nothing about their trip had gone according to plan. Bobby Ray drained the last of his vodka tonic and rested the empty glass on the brushed aluminum briefcase in his lap. Orlando Destry, the deadbeat gambler Tony had sent him to squeeze, rolled over like a dead fish. Apparently, details of his visit had preceded him. Bobby Ray suspected Tony had called and explained the *"or else"* option.

Destry arrived at the hotel even before they unpacked. He called their room from the lobby and asked Bobby Ray to meet him in the bar. Expecting a double-cross, the mobster arrived armed to the teeth. But Destry, who seemed surprisingly calm, set the briefcase on the table and handed him the key. Bobby Ray counted the money twice before nodding they were good. Their business concluded, Destry tossed a twenty on the table and excused himself without finishing his drink.

The rest of their LA layover was equally uneventful. Bobby Ray thought about going to Disneyland, but it rained two days in a row. He and Joey never ventured farther than the hotel bar. Most of the time, they hung out in their room watching pay-per-view porn.

"I'm staying with my brother F-F-Frank," Joey stammered. "H-H-He's picking me up at the airport." It was about the hundredth time he'd reminded him. The longer they were together, the worse his stuttering had gotten. His brother's trailer was in a low-rent part of town, but since Joey lived with his mom in a one-bedroom, basement apartment in Rego Park, even a single wide on cinder blocks was an upgrade in accommodations.

The plane shuddered as the tires touched down on the tarmac. Joey, his face the color of antifreeze, dug his fingernails into the armrests and didn't relax his grip until the plane rolled to a stop. The gangster enjoyed takeoffs and landings for the sheer terror they evoked in the mob boss's cousin. Bobby Ray jumped out of his seat and shoved his way into the aisle, using the briefcase to wedge himself between a woman and her small children.

Joey grabbed his bag and slipped in behind the two kids. As the sluggish snake of passengers emerged into the concourse, he stopped to look around, causing a traffic jam in the narrow gangway behind him.

"W-W-Welcome to Sodom and G-G-Gonorrhea," Joey said, a line he'd been rehearsing the whole flight.

"Great. Now you're a Biblical scholar," Bobby Ray muttered under his breath. As they plodded past the airport bar, he glimpsed

Monday Night Football on one of the TVs. The Redskins were playing the Giants. *The New York Giants*, Bobby Ray reminded himself. Nobody admitted to being from Jersey since Sinatra left.

The feeding frenzy in baggage claim looked like a suburban shopping mall the day before Christmas. Bobby Ray spotted his bags before they tumbled down the chute. He elbowed his way through the crowd, shoving aside a mousy woman reaching for her luggage. Too surprised to scream, she flailed wildly, trying to regain her balance, and stumbled backward onto the conveyor belt, sprawled across a backpack and a twill garment bag. Her two small children watched in horror as she made the slow loop around the carousel.

Bobby Ray telescoped the handle on his roller bag and balanced the duffle on top so he could carry the briefcase in his free hand. He was headed to the rental desk when a myopic movie fan rushed over, waving a ballpoint pen and a sheet of hotel stationery.

"Mr. DeVito," she said, swooning. "Can I please have your autograph? You can make it out to Gladys Little."

He glared at her apple-doll face and scowled. Without breaking stride, he grabbed her by the wrist, drew it to his mouth, and bit down hard. Bobby Ray stormed away, the woman wailing in his wake, blood spurting from her thumb like black crude from a wildcatter's strike.

"You stank in *Get Shorty!*" she screamed. "Did you hear me? You *sta-a-a-ank*." The words died in her throat in a wet gurgle.

Joey trailed a few steps behind him in stunned silence. When Bobby Ray got to the line at the rental desk, he rocked his roller bag upright and wedged the briefcase under the duffle. He glanced over his shoulder at the crowd collecting in front of the luggage carousel. The group included two airport security officers who were wrapping the woman's hand in a towel.

"Jesus. Can you believe that lady? DeVito's practically a *midget*." Despite his nearly spherical dimensions, he saw himself as the dashing, leading-man type.

Joey stood, mouth open, trying to think of something to say.

"I'm gonna wait over here for Frank," he stammered. "H-H-He's picking me up."

Bobby Ray was staying at a casino the Venetti family-controlled and was relieved he didn't have to offer Fat Tony's stuttering cousin a ride. That's when he noticed the stunning, twenty-something blonde staring his direction.

Honey Maxwell was exceptionally beautiful. Athletically built with straight, flaxen hair past her shoulders, she was standing with her back to a row of slots, scanning the main terminal. She was anxious to finish her class film project, a true-crime piece, by the weekend but was losing her nerve. Honey tried to tell herself she was the videographer of a college prank and not the co-conspirator in a felony, but the prospect of jacking another car didn't feel that way. It no longer seemed exciting, just risky and stupid.

The last thing she needed was a panic attack, but Virgil's stunt at the Circle K had shaken her badly. Despite the two black-and-whites parked out front, Virgil insisted on stopping for beef jerky and a case of Old Milwaukee. Honey waited in the car, nervously watching the cops, expecting to be dragged off in handcuffs. That she didn't wind up in a prison jumpsuit steeled what little determination she had to film a second job – that and forgetting to take the lens cap off the camcorder for the first one.

Thirty feet away across the concourse, Be-Bop, whose real name was Roy, rolled and re-rolled the sleeves of his Ronnie "Special KKK" Flowers T-shirt, trying to decide how to show off the iron crosses and swastikas tattooed on his wiry arms.

Virgil leaned against the wall beside him, an unlit cigarette dangling from his mouth, doing his best James Dean. Be-Bop hooked his thumbs through his belt loops, cocked his head to one side, and checked himself in Virgil's sunglasses. Dissatisfied with the effect, he unrolled his sleeves and started again in tighter folds this time.

When Honey's eyes briefly met Be-Bop's, he flicked the side of his nose with an index finger like Paul Newman in *The Sting*. Virgil and Be-Bop stayed up the night before, watching the video twice. Around her friends, Honey referred to them as the "Hitler Twins" or "*Sig Heil* and Roy." If they'd known, they probably would have been flattered.

Honey glanced at Virgil, who flashed a crooked, gap-toothed smile. He told skinhead friends he chipped the tooth fighting a "nigger cop," but Be-Bop had told her the real story: Virgil cracked his left incisor on the toilet seat, throwing up hotdog spaghetti and bathtub pruno homebrewed by a paroled Ely alum.

The car-theft scheme was hatched one night at Sinderella's, a strip club where Honey tended bar. The Hitler twins were drinking with Harper Valentine, a shift manager at Lucky Chucky's Cars. After their third pitcher, Valentine broached the idea of stealing rentals. To the Hitler twins, it sounded like easy money.

They planned to grab multiple cars on the same night from different rental companies, figuring insurance investigators would be less suspicious if they spread the thefts around. In a moment of beer-tinged bravado, Valentine and the twins toasted "moving up to the big time."

Honey overheard them talking and asked if she could shoot the thefts for a school film project. She rationalized stealing rental cars as ripping off insurance companies, which she thought of as one rung below cockroaches and one above attorneys.

In exchange for a cut of the chop-shop money, Valentine, a blubbery toad who gave her the creeps, provided a set of keys for the first theft: a Firebird Trans Am rented to an elderly Duluth couple staying at the Tahitian Princess.

It seemed like a straightforward proposition, but the twins had a gift for turning something simple into a long, involved process. Virgil drove his beat-up Yugo around the resort's parking garage for forty minutes until they finally stumbled across the red convertible. In their rush to get away, they forgot they needed the Yugo to drive back from the chop shop, piled into the soon-to-be stolen Trans Am, and, over Honey's objections, went joyriding in the desert.

Besides documenting the car thefts, her immediate role was simple: she was supposed to choose the mark. As she scouted travelers in the crowded McCarran terminal, Honey was having second thoughts. She glanced across the concourse at Virgil and Be-Bop and realized she had to pick out somebody soon. The boys were getting antsy.

The airport was unusually busy. There was a major medical convention in town, and doctors were flying in from all over. The plan was to tail one from the rental lot to their hotel and boost the car out of the garage.

Honey was assessing potential targets when a commotion erupted by the luggage carousel. A woman started screaming someone "stank" and was "short" and that she was going to "get him." Honey couldn't immediately sort out what was happening, but a bowling-ball-shaped guy in a rumpled suit was motoring toward the rental counter at escape velocity. The woman's thumb looked like it was gushing blood. Two airport security officers stopped to see what the fuss was about, drawing an even bigger crowd.

Honey decided the bowling-ball guy was too rattled to think clearly and was as good a mark as any. She was halfway out the door by the time the Hitler twins realized she was moving.

7

Morrison trudged down the hallway, too tired to overthink Digby's invitation to make himself at home. The kitchen was tidy with tiled counters and white cupboards. Hand-washed dishes were arranged in a rack by the sink. He could hear Digby, Elvis, and Jimi talking in the living room like there was nothing unusual about a sixty-year-old Elvis impersonator in a cleric's collar chatting with the real Elvis and an invisible man.

Morrison foraged through the foil-wrapped leftovers in the fridge before deciding he wasn't *that* hungry. The sell-by date on the orange juice was more than a week away, but he sniffed it anyway before he poured himself a glass and settled into a chair at the kitchen table. After playing the dad in their impromptu family for three, long days, he was glad to have a moment to himself.

As he sipped his juice, Morrison wondered how Elvis and Jimi came to be *his* responsibility. Part of it was driving. Sitting behind the wheel assumed a particular place in the pecking order. Part of it was his personality, paired with a basic rule he learned in high school physics: nature abhors a vacuum. The rest was like the *Three Stooges* French Foreign Legion sketch, where the captain asked three volunteers to step forward. When everyone else stepped back, Larry, Moe, and Curly "volunteered."

That's what happened to me, he realized. *I forgot to step back.*

Morrison felt like he'd been caught up in a misguided practical joke. The limo rolled to a dead stop in front of the *Chapel d'Love*. He knew, without checking, the chapel phone number was the one Cosmo had given Elvis, and there was the Special Delivery letter. The hard part was not the weirdness of it all but feeling like he was the only one not in on the gag. Morrison smiled softly, realizing he was enjoying whatever this was.

As he finished his juice, he heard somebody in the hallway. A woman in her mid-thirties, five-two or three, walked into the kitchen and slid an armful of grocery bags onto the counter. She was very pretty with mischievous, blue eyes, high cheekbones, and straight, red hair to the middle of her back.

"I knew you were here," she said anxiously. "I saw your car out front."

Morrison stood to introduce himself. "Hi, I'm..."

"Jim Morrison. Yes, I know. I'm Sparkle."

"Your dad said you were shopping."

"I couldn't decide what to make," she said, nodding at the grocery bags, "so I stocked up on staples. We could go out for something if you're hungry and not too tired."

"No, going out would be great."

"Help with the groceries, and we'll get the others."

"The others? Oh, right, you mean..." Morrison hesitated, not sure how to explain his friends.

After everything was put away, he followed her to the living room. Digby had fallen asleep in an oversized chair with Jaxx curled up at his feet. Elvis was sitting cross-legged in front of the TV, watching a black-and-white movie with the volume turned all the way down.

"Hi, I'm Sparkle."

Elvis stood and took her hand. "Elvis. Very nice to meet you."

"It's good to meet you too." Sparkle glanced at Digby. "So, what did we miss?"

"Your father and *his* dog," Elvis said, nodding toward Morrison, "got into a one-sided discussion about cold fusion."

"I hope they didn't stray to current events," Morrison interjected. "The mutt can get pretty passionate about politics." Jaxx sensed they were talking about him and sat up. Morrison bent over and patted him on the head. "It's okay. You wait here. We'll be right back." Jaxx stretched, circled twice, and curled up again at Digby's feet. "We're thinking about getting something to eat. You hungry?"

Elvis nodded. "Starving."

Morrison glanced around the room. "Any idea where Jimi might be?"

"To the extent someone who is already invisible can do so, Mr. Hendrix has disappeared." Elvis grinned. "You guys go ahead. I'm right behind you."

The screen door had barely snapped shut when Sparkle tugged Morrison's sleeve. "What did he mean by *invisible?*"

"Cosmo didn't explain that part?"

"No, he only said you were coming. He was vague about the details."

"Right. You should probably get used to that." Morrison rubbed the coarse stubble on his chin. "Let's see, where to begin?"

"How about the beginning?"

Morrison shook his head. "No, we haven't got that long. How about I skip to the part where I tell you Jimi *is* invisible?"

"Invisible? So, if he was standing right in front of me, I couldn't see him?"

"Yes, also if he was beside you or behind you even if you turned around."

"Hmmm." Sparkle's brow furrowed. "Is that possible?"

"Apparently. Military stuff. All very hush, hush." Morrison's expression turned serious. "Knowing that, we should probably keep a low profile."

At the end of the sidewalk, the limo and a white pickup were parked nose to tail. Sparkle turned and saw Elvis walking their direction. "That'll have to do for now. Looks like we're going out to eat." She dangled her keys. "How about I drive?"

"You fly, I'll buy."

"There's an all-night diner off the Strip where dad and I go sometimes. It will be mostly empty this late."

"Perfect."

They squeezed into Sparkle's truck with Elvis in the back. Mindful of Morrison's comment about keeping a low profile, she stuck to side streets and kept a watchful eye on the rearview mirror.

Across the street from the Dewdrop Inn was a vacant lot with oversized parking for eighteen-wheelers and RVs, empty except for a lone Winnebago. As she was backing in beside the motorhome, Sparkle misjudged the spacing and grazed a side panel with her rear bumper.

"Damn," she groaned, shaking her head. "I can't believe I did that." Sparkle yanked open the glove box, dug out a pen and notepad, and jotted down her name and phone number. As soon as she finished, Morrison plucked it from her hand.

"I'll take care of it." He slid from the truck and wedged the note in the crease between the screen door and the frame. As he was climbing back in the cab, he jerked his thumb toward the Viking Club banner draped across the RV's flank. "I think we passed these guys on the way into town."

Elvis grinned. "That so?"

Sparkle decided the accident was an omen and parked in front of the diner next to a red Cadillac. They waited by the register while a forty-something waitress with bleached-blonde hair and dark roots poured coffee for a guy at the counter. He glanced up from his paper and said something funny, and they both laughed.

The waitress was wearing a pink gingham jumper with a Peter Pan collar and big, white buttons down the front. Morrison wondered if the uniforms were original or if the restaurant was going for a campy-retro look. She set the pot on the warmer and headed their direction.

"Howdy, folks. My name's Edna. Welcome to the Dewdrop Inn."

Sparkle stood on her tiptoes and craned her neck. "I don't see her, but Millie's our next-door neighbor. Would it be okay if we sat in her section?"

Edna shook her head. "Millie's gone home already. She worked the morning shift. How about I sit you by the window? When it gets late, it's a good idea to keep an eye on your car." She popped her gum and gestured toward a row of booths arranged back-to-back along the front of the restaurant. "Deandre, the night cook, had his Pinto broken into last week. Some lowlife stole his Anne Murray tapes."

Sparkle glanced at her truck and nodded in agreement. Edna grabbed three menus from the stack under the register and motioned them to follow. As they sat down, Morrison glanced at the only diners besides the guy at the counter, an elderly couple and a much younger man sitting behind him. While they were deciding what to order, the couple walked past on the way to the restrooms. The man was holding his wife's hand and carrying a horned helmet in the other.

"My parents go everywhere together," the man explained as soon as they were out of earshot, "even the bathroom."

"That's nice." Sparkle was looking over photos of breakfast specials on the laminated menu.

The man took any response as permission to strike up a conversation. "They ate here on their honeymoon." He finished his coffee, scowling at the cup as he set it on the table. "I'm pretty sure that pot's been on the warmer since the last time they were here. Then again, I doubt you can get decent Arabica beans in Vegas."

Sparkle forced a smile.

"Dr. Richard Little," he said. "Call me, Dick." When he grinned, his teeth looked like two neatly-stacked rows of marshmallows.

"Sparkle."

"Another day or two in there, and I'm gonna have to check on them." He glanced over her shoulder toward the bathrooms. "Dad's in early-stage dementia. That's the obvious diagnosis anyway. Geriatrics is not my specialty."

"What do you specialize in?" Sparkle asked, reluctantly attempting conversation.

"Plastic surgery." He grinned again, displaying a perfectly-matched pair of dimples. "I'm in town for the convention. I'm chairing one of the seminars."

Sparkle barely looked up from her menu.

Dr. Dick leaned forward, hoping to impress her. "My main office is in Beverly Hills, but I have satellites all over LA. I run full-page ads in the sports section and have eager clients lined up around the block."

Morrison's brow furrowed. "Why would a plastic surgeon advertise in the sports section?"

"Where else would you market penile implants?" Dr. Dick wiped his hands on a napkin. "Of course, I don't do *all* the surgeries personally. I have six surgeons on staff in four clinics. The West Hollywood office is booked seven days a week." He picked up a fresh napkin and wiped his hands again.

"The Cadillac Seville's a rental. I have a Mercedes SL 320 back home: black leather interior, DVD player, and a personalized license plate with *Dick Doc*."

Morrison wasn't sure he'd heard him correctly. "Your license plate says *Dick Doc*?"

Dr. Dick nodded. "Came up with it myself." Morrison looked down, pretending to study the menu.

The waitress arrived to take their orders just as Dr. Dick's parents were returning arm-in-arm. The woman had a pinched, apple doll face and was wearing a purple baseball cap with *Viking Club* stitched across the front in gold. Her left hand hung limply by her side. The thumb had been wrapped in gauze and white tape.

"These are my folks, Elmo and Gladys Little."

Elvis smiled warmly. "My mother's name was Gladys."

"If you don't mind too much, how about calling me, Mother? Nearly everybody does."

"I'd like that."

Gladys smiled. "Well, that works out well, 'cause I'd like that too."

Elmo was a couple inches taller than his wife and slightly paunched. As they were shaking hands, he noticed Elvis staring at the helmet cradled in his left arm. It had a dull, hammered metal surface and curved, ten-inch horns hooking out of each side. Elmo mistook Elvis's calm demeanor for admiration. He raised it in both hands and slipped it on his head. Silvery wisps of hair stuck out at odd angles along the edges. He looked at Sparkle and Morrison and smiled, like he was enjoying a private joke.

"Oh, Dad," Dr. Dick muttered.

Elmo ignored him. "You gotta admit, it's a great little icebreaker." He was hard of hearing and spoke more loudly than you'd expect in polite conversation.

Gladys rolled her eyes. "Don't mind him. He takes that darn thing with him everywhere he goes."

"Got to," he said. "I'm a charter member of the Duluth Viking Club."

"Yes, but the rest of those old fools only wear theirs for *meetings*."

"I answer to a higher calling."

"I think you're just high." Gladys elbowed him in the ribs, and they both giggled.

"Is that your RV across the street?" Morrison asked.

"The one with the Viking Club banner?"

Morrison nodded. "I think we passed you guys driving into town."

"Well, if you came in from the south, maybe you did. Mother and I visited the Hoover Dam this afternoon. Did you know they poured three and a half million cubic yards of concrete during construction?"

"No, I hadn't heard that." Morrison shifted uncomfortably in his seat. "I'm afraid we owe you an apology."

Elmo looked bewildered. "How's that?"

"I backed into your RV when we were parking," Sparkle said. "We left a note with contact info in the door."

"That's all right, Missy. Leave it to the insurance folks to sort out. In the meantime, I'd like some pie." Elmo looked around for the waitress. She was at the far end of the counter refilling salt and pepper shakers.

"The Duluth Viking Club," Morrison asked, "like the football team?"

Elmo circled his arm around his wife's scrawny shoulders. "No, we started the club right after the war, more than a decade before the NFL came to Minnesota. We're a service organization like Rotary. We called ourselves Vikings because most of the guys are descendants of the real McCoys."

Sparkle looked perplexed. "Little doesn't sound Scandinavian."

Elmo grinned. "We Littles hail from the Scottish Highlands, but, except for myself and a handsome Irishman named Tom Martin, everyone else is Norwegian. We used to have our meetings at the lunch counter in my dad's drugstore. When Jorma Jormasen called roll, it sounded like he was stuttering – Olaf Olafsen, Nils Nilsen, Magnus Magnusen, Soren Sorensen, Jen Jensen."

"Norsemen are a hale and hearty bunch," Gladys added, "but not very imaginative." She squeezed her husband's hand. "They asked Elmo to join because they'd been together since grade school and fought in the war together."

Elmo stared at his nearly empty coffee cup. "But that was a long time ago, and now we're all retired."

"And finally have time to travel," Gladys explained. "We use the club to arrange RV tours so we can get group discounts."

"Oh, Mother. You better stop before you blab the secret password."

Gladys gave her husband another bony elbow, and they giggled again. "We don't actually own a motorhome. We rented an RV from The Happy Hobo in Duluth. We're here for our second honeymoon."

"Well, Mother, we've had more than *two*," Elmo corrected, setting off another round of giggles.

As she dabbed her eye with a napkin, Gladys noticed Sparkle

staring at her bandaged thumb. "It happened at the airport," she explained. "We were meeting friends flying in from Minnesota. He has piles and doesn't travel well. They were afraid the long drive would be too much. We barely got to town in time because Elmo kept veering off on sightseeing detours. When we were in Kansas, Elmo drove sixty miles out of our way to see the world's largest..."

"Your *thumb*," Dr. Dick interrupted.

Gladys shot her son a peevish glance. "Are you gonna tell the story, or am I?" Dr. Dick picked up his fork and poked at the orange rind and sprig of parsley on his otherwise empty plate. "*Anyway*, Elmo and I were waiting by the luggage carousel when I saw Danny DeVito, you know, the actor in *Get Shorty?* When I asked for an autograph, he bit me." Gladys held up her bandaged hand.

"I rushed Mother to Urgent Care to get her patched up."

"The doctor gave me a tetanus shot," Gladys added. "Who knows where that vile, little mouth has been?"

When Edna stopped to see if they needed anything, the Littles ordered apple pie. Elmo patted his wife's arm. "You know, Mother, that wasn't *really* Danny DeVito." Gladys turned her withering stare on him, but he was not deterred. "My wife has a history of celebrity sightings. Two summers ago, she thought Whoopi Goldberg was working at the Dairy Queen, and last spring told everybody in town Tom Cruise was delivering our mail."

Before she could say anything, Edna returned with the pie. Gladys helped herself to a bite and used her napkin to wipe a smudge of filling from the corner of her mouth.

"Now Elmo," she protested, "I only said the waitress *looked* like Whoopi Goldberg, but that really was Tom Cruise when our regular mailman took his family to Niagara Falls." Gladys lightly drummed her fingers on her cheek. "I think sometimes famous people just wanna get away from being famous."

Elmo had stopped listening and was staring intently at Morrison. The talk about celebrities had triggered something. "I know you," he said, satisfaction evident in his face. "You're, you're..." Elmo stared blankly into space as the thought fluttered away. Morrison looked visibly unsettled.

"Dad's right," Dr. Dick added. "You *do* look familiar."

Morrison shrugged. "One of those faces, I guess."

Dr. Dick studied Morrison for a moment. "I was better with faces before I figured out the *real* money was in penile enhancement."

Gladys and her husband glanced at each other and rolled their eyes. Elmo finished the last of his pie and stood to leave. "We're gonna head back to the hotel. We're kinda tuckered."

"That's fine. I'll get the check and see you in the morning."

"It was mighty nice meeting you folks," Elmo said. "Next time you're in Duluth, look us up."

Morrison smiled. "It was mighty nice meeting you too."

Gladys leaned forward and gave him a hug. "Remember to call me, Mother," she reminded him. "You can call Elmo anything you want. He's deaf as a post."

She elbowed him again, setting off another round of giggles. Elmo laughed so hard he had to straighten his helmet. Gladys shook her head. "He only wears the damn thing so he can tell people he's horny."

Elmo glanced at Sparkle and Morrison and grinned. "You know how it is when you wake up every morning next to a beautiful woman. We just can't help ourselves."

Morrison started to explain how he and Sparkle weren't a couple, but before he could, Elmo, smiling impishly, leaned forward and patted Sparkle's hand. "You know the great thing about living as long as I have?"

"Besides being able to hide your own Easter eggs?" Gladys teased.

"Well, that too, but the best thing is, I get to see all my lies come true." Elmo winked as if sharing a great secret. "Now, if you folks will excuse us, we're gonna mosey along."

As the Littles strolled out the door holding hands, the waitress brought plates piled high with steaming mounds of pancakes and fried potatoes.

"Your parents are very nice," Sparkle said, taking a bite of scrambled eggs. "I hope I'm that happy when I'm their age."

Dr. Dick shrugged. "I keep marrying my nurses. The last divorce was number four. Ex-employees don't collect unemployment. I pay them spousal support."

Morrison and Sparkle chuckled. Even Elvis had to smile, but Dr. Dick appeared distracted. "I know who you look like," he said, pointing at Morrison. "Kirk Russell. You have Kirk Russell's face."

"*Kurt* Russell?"

"Right. I'm great with faces, lousy with names. You could make good money, special appearances, kid's parties, stuff like that. Celebrity lookalikes are big business in LA. You should come out to the coast." Morrison hunched over his pancakes and sausage, trying to evade his stare. Dr. Dick, smiling smugly, slid out of the booth.

"It was nice meeting you folks. Enjoy your evening." He glanced again at Sparkle before strolling to the register.

Morrison was reaching for the maple syrup when they heard tires screaming and the explosive impact of metal on metal. Morrison, Elvis, and Sparkle jumped up and charged out the door with Dr. Dick close behind them.

8

The stunning blonde disappeared into the surge of people streaming out the terminal doors. Bobby Ray tried to single her out of the bobbing sea of heads but lost her in the crowd. Behind him, the ferret-faced woman at the rental desk cleared her throat.

"Can I help you?" Her voice was as soothing as a dentist's drill. She folded her arms across her chest and appraised him over the top of her bifocals, resurrecting memories of the nuns who terrorized him in parochial school.

Bobby Ray stared at his loafers, unable to make eye contact. "I'm here to pick up my car," he mumbled, barely loud enough to be heard.

"License and credit card, please."

Bobby Ray fumbled through his wallet and slid them across the counter. For a frustratingly long time, her attention flitted back and forth between the monitor and a ringed binder open in front of her. Finally, she leaned over and whispered something to a pudgy guy in a short-sleeved dress shirt and clip-on tie. He was helping another customer but glanced up long enough to nod.

"I'm sorry, sir, the Seville you requested is not available. There's a doctors convention in town, and every luxury car was overbooked." Before Bobby Ray could react, she folded her arms across her chest again, cowing him with her stare. "How about a nice *Pontiac*?" She nodded to the man standing beside her. "Mr. Valentine has authorized me to make a Grand Prix available at the compact-car rate."

She pushed a pile of paperwork across the counter. Too bullied to react, Bobby Ray grabbed the pen and scribbled his name.

"Thank you, sir. Enjoy your stay in Las Vegas."

Bobby Ray snatched the key and folder from the counter and stormed outside to catch the shuttle. He ignored the pedestrian crossing and stepped in front of a yellow cab as it was pulling away from the curb. The taxi lurched to a stop, tires squealing, inches short of hitting him. The driver leaned out the window and shook his fist. Bobby Ray flipped him off without glancing his direction or even slowing down.

After the short shuttle ride, he wandered around the rental lot until he found his silver Grand Prix in a rainbow-hued herd of minivans. He tossed his bags and the briefcase onto the passenger seat and drove around to the exit. After the guard reviewed his paperwork, he gunned the engine and accelerated onto Tropicana Boulevard.

Halfway to the Tahitian Princess, Bobby Ray fished the .38 from his travel bag. Before he could slide it into his shoulder holster, a black-and-white stopped beside him at a red light. Even before the cop glanced his direction, he let the gun fall to the floor and pushed it under the seat with his heel.

When he got to the casino, Bobby Ray pulled into the parking garage and found a spot near the elevator, oblivious to the beat-up Yugo that tailed him from the airport. He grabbed his bags and made his way through the frenzied whirl of slot machines to the registration desk. While waiting behind an elderly couple in purple baseball caps, Bobby Ray realized he'd left his gun in the car.

"Damn," he muttered, loud enough to be heard.

"Watch your language," the woman standing behind him snapped. Because her back was toward him at the time, she didn't recognize Bobby Ray from the tumble at the luggage carrousel, but her kids did. They wrapped themselves so tightly around her legs, she almost lost her balance again.

"Watch it yourself," Bobby Ray growled as he stormed past. When he exited the elevator, he nearly bowled over a blonde shooting video with a hand-held camera. Bobby Ray was almost to the car when he recognized her from the airport. He started to turn to say something when he saw two guys slim-jimming the door on his

Grand Prix. They had their backs to him, and Bobby Ray was on top of them before they realized he was there.

"Well, whatta we got here? Looks like a couple of scumbags breaking into *my* car."

The skinny guy looked up in a panic, but the stocky one frantically pumped the flat rod up and down until the door popped open. He leaned inside and picked up Bobby Ray's .38, which had slid out from under the seat.

"A couple scumbags with your gun," he said, pointing the revolver at Bobby Ray's chest. "I believe that makes me *Mr. Scumbag* to you."

Bobby Ray froze mid-step as the girl came up behind him. "What the hell are you doing?" she screeched.

"It's okay. Everything's under control. Isn't that right?" Virgil was looking at Bobby Ray.

"Oh, everything's just peachy, *Mr.* Scumbag."

"This *wasn't* the plan." Her voice was quivering.

"Well, we got ourselves a brand-new plan. Gimme the keys." When he hesitated, Virgil pressed the .38 into the soft skin under the gangster's chin. Bobby Ray fished the keys out of his jacket and dropped them on the hood. Virgil picked them up, walked to the back of the car, and popped the trunk.

"Dump your stuff in here." Bobby Ray tossed in his bags and the briefcase and slammed the lid. Virgil waved the revolver, motioning him toward the front passenger seat. "All right. Everybody in the car."

Virgil tossed Be-Bop the keys and slid in behind Bobby Ray, snuggling the muzzle of the .38 against the base of his skull. Honey got in the back seat beside Virgil and stared sullenly out the window.

The Hitler twins drove around bickering for twenty minutes before finally deciding to dump Bobby Ray at an all-night diner. Be-Bop pulled into the lot across the street and parked beside a Winnebago.

"Get out of the car," Virgil demanded, "and take off your clothes."

"Take off my clothes? Are you nuts?"

"Down to your tidy whities." Virgil cocked the hammer on the .38. "Now."

Bobby Ray slid out of the car, stripped to his underwear and socks, and tossed his clothes and shoes on the passenger seat.

"Honey, you shrunk the squid," Be-Bop sneered, pointing at Bobby Ray's crotch. Virgil squealed with laughter. Honey's reaction was more of a nervous twitter.

Bobby Ray jabbed his finger their direction. "You won't think this is so *effing* funny when I catch up with you bozos."

Virgil kicked Bobby Ray's clothes onto the floor as he climbed over the seat. "Well, I guess we'll see you tomorrow then." He slammed the door, and Be-Bop punched the gas pedal. The Pontiac burned rubber out of the parking lot, kicking up clouds of gravel and dust.

"Yeah, you'll see me tomorrow," Bobby Ray growled as the Grand Prix disappeared around the corner. "You can count on that."

The lot was empty except for the RV and a payphone on the corner. Bobby Ray scuttled to the phone and punched 4-1-1. Directory assistance gave him Frank Cozzaglio's number and connected the call. Frank didn't pick up until the fifth ring.

"Hello?"

"Will you accept a collect call from Bobby Ray Darling?"

"From who?"

"Bobby Ray Darling."

"Who?"

"Take the damn call," Bobby Ray growled.

"Ah, yes, ma'am. I'll accept the charges."

"Frank, come pick me up right now."

"Hold on, I'm watching *Bonanza*. I'll get Joey."

"Frank!" Bobby Ray screamed, but he was already gone. He seethed for nearly a minute, waiting for Joey to come to the phone.

"H-H-Hello."

"Joey. I'm across the street from some shitty little diner, the Dewdrop Inn. You and your brother gotta pick me up."

"Pick you up? What about your car?"

"Never mind my car. Come pick me up. You know the place?"

"Hold on a second." There was another maddening pause while Joey went to ask his brother. "Frank says he has waffles there sometimes. We'll be over after *Bonanza*."

"No, Joey." Bobby Ray's jaws were clenched so tightly he could barely speak. "You're gonna get here sooner than right now."

"B-B-But Hoss's gonna fight the Duke of London."

"You better be here before I hang up!" he screamed.

"Jeez, okay. W-W-We'll be right over."

Instead of hanging up, Bobby Ray slammed the handset against the phone until it shattered. The mouthpiece, still attached by the silver cord, dangled from the receiver like the guest of honor at a lynching.

From the waist up, Bobby Ray looked like he had on a cashmere sweater but knew if he stayed in the well-lit phone booth long enough, somebody would try to stuff dollar bills in his Fruit of the Looms. He shoved open the door and stormed across the lot to wait beside the motorhome.

As angry as he was about getting carjacked, Bobby Ray wasn't going to call the cops. The stolen Grand Prix was the rental company's problem, but he planned to turn over every rock in Vegas until he found the crew.

"I'll start with the guys with the swastika tattoos," he muttered. "Somebody will remember those two. Social outcasts make an impression."

He was waiting in the shadows when an elderly couple strolled across the street from the diner. The woman nearly bumped into him, then froze, staring at the squat, furry figure stripped to his underwear.

"Whaddya looking at, lady?" he growled.

"Elmo, it's a naked man!" she shrieked.

The old guy in the Viking helmet hadn't noticed Bobby Ray, even though they were only a few feet apart. "A sacred ram?" he asked hopefully. Elmo stretched out his arms, palms up, and stared skyward as if giving thanks to the cosmos.

"The old coot's as crazy as a shithouse rat," Bobby Ray mumbled.

Gladys, horrified when she recognized him from the airport, grabbed her husband by the wrist and dragged him into the motorhome, screaming, "Don't look back!" as if one more glance at Bobby Ray would have turned them into pillars of salt.

Sparkle, Morrison, Elvis, and Dr. Dick could see the not-so-late-model Cadillac that had crashed demolition-derby style into the Little's Winnebago from the diner steps. A short, round guy in briefs and black socks was pummeling the side of motorhome with his fists. He shouted something they couldn't hear, slid back behind the wheel, and pulled ten or fifteen feet forward. Bot passengers held up their hands, pleading with him to stop, but he shifted into reverse and punched the accelerator. The convertible plowed into the motorhome's midsection, impaling the RV almost to the Caddy's back seat. Apparently satisfied with the level of destruction, he revved the engine and roared away, tires screaming.

Before the others could react, Sparkle broke ranks and sprinted across the street. When she reached the motorhome, a badly shaken Gladys Little had mustered enough courage to peek out the kitchen window. Through a Cadillac-sized hole in the RV, Sparkle could see Elmo sitting on the john, still wearing his Viking helmet, his pants around his ankles.

"You guys okay?" she very nearly shouted. Gladys nodded weakly. Elmo leaned forward and flashed two thumbs up. By that time, the others had caught up with her. Sparkle patted Dr. Dick's arm. "At least they're all right."

He blinked twice, rooted to the asphalt. His mouth ratcheted open and shut, but no words came out. Water from the RV's ruptured plumbing line splashed against his slacks and beaded on his Italian loafers. "Yes, at least they're all right," he repeated. His wispy, blond hair was plastered against his skull with sweat and his head bounced up and down like a baby chick's when he said it.

Sparkle patted his arm again. "You should call the police."

"Right, the police." He pulled a cell phone from his pocket and stared at it for a moment before haltingly punching 9-1-1 into the keypad. The emergency operator picked up on the second ring. "Hello, I want to report a, well, a crime, I guess."

Morrison leaned closer to Sparkle. "I wondered if it's occurred to his celebrity-sighting mother, he looks like Niles on *Frasier?*" Sparkle tried to look stern, but Morrison saw traces of wry amusement in her eyes.

While Dr. Dick was on the phone explaining the situation, Elmo hitched up his pants. With help from Morrison and Elvis, he and Gladys climbed out through the gaping wound in the RV. The motorhome looked like it'd been gored by a giant, steroid-addled bull. Shards of laminated fiberglass, splintered two-by-two framing, and chunks of Styrofoam insulation were strewn everywhere.

Elmo shook his head as he appraised the damage. "It's gonna take more than duct tape to make that right."

Over Elvis's shoulder, Morrison saw the flashing lights of a black-and-white headed their direction. While everyone else was focused on the police car, he picked up Sparkle's note, dislodged from the door jamb when the Littles rushed inside, and stuffed it into his pocket.

The police cruiser rolled to a stop fifteen feet away, illuminating the scene in its headlights. After taking a moment to assess things, a uniformed officer stepped from the car. He was about Morrison's height, thick through the shoulders, with thinning brown hair. Backlit by the lights from his cruiser, his boyish features were barely visible.

"Everybody okay?" His attention flitted back and forth between the faces in the headlights and the gored motorhome. Six heads coalesced in a chorus of nods. "I'm Officer Costanza." He glanced over his shoulder as another unit arrived.

The second policeman was shorter, Hispanic, and looked like a gym rat. "I'm Officer Martinez," he said as he pulled the cap off his pen with his teeth. "Who wants to go first?"

By the time Detective Hennigan arrived, Martinez and Costanza had finished with the Littles. Gladys's statement was fairly detailed, but Elmo's consisted almost entirely of vague ramblings about "a sacred ram." Hennigan, a twenty-year police vet, was a shade over six feet tall with dark hair and movie-star good looks. He would have been content to just observe, but sensing he was a man of some importance, Gladys dogged him around the crime scene, trying to get his attention.

She finally caught up with him by Costanza's black-and-white. After overhearing bits and pieces of her husband's statement, she was feeling defensive. She glanced at Elmo, who was standing beside the Winnebago, humming quietly to himself.

"Since Elmo's gotten forgetful, I'm the co-pilot and navigator," Gladys explained. "I never let him drive by himself."

"I get a little forgetful myself," Hennigan said reassuringly. He hadn't seen Costanza's report about the sacred ram yet.

"I just wanted you to know."

"I'll see it's in the report." Hennigan was careful to use his *make-the-old-lady-feels-safe* voice. He excused himself and walked over to check in with Costanza.

Confident she'd made her point, Gladys squeezed Elmo's hand. "See that nice detective? He reminds me of Colombo, only better looking. And the officer over there," she said, pointing at Martinez, "looks like Eric Estrada."

Hennigan, who was still close enough to hear, bit his lip, trying not to smile.

Elmo glanced at Hennigan, then Martinez. "You know, you're right. I guess they kinda do."

"Well, I said they looked like them. I never said they *were* Colombo and Eric Estrada." Gladys squeezed Elmo's hand a little tighter. "I think it's important to make that distinction. I wouldn't want you getting confused again."

Elmo rubbed his chin as he remembered something that came to him when they were in the diner. "That fella's Jim Morrison," he said softly, "and the other one is..."

"Oh, Elmo," she interrupted before he could say, Elvis Presley. "We don't have time for that now." Elmo started to object, but one look at his wife told him his revelation could wait.

Costanza was leaning against the black-and-white working on his report. He glanced up when he saw the detective walking toward him. An all-state linebacker in high school, Hennigan partnered with Tommy's dad at Metro Homicide and went to every game his senior year. College recruiters were beating down the door until he tore his ACL.

Except that his sandy-blond crew cut had begun a hasty retreat at the temples and he'd put on twenty pounds, Tommy looked pretty much the same as the day he hobbled across the auditorium stage on crutches and picked up his diploma. As he slouched against the police cruiser, Hennigan noticed how hard the buttons were straining to hold his uniform closed.

Maybe thirty pounds, he conceded.

"I heard the call. Indecent exposure's not my usual area of expertise, but since I was in the neighborhood, I decided to stop and see if you boys needed help."

Costanza folded his arms across his chest and rolled his head to one side. "And I thought you're just fishing for ideas for your next bestseller."

Hennigan smiled. He still got occasional grief over *The King Kong Case.* The plotline grew out of a late-night vice raid on Discount Dan's, a mattress store moonlighting as a whorehouse. The bust netted a dozen bleach-blonde hookers, a trunk full of gorilla suits, a busload of Taiwanese businessmen, and two presidential candidates. Inventing a dashing lead detective and a little poetic license was all it took to turn the story into a modestly successful paperback.

"Why?" he asked, feigning nonchalance. "You think a naked guy playing bumper cars with an RV might make a good page-turner?"

"Snoop around all you like, but I'm pretty sure the perp's long gone."

Hennigan shook his head. "Still the wise guy, huh? Just like your old man. How is Jackie, anyway? Staying busy working casino security?"

"Yeah, the Tahitian Princess. Mom says he only took the job for the showgirls."

"Sounds about right." Hennigan glanced over his shoulder at the motorhome. "So, whatta we got here?"

Costanza checked to make sure only Hennigan could hear. "In twenty-five words or less, even with the physical evidence and the testimony of five eyewitnesses, not counting the old man, I think they made the whole thing up."

Hennigan chuckled. "Maybe we should take 'em downtown for a session with rolled newspapers and rubber hoses."

Costanza glanced at Morrison, who was talking with Martinez. "Probably just some down-on-his-luck gambler who lost his shirt."

"*And* his pants," Hennigan added, and they both laughed. "Well, since I'm here, at least give me the highlights."

"All righty, then. You're the detective. The old lady swears the perp was Danny DeVito."

"You put out an APB?"

Costanza held his fist in front of his mouth like he was holding a microphone. "Attention, all units. Be on the lookout for a naked Danny DeVito making a last, desperate pass at the crap tables."

They were still chuckling when they got to Martinez, who was finishing up the last interview. When he was Hennigan's training officer, Jack Costanza, Tommy's old man, warned him about playing poker with a detective. "A shield's a human lie detector," he told him. "They can read you like a book."

Hennigan's detective instincts prickled. Even at a glance, he could tell Morrison was hiding something. Suspects lied to him. Witnesses lied to him, but his instincts never did. He'd been on the job long enough to tell good guys from bad guys, even if he couldn't prove it beyond a reasonable doubt. Hennigan's cop sense told him this was a good guy.

"He was short with a chip on his shoulder," Morrison told Martinez, "and walked like this." Morrison waddled halfway to the ruined RV and back, mimicking Bobby Ray's self-important, corncob strut. "You know, the kind of guy who drives a Porsche."

Martinez and Costanza both laughed, but Morrison didn't know the real reason why. Even though his Porsche was fifteen years old and picked up at a DEA auction, when he wasn't behind the wheel of an unmarked police car, Hennigan drove a 911.

9

After everything salvaged from the RV was loaded into Dr. Dick's Seville, there was another round of goodbye hugs, the Littles left for their hotel, and Sparkle, Morrison, and Elvis went inside to finish eating.

While Costanza and Martinez completed their reports, Hennigan leaned against the hood of his car, closed his eyes, and pictured himself fly-fishing in a mountain stream. He could almost hear the music filament makes whipping through the air and the faint pop of a jig hitting the water when Costanza cleared his throat.

"Sleeping on the job?"

Hennigan shook his head. "Just thinking about taking some vacation time."

"If I go anywhere, I gotta take the family. After a couple of days with Rochelle and the kids, I'm ready to be back at work."

"I can see how you wouldn't wanna miss all this."

Costanza shrugged. "I don't know. This is just the sort of case I was hoping would come along and jumpstart my literary career."

Hennigan rolled his eyes. "I should've published that damn book under a pseudonym."

"Anonymous authors don't get invited to *Oprah*."

"Well, neither did I." Hennigan jerked his chin toward the strip mall behind the diner. "Discount Dan's was where the food court is now."

"I remember. Rochelle and I bought a sofa there after breakfast at the diner. The kids love the waffles."

Hennigan could see Sparkle, Morrison, and Elvis through the window. "The Dewdrop Inn's where I proposed to Sheila. We were sitting in the same booth as our witnesses. Hey, what's today?"

"The twenty-eighth."

Hennigan sighed. "Nine years ago, *today*."

"Happy anniversary."

"Thanks, I guess. She ordered the Shrimp Louie, dressing on the side. I had the chicken-fried steak and a glass of the delightful house red."

"Steeling your resolve?"

"I was less terrified my first time in combat. After Sheila said "yes," I went to the bathroom and threw up on my shoes."

"You probably shoulda seen that as an omen."

"Hindsight's 20/20." Hennigan half turned and glanced at the convenience store on the corner. "See the Circle K? That's where Chestakowski body-slammed a would-be Cheeto thief across the windshield of a Plymouth Voyager."

"I heard about Cheezesteak's suspension."

"He brought it on himself."

"Yeah, but…"

"He brought it on himself," Hennigan repeated, more firmly this time. Costanza's radio buzzed as a call came in from dispatch. A truck reported stolen had turned up in the alley behind the strip mall. Martinez radioed they'd take the call.

"We're gonna roll if that's okay."

"No problem. I'll hang here till the cavalry arrives."

"You sure?"

"Positive. I'll lock up and turn out the lights."

Costanza and Martinez climbed into their cruisers and had barely disappeared around the corner when the tow truck arrived. The driver swung the rig around, backed up to the RV, then heaved himself out of the cab and stood for a moment, surveying the scene.

"I'm Walt," he said, tugging on the brim of his Runnin' Rebels baseball cap.

Hennigan had already read his name embroidered over the pocket of his coveralls. "Detective Hennigan. Metro Homicide."

"Homicide, huh? You don't need to wait for the coroner's report. Pretty sure the COD was blunt force trauma."

"Yeah, kind of a long story."

"I can believe that." Walt pulled off his cap and ran his fingers through a greasy matt of dark hair. "Jeez, what a mess."

The detective gave him a half-smile and tried to look sympathetic. "Then I guess you better get started."

Walt walked around the motorhome, deciding where to begin. After the second lap, he folded his arms across his chest and shook his head. "This has gotta be more than the regular rate."

"Do you guys *always* angle for more money?"

"Come on," he pleaded. "Look at this mess. And we practically do city jobs for free. This has gotta be extra."

Hennigan held up his hands, palms forward. "I'll see what I can do."

Walt figured that was as good as he was going to get and went to work loading the Winnebago. Hennigan thought his accent sounded like New York or maybe Jersey. Nobody, it seemed, was from Las Vegas.

Hennigan was also a transplant, born and raised in Framingham, a small town outside Boston. After getting out of the Marine Corps, he stopped to visit Jack Costanza, his staff sergeant in Viet Nam, and stayed long enough to interview with Metro PD. Since graduating from the police academy, he'd only been back to Massachusetts three times. Once for his mom's funeral and twice for Christmas with his dad.

In less than thirty minutes, Walt had the RV loaded and strapped to the truck bed, ready for transport to the city yards. After checking to make sure everything was secure, he climbed in the truck cab, nodded goodbye, and rumbled out of the parking lot.

Hennigan pulled the Crown Vic around to the alley behind the strip center. Costanza and Martinez were there along with the stolen delivery truck, an ambulance, a fire engine, and a third black-and-white. He parked and walked to Costanza, who was leaning on the hood of his cruiser, filling out a report. He barely looked up from his clipboard.

"Sniffing out more ideas for your next bestseller?"

Hennigan ignored him. "Busy night."

Costanza grunted in agreement. The alley was squeezed between a cinderblock wall and the back of the strip center. The ambulance and fire truck crews were joking with the third officer as he strung yellow police tape between the building and the wall. Hennigan didn't recognize him and assumed he was a rookie.

"What throngs of lookie-loos is he keeping out of the crime scene?" Hennigan rubbed his temples again. His headache was getting worse.

"He's only doing the job he was taught at the Academy."

"Those who *can,* do."

"And those who can't, teach at the Academy."

Hennigan grinned. Costanza's old man said that a lot when they were partners. Between the two of them, he and Tommy had probably heard it a million times. "How about we finish this up?" he asked. "Is there an inventory so we can figure out what's missing?"

"Martinez has it. The truck's full of Elvis junk."

"Around here, he's still a headliner."

Costanza grabbed a sequined, white cape from a box in the back of the truck, draped it over his shoulders, and whirled around, his lip curled in an exaggerated sneer. "Viva, Las Vegas," he crooned, badly off-key.

"Long live the King!" one of the firemen shouted.

Costanza windmilled his arms, dropped to one knee, and pumped his fist in the air. Caught up in his antics, the ambulance and fire crews broke out in applause.

"Quit playing with the evidence," Hennigan scolded, pretending to be stern. "I'd like to be home before the sun gets up."

Costanza used the liftgate to pull himself to his feet and leaned against the truck bed, trying to catch his breath. "Hurry up in there!" he shouted. "There's someplace our detective would rather be."

"We'd be done already if you weren't completely useless," Martinez shouted back.

Costanza balled up the cape and tossed it back in the box. He rummaged through the next carton and pulled out a lava lamp with a leather-jacketed Elvis strumming a guitar. "Hey, Hennigan, you should get one of these for Amanda."

"What would my four-year-old daughter want with one of those?"

"I don't know. I was just saying."

"Tommy, don't make me shoot you."

Costanza's brow furrowed. "I don't get it. Who'd wanna steal this stuff?"

"You don't think a black velvet painting of Elvis at the Last Supper is a fashionably ironic Da Vinci homage?"

"I'm more of a dogs-playing-poker kinda guy."

"Perfectly suitable man-cave decor, but works like this are meant for public spaces."

"Like behind the busted refrigerator Rochelle's been bugging me to haul to the dump?"

"Exactly!"

Costanza shook his head. "This has gotta be a publicity stunt, right? Local networks monitor the police band. Maybe this is some marketing genius's ploy for free TV time."

"Any minute now, the place will be crawling with camera crews zooming in for headshots."

Costanza fished a roll of Certs from his pocket, thumbed one out of the foil, and popped it in his mouth. "All right, Mr. DeMille, I'm ready for my close-up."

"Wow, crime-fighting super cop *and* Gloria Swanson. That's *some* range."

Martinez held up a black dinner plate with a Vegas-era Elvis in a sparkly, white jumpsuit. "I've found everything except twenty-four place settings."

Hennigan's shoulders slumped. "I remember that china from my wedding." He used the liftgate as a step stool and climbed into the truck. Martinez ran his finger down the inventory until he came to the dishes. He tapped the entry twice and handed the clipboard to Hennigan.

While they were searching for the AWOL dishes, Spencer Orange, the Assistant Special Agent in charge of the FBI's Nevada field office, showed up with a guy Hennigan didn't recognize. He remembered Cheezesteak saying something about a hotshot, new fed in town before he got suspended. Hennigan suspected his inside information came from the Bureau's top-heavy receptionist. Cheezesteak had plied her with copious amounts of alcohol at an interagency meet-and-greet. When Hennigan and Martinez finished, the feds were still chatting with Costanza.

"Good evening, Detective Hennigan."

"Good evening, Special Agent Orange."

"This is Special Agent Newman."

Hennigan jumped down, and they shook hands. The uniformed officers took that as their cue to leave. Costanza jerked a thumb toward his police cruiser. "We gotta go protect and -- what was that other thing?" He cocked his head to one side and looked at the FBI agents feigning bewilderment.

"*Serve*, Officer Costanza," Newman chimed in, trying to be helpful. "I believe *serve* is the word you're looking for."

"Yeah, right." Costanza rolled his eyes. "Thanks, kid. You could teach at the Academy."

He clapped Newman hard between the shoulder blades. The FBI agent staggered a half step forward before regaining his balance. Costanza and Martinez were still chuckling as they climbed into their black-and-whites. The ink hadn't dried on their reports when Special Agent Orange started asking Hennigan some very peculiar questions.

Long after everyone else had gone, the lights were still on in Agent Orange's office. Not much of a morning person, he preferred late-night meetings. Besides, they fostered the illusion of working long hours.

Richard "Newmeat" Newman was sitting across the desk from him, holding a photograph in each hand. One had "Bobby Ray Darling" written in blocky letters on the back; the other "Carmine Verduci" in a lilting, feminine script. Bobby Ray's was a mug shot from one of his arrests. Verduci's was from the media packet the White House passed out to reporters and tourists.

In the next few days, the federal grand jury in the Southern District of New York was issuing warrants for seventeen members of the Venetti crime family. Bobby Ray Darling was already in Vegas, and Verduci would be arriving soon. Major arrests always looked good on an agent's record, even if they amounted to nothing more than being in the right place at the right time. Slapping cuffs on Verduci and Darling oozed career-defining potential.

Newmeat set the headshots aside and thumbed through a stack of "surveillance" photos he took with his cell phone camera during the flight from LA. Like most junior agents, he was fascinated with gadgets. Newmeat lingered on one of Bobby Ray and an unidentified man in a Mets cap. Unidentified individuals were always classified "as-of-yet" per Bureau policy.

"So, this is our guy," he said matter-of-factly in his best FBI voice. In Orange's experience, most new agents talked like movie G-Men. "He doesn't look like a Mafia hitman."

Orange had to concede Newmeat was right. Bobby Ray was less steely-eyed and calculating than balding and flatulent. Pencil in a thin mustache and slap on a fedora and black trench coat, and he'd make the perfect cartoon villain.

Orange picked up the file. "Verduci went to Annapolis."

Newmeat glanced up as if he'd said something transcendent. "So, he's an Academy man?" He said *Academy man* like it was sacred.

"Verduci was appointed to the Naval Academy on the recommendation of Warner Hoskins, Don Bruno's Senator. Not *his* Senator because he represented the don's state but *his* Senator because Venetti owned him. Verduci was flunking out his first semester when photos of Hoskins and a couple hookers arrived at the Senator's office with a note strongly suggesting he pass. The don's letter gives *correspondence course* a whole new meaning."

Orange's attempt at humor sailed right past Newmeat. He was staring at the airplane photos again, his eyes as glazed as a cop's doughnut. Orange flipped through the file until he came to pictures of Hoskins and the hookers. "I don't remember meeting Mrs. Senator, but I'm pretty sure neither of these young ladies is his wife."

Newmeat leaned forward and tapped his finger on one of the pictures. "She must do a lot of yoga." Orange slid the photos back in the file, confident the Bureau could count on Hoskins' support for the upcoming FBI appropriations bill.

"Verduci graduated last in his class, without ever actually going to class. He spent his undistinguished, six-year service career drinking at the officer's club and fraternizing with noncoms." Orange realized his partner wasn't following the subtext. His eyes had glazed over again. "Fraternizing being a euphemism for behavior generally characterized as *don't ask, don't tell.*"

"Oh, you mean he was —"

Orange nodded. The American intelligence community didn't have a clue who killed Kennedy or about homegrown terrorists plotting to blow up the federal building in OKC, but if you wanted the dirty lowdown on who was sleeping with whom, they had you covered. With J. Edgar's fondness for high heels, simple black dresses, and feather boas, it seemed like a curious legacy.

"As his service commitment was winding down, Verduci got caught playing priest and the altar boy in the barrack showers. Given the face-saving choice of pursuing a career as a civilian and a court-martial, he resigned his commission."

Around Washington, there were still people who referred to him as *"Father Verduci."* That and that, even in his late forties, he was a chronic bed wetter, were not in the file.

"After Verduci was discharged, he joined the reserves and climbed through the ranks from captain to lieutenant colonel without ever showing up for monthly training exercises or meeting his annual service commitment. He has an extensive goat porn collection and sneaks into the White House Media Room for late-night movie marathons." That wasn't in the file either, but Orange couldn't resist sharing it with his junior partner.

Newmeat wore the blank expression of an obedient dog told to wait. "Are we going to involve local law enforcement?"

Orange shook his head. "Not right away. Too many security concerns." He didn't say so but planned to wait until they needed help with the heavy lifting.

"I only ask because you brought the detective in on that other matter."

Agent Orange glanced at the second file with obvious disgust. It held a single sheet of paper: an unsigned memo advising the Vegas field office to be on the lookout for Elvis Presley. On the offhand chance it wasn't a prank, talking with Hennigan would cover his ass if Washington *seriously* expected him to look for Elvis. Until circumstances dictated otherwise, he was going to consider the request a practical joke.

"I'm not gonna waste time chasing a ghost." Orange pushed the file to the far corner of his desk. "We'll toss out some feelers. If Hennigan or some other flatfoot stumbles across anything useful, we'll step in and take credit. Until then, consider the matter low-priority."

Orange was thinking about grabbing a steak at Binion's. He liked walking past the Million Dollar Display. As he flipped the Venetti file closed, one of Newmeat's airplane photos fluttered out and landed on the desk. Orange sighed.

"In the old days, the FBI hunted *real* bad guys like Dillinger and Machine Gun Kelly. We get Boris Badanov. I wonder how long before Natasha shows up."

As things worked out, he wouldn't have to wait long at all.

Streaked in shades of industrial gray, Tokyo's afternoon sky looked like a TV tuned to a dead channel. Cleopatra Takahara lit another cigarette and checked the time on her phone. She was waiting for her uncle and had taken refuge from the light drizzle in her building's foyer. She was surprised when Hiro offered her a ride to the airport — waiting and wondering *why* ate at her.

Cleopatra would have been willowy if she was taller, but at five-six, was only thin. Her narrow face was framed with square-cut bangs nearly to her eyebrows and straight black hair past her shoulders. Almost forty, lines had begun to etch their way into the corners of her eyes. She finished her coffee, crushed the empty cup, and tossed it into the trash bin by the mailboxes.

When her uncle's limousine pulled up to the curb, he was invisible behind smoked windows of bulletproof glass. Hiroshi Shinozawa was *oyabun*, the godfather of Japan's most powerful criminal family, and the most calculating man she'd ever known. Everything he did was precisely planned and carried out with the utmost attention to detail. Briefings were almost always handled by Noguchi, his security chief, whose car pulled in and parked behind the limo. For Hiro to brief her personally was out of the ordinary. Halfway to the curb, she took a last drag on her cigarette, dropped the butt onto the pavement, and ground it out with her boot.

Four bodyguards in matching black suits and wraparound sunglasses emerged from Noguchi's car. Three took up positions around the *oyabun's* limo, their heads swiveling back and forth in overlapping fields of fire. The fourth walked stiffly to Cleopatra's side, opened the door, and stowed her bags in the trunk. None of them acknowledged her as she slid in beside her uncle. In the front seat, the driver and another bodyguard sat stone-faced, staring straight ahead. Hiro raised the partition so he and Cleopatra could talk privately.

The air inside the limo was cool, but Hiro was sweating profusely. As the cars pulled away from the curb, he dabbed his face with a silk handkerchief, stuffed it into the sleeve behind the seat, and retrieved a fresh one. Built like a sumo wrestler, even being alone with him in the back seat felt claustrophobic. Hiro hefted his huge, toady body to one side so he could face her.

"Are you well, Uncle?" Cleopatra asked, uncomfortable with the protracted silence.

His eyes narrowed as he waggled a fat sausage-like finger in her direction. "You need not worry about me, young gentlewoman," he said, pretending to scold her. "I have been dying my whole life." The faintest suggestion of a smile flickered across his face. The tension, suddenly and unexpectedly broken, Cleopatra relaxed a little.

"We are in sensitive negotiations with our American associates." He spoke softly, but she heard the seriousness in his voice. "I am flying to Las Vegas tomorrow on my jet. You are leaving today because I have special work for you."

She leaned a little closer. "*Special work*" sounded like an assassination. He closed his eyes and collected himself. When he opened them, he seemed to be studying her.

"What would you have me do?"

"Wait."

Cleopatra looked puzzled. Hiro retrieved a computer disc in a plastic sleeve from his pocket and handed it to her. "Noguchi prepared some files for you. After you have read them, destroy the disc."

She nodded and slipped the sleeve into her jacket. While the limo was idling at a red light, she watched kids in school blazers playing in the rain. One of them, a girl about nine or ten, glanced their direction. Cleopatra started to wave but realized she couldn't see her behind the darkly-tinted windows. She rocked forward and

114

rested her forehead against the glass. Cleopatra could not recall playing as a child. A nagging sense of loss tugged at her. Hiro seemed to sense what she was feeling.

"What do you remember of your mother?"

"I remember she was sad."

"I remember that too." Hiro cleared his throat and waited until she'd turned to face him. "And what do you remember of your father?" Cleopatra bit the inside of her cheek. The question had caught her off guard. Until that moment, they'd never spoken of him, even when her mother died.

"Only that he went away."

"And nothing else?"

Cleopatra hesitated before answering. "I heard you worked together after the war."

"We will talk of him when we get back." Hiro picked up the newspaper folded on the seat beside him and opened it to the sports section. Cleopatra stared out the window, questions raging inside her like squall lines in a typhoon.

The ritual of her pickup was repeated at Narita. Three bodyguards stood watch while a fourth helped her from the car, retrieved her bags from the trunk, and checked them with the skycap. When Cleopatra turned to say goodbye, Hiro was invisible behind the smoke-black windows but bowed curtly just the same.

She walked briskly through the terminal and arrived at the gate as her flight was being called. Cleopatra boarded with the other first-class passengers, set her laptop on the aisle seat, and tossed her denim jacket to the window one. She had her half of the row to herself. In a crowded country like Japan, the empty seat spoke volumes about the wealth and power of Hiroshi Shinozawa. The message was not lost on the flight attendants who offered her champagne before she sat down.

An hour into the flight, Cleopatra pushed aside the in-flight meal, retrieved the silver data disc Hiro had given her and slid it into her laptop. She studied the notes and pictures of the American gangsters her uncle was meeting in Las Vegas but found herself drawn to the same one again and again.

"Bobby Ray Darling," she read, mouthing his name. *Are you my special work?*

Cleopatra skimmed the entire folder one more time, dragged the icon to the trash, and ejected the disc. She bent it until it snapped, repeating the process, breaking the halves into quarters and the quarters into eighths. When the flight attendant arrived to bus her dishes, Cleopatra collected the plastic shards and piled them onto her dinner plate. She switched off her laptop, zipped it into the carrying case, and reclined her seat.

Growing up fatherless in post-war Japan was difficult. Her mother's steadfast reluctance to talk about him only made things harder. All she'd ever said was he was a GI who went home to America before she was born.

Somewhere over the Pacific, Cleopatra dozed off. She slept fitfully, haunted by dreams of her mother. Jolted by a patch of turbulence, she awoke in a cold sweat. Cleopatra slipped on her jacket and tucked her fists under her elbows, trying to get warm.

In the last dream, the one she remembered, she was standing beside a manmade pond. A wooden footbridge and stands of dwarf pine, cypress, and willows were arranged around it in a stylized, miniature landscape. A cloying mist collected in a cool film against her skin.

Her mother, dressed in a black kimono with cherry blossoms and white cranes, was sitting on a granite boulder, dangling her silk slippers over the pond. Colorful koi looped in and out of patches of lotuses and water lilies. She chose a pea from the lacquered bowl in her lap and tossed it into the water. A white koi with an orange sunburst on its forehead gobbled it up and circled lazily back for more. Her mother's face glowed with the same childlike amusement Cleopatra remembered from before she got sick.

When her mother realized she was there, she folded her hands one on top of the other like she did when she had something

116

important to say. Cleopatra could see her mouth the words but couldn't hear what she was saying. She frantically repeated herself several times and was getting increasingly agitated when the plane hit a patch of turbulence that startled her awake.

Determined not to sleep the rest of the flight, she asked the attendant for black coffee. Cleopatra stared dully out the window, wondering about the dream and what Hiro would tell her about her father.

10

Morrison slept on the downstairs sofa. He'd barely opened his eyes when Jaxx trotted over, wagging his tail.

"Getting to be that time, boy?"

Morrison trudged to the kitchen, where he found Jimi visible but wispy around the edges, stacking dishes on the counter. His short Afro had grayed, but he looked surprisingly fit.

"Damn, it's good to see you."

"Now, don't get all teary-eyed. I'm just pacing myself. Here, check these out." Jimi handed Morrison a black dinner plate with a Vegas-era Elvis in a sparkly, white jumpsuit.

"Expecting company?"

"Ask him. I'm not in the fortune-telling business, but the price was right."

"So, how affordable was all this?" Morrison made a circling gesture with his index finger.

"Fell-off-the-back-of-the-truck cheap. There was a whole load of Elvis stuff, but two boxes was all I could carry."

"You know, you never finished your story."

"Not much to tell, really. I spent twenty-five years in a guest cottage at the Agency's Maui compound where CIA bigwigs take their secretaries for *working* weekends." Jimi slid a stack of plates onto the shelf. "Remember Janis?"

"Joplin?"

Jimi nodded.

"She and I did some serious drinking at Barney's."

"Before you—"

"—Right," Morrison interrupted. "Before my lifetime ban."

Jimi grinned. "Janis was there toward the end. They wanted her isolated in case she completely unwound."

118

The end of what? Morrison, too uncomfortable to ask, forced a smile.

"She and I had *relationship* issues." Jimi bracketed "relationship" in air quotes. "Janis got horny when she drank, and she was drunk most of the time. When I showed no interest, there were hard feelings. Her last stint in rehab, she got that old-time religion in a passing-out-Bibles kinda way. The thought of her going door-to-door confessing their sins made the Agency uncomfortable. Some higher up decided it was best if she drank herself to death."

Morrison nodded he understood. He was thinking about Pamela. Jimi slid the last stack of dishes onto the shelf, closed the cupboard, and packed himself a bowl from the pouch around his neck.

"While you finish here, the dog and I are going for a walk."

Jimi raised the mermaid pipe in a mock toast. "Happy trails."

Morrison draped the leash over his shoulder, and he and Jaxx took a leisurely stroll around the block. On the way back, he stopped at the limo to grab the rest of his things. The trunk lid was ajar, and there were fresh tool marks around the lock where it had been jimmied. When he poked his head inside, he saw the trunk was empty. Morrison heard somebody coming up behind him and glanced over his shoulder, but all he saw was a smoldering pipe dancing in the air. Jimi was back to sight unseen.

"Somebody stole the blanket and a bag of laundry. They even took the spare tire."

"It's high time we went shopping. There's a vintage clothing store around the corner. With just one set of clothes, my wardrobe's becoming a hygiene issue. Wanna tag along?"

"No, thanks. Maybe later." As Jimi disappeared down the street in a puff of smoke, Morrison patted Jaxx on the head. "Come on, boy. Let's get something to eat." Sparkle was standing by the stove still half-asleep. Her disheveled hair hung loosely past her shoulders.

"Good morning, stranger."

She looked up bleary-eyed from a steaming cup of tea and grinned sheepishly. "So, it wasn't a dream."

"Sorry, I'm afraid the nightmare continues." Morrison stared at her intently, trying to divine the significance of her remark.

"Well, it wasn't as bad as all that. I got to hang out with a couple rock legends, meet some nice folks from Minnesota, *and* star in a *Cops* episode."

"At least nobody wound up in handcuffs, and I thought Dr. Dick was going to offer you a job."

Sparkle sipped her tea. "I already have a job."

"Helping out here with your dad?"

"No, teaching high school English. I took a year off to finish my masters."

Morrison petted the dog again. "Jaxx, if my teachers looked like her, I might have gone to class."

She rolled her head to one side and grinned. "Would you like a cup?"

"No, thanks. I'm good."

Sparkle grabbed a stack of postcards from the counter and waved them at Morrison. "We started getting these last Monday." She bent back a corner with her thumb and flipped through them like playing cards.

Morrison shook his head. "I don't know what to tell you."

"I saw Elvis when I came downstairs. How about we ask him?"

They found Elvis in the living room sitting cross-legged on the floor. He was watching the local news, but the sound was muted. An Asian woman draped in a white, rhinestone cape was reporting from the back of a delivery truck. Sparkle handed him the stack of postcards.

"We got five or six every day this week." Elvis studied the front photo and read the writing on the back of the first couple cards.

"Check out the postmarks," Sparkle suggested. "Your friend's quite the world traveler. He liked Vancouver but thought Tokyo was pricey. He wrote something about the yen-to-dollar exchange rate. I was reading them until we got the Special Delivery letter. Since they were mailed to Elvis at this address, I thought they were for Digby."

Elvis shuffled through the cards again and handed them to Sparkle.

"So, who's Cosmo? In all the excitement, I didn't get a chance to ask last night."

"My cat."

"Your *cat* sends you postcards?"

"Well, he's not really mine. Cosmo's more his own cat. Did you notice most of his stops are port cities? He's partial to seafood."

"Vienna?"

"His other weakness. Cosmo loves a good strudel."

Sparkle flipped through the postcards again. "On Tuesday, he wrote from Boston, Bangkok, Cape Town, Anchorage, Rio, and Key West."

"Rio? That's surprising. Carnival's not till February."

She took a deep breath, trying to compose herself. "On Wednesday, he wrote from Palermo, Seattle, Sydney, Hong Kong, New Orleans, and Phuket."

"He's always loved Thailand. You can't tell from his coloring, but I think he's part Siamese."

Morrison draped his arm across Sparkle's shoulders and grinned. "Welcome to my world."

Detective Hennigan didn't get to Metro Homicide until late morning. He was wearing gray slacks and a navy blazer. Both showed a lot of wear, and his shirt had a coffee stain on the collar. While not obsessively neat, he usually put some effort into looking professional. But with Phillip "Cheezesteak" Chestakowski on administrative leave and the hours and caseload wearing on him, Hennigan had, as Gladys Little suggested, fallen back on a rumpled, *Colombo* look.

Hennigan and Cheezesteak ignored rotation protocols and worked most of their cases together. Even the five other detectives in their unit thought of them as partners. Since nobody liked working with either of them, the lieutenant gave Hennigan a lot of latitude. Besides, their pseudo partnership worked, and he was old-school enough not to fix what wasn't broken.

Hennigan finished the last of his coffee and stole a weary glance at the pile of paperwork in his out-basket. Besides sharing the workload, another reason he missed his AWOL partner was he had excellent penmanship and completed most of their reports.

Cheezesteak had been suspended over an off-duty incident when he stopped at a Circle K for chilidogs and a Diet Coke. As he was reaching for the door, a teenage boy charged past him with a bag of Cheetos poking out of his hoodie and the store clerk in hot pursuit. Cheezesteak wrestled the would-be thief to the ground and was cuffing him when the situation escalated. By the time uniforms arrived, the kid was screaming about police brutality. Charges were dropped after the *alleged* shoplifter signed a release agreeing not to sue the department. A hearing was scheduled so a review board and the union rep could sort things out.

In twenty plus years on the job, Hennigan had only lost his Irish temper once when a fellow officer called another cop the n-word. His reaction was ironic since Hennigan didn't like the black cop, who he suspected was using preferential treatment to leverage hookers for sexual favors.

Cheezesteak's recent separation didn't excuse his behavior, but Hennigan understood what he was going through. In his last few months with Sheila, any interaction became an excuse for a confrontation. The proverbial last straw was an argument over storing leftovers. Who knew Tupperware could be a euphemism for irreconcilable differences?

Since moving out a year ago, he'd been renting a one-bedroom apartment near Big Mike's Sports Bar. The decor was new-bachelor minimalism: a sink full of dishes, piles of dirty laundry on the floor, and pizza boxes on the coffee table. Since August, he'd been seeing Elizabeth Booth, a fourth-grade teacher at his daughter's school.

After one trip to his apartment, she decided conjugal visits would be at her place.

Hennigan lived up to the stereotype of a big city detective with two exceptions: he didn't smoke and barely drank, but did enjoy an occasional glass of red wine or an after-work beer with Cheezesteak. Elizabeth was partial to Chardonnays, but they were working it out.

When the phone rang, he let it ring four or five times before answering. "Hennigan, Metro Homicide."

"Hello, Peter." It was his soon-to-be ex-wife.

"Hello, Sheila."

"We need to get together for lunch tomorrow." Hennigan scowled. Lunch would be about money. With Sheila, it was *always* about money.

"I have plans," he said, trying to sound gruff.

"With *her*? With *Betty Boobs*?"

Hennigan clenched his teeth and tried not to overreact. Talking to one of the Neanderthals in Traffic, he had, in a stupid moment of macho posturing, summed up his new love interest as "great tits." The remark got back to Sheila, and she never let him forget it.

"Yes, with Elizabeth," he said flatly. "It's my weekend. I'll pick Amanda up from school on Friday."

"I talked with my attorney."

Hennigan knew what that meant – *meet me or else*. Sheila's attorney, his future ex-brother-in-law Winston DeBoer, was a smarmy, little troll with a 70's porn star mustache and a bad comb-over. He jumped on every opportunity to cost Hennigan time or money. Usually an ambulance chaser, he was handling Sheila's side of the divorce "at a substantial discount."

"How *is* your brother?"

"He's fine." Her voice was edged with sarcasm.

They lapsed into an awkward silence. Hennigan shuffled papers around his desk and wondered if this was Sheila's new tactic to drive him crazy. He would be damned if he was going to let her know how well it was working.

"Anyway," she said finally, "Winston told me we could save money if we didn't get the attorneys out counting pots and pans."

Hennigan stared at the ceiling. Their divorce was a dreamlike, out-of-body experience, except for the astounding amount of money he was paying his lawyer.

"Are you listening?" Sheila sounded petulant.

Hennigan had reached the point where he'd agree to almost anything to get her off the phone. "Yeah, sure. Tomorrow lunch."

"Meet me in the Tiki Lounge at the Tahitian Princess. One o'clock. And don't be late."

"Fine. I'll be there." He gritted his teeth and slammed down the phone. Hennigan was always punctual. Sheila had never been on time for anything in her life. He loosened his tie and stared glumly out the window. When the phone rang again, he let it go to voicemail.

Though mildly bizarre, even by Las Vegas standards, the hijacked truck and stolen Elvis plates had not aroused him from his stupor. Hennigan fulfilled all the by-the-book requirements. He faithfully walked the scene and scribbled notes in his scratchy, cop shorthand without once wondering *what the hell happened?*

Even the FBI's sudden interest in Elvis Presley had failed to pique his curiosity. Hennigan was having a hard time caring about much of anything. The divorce was sucking the life out of him like an emotional vampire.

After battering the hapless Winnebago into submission, Bobby Ray and the Cozzaglios stopped by Frank's trailer for a pair of sweats. They fit snuggly, but the mobster couldn't check into the Tahitian Princess wearing only socks and underwear. By the time they got to the resort, it was half-past two in the morning. Since he hadn't arranged for a late arrival, the desk clerk explained they didn't hold his reservation and that the nicest available room was a honeymoon suite. Too exhausted to argue, Bobby Ray traipsed upstairs, collapsed on the heart-shaped bed, and didn't open his eyes until early afternoon.

After showering, he phoned Frank to see if they'd tracked down the delinquents who jacked his car. The answering machine picked up on the fifth ring. He left a message, ordered a steak sandwich from room service, and got busy emptying the minibar.

A half dozen unanswered calls later, Bobby Ray stumbled downstairs. His bags were stolen with the Grand Prix, and he desperately needed clothes. When you're barely five-five and wear a size forty-eight jacket, you can't exactly buy suits off the rack.

The casino gift shop's selection was limited, but he found a pair of khaki cargo shorts, lime-green flip-flops, and three Hawaiian print shirts in his size. He changed in the gift-shop fitting room and walked out of the store looking like a wayward hobbit who got lost on his there-and-back to the shire and went native in Waikiki.

Cleopatra Takahara was stuck in the San Francisco International Terminal. She was traveling under an alias on a Canadian passport. When biometric screening at the INSPASS kiosk suggested she resembled a Japanese national on an Interpol watch list, her entry into the United States ground to a halt. A man in a dark blue Customs uniform directed her to a secondary station so her visa and identification documents could be reviewed manually.

She waited, drumming her black-lacquered nails on the counter while fellow travelers streamed through the doors to connecting flights. As the agent flipped through her passport for the third time, she stared at him hard enough to carve diamonds.

"What time, please?" Cleopatra asked, her heavily accented words barely intelligible. She spoke English quite fluently but liked to affect otherwise when the situation dictated.

"Four forty-five."

She glanced at her watch, still set to Tokyo time, and checked her itinerary. "My plane leave soon."

"Sorry, ma'am. I'm processing your paperwork as quickly as I can."

Cleopatra felt a tickle in the back of her throat. Once, as she was boarding a flight from Tokyo to Bangkok, she sneezed, and her ben-wa balls accelerated from zero to escape velocity. She had on a short skirt but no panties and left little steel balls rolling around Narita like a pachinko machine's wayward children. One good cough away from leaving more than her heart in San Francisco, Cleopatra cleared her throat and sucked a lozenge from the roll in her pocket.

The customs agent flipped through her passport again, deliberately avoiding eye contact. Cleopatra leaned across the counter so she could see her face and a list of known Yakuza associates on his monitor. "This because we *all* look alike to you," she growled.

The agent was sweating profusely. It was his second day in the field, and his training supervisor had gone to lunch without him. Everyone else in customs was busy drinking coffee or had snuck off for a cigarette. He opened her suitcase to finish his inspection. A black lacquer box drew his immediate attention.

Cleopatra tensed. "Be careful. That special gift."

He gently lifted the box and set it on the counter. Inside was a velvet, form-fitting insert and a snow globe swaddled in silk scarves.

"Birthday present for my niece," she lied.

The globe was a souvenir from the 1939 World's Fair and all that Cleopatra had of her father's. When she was little, she pretended he left it as a gift, impossible since he abandoned her mother not knowing she was pregnant. The water inside was nearly opaque, but she treasured the globe and brought it with her wherever she traveled.

Satisfied it wasn't contraband, the agent nestled the globe back in the box and rifled through the rest of her things. He didn't glance in her direction until he came across her vibrator.

"Curling iron," she offered dryly. For traveling, she favored vibrators that could pass for household appliances. They tended to evoke fewer prying questions from anxious security people. Like her American Express Card, she never left home without one. This trip's facsimile of choice was a Venus Wand, a battery-operated, lipstick-shaped model.

The flustered agent stuffed her things back in her bag and waved her through customs. She stopped at the airline counter and exchanged her ticket for the first available flight. The last leg to Las Vegas was uncomfortably crowded but uneventful.

As soon as the taxi dropped her at the Tahitian Princess, she trudged to the front desk. After checking in, she handed a bellhop ten dollars, asked him to take her bags to her room, and got directions to the bar.

She spied Bobby Ray as soon as she walked in. He was sipping an orange-colored cocktail from a highball glass with a paper umbrella. Cleopatra strolled casually across the bar and sat down.

Well into his third Mai Tai, Bobby Ray was slow to react when the modestly attractive Asian woman slid into the booth across from him. He meant to leer at her but could only manage a lop-sided grin.

"Mind if I join you?"

"Not at all. Sit yourself down." His words were slurred, and he failed to take into account she was already sitting.

"Cleopatra Takahara," she purred, offering her hand.

He grabbed it clumsily. "Bobby Ray Darling. Can I buy you a drink?"

"Whatever you're having." Her smile was predatory, but the effect was lost on Bobby Ray. He flagged down a cocktail waitress and held up two pudgy fingers.

"Mai Tais. Doubles." She looked quizzically at Cleopatra then back to Bobby Ray.

"Yes, sir. Two Mai Tai doubles coming right up."

Bobby Ray possessed only two remotely successful strategies with women. One was to ply them with excessive amounts of alcohol. The other was to offer money. In theory, he favored the former, but all of his success, stretching back to when he dropped out of high school, involved the latter.

Bobby Ray fidgeted with his cocktail napkin, trying to decide if she was a hooker or if his luck had turned. He took a long draw on his drink, collecting his nerve and meager resources.

"So, what's a sweet dame like you doin' in a dive like this?"

The effect was galvanizing. To Cleopatra, who was obsessed with American movies, he looked like a film noir character who could sit on the stool next to Bogie and drink bathtub gin.

The waitress returned with their drinks. As he raised the cocktail to his lips, Bobby Ray poked himself in the nose with the paper umbrella. It took several fumbling attempts before he finally reached the straw. "Ever been to Vegas?"

"No, my first visit to Sin City," she answered coyly over the rim of her glass. "I'm in town looking for a little fun."

Bobby Ray took another sip of his Mai Tai. "We should hang out together. A little fun's practically my middle name." His droopy stare kept finding its way to her blouse, though it was as much out of intoxication as lust.

"Great. I got a few days to kill." Usually self-conscious about being flat-chested, Cleopatra found his probing stare exciting. She was so aroused her ben-wa balls slipped.

"Stick with me, kid," Bobby Ray snorted drunkenly. "I'm a man. You're a woman. Do da math."

He intended to order another round before things cooled off, but their waitress had disappeared into the kitchen. Another round proved unnecessary. Before they finished the first, they were making out hot and heavy the entire elevator ride to his floor.

11

Morrison was sprawled across the living room sofa, nibbling cold delivery pizza, and watching *America's Most Wanted*. He half expected to be featured in the evening's episode, and his anxiety level didn't drop until the final credits scrolled past.

Jimi was sitting beside him, or so Morrison assumed from the sag in the overstuffed chair, occasional bits of conversation, and the pungent aromas of dope and patchouli oil. Everyone else was at a wedding. The Chapel doors were cracked wide enough for Morrison to see Reverend Elvis belting out a karaoke version of "Love Me Tender."

"Digby's got a decent voice."

"Yes," Morrison agreed.

"Speaking of which, it's getting to be that time." Morrison heard rustling noises as Jimi got up from his chair. "I'm playing a club off the Strip."

The color flushed from Morrison's cheeks. "You're playing *tonight*?"

"I've been sitting in with these guys," he explained, "Moby Dix and the Ahabs. Reggae mostly. Steel drums. That sorta vibe."

Morrison shook his head. "That can't be good."

"No, it's cool. The band's stoned enough to believe I'm the ghost of Bob Marley, and the audience's preoccupied with the dancers."

"The dancers?"

"At Sinderella's."

It took Morrison a moment to realize by dancers, Jimi meant *exotic* dancers. "You're playing a strip club?"

Jimi laughed. "Talk about preoccupied."

Morrison glanced at Sparkle through the crack in the Chapel doors. He couldn't see his face but imagined Jimi grinning wickedly.

129

"No token gesture of resistance? No half-hearted defense?"

"Well, I..." Morrison's voice trailed off as he heard footsteps headed toward the front door that appeared to open and then close on its own. "The ghost of Bob Marley," he muttered, trying to imagine a scenario that didn't turn out badly.

Morrison was aimlessly channel surfing when he realized Sparkle was behind him and handed her the remote. She switched to the local news, hovering close enough to make him antsy, one hand on her hip, the other with the remote aimed at the TV. Morrison fidgeted with his napkin until all that remained was a greasy wad of shreds. When he thought she wasn't looking, he rolled them into a ball and tossed them into the pizza box.

The news segued from the anchor desk to an exterior shot of the Event Center at the Tahitian Princess. The camera panned to an Asian woman with square-cut bangs holding a microphone. She was down on one knee, interviewing two men, neither of whom looked more than three feet tall. One was dressed as a young, black-leather Elvis, and the other as a sequined-and-white-fringed Elvis. When the station broke for a commercial, Morrison turned to face her.

"Any chance you've seen my keys? In all the commotion with the Littles and the police, I think I left them at the diner." He rocked back on the sofa and patted his pockets for effect.

"What do they look like?"

"Three keys and a coach's whistle on a silver ring."

Sparkle smiled coyly. "A coach's whistle? Oh, do tell."

"It's a long story."

"Come now. There are no secrets in Reverend Bible's house."

Morrison glanced at Jaxx, who had curled up at his feet. "I bought a dog training program I saw on a late-night infomercial. It came with tapes and a manual."

"And a whistle."

"Right, and a whistle. But, after a couple sessions, we pretty much lost interest."

"Hmm. Sounds like Jaxx did a better job training you than you did training him."

"That's probably true. I hardly ever pee on the carpet or chew up slippers anymore." When she laughed, Morrison was thinking how beautiful she was.

Sparkle handed him the remote. "How about I check with the diner and see if anybody found your keys?"

While she was on the phone, Morrison collected the leftovers and took them to the kitchen. He wrapped the last few slices in foil and stacked the empty boxes on the trash can. Sparkle was waiting when he got back.

"I talked with Edna. Your keys are in the lost-and-found box under the register. I told her we'll swing by tomorrow and pick them up."

"Thanks." Morrison smiled appreciatively.

"I'm bushed. I'm going to call it a day. You need anything?"

Morrison shook his head. "No, I'm good." He was thinking again how beautiful she was.

As she climbed the stairs, Sparkle half-turned toward Morrison and smiled. A few minutes later, he was on his way to the bathroom when he literally ran into her headed the opposite direction after brushing her teeth. Morrison caught her, at first to keep her from falling, but when their eyes met, he pulled her closer. He used his thumb to wipe away a smudge of toothpaste, tilted her chin up slightly, and gently kissed her. When he pulled back enough to see she was smiling, he kissed her again. This time she kissed him back.

They barely made it to her room. He lifted her in his arms and gently laid her on the bed. Sparkle had changed into sweats. The drawstring was in a slipknot Morrison untied with his teeth. He pulled off the bottoms in one motion. She arched her back and raised her hips as he slipped her panties down around one ankle. Sparkle flicked them casually across the room.

"See, I *am* a natural redhead."

Morrison looked up, surprised. He hadn't noticed she had red hair. In the short time they'd spent together, he hadn't gotten past her eyes.

Morrison was drifting off to sleep when Sparkle snuggled up against him. He rolled over and kissed her on the neck. Almost immediately, he felt himself poking her in the side.

"O trespass sweetly urged," she cooed softly.

"You're irresistible when you quote Shakespeare."

Sparkle ran her hand along his inner thigh. "Apparently so, but then again, Elvis said you were a hard man."

Morrison brushed away a lock of hair that had fallen across her face -- red hair, he made a point of noticing. "That's true, but he meant it as a compliment."

"And they said you had no redeeming social value," Sparkle giggled.

"Well, there's that, *and* I can lick my eyebrows."

"Or so I've heard."

"Ahhh, how quickly they forget."

Sparkle tapped playfully him on the nose with her index finger. "You're just going to have to remind me."

Morrison grinned. "It is important to confirm you *really* are a natural redhead. It would be irresponsible not to verify my previous research."

He kissed her twice on the lips and slid down her body, kissing her left nipple, pink and pouty, as soft as chewed bubble gum. He kissed her again, this time just below the navel. Her body trembled with anticipation.

"So, *now* you're the strong silent type?"

Morrison looked up and smiled. "Just minding my manners. I was raised not to talk with my mouth full."

He slid a little lower. If Sparkle had a snappy comeback, the words died in her throat. Her eyes glassed over, she arched her back, and her whole body quivered.

Morrison was at the bedroom window watching the sunrise when he heard Sparkle coming up the stairs. She balanced a wicker tray on one arm and pushed open the door with the other.

"Well, good morning, sleepyhead." She was wearing his flannel shirt. Given the difference in their sizes, the shoulders were almost to her elbows. Even rolled up, the sleeves reached her wrists.

Sparkle tucked a wisp of hair behind her ear. "You know, Jim Morrison, you've come a ways from the guy who woke up at the crack of noon and had himself a beer?"

"Noon? I never got up that early, and *always* had more than one." They both laughed.

Sparkle set the tray on the nightstand and poured them each a cup of tea. Before sliding into bed, she handed him a muffin and grabbed one for herself. Morrison climbed in beside her, suspiciously eyeing the steaming mug of chamomile.

"No caffeine, right?"

Sparkle held up her right hand, index and middle fingers erect, as if taking an oath. "Scout's honor."

"How can I be sure you were a scout?"

"Come over here, and I'll show you my merit badges," she giggled as she tore off a bite of muffin and stuffed it in his mouth. "Sorry about the unmade bed and the furry-monkey-leg thing." Sparkle brushed her hand self-consciously across her thigh. "I thought it would take longer to get you upstairs." Morrison looked bewildered. That she hadn't just shaved her legs was another detail he'd failed to notice.

"Oh, right, you assumed this was all *your* idea," she teased, misunderstanding the look on his face. "How about a little show and tell?" Sparkle took another sip of tea and studied him over the rim of her cup. "Here, I'll go first. This scar's from when I got hit in the face with a swing when I was five." She tapped a quarter-inch indentation in her upper lip with the tip of her index finger. Sparkle flexed her right leg and pointed to a birthmark halfway to her ankle. "However, the California-shaped birthmark on my shin, I was born with."

"Thanks for sharing."

"Now, it's your turn. Elvis told me you guys, how did he say it, *muled secret government documents.* When the Russians found out, the CIA faked your deaths and set you up in a dead rock star protection program."

"That's the shorthand version."

"Were the three of you together?"

"No, Jimi was on Maui, and I was in northern Virginia."

"And Elvis?"

"No idea. I've asked a couple times but can't get a straight answer." Morrison took another bite of muffin and chewed it thoughtfully. "I'd been kicking around the idea of being somebody else for a while. Dying and my subsequent resurrection in anonymity pretty much clinched it. I hung around Langley doing grunt work until the Agency brought Pamela in."

Sparkle's eyes narrowed, but she didn't say anything.

"We'd always had a stormy relationship, and that part hadn't changed. Being together was less a reunion than a rematch. We didn't need a marriage counselor. We needed an exorcist. Her mood swings got worse after I started grad school."

"My mom was like that. One minute she was high as a kite, the next angry and depressed. When I got old enough to know what was coming, I tried to be somewhere else."

Morrison nodded. "I went out of *my* way to stay out of *her* way. I kept to myself, read a lot, and focused on school until the morning I found her curled up on the bathroom floor with an empty bottle of Jack Daniels. I knew we couldn't keep pretending, but for me, the four most frightening words in the English language are *we have to talk.*"

"How'd she react?"

"Like a cornered animal. Pamela swore she wasn't drinking. After hours of mostly her talking, she admitted *maybe* she drank a little. A couple hours after that, she conceded *maybe* she drank a lot, but it was my fault."

As Sparkle reached to comfort him, she traced her finger along a fleshy, pink scar on his shoulder. Morrison flinched.

"Old war wound," he said self-consciously.

Sparkle tucked her hand beneath the pillow. "Sorry."

"It's okay. I'm getting to that part." Morrison took a moment to collect himself. "It wasn't just the drinking. The bathroom counter was a wall-to-wall pharmacy. My one-man intervention went poorly." Morrison stared into his teacup as if trying to divine the past. "The bad days kept getting worse and the good ones fewer and farther between. Finally, I called her doctor. He recommended a private clinic. She stayed ten weeks. When she came home, things were okay for a while. She decorated the house, country French, did an amazing job. She really had a knack for it, but after a while, the mood swings came back, and I knew she was using."

"As bad as before?"

"Worse. She tried killing herself, swallowed half a bottle of sleeping pills. The emergency room visit should have been a wake-up call, but it wasn't. One night during an argument, she came at me with a butcher knife."

"The scar?"

Morrison nodded. "After that, we didn't just sleep in separate rooms. I slept in a separate room with the door locked. "I can't explain why I spent ten years in that relationship any more than why I spent ten years after that alone. I guess I got comfortable with being miserable."

Not sure what to say, Sparkle squeezed his arm.

"It took a week of fighting, but she agreed to give rehab another try." Morrison spoke softly, barely loud enough to hear. "There was a guy, I don't remember his name, just some junkie she met in group. They snuck out one night and scored some heroin. He turned up dead behind a dumpster. The day after that, police found her body in an alley with the needle still in her arm."

Morrison raised himself on an elbow. "Sorry to hit the pause button, but I need to use the little boy's room." He rolled out of bed, pulled on his jeans, and headed down the hallway. As soon as he was gone, Jaxx jumped on the comforter and curled up at Sparkle's feet.

"Do you want me to tell him to get down?" Morrison asked when he got back.

"You forgot your whistle at the restaurant, remember?"

"Funny."

"That's okay. It's kind of special sharing my bed with two such handsome rascals." Sparkle broke off another bite of muffin and popped it in her mouth. "You know, we don't have to do this right now."

Morrison slipped off his jeans and slid in beside her. "We should start clean. How about you? Any dark tales to tell?"

Sparkle shook her head. "No skeletons in my closet."

"You said there were *no* secrets in Reverend Elvis's house."

Sparkle pursed her lips. "I have a daughter," she said softly. Morrison pictured a five-or-six-year-old version of Sparkle in freckles and pigtails bursting in and bouncing on the bed.

"Dad's weekend?"

Sparkle shook her head. There was something in her expression Morrison couldn't read. She rolled onto her back, folded down the top sheet, and tucked it under her chin. "She has her own place. She's a senior at UNLV, studying broadcast journalism."

"She's grown then?"

Sparkle smiled. "She's tall anyway."

"Well, that's a start." Morrison wanted to hear more but sensed Sparkle's reluctance to talk about her daughter. "Sorry for going on so long, but I wanted you to have an idea of what you're getting into."

"Exorcising ghosts of relationships past?"

Morrison propped himself on an elbow. "I guess. After ten years of living alone, Elvis showed up on my doorstep one night, and the next thing I knew, the mutt and I were trucking across the country on a middle-aged children's crusade."

"And that's a bad thing?"

Morrison shook his head. "No, at some level, I knew I was coming here."

"To Vegas?"

"No, Sparkle, to you." He curled his index finger under her chin and lifted her head. "Be gentle. My people skills are rusty. For a decade, cold showers were the basis of my social life."

"Well, it's true then. It *is* like riding a bicycle."

Morrison pretended to scowl. "I'm trying to be serious."

"I *am* being serious. How about we take this a day at a time and see how things go?"

Morrison nodded, not sure what he'd agreed to. He smiled sheepishly as he leaned over and kissed her. "Then again, the doctor told me to stay in bed until the swelling goes down."

Sparkle tapped him playfully on the tip of his nose. "Jim Morrison, you're incorrigible."

"And you said I had no redeeming social value." He pulled her close and kissed her until they fell asleep, sweaty and exhausted, in each other's arms.

12

Bobby Ray was posturing in front of the mirror, threatening his reflection with a Smith & Wesson Model 29 and the few lines he remembered from *Dirty Harry*. It had been more than a day and a night since the carjacking, and he still hadn't heard from the Cozzaglios. Used to snub-nosed revolvers, the nearly eight and a half-inch barrel took forever to get out of the shoulder holster and kept snagging on the front sight. The gun was unwieldy, but he was going to use it to impress Joey and Frank with the seriousness of their assignment.

After he begrudgingly reported the stolen Pontiac to the police, the rental agency provided a replacement Grand Prix, a black one this time. Then Bobby Ray called a local gun dealer the family did business with and had a small armory delivered to his room: a pair of TEC-9s, a semi-automatic Remington 12 gauge, two AR-15s, a .38 with skull-and-crossbones tape on the grip, and three dozen boxes of ammunition were strewn across the heart-shaped bed.

By the time Joey and Frank finally showed up half an hour late, he'd worked himself into a lather. Bobby Ray met them at the door, waving the giant hand cannon. The subtext was not lost on the brothers.

"Where are the delinquents who jacked my car?" he growled.

"W-w-we got *several* promising leads." Joey's eyes were the size of tennis balls. He looked like a manic teenager bingeing on Red Bull.

"I don't want leads. I want that crew, and I want them yesterday." Bobby Ray suspected their entire effort amounted to watching TV and had to stifle the urge to shoot them on the spot.

"But w-w-what if we can't find them?" Since the run-in with the Winnebago, Joey's stuttering had gotten progressively worse.

"And what about my Caddy?"

"Stop whining about a couple scratches and find those assholes. She's a looker, and the guys are inked up. Ask around. Somebody's gotta know that crew." The brothers nodded in jerking motions like synchronized bobbleheads. Bobby Ray jammed the muzzle of the .44 into Frank's sternum.

"I'm meeting somebody downstairs for breakfast. If you don't find 'em by the time I finish my second cup of coffee, I'm gonna rope you two across the Cadillac's trunk like prize stags and go looking for another RV." Joey and Frank did the spastic thing approaching a nod again.

Bobby Ray tossed the magnum on the bed. Without a jacket, he couldn't walk around the casino strapped. He slipped on the lime-green flip-flops and motioned for the brothers to follow. The mobster waggled a stubby finger at the brothers as the elevator lurched to a stop.

"Till my second cup of coffee," he reminded them as the doors slid open.

"R-R-Right," Joey said as he and Frank scurried out of the elevator toward the exit.

Bobby Ray was halfway across the lobby before he spotted Carmine Verduci. When he waved, his cousin reluctantly waved back.

At weddings, baptisms, and funerals, Verduci avoided Bobby Ray, who always had something to say at his expense. For no obvious reason, they were the favorite nephews of Fiametta, the don's spinster sister, who made them promise to get together in Las Vegas.

When they were schoolboys, Carmine and Bobby Ray thought she was a gnarled, old crone. In the forty years since, she'd gotten older and crazier. Fiametta had not ventured beyond the front porch of the Don's Brooklyn brownstone in over a decade, shuffling from room to room in slippers and a worn housecoat, mumbling words that might have once been Sicilian but that had, over time, devolved into her own, mostly incomprehensible language. Everyone, including the don, gave her a wide berth, believing she was a *jettatora* and could cast an evil eye.

The cousins greeted each other with the closest approximation of a hug their stubby arms and round bodies would allow.

"So, Carmine, how's things at the White House?"

"Great. How's Vegas? Killed anybody yet?"

Bobby Ray shook his head. "No, but I've only been in town a couple days."

"Lemme get a look at you." Verduci stepped back to better view the bare-breasted Polynesian women frolicking on Bobby Ray's mustard-yellow shirt. "You can wear stuff like that in public?"

"Gauguin," Bobby Ray said, repeating what the girl in the gift shop had told him.

"He some fancy, new designer?"

"Yeah, that's the guy." Bobby Ray held his arms out straight and did a slow three-sixty. "Swing by later for my GQ shoot. I'm next month's cover."

"When the Cubs win the Super Bowl," Verduci laughed, snorting through his nose.

While they were waiting to be seated, Verduci, who fraternized obsessively with anyone in uniform, snapped to attention when the twenty-something kid in a tux asked how many were in their party. Bobby Ray held up three pudgy fingers before his cousin could do anything embarrassing.

The hostess seated them in a corner booth, handed them each a menu, and left to fetch coffee. Bobby Ray was trying to decide between waffles and French Toast when he saw Ernie "Bad Dog" Badoglio, the Tahitian Princess GM, strolling their direction with a tall, platinum blonde.

"Boy, have we got a surprise for you," he crowed, nodding toward the woman.

"Great." Verduci didn't bother feigning enthusiasm.

Like Aunt Fiametta, Bobby Ray and Bad Dog subscribed to a theory popular with the family: Carmine just hadn't met the right girl. It hadn't occurred to them a two hundred dollar-an-hour hooker might not be the right girl either. However, the kid in the tux at the hostess station could get serious as-is consideration.

"Hey, good to see you boys again." Bad Dog stuck out a meaty paw and shook hands. "There's somebody I want you to meet. Bobby Ray Darling and Carmine Verduci, this is..."

"Miss Vikki," she said, offering her hand. "Pleased to make your acquaintance." Her raspy voice mismatched her limp-wristed handshake. Bobby Ray stood and motioned for her to sit down.

"Please, join us."

"I'd love to," she answered drolly as she slid into the booth between them.

Bad Dog clasped his hands together. "Listen, I can't stay, but while you're here, if you need anything, just lemme know." The waitress arrived with a fresh pot of coffee. Bad Dog put his arm around her. She forced a half-smile, trying not to cringe at his touch.

"These folks are family. Whatever they want, put it on my tab."

"Yes, sir. I'll take good care of them, Mr. Badoglio."

Bad Dog's coat hummed. He retrieved his pager and squinted at the tiny screen. "It's a pit boss. We gotta problem with one of the guests."

"No rest for the wicked," Bobby Ray grinned.

Bad Dog glanced at Verduci, then Vikki, and winked. "Hope you two don't get any rest either."

As Badoglio motored across the gaming floor, Bobby Ray spotted Cleopatra at the hostess station and waved her over. After a moment's hesitation, she strolled across the room and slid into the booth beside him. There was another round of introductions, followed by more coffee, mimosas, and, finally, breakfast.

When Bobby Ray finished eating, he used the last of his waffle to swab up a puddle of syrup, wadded his napkin into a ball, and dropped it onto his plate.

"If everybody's done, I suggest we retire to the lounge." His speech was noticeably slurred. The group slid out of the booth and trouped behind the mobster as he slogged unsteadily toward the bar.

Cleopatra was standing in the café line when she saw Bobby Ray with another man and a woman with teased-up, platinum hair. Disappointed with the brutishness and brevity of the previous night's encounter, Cleopatra intended to ignore him until she realized the guy beside him was the White House chief of staff. She recognized Verduci from a CNN piece about allegations of bribery and tax evasion. That was enough to arouse her curiosity.

But halfway through her first mimosa, she was beyond bored. Bobby Ray made no effort to include her, and each round of laughter made her feel more left out. She entertained herself raking her nails up his inner thigh. Cleopatra enjoyed watching him fumble with his dinnerware, and several of his mealtime remarks were punctuated with high-pitched squeals.

After a morning of steady drinking, the two men were several sheets to the wind, but Miss Vikki seemed unaffected by the copious volume of rum she'd consumed. Cleopatra switched to Pepsi after her second drink. She was foraging in her purse for gum when Bobby Ray rapped his knuckles on the table to get everybody's attention. Verduci flagged down the cocktail waitress and ordered another round. Whatever Bobby Ray had to say, he had no intention of hearing sober.

"Carmine here was Turtle Creek Clinic's first three-time loser."

"The Turtle Creek Clinic?" Miss Vikki was munching the pineapple wedge from her drink. She flicked out her tongue and caught a trickle of juice dribbling down her chin.

Bobby Ray took a slow pull on his Mai Tai. "It's Betty Ford for big boys fond of little boys. They closed after an incident involving the director's fifteen-year-old son." He turned toward Verduci and smiled. "I don't think *but he looked sixteen* would have been much of a legal defense, do you, Mr. Big Shot attorney?"

Verduci made a feral noise between a growl and a burp. As he leaned over his drink, Bobby Ray glanced at his cousin. His lips reached for the straw, but the tip of the paper umbrella poked him in the nose.

"Serves you right," Verduci muttered. Bobby Ray yanked out the tiny parasol and tossed it on the table. He was still glaring at it when the waitress arrived with another round.

"You know why his shower buddies at Turtle Creek called Carmine here *Big Papa*?" Miss Vikki and Cleopatra shook their heads. Verduci buried his face in his hands.

Bobby Ray made a fist and wiggled his pinky finger like a worm on a hook. "Because he's got a tiny little thing like this."

Bobby Ray laughed uproariously. Miss Vikki barely rolled her eyes. Cleopatra sat stone-faced, but Verduci looked like he'd been kicked in his tiny, little thing.

By the time Agent Orange and his new partner got to the Dewdrop Inn, it was early afternoon. They were sitting across from each other in the row of booths by the register. Newmeat's back was to the door. He'd almost finished coloring the kid's menu fire engine when the waitress brought their breakfasts. She didn't recognize Newmeat, but Orange ate there often enough to be considered a regular. Unlike the local cops, he was a notoriously bad tipper.

Orange was having his usual: a grilled ham steak, extra-crispy hash browns, sourdough toast, and eggs over easy. Newmeat was having the same thing. Imitation might be the sincerest form of flattery, but the junior agent's habit of ordering whatever Orange ordered was getting on his nerves.

There're photos of a dozen breakfast specials on the menu. Can't he just pick something out and point?

Orange sorted through the basket of jams and jellies with his index finger, pushing aside a concord grape and two mixed fruits only to find more of the same underneath. Newmeat was slathering his toast with what looked like the last of the strawberry preserves.

Orange opened the file beside his plate and spread out photos of Carmine Verduci and Bobby Ray Darling having breakfast with two unidentified women. Verduci looked stressed enough to turn a well-placed lump of coal into a diamond. Orange assumed the women were hookers.

"I'll have Hennigan run the pictures by Vice and see if anyone recognizes them. Newmeat, who'd was shoveling a heaping forkful of hash browns into his mouth, nodded.

The Venetti Family arrests were imminent, and the White House chief of staff was included in the indictments. Director Reynolds, an appointee and not a career FBI man himself, had not thought through the implications of the Oval Office getting a tit caught in the ringer.

Orange slid the manila envelope that had arrived by courier that morning from under the surveillance photos. *Special Assignment* had been stamped in red ink where the addressee info would typically be. The follow-up to the original Elvis letter was short on details. Orange surmised from the one-page memo the DOD had requested the Bureau's help in a manhunt. A cross-country trail of credit card charges and ATM withdrawals suggested the two fugitives, identified as James Douglas Morrison and Elvis Aaron Presley, along with several AKAs, were headed their direction.

Photographs of the men were included. The one identified as Elvis was in his forties with cherubic good looks. He was wearing a black, crewneck sweater, blue jeans, and a tweed jacket. Orange thought he looked more like a college professor than Presley's second coming. The other man, identified as Morrison, was a few years older with soft, soulful eyes, white hair past his shoulders, and a baggy linen shirt. Orange could tell at a glance Scruffy Jesus was a serious wack job. He didn't recognize Morrison's name, and it didn't occur to him or anyone else at the Bureau, the names had been transposed.

Orange was ready for more coffee and was looking around for the waitress when he spotted her at the register talking with two men and a petite redhead. She handed one of the men a set of keys. Orange was waving his cup to get her attention when he realized the two men were the professor and Scruffy Jesus. He quickly counted out enough fives and ones for the breakfasts and slid them under his plate. Orange reached across the table and grabbed his startled partner by the wrist.

"We're leaving *now.*"

"I'm not finished."

"Now!" Orange repeated more forcefully this time.

Newmeat stuffed a bite of sourdough toast in his mouth, grabbed the crayons and the kid's menu, and followed him out the door. Orange came to an abrupt halt halfway across the parking lot, waving the manila envelope in one hand and pointing toward the restaurant with the other.

"You know the Bureau's wild goose chase? The guys we're looking for are inside."

Newmeat, crouching slightly in the shooter's stance he was taught at the Academy, reached for his gun. As he was spinning around, the Glock snagged on his shoulder holster and was wrenched from his hand. It clattered across the pavement and came to rest at the feet of the fugitives and the woman who had finished at the diner. Scruffy Jesus picked up the gun by the barrel and offered it to Newmeat.

"I believe this is yours," he said softly.

Newmeat grabbed the Glock and aimed it unsteadily at Elvis. "You're the Federal Bureau of Investigation, and we're under arrest." The professor wrapped his arm protectively around the redhead. Scruffy Jesus just stood there, smiling.

"What's this about?" the woman demanded.

"The FBI's looking for your friends," Newmeat growled.

"Everything will be okay," Scruffy Jesus assured her.

"Not till the Bureau says it's okay." Newmeat was using his Special Agent voice. "Let's see some ID."

The woman slipped the driver's license out of her wallet and handed it to Newmeat. The professor looked disconsolate, but the Jesus wacko was still grinning in a way that made Orange uncomfortable.

"The female accomplice's name is Sparkle Stiff. Sounds like an AKA." Newmeat handed Orange her license. "The address is local. We'd better check it out. There could be others involved."

"How about we take 'em to the office for questioning first?"

"Right. We'll hold them there and await further orders." Newmeat was herding the prisoners to the car when a disembodied presence in a cloud of marijuana smoke snatched the gun from his hand.

"All right, you dirty coppers, grab some sky," Jimi commanded in an over-the-top, movie gangster voice. Newmeat held up his hands, whimpering softly. Orange stared at the Glock suspended in midair until the click of a cocking hammer snapped him into the moment. Morrison plucked the driver's license from Orange and handed it to Sparkle while Jimi collected Orange's Glock and patted down both agents for backups.

"Cuff yourselves together," the bodiless voice demanded. Orange unclasped the handcuffs from his belt and manacled himself to Newmeat. Morrison made sure they were on good and tight.

"Now, you boys march yourselves around back." Newmeat's Glock made small twitching motions, directing the FBI agents across the lot to the bathroom behind the Circle K. At gunpoint, Jimi sat them down facing each other with their arms wrapped around the toilet while Morrison shackled their free hands together with Newmeat's cuffs.

When the bathroom door slammed shut, the two subjects escaped, along with their female accomplice and person or persons unknown and apparently invisible.

While waiting in line at Mogi's Do-Nuts, Hennigan had one of those transcendent epiphanies that usually came when he was sitting on the john. As soon as he picked up his order, he called Cheezesteak, who sounded like he'd guzzled a six-pack for brunch and dozed off watching the Playboy Channel.

"Cheeze, I need your help with something, kind of a side job, a private dick sort of thing." He heard the La-Z-Boy moan as his partner shifted his weight. "Okay if I swing by?"

"My dance card's pretty full, but seeing how you're practically family, I'll have my secretary squeeze you in." Cheezesteak had a gift for lightening the moment. When you work homicides, it's a handy survival skill.

"I'll be there in ten minutes." Hennigan hid the donuts in the trunk and drove straight over. Cheezesteak was leaning against the mailbox when he got there. He looked like he'd been wearing the same rumpled Hooter's T-shirt all week.

An inch or two shorter than his partner, Philip Chestakowski was as round as a Butterball turkey with curly, burnt-orange hair. When he needed a haircut, which always seemed to be the case, his scruffy locks seemed better suited for a rodeo clown than a homicide detective. His workday wardrobe consisted of short sleeve dress shirts with frayed collars and clip-on ties that looked like he used them for napkins when he ate -- which was pretty much all the time. The car groaned as he wedged himself into the passenger seat.

"Glad to see you haven't wasted any time off hanging out at the gym."

Cheezesteak grinned sheepishly and pretended to raise a bottle to his lips, alternating between his left and right arms. "I did work in a few Genuine Draft curls."

Hennigan checked the rearview mirror as he pulled away from the curb. "Hungry?"

"That a trick question?"

"How about Mike's?"

Cheezesteak grinned. "Works for me."

Big Mike's was a sports bar near Metro Homicide much revered for their cheesesteak sandwiches. Cheezesteak ate lunch there almost every day, even on his days off. One afternoon, grease dribbling down his chins, Big Mike dubbed him *Fat Philly Cheesesteak* in an impromptu ceremony, knighting him with a butter knife. The nickname quickly devolved to Cheezesteak.

While they were idling at a light, Hennigan glanced at his partner. "I miss having you around. It's not like we take moonlit walks on the beach, but we're friends, and that counts for something."

"Thanks." Cheezesteak stared sadly out the window. "Look, I get I screwed up. I managed to turn a stolen bag of chips into a hot mess."

"Cheetos," Hennigan corrected and immediately wished he hadn't.

"Right. Cheetos." Cheezesteak's sigh was almost a groan. "Everything caught up with me. I just snapped."

"It happens." Hennigan tried to sound sympathetic.

"Yeah, but it happened to me." Cheezesteak's voice was almost a whisper.

And to a kid who snatched a bag of Cheetos, Hennigan reminded himself. "You're one smooth move away from getting busted down to bike patrol, and you pedaling down Fremont Street in short shorts answering dumb tourist questions doesn't paint a pretty picture."

"Hopefully, it won't come to that. The union rep's negotiating a deal: six months of anger management and a one-week suspension, twenty hours without pay and twenty hours of vacation time."

"Sounds fair."

"If the brass agrees, I can skip the review board hearing. In the meantime, what's the mission impossible you've cooked up for me?"

"You know Spencer Orange?"

"The local FBI guy?"

"Right. A couple nights ago, I was helping Costanza with a stolen delivery truck, and he and his new partner stopped by and asked if I'd seen Elvis."

"You put out a BOLO for a pink, rag-top Caddy?"

"Funny, but I'm serious, or at least he was, and I wanna know why. How about nosing around and see if you can figure out why the FBI's hot and bothered about Elvis all of the sudden?"

Cops are naturally suspicious, and Agent Orange's oddball questions had finally piqued his curiosity.

13

By the time they got back to the Chapel d'Love, Jimi, as near as anybody could tell, had disappeared again. Elvis settled into his spot in front of the TV, and Sparkle headed down the hallway with Morrison a half step behind. She saw her father drinking coffee at the table but didn't realize her daughter was there too until they got to the kitchen.

"Hey, look who's here." Digby stood to make introductions. "Jim, this is my granddaughter, Honey."

Morrison immediately recognized her as the blonde from the convertible they saw driving into town.

"Hi, I'm Jim," he said, trying not to look at her shirt. The band's logo and his likeness from the rock-n-roll days was on the front."

Honey stole a sideways glance at her mom as she took his hand. "Nice to meet you, Jim."

"You guys wanna join us?"

"No, thanks. Not a coffee drinker."

Sparkle shook her head. "I'm good."

As Honey and Digby sat down again, Morrison grabbed Sparkle by the sleeve and very nearly dragged her out of the kitchen.

"That's your daughter?" he asked as soon as they were out of earshot. Morrison could tell by her reaction he'd hit a nerve and started backpedaling. "I didn't mean that or whatever you thought I meant. I mean, I mean – wait. What did you *think* I meant?" Sparkle didn't answer, but her teeth were clenched together, her cheeks as taut as drumheads. "I saw her with a couple tatted-up skinheads when we were driving into Vegas."

"Swastikas and Iron Crosses?"

Morrison nodded.

She seemed to relax a little. "Sounds like the Hitler twins."

"The Hitler twins?"

Sparkle hesitated, still connecting the dots. "Virgil and Be-Bop, two guys she hangs out with sometimes. That's what she calls them. They're in one of her classes, and I think Virgil's brother's the bouncer at the club where she works." Sparkle looked around to make sure it was just the two of them. "And Virgil's father's Garland Thibodeaux."

"The whack job who ran as Hartley's VP?" Before she could answer, Sparkle saw Honey and her father coming down the hallway.

"You guys have a busy morning?" Digby arched his bushy eyebrows. He looked amused.

Sparkle was deciding what to say when the doorbell rang. Her eyes wide with fear, she glanced at Morrison and mouthed, "FBI?"

His heart pounding in his chest, Morrison jerked his thumb toward the door. "I'll get that." He took a deep breath and two quick steps and leaned into the peephole. He could see a barely visible Jimi Hendrix, three slender, black men with braided hair, a dozen young women in halter tops and cutoffs, and, in the back, an enormous man with nearly translucent skin in a white duster and wide-brimmed Panama hat.

Morrison looked over his shoulder at Sparkle and nodded reassuringly. "Just Jimi and some friends," he said as he opened the door.

"We were in the neighborhood and stopped to see if you wanna join us at Moby's." Jimi gestured toward the massive guy in the duster. "We're working on some new material and thought maybe you'd like to sit in."

"You can practice here." Digby had worked his way past Sparkle and was standing in the foyer. "We don't have any weddings scheduled, and the neighbors are used to the noise."

"Thanks, Reverend. It'd be great to have the extra room."

Moby raised his hands over his head and clapped. "All right, ladies, let's get this party started."

Scantily-clad women began unloading band equipment and enough food and beer to feed the neighborhood from a battered Econoline van. A leggy blonde in bejeweled flip-flops lit the barbecue on the back patio and set Saran-wrapped plates of skewered shrimp and jerk chicken on the brickwork while the grill got hot. A brunette in a denim bikini top and bright white Daisy Dukes emptied bags of plantain chips into bowls. Morrison was stepping out of the way of a redhead wheeling a dolly loaded with cases of Red Stripe when he realized Hendrix was standing beside him.

Jimi made a sweeping gesture. "The most beautiful ladies in Vegas -- says so on the marquis."

"So, they're like dancers?"

"*Exactly* like dancers."

"Groupies multitasking as roadies. Clever boy. That'll cut down on overhead."

Jimi rested a wispy hand on Morrison's shoulder. "You get over a lot of things, but you *never* get over head." They were still laughing when a petite Asian woman handed Jimi a black Stratocaster. Morrison eyed the guitar suspiciously.

"A gift from Moby, scout's honor." Hendrix held up two fingers as if taking a pledge. "Now, if you'll excuse me, duty calls."

Jimi helped two *roadies* in pink bikinis push the sofa and chairs against the wall to clear a space for the band. Then he strapped on the guitar, played a couple short progressions, and adjusted the tuning. When he was satisfied, he left the Stratocaster leaning against an amp and went outside to fire his pipe.

After everything was set up and they'd finished their soundchecks, the Ahabs started things off with a couple Elvis songs. Digby, still wearing his collar and oversized sunglasses, was standing in for Moby. Half a verse into "Hound Dog," the Chapel d'Love was rocking.

Sparkle and Morrison settled into an open spot by the stairs, far enough from the band they could talk. "Is your dad okay with all this?"

"With the party or are you asking how he feels about harboring three presumed dead rock icons, including one who's invisible?"

Morrison shrugged. "Both, I guess."

"I don't think he's given any thought to who you are. As to our ghost, you'd have to ask him."

"Ask away."

"Jesus, Jimi. You can't sneak up like that."

"Sorry, but just 'cause I'm invisible doesn't mean you can talk about me like I'm not here. But, to answer your question, the night we showed up, he called me a new paradigm and hasn't mentioned it since."

"That's Dad. One moment, he doesn't see the elephant in the room, and the next, he's obsessed with some incomprehensibly tiny detail."

"Speaking of details, I'm going to get myself a beer. You want one?" Morrison asked.

Sparkle nodded and held her fist up to her mouth like a microphone: "…'cause the future's uncertain, and the end is always near."

Morrison followed Jimi to the coolers of Red Stripe and returned with a bottle in each hand. His view of the stage was partially blocked by the band's usual frontman. He was deciding how to strike up a conversation when Moby spoke up first.

"Good to meet you, Mr. Morrison," he said without turning around. His voice was deep with an upper-crust British lilt.

"Jim, please."

"Good to meet you, Jim." Morrison intended to introduce Sparkle, but Moby was still standing with his back to them. "When I was eight, my father took me to one of his last performances. That bloated parody was the original Elvis impersonator. I hope he wouldn't take it personally, but dying was a great career move."

Morrison glanced at Elvis, who was across the room, staring intently at his computer. "I think he'd be okay with that. He said as much himself."

Moby didn't say anything. He leaned against the doorframe, sipping a beer, his massive body swaying in time with the music. When the song finished, he turned around. "And you would be Sparkle." She smiled and took his hand.

Moby's jowly face was impassive. His neck bunched in folds, supporting an improbably large head. He was still wearing the Panama hat. His rheumy eyes were set close together, nestled deeply in his cheek pouches like shelled oysters, with black dots for pupils and pale, blue-gray irises.

"Jimi told me you got up close and personal with the FBI this morning."

Morrison nodded. "We're lucky he showed up when he did."

"Given what I assume are your security concerns, his public appearances, or more correctly his disappearances, are problematic. An invisible guitar player *will* garner attention." One of the brothers counted down, and Jimi's floating Stratocaster launched into an explosive riff. "Since it appears he's going to be a regular with the band, he's welcome to stay with me."

"Thanks. That would be helpful."

"Good. I will extend the invitation."

"How long have you been playing Sinderella's?" Morrison asked changing the subject.

"For two years on the regular DJ's night off. We work for tips, but it's really just a place to practice in front of a live audience."

Ishmael, one of the band's drummers, walked by carrying two Red Stripes bottles by the neck in each hand. "Like so much genius, we're unappreciated in our lifetime. My old granny used to say that nobody goes to Hooters for the wings, and nobody goes to

Sinderella's for the music. A couple nights a week, surrounded by naked women, we suffer for our art."

"Beats cutting sugar cane," Moby grunted.

"Says the man whose family owns the largest plantation on the island."

Moby waved his hand dismissively. "Don't mind him. We've known each other since boarding school. He's always had an attitude."

Ishmael rolled his eyes. "We didn't go to school together. You were a student at Munro, and my father was the groundskeeper."

"If you're really *that* homesick, my good Jamaican brother, there are a dozen flights a day with connections to Kingston."

"It pains my heart to hear such things. You know I came here seeking religious freedom."

"Obeah, the Jamaican version of Voodoo," Moby explained before Sparkle could ask. "Don't get him started. He'll want to sacrifice a chicken in your living room."

Ishmael threw back his head and cackled. "You know me *too* well." He raised the beers over his head and danced like he was leading a Conga line to the improvised bandstand.

"It's true, though," Moby admitted, "I am from a wealthy planter family, heir apparent and last of the lineage, unless my sexual proclivities take a decidedly U-turn." He shifted his considerable bulk and raised his chin slightly to appraise them. You two have a glow that suggests you're not only taking a more traditional approach to breeding but that you're taking it together."

Sparkle covered her mouth, hiding a smile. "We're glowing?"

"You positively illuminate the room. I have to warn you though, Jimi invited several *nice* girls from the club. Now that your boy's gone and made himself unavailable, Jimi's going to have to entertain them himself."

"Well, it's a dirty job."

"If it's not, he's going to be disappointed. Now, if you'll excuse me. I'm going to sit in on the next set before your father hijacks my band."

Moby strolled to the makeshift stage, said something to Jimi, and joined Digby for a reggae-style medley of Righteous Brothers hits. Morrison finished his beer as they were winding down an extended version of "You've Lost That Lovin' Feeling."

"This is sensory overload. I'm not used to being around this many people."

"Well, Jimi came with you, and everybody else came with him."

"I know. I'm sorry."

"You can make it up to me later. In the meantime, how about checking on Elvis? He's not where we left him." As he was turning to walk away, Sparkle tugged at Morrison's sleeve. "I'm worried about the FBI."

"Me too. Maybe it's time we went public."

"You should talk with Elvis and Jimi. You'd be less in harm's way if you were more in the public eye."

"I know a guy at *Rolling Stone*. If we don't come up with a better plan by then, I'll call him Monday morning."

Sparkle looked anxious. It was only Thursday afternoon, and a lot could happen between now and then.

When Honey realized her mom was by herself, she decided it was time for a mother-daughter chat and beelined across the room. "I've been watching you all afternoon," she said softly, "and unless I'm very, very wrong, you're in love."

"Oh, Honey…" Sparkle's voice trailed off.

"That's a non-denial, denial if ever I heard one." Honey wrapped her arms around her mom and squeezed. "I've been waiting a long time to see that look. I'm so happy for you."

The band was playing a song from an early sixties trio that Jimi, in his medicated state, introduced as a classic from Peter Pan and

Mary. Hendrix had slowed his intake to the point you could see his fingers dance across the fretwork. Honey looked around to make sure nobody was close enough to hear.

"Ishmael told me that guy's the ghost of Bob Marley, like in *Ebenezer Scrooge*."

"*A Christmas Carol*," Sparkle corrected, "and that was the ghost of *Jacob* Marley." Sparkle gnawed her lip. "But that's not the ghost of Bob Marley. It's Jimi Hendrix."

"That's the ghost of Jimi Hendrix?"

"No, just Jimi Hendrix, only invisible."

Honey glanced at the wispy figure playing the Stratocaster. "We should stick with the Bob Marley story."

"Perhaps that would be best," Sparkle agreed.

"And that guy, *your* guy, looks like…" Honey pointed to the face on her T-shirt.

Sparkle took a deep breath. "He is, but you can't tell a soul." Honey started to say something, but Sparkle held up her hand. "It's a long story."

"I'm listening."

"This isn't a good time, and, until it is, you *have* to keep quiet. The FBI and probably the CIA are looking for him."

"Really? Are you sure?"

Sparkle forced a smile. "Pretty sure."

"That's amazing. Jim Morrison, I mean *the* Jim Morrison and some invisible guy are in our living room." Honey thought about it for a moment. "And I bet there's lots you're not telling me."

Sparkle glanced across the room at Morrison. He was standing beside Elvis, watching Jimi play. "You have *no* idea. And just this second, I wouldn't know where to begin."

The afternoon heat had turned the Circle K bathroom into a urine-infused sauna. Orange settled in as comfortably as he could and tried to focus on breathing through his mouth. The cloying veneer of pine-scented air freshener was no match for the puddles on the floor. Several male guests would not be getting merit badges for marksmanship.

The more Orange thought about the CIA neglecting to mention the invisible man, the angrier he got. Because the situation involved another government agency, he assumed his current misfortune resulted from interagency parochialism. He neglected to consider an equally obvious and, in this case, valid conclusion: except for Carver Hawkings, Morrison's old handler, who had looped himself out of the process, the folks at Langley putting the file together didn't have a clue.

Newmeat made a noise between a groan and whimper. His forehead rested on the toilet seat, his chin burrowed so deeply in his chest, all Orange could see was the top of his head. He couldn't tell if Newmeat was praying or getting ready to throw up.

"Okay," Orange said, rousting him from his stupor. "Here's the plan. We work loose the bolts securing the base to the floor, lift the toilet, and get the hell outta here."

Newmeat looked up and nodded. There was a red furrow across his forehead from the toilet seat. Orange used his teeth to slide a shirtsleeve over his fingers to better grip the rusty bolts. After several minutes of painstaking effort, he managed to work them free.

"I got mine. How you doing on yours?"

"The back's off, but the front won't budge. Grab the toilet and rock it forward. Maybe we can loosen it that way."

As they rocked the toilet back and forth, the gasket between the base and floor ruptured. Water flooded everywhere. They were frantically thrashing around when Newmeat accidentally flushed the toilet. More water gushed out as the tank drained to refill the bowl. By the time Orange twisted the shut-off valve closed, they were in water almost an inch deep.

Newmeat was staring at his fingers, the tips bloody and raw from unscrewing the toilet, when he heard footsteps and the doorknob turned. "Maybe it's *them*," he whispered, "back to finish the job."

"Exactly which part's *unfinished*?" Orange growled as the heavy metal door swung open and banged into his leg. "Arrrrrrrrgh!" The scream died in his throat in a wet gurgle. He blinked away tears as he looked up at the elderly woman standing over him.

"Perverts!" she screamed as she swung her handbag in a wide arc. Handcuffed and unable to protect themselves, the first salvo caught Newmeat high on the right cheek. The next struck Orange across the mouth.

"Lady, wait!" Orange pleaded, blood trickling from a split lip.

"I'm calling the cops!" she screamed as she battered them repeatedly. Her rage finally spent, she turned and stormed out in a huff. The door slammed behind her with a dull thud.

"Maybe she's gone for help," Newmeat croaked weakly. A blotchy mouse had blossomed under his eye.

Furious enough to take out their predicament on his partner, Orange was ready to rip off the toilet seat and bludgeon Newmeat with it before more witnesses showed up. As he spit out a mouthful of blood, Orange realized he'd chipped a tooth.

"Which part of she's calling the cops didn't you understand?"

The more he thought about the DOD neglecting to mention the invisible man in their report, the angrier he got. Because the matter involved another governmental agency, Orange decided their current misfortune was due to interagency parochialism.

Ten minutes later, they were rousted by the squeal of tires on pavement and the distinctive crackle of a police radio. A car door opened and slammed shut. Orange braced himself, trying to protect his battered leg, knowing any moment one of Las Vegas's finest was going to kick open the bathroom door with his gun drawn.

Another vehicle pulled up, and Agent Orange recognized the voices of Detective Hennigan and his partner. Moments later, a thunderous fist pounded the door: "Las Vegas Police Department!"

"Hennigan, it's me! Spencer Orange."

The door crashed open, banging into the agent's already throbbing leg.

Hennigan holstered his weapon. "Detective Chestakowski, you remember Senior Special Agent Spencer Orange."

Cheezesteak thrust out a meaty paw. "Agent Orange. Good to see you again."

Orange scowled in disgust. "Excuse me for not shaking hands."

"An unforgivable breach of etiquette."

"And this is his associate, Special Agent Richard Newman."

Orange glared at the detectives. "Will you two assholes get these damn cuffs off?"

Hennigan grinned and jerked his thumb toward his partner. Cheezesteak was standing behind him, holding a camera. "Sure thing. As soon as he's done taking crime scene photos."

The feral noise escaping Agent Orange was close to a howl.

After Cheezesteak got around to unlocking the cuffs, Orange grabbed the sink and pulled himself to his feet. His whole body ached, and his urine-soaked slacks clung to his legs like a spray-on tan. While Newmeat was explaining to the detectives he couldn't recall any details from the female suspect's license, Orange shoved open the door and walked stiffly past a red Cadillac, ignoring the woman talking with a uniformed officer and the guy beside her in a horned helmet.

"Jeez," he muttered, shaking his head. "What else can go wrong?"

Halfway across the parking lot, Orange was reaching into his pocket for the keys when he realized somebody had stolen their car.

14

After they finished at the Circle K, Hennigan and Cheezesteak stopped by the Tahitian Princess for a beer with Jackie Costanza. When the Venettis decided to convert the old coffee shop to a Polynesian-themed bar and grill, Ernie "Bad Dog" Badoglio, the casino GM, wanted to call it the Enchanted Tiki Room. Disney got word and filed an injunction. The Tiki Lounge was the lawyerly compromise.

Cheezesteak thought about getting a Pu-Pu Platter even though Costanza had suggested skipping the food. Bad Dog ignored overtures from several B-List celebrity chefs and contracted with a company that mass-produced cafeteria-style meals for airlines and prisons. Cheezesteak decided he wasn't that hungry and slid the happy hour menu back in the condiment caddy.

Three guys in yellow hardhats were installing a palm-thatched roof section over the hostess station. Cheezesteak helped himself to another hammy fistful of pretzels. "Looks like they're finally fixing the place up."

"Your uncanny powers of observation are what make you one of the world's great detectives."

"That's me, a regular Sherlock Holmes."

"It's gonna take more than plastic leis and Don Ho tunes to turn this into a tourist hot spot."

"Don't forget the wall décor." Cheezesteak jerked his thumb toward a cluster of sepia-toned photographs. "Like Victoria's Secret in grass skirts."

Hennigan glanced at one taken on Waikiki, where he and Sheila stayed on their honeymoon. "Like déjà vu all over again," he muttered.

"How's that?"

"I'm meeting my soon-to-be ex-wife here tomorrow for lunch."

Cheezesteak arched his eyebrows. "You *sly* dog. Liquoring her up for a last tawdry roll in the hay."

"Not *here* in the hotel, here in the restaurant," Hennigan answered defensively. "Sheila called and demanded we talk face-to-face. And you know she's going to be late. Sheila's *always* late."

"Women. What are you gonna do? Can't live with 'em, can't stuff 'em down the garbage disposal." Cheezesteak reached for another handful of pretzels. "Wait, I got a Badger 5XP in the sink at home. That might just chew the bitch up."

"Can I think it over and get back to you?" Over his partner's shoulder, he saw Costanza hurrying their direction.

"Sorry, guys," he wheezed, badly out of breath. "Got here as soon as I could."

Hennigan held up his almost empty glass. "In your absence, my partner was waxing poetically about the virtues of *true* love, and I'm not gonna listen to that crap sober."

"So, has he talked you into whacking Sheila?"

Cheezesteak waggled a pudgy finger at Costanza as he slid into the seat across from him. "We were working out the details when you butted in. So, you want it to look like an accident or are you leaning toward an anonymous hole in the desert?"

"Don't tempt me. Shelia's jerking me around on visitation, and I haven't had enough to drink to believe it was *all* my fault." Hennigan drained the last of his beer. "So, Jackie, what's important enough to make you late for a drink with old friends?"

"We got a big promotional event tomorrow, and management wants to make sure we got our ducks in a row. You know how it goes. The guys in charge have no clue and think it's their job to bother the guys who do."

The barmaid arrived for their drink orders. She bent over and gave Costanza a peck on the cheek. "Delores, this is Peter Hennigan and Phillip Chestakowski."

"Pleased to make my acquaintance, I'm sure."

Costanza pointed at the two nearly empty glasses. "My friends are thirsty."

"Any friends of yours, Jackie." The barmaid gave them an exaggerated wink. "The usual for you and another round for these two?"

"That'll work."

"Be right back."

Hennigan offered his old partner a napkin. "You might want to wipe off the lipstick."

Costanza shook his head. "It'll give Carla something to talk about besides *Oprah*."

When Delores returned with their drinks, Cheezesteak gave her a beery smile. "*So* nice to see you again."

She gave him a small curtsy before dealing out new coasters as smoothly as a blackjack dealer, set a beer on top of each one, and picked up the empties. "I'll be 'round."

Costanza watched as she walked toward three men in a booth across the bar. "See the guy in the suit with the two grease balls? That's Ernie Badoglio, the casino GM, the guy the marketing geniuses sold on the promotion. It's supposed to be our one-millionth guest, but nobody's counting. They're gonna pick some schmuck outta the crowd who looks like the ad guy's idea of our target audience." Costanza bracketed *target audience* in air quotes. "My job's to babysit the TV lady and make sure nothing funny happens."

"Hey, I saw your boy the other night," Hennigan said, changing the subject. "He and Martinez got called out on a domestic disturbance between an RV and a Cadillac."

"Tommy told me when he stopped by for breakfast. He said the crime scene looked like a demolition derby."

"We haven't found the Caddy, but I'm pretty sure the motorhome got the worst of it."

"So, what else is new in the wonderful world of law enforcement?"

Hennigan munched a pretzel. "You mean *besides* the FBI's sudden fascination with Elvis?"

Costanza grinned. "Tommy kinda mentioned that too."

"You know Special Agent Orange?"

"Sure, the local FBI guy."

"I can't turn around without tripping over him, and every time we chat, Elvis is the hot topic."

"Weird." Costanza leaned forward and rested his elbows on the table. "I wonder why the FBI's panties are in a bunch about a dead guy?"

Cheezesteak set his glass on the table. "Maybe they think his death wasn't an accident. There's no statute of limitations on murder."

Hennigan shook his head. "I doubt it. They'd be playing a celebrity homicide closer to the vest. They're probably just stumbling around in the dark."

"That's the feds for you," Costanza chuckled.

"Did Tommy tell you we found Orange and his partner cuffed together in the bathroom?"

"The subject did come up. That must've been pretty funny."

Cheezesteak broke out in giggles, dribbling beer down his chins. "It was effing hilarious." He reached across the table and grabbed a fistful of napkins. "Remind me to show you the crime scene photos. The camera's in the car."

Costanza grinned. "*That* I'll remember."

Hennigan looked puzzled. "Something's going on with this Elvis business. I just can't figure it out."

Costanza stabbed at him with his index finger. "You're a detective. Keep working on it. It'll come to you."

"I hope so," he sighed. "It's starting to keep me up nights."

"Don't take the job home with you."

"Like you didn't."

"Like I did. That's why I'm working hotel security."

"Before I forget, Tommy told me he's taking the detective's exam. He's gonna do you proud."

"To a good cop." Cheezesteak raised his glass. He was starting to slur his words. "Just like his old man."

Costanza nodded. "Thanks."

"No, thank you," Hennigan added. "You taught me everything I know about police work, at least the part worth knowing."

"God, don't blame that on me."

Cheezesteak tilted back his head and drained the last of his beer. "There's something I've always wondered. How'd a nice Italian boy like you wind up a Jackie?"

"No big mystery. I was named after my father's uncle."

Cheezesteak's brow furrowed. "I don't care how many red-checkered tablecloths you've got in your family tree, I don't see Jackies jumping to the front of the enlistment line for the Sons of Italy."

"First of all, that's a strictly fraternal organization."

"And you'd be the only member of the local chapter without *the* for a middle name."

"…and," Costanza continued, ignoring him, "I was born and baptized Jacopo. That *paisan* enough for you?"

"Jacopo? I can see why you Anglicized it."

Costanza tipped the beer to his lips and sipped it thoughtfully. "I've heard the Polack's story. How'd an Irish bug like you wind up a noble crime fighter?"

"You mean besides the part about me following in the footsteps of my platoon sergeant?"

Costanza rolled his eyes. "So, you being a cop's my fault too?"

Hennigan grinned and glanced at his old partner. "My grandfather and great grandfather drove the paddy wagon. We Hennigans have a long and storied tradition of locking up drunks."

Cheezesteak picked up his glass and looked for Delores. "I'll drink to that."

"Your grandfather and his father, but not yours?"

"Not Kevin Patrick Hennigan. My dad lied about his age and enlisted in the Marines the day after Pearl Harbor. He wound up in Supply and worked his way to sergeant."

Costanza grinned. "My grandfather was in Supply too, so long ago he called it the Quartermaster Corps. He counted *everything*. Your old man that tight?"

"I heard him tell a drinking buddy he wouldn't let a Corpsman take his temperature without signing for it. The last time I was home, we spent a pleasant evening in the neighborhood bar. He's known every guy in the place since grade school. Except for a couple years overseas, he's lived in Framingham his whole life."

"Massachusetts?"

Hennigan nodded. "Just outside Boston. Mom passed ten years ago, so it's just dad and an Irish setter."

Costanza glanced at Cheezesteak. His eyes were closed, and he'd started to snore. Costanza turned up his palms and shrugged. "Past his bedtime. So, what'd your dad do after the Marine Corps?"

"He worked for the Postal Service and walked the same route, rain, sleet, or snow, for more than forty years. He's past president of the local VFW, grows prize-winning azaleas for the state fair, and month after next, he's gonna be the Grand Marshal of the Veteran's Day Parade. He fishes any day the roads are clear and hauls firewood to every widow on his old postal route."

"Sounds like somebody I'd like to meet."

"You might get the chance. He's threatening to come out for Christmas."

"Let me know. We'll have you over for dinner."

"Better keep a weather eye on Carla. Dad's quite a charmer."

Costanza jerked his thumb toward Cheezesteak. "If they run off together, it'll save me the trouble of hiring Sleeping Beauty when he finishes your side job." Startled awake by his own snoring, Cheezesteak looked up and blinked twice.

Hennigan tipped his glass to his partner. "Welcome back."

"Did I go somewhere?"

Hennigan grinned. "The important thing is you're here now."

Cheezesteak rubbed his eyes and looked around for Delores. "Everybody should believe in something," he mumbled. "I believe I'm gonna have another beer."

On the far side of the lounge, Bobby Ray was droning on about the only thing that interested him – Bobby Ray. Verduci, already several sheets to the wind, was building a log cabin out of toothpicks. Bad Dog, preoccupied with the One Millionth Guest promotion, was resisting the urge to drink enough to make their company tolerable.

Bobby Ray drained his vodka tonic, raised the empty glass, and waved it at the barmaid, who nodded in acknowledgment. He slid his glass onto the table and went back to his story. "My dad was in Tokyo after the war," he explained, "and ran the *whole* black market."

Verduci looked confused. "The black market?"

"When the war ended, the stores were empty. There was *nothing* on the shelves. My dad was selling regular stuff like Hershey Bars and Lucky Strikes for a small fortune."

"Where did he get candy bars and cigarettes?"

"He worked in Supply. Some of the stuff he diverted from inventory like when something falls off the back of a truck. The rest he smuggled in from the states."

Bad Dog glanced at Bobby Ray over the rim of his glass. He'd reminded Delores to bring *real* Johnnie Walker, not the cheap well scotch the barman used to refill the distinctively black-striped empties. He loosened his tie and stretched his arms across the top of the booth. "Weren't you born in Japan?"

Bobby Ray nodded.

"So, you're like half Japanese?" Verduci giggled.

"How could I be half Japanese? I don't even like rice."

"Well, you don't have a *real* Italian name."

"Does Darling sound Japanese to you?" Bobby Ray jabbed a chubby finger at his cousin. "Dante's my real name. My parents are as American as you and me. I was just born there."

Verduci peeled a mint leaf from his front tooth and flicked it on the carpet. Bobby Ray gave him another dirty look. "When I was a year old, mom died, so it was just dad and me. After he was discharged, we moved to Brooklyn and lived with dad's kid sister Nympha. When we was overseas, she and John eloped on account of Primo, my dad's older brother."

"And on account of her being pregnant," Verduci mumbled.

Bobby Ray scowled. "No, on account of John not being Italian."

Bad Dog looked up from his scotch. "I knew Primo. He *was* old school. His baby sister marrying somebody who wasn't Italian wouldn't sit well with a guy like that."

"That's why they eloped." Bobby Ray glared at Verduci. "Catholics ask for forgiveness, not permission. To appease Nympha, my dad tried going straight. His job in a lady's shoe store lasted most of an afternoon. He was in the backroom looking for a pair of baby doll pumps when the owner, a fat guy named Bonfigleo, strutted by in pink chiffon. He punched the little fairy, paid himself a week's severance out of the cash drawer, and hit the street."

The conversation hushed as the barmaid brought another round of cocktails and collected glasses even though Bad Dog had barely touched his. "Can I get you boys anything else?"

Bad Dog waved her off. "No, I think we're good."

She smiled curtly. "Well, if you need anything, just let me know."

As she crossed the room to tend the only other people in the bar, Bad Dog rocked forward and rested his elbows on the table. "When we're done here, I gotta have a fatherly chat with the resident mixologist. Security says he's comping drinks for underage girls. *Again*."

Verduci sat a little straighter in his seat. "The don wouldn't be pleased if your liquor license got yanked."

"Like you gotta remind me." Bad Dog stubbed out a half-smoked cigarette and glared angrily at the pimple-faced Casanova tending bar.

"So, what happened to your dad, I mean after the shoe place?" Verduci was trying to suck up after the half-Japanese debacle.

"He sold insurance. When that didn't turn out so good either, he went to work with Primo. Next time he was in Bonfigleo's shop, he was collecting protection money." Bobby Ray's voice trailed off. "A few weeks before Christmas, kids fishing in the East River found his body. I was already living with John and Nympha, and a couple years after that, they adopted me. John wasn't too keen on the idea, but after a while, she wore him down."

"Women are like that." Verduci looked up and managed a crème de menthe-tinged smile. "That's why I'm a confirmed old bachelor."

Bobby Ray smirked. He could think of at least one other reason. "When I was six, John took a headfirst dive through an open manhole on Newkirk Avenue. I think Primo caught him sneaking off for lunches with his daughter." Bobby Ray finished his drink and set the empty glass on the table. "That's the long and short of how I grew up in a Flatbush row house with pink flamingos on the lawn. Now, if you boys will excuse me, I gotta drain the lizard."

Bad Dog waited until Bobby Ray was out of earshot before jerking a thumb toward his empty seat. "Can you believe that crock of shit? You guys grew up together, right?"

Verduci nodded.

"He was a greasy, little meatball the other delinquents used for a punching bag."

"And he smelled like burnt fur," Verduci mumbled. "I remember that."

Bad Dog grinned wide enough to show canines. "Besides getting beaten up, the only two things he was ever good at was torturing cats and jerking off." He looked over to make sure Bobby

169

Ray was still in the bathroom. "When I was a kid, I ran numbers for Primo. I know what *really* happened, and it sure as hell wasn't the fairy tale he told us."

Titillated by the prospect of getting dirt on his cousin, Verduci sat up straighter in his chair.

"Primo wasn't as ambitious as his baby brother, but he knew plenty Aldo could learn, starting with the secret of living to a ripe, old age." Bad Dog tapped a well-manicured nail on the table. "You know what that is?"

The gesture startled Verduci, who had drifted off again.

Bad Dog chuckled. "Don't die young." He tilted his head back and drained his scotch. "Primo figured Aldo could live and learn. Trouble was, he wasn't too good at either one. He'd was used to wheeling-and-dealing and was *always* looking for shortcuts."

Dolores looked in their direction, but Bad Dog waved her off.

"Experience wasn't the only thing Aldo picked up. Some of the things he picked up were Don Bruno's, and he's very proprietary about what's his. Selling cigarettes and candy stolen from the government's one thing but stealing from the don's an exercise in *fatality*."

Bad Dog chuckled at his own cleverness. "A couple weeks before Christmas, Aldo got busted for loan sharking. The cops squeezed a little, and he turned into a one-man Vienna Boys Choir. Half the precinct was on his payroll so Don Bruno heard about it right away."

Bad Dog changed his mind about another scotch and glanced around the room for Delores. He spied her snacking on olives from the barman's set up. When she glanced their direction, he waggled his empty glass until she nodded.

"The don posted his bail, arranged a homecoming party, and Aldo choked on a meatball." Bad Dog made a gun with his thumb and index finger. "One in the throat, two in the chest, and three in the back of his head."

Verduci's Adam's apple bobbed up and down. His mouth opened, but no words came out.

Bad Dog wiped his hands on a cocktail napkin, wadded it into a ball, and glanced over his shoulder again at the bathroom. "I heard Primo took care of it personally."

"Jeez, his own brother?"

Bad Dog shrugged. "That's the kinda guy Primo was. The *family* came first, even before his family. He didn't want Aldo's blood on nobody else's hands."

He looked up and saw Bobby Ray walking toward them. "Here, he comes. Not a word. *Capiche*?"

"I wasn't here," Verduci said, "and if I was..." He pitched forward, and his head struck the table with a dull thud.

"I was passed out drunk," Bad Dog finished.

The Chapel d'Love was still rocking when Sparkle and Morrison excused themselves and trudged upstairs to bed. It was still dark when he awoke a little after four. Restless and alert, he stared at the ceiling for half an hour before slipping on a T-shirt and pair of jeans. Relieved to find the downstairs didn't look like Jonestown the morning after, Morrison filled the kettle at the sink and set it on the stove. When the water heated through, he brewed a cup of chamomile and sat down at the kitchen table.

Morrison knew he wasn't good at relationships. The son of a career naval officer, every year meant a new school and new friends. Growing up, he learned to live with one foot out the door.

Besides being obsessively attached to each other, all he and Pamela shared was vices. Insulated by drugs and lovers, they kept each other at arm's length. Their last few years together, they didn't even have that. After she died, he shut himself away and walled off the world.

But things were different with Sparkle. Being with her felt like the chance to reinvent himself he went looking for in Paris. Morrison smiled, remembering something Twain said about cats and cold stoves. That was the challenge: he had to learn to sit on a cold stove.

Morrison finished his tea, feeling the same sense of calmness he felt around Elvis. He was thinking about what Sparkle said about taking things a day at a time.

"Good advice, huh, fella?" Jaxx, who had curled up at his feet, wagged his tail.

Morrison rinsed the mug, left it in the rack to dry, and tiptoed upstairs. Sparkle was still asleep. He collected pens and a spiral notebook from the nightstand, turned on the light in the closet, and stretched out on the floor to write.

The bedroom was dark. As she rolled over, trying not to wake him, Sparkle realized the closet light was on. Through the open door, she could see Morrison scribbling furiously. She smiled softly, pulled the comforter around her shoulders, and went back to sleep.

15

When he looked up and realized he could see sunlight through the curtains, Morrison slipped downstairs again and took Jaxx for a walk. They stopped at the corner market for eggs and English muffins, two more spiral notebooks, and a box of pens.

By the time Sparkle came down, he'd finished most of the prep. She was wearing sweat pants and his flannel shirt. Sleepy-eyed, she slid a paper bag onto the counter and snuggled up against him.

"What's that?" he asked, nodding toward the bag.

"For our field trip."

Morrison gave her a puzzled look.

"I'm a school teacher, remember?"

"Right. And I thought you were a cold stove."

"A cold stove?"

"Mark Twain said a cat would only sit on a hot stove once, but after that, wouldn't sit on a cold stove either." He curled his index finger under her chin and lifted her head until their eyes met. "Just reminding myself, with no disrespect to Cosmo, I'm not a cat."

"Maybe you should wait until I've had my coffee before you get all heavy."

"But you don't drink coffee."

Sparkle brushed aside a lock of hair that had fallen across her face. "Then I guess you'll be chilling for a while." She pointed at the pens and notebooks on the counter. "Don't you think it's time you came out of the closet on the writing thing?"

"Sorry. Didn't mean to wake you."

"I'm just glad you're writing."

Morrison set a low flame under the saucepan with the butter. "It's been a long time, since Paris really."

"What was it like, Paris, I mean?"

173

"I was a stranger in a strange land," he said softly, his voice almost a whisper. "I thought things would be less crazy in Paris, but nothing really changed."

"Maybe you expected too much."

"I guess." Morrison stirred the melted butter with a whisk and stared at the soft, yellow contrails in the wake. "The only French I learned from Pamela and her friends was *la Chinoise blanche*. I couldn't even slip into a charming neighborhood bistro and get something to eat.

"Or, sadder still, slip into a charming neighborhood bar for a beer."

Morrison grinned. "I learned to grunt and point a little. If you wave enough francs at a bartender, even a French one, they get the idea." He leaned over and kissed her full on the lips. Jaxx looked up and yelped.

"Oh, Jimmy," she teased. "Not in front of the children."

"I think it's important he sees mommy and daddy like each other."

"Like? Well, that's a start." Sparkle rested her head on his shoulder. "You never told me what Jimi and Elvis said when you told them we were together."

"Honestly, they didn't seem surprised. I guess everybody knew where things were headed except us." Sparkle tilted her head and smiled. "Okay, maybe except me."

"The handsome rascal. Always the last to know."

"Anyway, I told them you yanked open your blouse and flashed your boobs, temporarily disabling me, and the next thing I knew, we were in bed, and you'd had your way with me. I also said my recollections were fuzzy and that you probably drugged my pizza."

Sparkle covered her face with her hands and shook her head. "I'll never be able to show my face in this town again. What am I going to do with you?"

"Well, I was hoping for more of the same," Morrison said softly. "Actually, much, much more of the same."

Sparkle spread her fingers wide enough to peek out between them. "Okay, but you gotta feed me first."

"Your terms are acceptable." Morrison grabbed the bowl of yolks and whisked them into the melted butter. As he was stirring, he nodded toward a leather-bound journal next to the spiral notebooks. "I found that this morning. I had it in Paris but didn't realize it was packed until I stumbled across it looking for socks."

Sparkle picked up the book and thumbed through the yellowed pages. They were blank except for the cryptic notation on the first page – "let the poets decide." Morrison was leaning in for another kiss when he heard Elvis in the hallway.

"I hope I'm interrupting something."

"Just making breakfast. Hungry?"

"Famished, actually."

"Great. How about setting the table?"

Morrison finished the Benedicts while Sparkle and Elvis grabbed napkins and silverware and poured juice. Morrison slid breakfast onto the table, leaving the Canadian bacon off Elvis's plate.

"Wow! This looks amazing." Elvis punctured the egg, spilling yolk down the side of his muffin.

"Thanks. I'm considering a career move." Morrison ground fresh pepper over his Benedict and reached for a fork.

"In the meantime, how about a field trip? Elmo and Gladys are staying at the Tahitian Princess. We could get together for lunch." Sparkle retrieved the paper bag from the counter and pulled out two fake beards. "After our close encounter with the FBI, I think you guys should be harder to recognize."

Morrison jerked his thumb toward Elvis. "We're not cruising around Vegas looking like Billy Gibbons and Dusty Hill. How about I wear a hat and sunglasses?"

"You *always* wear a hat and sunglasses."

"We'll stop at a souvenir shop, and you can pick out a new hat."

"James Douglas Morrison, you're impossible!"

"I thought I was incorrigible."

"Apparently, you're diversifying. Honey figured out who you are without any help, and, in case you haven't noticed, Jimi's becoming a public figure."

"As much as an invisible guy can."

Sparkle waggled a finger in his direction. "Joke if you want, but if you're not careful, you're going to wind up front-page news, and not just in the *National Enquirer.*"

Elvis swabbed the last of the Hollandaise with a bite of muffin, refolded his napkin, and tucked it beside his plate. "We can't hide from what's coming."

Morrison's eyes narrowed. "You sound like we're about to be tested."

"Let's call it a hunch."

Sparkle glanced again at the bag of beards. "And I'm guessing there's no such thing as a free hunch."

Morrison's shoulders slumped. "You know it's not that simple."

Elvis pushed aside his plate. "It's *always* that simple. It's just not easy. There's only right and wrong. It's about choosing sides, one of the two universal truths."

"I'm afraid to ask."

Elvis flashed a bemused smile. "Like the man said, *no one here gets out alive.*"

Morrison shifted uneasily in his chair and stared out the window. "What did Elmo say," he muttered softly, "about how eventually all of our lies come true?"

Cleopatra lay stiffly on the edge of the heart-shaped bed staring at the ceiling. It wasn't the rattle of the air conditioner or Bobby Ray's snoring that was keeping her awake, it was her own troubling behavior. Physical intimacy made her claustrophobic, and she was behaving like a giddy schoolgirl.

After brunch and cocktails, she and Bobby Ray made out the whole elevator ride, as titillated as rutting teenagers. He suggested his room because the Honeymoon suite was closer. They barely made it inside with their clothes on.

"What would Hiro think?" she mumbled softly. Cleopatra heard Michael Corleone in her head: *Keep your friends close but your enemies closer.* That sounded like something Hiro would say, but she doubted jumping into bed with Bobby Ray was what he'd have in mind.

Cleopatra grabbed the remote and flipped through the channels. All she found was soaps, sitcom reruns, and the Vegas Visitor's Guide. She settled on *Gilligan's Island.* Bobby Ray grunted and rolled over, dragging the bologna-colored comforter with him. Cleopatra yanked the top sheet, trying to cover herself. He came too, draping a squat, furry arm across her stomach. Resigned to being groped in his sleep, she muted the toothy blonde hawking Maxi Pads.

Sex with her first American was disappointing. Thirty seconds of sweaty, grunting passion wasn't worth the trouble of getting undressed. Grunting, anyway. Bobby Ray didn't carry on long enough to work up a sweat.

Cleopatra checked to make sure he was sleeping and reached into her bag for her vibrator. She adjusted her pillows and sat up a little straighter, hoping the batteries in her "curling iron" were still charged.

Bobby Ray slept soundly. He wasn't restless and fretful like Cleopatra. She needed a reason. He only needed a place.

Until he dropped out of high school, his love life consisted of girlie magazines and stalking cheerleaders. Since then, his would-be romances mostly involved strippers, but gorilla-sized bouncers always seemed to arrive at inopportune moments and nipped those fledgling relationships in the bud.

Rousted by Ginger's high-pitched scream, Bobby Ray sat up and scowled at the TV. "Obscene, not heard," he grumbled. It was something he remembered his father saying. The mobster yawned and stretched, leaned over, and kissed Cleopatra roughly on the neck. Both repulsed and excited, a familiar queasiness surged through her body.

The second of the afternoon's sessions lasted nearly through a McDonald's commercial.

Daytime temperatures in Vegas can be oppressive, even in late September. The short walk from the Chapel d'Love to Sparkle's pickup felt like a slog through a smelter. Every time Morrison inhaled, scorching, bone-dry heat seared his lungs. As he slid into the passenger seat, he saw the bag of beards at his feet.

"In case you change your mind," Sparkle said as she twisted the key in the ignition. Traffic crawled along at a snail's pace along the Strip. They rolled to a stop behind a minivan as the light turned red.

"See that group of men sitting in front of Mickey D's?" Sparkle asked, pointing out the window.

Morrison hunched forward. "The guys in suits and dark glasses?"

Sparkle nodded. "Do you know how to tell they're *foreign* guests?"

Morrison had focused on the man the others seemed to defer to. Built like a sumo wrestler, his eyes were unreadable behind black-on-black Wayfarers. "Something besides wearing suits to a McDonald's?"

"They're eating milkshakes with spoons."

The light changed, but as she rolled into the intersection, a drunken frat boy, slurping a neon-blue margarita from a plastic yard glass, stumbled into the narrow crease between her pickup and the minivan. Sparkle stomped hard on the brake pedal. The truck lurched abruptly to a stop. Morrison had to stiff-arm the dash to keep from pancaking against the windshield.

"You guys okay?" Morrison and Elvis nodded. The frat boy, indifferent to his near-death experience, did an about-face and staggered back to the curb. The commotion drew the attention of sumo man, who craned his neck to see what was happening. Even several blocks later, when he could no longer pick him out of the crowd, Morrison couldn't shake the feeling he was still watching them.

Sparkle turned into the Tahitian Princess parking structure and found an open spot between a black Grand Prix and a red Seville. As they were walking toward the ten-foot-tall Tikis bookending the double doors, Sparkle pointed at a small, black dome on the ceiling. "Big Brother's watching," she reminded them. Morrison pulled his cap almost to his eyebrows and stole a furtive look around.

As they navigated the gauntlet of players furiously pumping coins into the slots, the low hum dissolved into blurry, featureless static. Beneath the frenetic buzz, Morrison sensed the throbbing ebb and flow of quiet desperation.

They were almost to the restaurant when Sparkle stopped to feed a quarter into a slot machine. She punched the red button, and reels of oranges, cherries, lemons, grapes, and sevens started spinning and then slowed to a stop. She shook her head, but her bemused smile suggested more mischief than disappointment. "You know what they say -- unlucky in slots, lucky in love."

Morrison bent over and kissed her on the neck. "If I was wearing a beard, that would've been a scratchy kiss."

"You're not getting off that easily."

"Well, the important thing is I get off."

"See? You *are* incorrigible."

"Isn't it good to know in a world that's constantly changing, there are some things you can always count on?"

"Death, taxes, and you being incorrigible?" As she said it, Sparkle counted them on her fingers. Three rows over, an explosion of lights, bells, and whistles erupted as a woman jumped from her seat and danced around as nickels spilled down a chute into a plastic bucket.

Morrison grinned. "I guess she's unlucky in love, then again, my dad used to say he'd rather be lucky than good."

"So, which one were you?"

"If those are the two options, I must have been lucky because we both know I was very, very wicked."

Even Elvis had to bite his lip to keep from laughing.

16

Morrison, Sparkle, and Elvis waited under the thatched overhang by the register while a woman with two small children was seated. The hostess scurried to greet them, shuffling her feet so she wouldn't stumble in her high-heeled flip-flops.

"Welcome to the Tiki Lounge," she said, slightly out of breath. "Three for lunch?"

"We're meeting another couple," Sparkle explained as she pointed toward the Littles, who were sitting in an oversized circular booth in the corner. The hostess led them across the nearly empty restaurant and spread menus on the table.

"Your server will be right with you."

Elmo, who was wearing the plastic orchid from his Mai Tai behind his ear, looked up and grinned. "Good to see you guys again."

Sparkle smiled back. "Good to see you too."

"Please, sit down." He gestured toward the empty arc of seating beside his wife.

Elvis slid in next to Gladys, who squeezed his arm, careful to protect her bandaged thumb. "Remember to call me Mother," she reminded them.

Sparkle scooted in beside Elvis, and Morrison beside her, pushing an empty hi-ball glass and a discarded paper umbrella to the middle of the table.

"You just missed Atlas Shrugg," Gladys explained. "He's one of the favorites in tomorrow night's Itty Bitty Elvis contest."

"*And,* an honorary Viking," Elmo added.

Sparkle unrolled the napkin wrapped around her silverware and arranged it on her lap. "I remember seeing something about that on the news."

Elmo sat up a little straighter in his seat. "Mother and I were there when the TV lady interviewed him. Did you know nearly all the contestants were on the Midget Wrestling circuit?"

Sparkle shook her head. "No, I hadn't heard that."

Morrison didn't recall the news piece clearly and wasn't really listening. Hungry and preoccupied with the menu, he was relieved when the waitress arrived to take their orders.

Gladys was explaining how the restaurant had been closed for a remodel when their food arrived. The garland of plastic flowers around the server's neck dragged across Morrison's plate as she slid it onto the table.

"Ma'am, your lei," he stammered.

"They're available in our gift shop," she answered cheerfully. "Can I get you folks anything else?"

Morrison was staring at kernels of fried rice clinging to the plastic petals when Sparkle reached over and squeezed his hand. "No, I think we're good."

"A *faux*-flower lei," Elvis remarked as soon as she was out of earshot. "Just what every devout pilgrim needs, a plastic relic from their Vegas pilgrimage." Everybody laughed. Elvis had been more animated than usual since they sat down.

Morrison stabbed a piece of chicken and tried to slide it down the bamboo skewer with his fork, but it steadfastly resisted his best efforts. After several failed attempts, he raised the kabob to his lips and nibbled it like an ear of corn. Nobody seemed to notice. They were focused on Elmo and Gladys, who were recounting their previous afternoon's adventure.

"I heard sometimes criminals return to the scene of the crime," Gladys explained, "so we borrowed Dickie's car and drove to the Dewdrop Inn for a *stakeout*."

Sparkle was intrigued. "A stakeout?"

"Mother loves cop jargon. She picks it up watching reality crime shows, like *City Confidential* and *American Justice*," Elmo explained.

"And *FBI Files*," Gladys added. "That's my favorite."

"She's planning the perfect crime. I've tried telling her they're not do-it-yourself shows, but does she listen?"

"I *am* planning the perfect crime. I'm going to murder you and make it look like an accident." She elbowed her husband in the ribs, and they both giggled.

Elmo nodded Sparkle's direction. "If I die under mysterious circumstances, make sure things get *thoroughly* investigated."

Elvis grinned. "We'll tell the coroner to look for evidence of fifty years of marriage." Gladys reached over and patted his hand.

"There you go, Mother," Elmo teased, scooting out of range of his wife's elbow. "You've gone and entangled these nice folks in your wicked conspiracy."

Gladys rolled her eyes. "*Anyway*, we parked off to one side where we could see the whole lot but still be inconspicuous. That's the key to a really good stakeout. You gotta be inconspicuous." She tapped her bony finger on the table to emphasize the point.

"We left the engine running for the air conditioner," Elmo added.

"Land sakes, yes. Otherwise, we'd have roasted alive."

Morrison, mindful of their close encounter with the FBI, glanced at Sparkle. "So, what time was that?" he asked, doing his best to sound casual.

Gladys puzzled over the question. "I think it was about this time."

Morrison stole another glance at Sparkle. *Almost one-thirty. The same time we were there.*

Elmo dipped his napkin in the water glass and dabbed at a mustard spot on his shirt. "We pretended to read a newspaper but cut peepholes in it so we could see."

"That was my idea," Gladys pointed out proudly.

"And your idea worked perfectly. Too bad we didn't get to work it very long. We'd only been there a couple of minutes when Mother had to use the restroom. I reminded her to go before we left the hotel."

"Well, I didn't have to go *before* we left," she said firmly. "I didn't want to go in the restaurant in case the perp was casing the joint, so I used the one at the Circle K."

"When Mother opened the bathroom door, there were two creeps handcuffed together, doing some strange sex thing." Morrison and Sparkle exchanged knowing looks.

"Humph," Elmo grumbled. "With all the hotels in Vegas, you'd think they'd get a room."

"The two officers we met after our run-in with the Cadillac showed up and then that nice detective. He told me not to worry and said he'd see the perverts in the bathroom were properly punished. I think he thought the whole thing was kinda funny."

Sparkle shrugged. "Police get jaded, especially in a town like this. After a while, they've probably seen everything."

"I suppose that's true. It's just that—" Gladys didn't finish the thought as she spied a familiar face. "Look," she said, pointing at a man across the restaurant. "There's our detective."

The others craned their necks, trying to get a better look. Since his back was to them, they hadn't seen his face until he stood to greet a woman who was joining him.

"What was his name?" Sparkle wondered out loud. "Something Irish, I think."

Gladys was still pointing at the detective. "I don't remember. I call him Colombo on account of, well, you know."

Sparkle studied the woman sliding into the booth across from him. "I wonder who she is."

"Probably a suspect," Elmo suggested.

Gladys stacked her silverware on her plate. "Well, I'm gonna ask if those nice policemen have made an arrest yet."

Elmo, who was sitting on the outside of the booth, didn't budge. "Mother, just let them do their job."

Gladys fretted with her napkin. "I guess you're right. It seems like we should've heard something by now."

Elmo stood to leave. "The police will call as soon as they have anything to tell us. Now, if everybody's finished, let's settle our checks."

As she was getting up, Elmo took his wife by the hand. *Such a tender gesture for a couple married half a century*, Morrison thought, before realizing how hard she was straining to get away. He was headed for the register, but Gladys was pulling the opposite direction toward the detective. Elmo very nearly had to drag his wife out of the restaurant.

They crossed the gaming floor and were almost to the exit when Morrison noticed the guy from McDonald's surrounded by his entourage. Sumo man was wearing sunglasses, but Morrison had the impression he was watching them. When Morrison tugged on the brim of his cap, he nodded back. He was puzzling over the gesture and took no particular interest in the odd assortment of people milling around the double doors.

At Glady's suggestion, they'd decided to stroll down the Strip to do a little shopping and walk off lunch. With the Littles in the lead and Elvis a few steps behind, they were almost to the corner before Morrison tugged at Sparkle's sleeve.

"You know the guys we saw at the McDonald's?"

"The ones eating milkshakes with spoons?"

Morrison nodded. "We passed them as we were leaving the casino."

"Small world."

"That's not the weird part. When I—" Morrison turned to look for Elvis. He'd done a one-eighty and was walking back toward the Tahitian Princess. "Christ, where's he going?"

Morrison hurried after him with Sparkle a step behind. As they passed one of the hotel's security people talking on a cell phone, Morrison realized he was describing Elvis then counted down from five to zero as Presley approached the casino's double doors.

Sometimes Cosmo's e-mails were cryptic and obtuse. Other times, they wandered on about nothing in particular. Elvis assumed it had something to do with the feline's non-human perspective. But every once in a while, they offered brief glimpses into the everyday workings of the Universe. The e-mail Elvis got that morning was one of those:

```
    Heaven's a very specialized place. Take Flynn,
the angel in charge of stray bullets. Born Irish,
he's exceedingly fond of whiskey and nearsighted
to boot. Lately, and remember in Heaven, "lately"
takes on a whole new meaning, when Flynn goes to
choir practice, he hides a flask of Bushmills in
one of the pews.
    Like God doesn't know. Of course, He knows.
    Cynics can argue it's more proof He's losing
control or dead, but it's really about free will.
God doesn't muck about in the details. He's all
about the big-picture. The rest you can chalk up
to His peculiar sense of humor.
```

The paths of the patron angel of stray bullets and the First Lady and her bloodline had crossed many times. Just as certain types of cancer or a predisposition to heart disease run in families, hers had demonstrated a bizarre penchant for accidental headshots.

While Gladys and Elmo were telling their story of two men handcuffed in the bathroom of a Circle K, twenty-four hundred miles away at the White House, Secret Service agents were laughing over several Flynn projects, including a perfectly engineered shot banked off a Magic 8 Ball and an Easy Bake Oven.

Minnesota Fats eat your heart out.

When Abrams McCullough and his aide arrived to brief the president, they were directed to the Theater Room, where McDannold and his wife were in a shouting match over the suspicious disappearance of the TV remote. The First Lady seized the opportunity to make good her escape and stormed out in a theatrical flurry, screaming at the top of her lungs all the way to the rotunda.

McDannold was left standing by the sofa, wringing his hands. "Damned difficult woman," he grumbled.

McCullough nodded sympathetically. "Aren't they all, Mr. President? Colonel, if you don't mind, I'd like to brief the president privately."

Timkins snapped to attention. "Not at all, sir. I'll wait outside." He pivoted about-face and quick-timed out of the room, happy for any measure of plausible deniability, a practical necessity for a simple soldier treading political minefields. The colonel had good reason for concern: being McCullough's aide had been a steppingstone to early retirement for several good men.

Across the hallway, half a dozen Secret Service agents were milling around a box of muffins in the breakroom. Timkins recognized Aaron Kozlowski, who'd worked in the Presidential Protective Division since the Carter administration. Kozlowski introduced everybody before finishing a story about the First Lady, who nobody seemed to like.

"When she was eight, neighborhood kids were outside playing cops and robbers. A half-wit bully named Buddy Poteet squeezed off a couple rounds from his daddy's .22. Phyllis was upstairs having a tea party with doll friends. One of Poteet's shots shattered the window, was deflected by the Magic 8 Ball on her dresser, ricocheted off her Easy Bake Oven, and pierced her right cheek just above the jawline."

Timkins poured some coffee and helped himself to a blueberry scone. "I bet that left a mark."

Kozlowski nodded. "The zigzag lightning bolt under her left ear. She slathers on makeup with a masonry trowel, but when she's angry, which is most of the time, it glows like a red-hot poker." He jerked his thumb toward the lanky, African-American agent beside him. "Washburn thinks her family's being hunted by the magic bullet from the Warren Report."

Timkins chuckled, added two pumps of creamer to his coffee, and blended them with a wooden stir stick.

"It sounds crazy, but there *is* supporting evidence," Washburn insisted. "Her father was killed on a hunting trip. Drinking buddies mistook him for a bright-orange, bipedal deer and filled him full of twelve gauge. The coroner ruled the death accidental, but the Park Ranger cited the hunters because deer weren't in season. Her brother was shot in a drive-by gang initiation for a Compton kid named *Oz Dog*. Nowadays, he lounges around the house in Depends watching C-SPAN and *Jerry Springer*."

"If her family's half as unpleasant as she is," Kozlowski suggested, "it's understandable. I've considered shooting her myself."

Because he hadn't heard the story, Washburn didn't include the one about her uncle, a Navy corpsman in Vietnam. One night a young marine lieutenant was stumbling back drunk from a poker game, fell into a latrine trench, and broke his ankle. His screams startled a dozing sentry, who panicked and fired into the air. Exhausted by friction and overcome by gravity, the bullet did a slow one-eighty, punctured the roof of the MASH tent where Uncle Ned was swabbing out bedpans and grazed his left occipital lobe. He came home with a full disability pension, a pronounced stutter, and a tendency to drool.

"Isn't the president troubled by his wife's family curse?" Timkins asked.

Kozlowski shook his head. "It only seems to afflict blood relatives."

Everyone hushed as the door to the Theater Room opened, and McCullough emerged with the president. McDannold was wearing the same bewildered expression he wore when contemplating anything more complicated than a carton of ice cream.

"Now, if you'll excuse me, Mr. President, I'm gonna make sure mission resources are on the ready line." McCullough motioned for Timkins to follow, and they marched in lockstep down the hall.

McDannold had already finished a carton of Chunky Monkey and was watching *Scooby-Doo* in the Theater Room when he realized he'd forgotten to call his chief of staff. He grabbed the phone and asked the White House operator to dial the number for him. Verduci picked up on the fourth ring.

"Carmine. It's me. You know, the president."

"Yes, Mr. President."

"I had a meeting with the guy with all the stars."

"McCullough? The chairman of the Joint Chiefs?"

"Right, him. He said the Red Chinese are on the verge of a breakthrough."

Verduci cupped his hand over the mouthpiece and whispered: "With invisibility?"

The president nodded even though his chief of staff couldn't see him through the phone. "He said the launch window for the Jamaican mission's been moved to right after you get back."

Verduci saw the barmaid headed their direction and drained the last of his Mojito. "Did he say anything else?"

McDannold nodded again. "He said we should use National Guard units instead of regular military for security reasons. He said to tell 'em Jamaica's a training exercise."

Verduci used his index finger to dislodge a mint leaf clinging to his tooth. "I'm flying in the day after tomorrow. I'll fine-tune the invasion plan as soon as I get back."

"I know you already told me, but I've forgotten why you're in Vegas."

"*Family* business," Verduci answered drolly. Bad Dog and Bobby Ray, who could hear his half of the conversation, snickered. McDannold stared blankly at the TV.

As usual, he didn't get the joke.

Elvis was mobbed by security people and hustled up the steps of a makeshift stage as he soon as he stepped inside the Tahitian Princess. Fearful they'd been discovered, Sparkle and Morrison frantically searched the crowd, trying to locate the FBI guys. Stifling a knee-jerk reaction to storm in and rescue Elvis, Morrison pulled his hat lower on his forehead and tried to blend in.

A KVIG news crew elbowed their way past him and set up for a remote broadcast in front of the stage. When everybody was in position, the reporter, an Asian woman with square-cut bangs, tugged the hem of her blazer and nodded to the cameraman she was ready.

Behind her, a little Elvis in a sequined-and-white-fringed jumpsuit was standing beside a plastic palm tree, looking bored. Moby and the Ahabs were on the opposite side of the stage, dressed as their Polynesian alter egos. Elvis was in the middle, casually waving to the crowd. He didn't look the least bit ruffled.

The bowling-ball-shaped guy who crashed the Cadillac into the Littles RV was in the back with several casino executives. Sparkle and Morrison didn't recognize him in an aloha shirt and lime-green flip-flops.

A broad-shouldered man in a tailored suit strutted to the front of the platform, microphone in hand, and waved to the crowd. He cleared his throat and nodded to the band, cuing them for a drum roll. As the thunderous pounding subsided, he raised his hand to quiet the crowd.

"Good afternoon, everybody. I'm Ernie Badoglio, President of Operations here at the fabulous Tahitian Princess Resort and Casino. Is everybody having a good time?" There was a smattering of applause as he motioned Elvis forward. "First of all, I wanna congratulate you on being the casino's one-millionth guest."

"Well, thank you, thank you very much," Elvis said, grinning.

Bad Dog put an arm around him. "As the casino's one-millionth guest, I have the great pleasure of awarding you these fabulous prizes: a four-day, three-night stay in our luxurious VIP suite, meal vouchers and drink coupons redeemable at any of the resort's bars and restaurants, and a coconut full of quarters for the slots. And, best of all, tomorrow night, you'll be the special guest judge at the Itty Bitty Elvis Contest."

There was another thunderous round of steel drumming as Bad Dog and Elvis disappeared in a swarm of Tahitian dancers that suddenly appeared from both sides of the stage. The little Elvis sauntered to the center of the platform, grabbed the mic stand, and pulled it down at a forty-five-degree angle to the floor. He yanked out the microphone, spun it by the cord through several full circles, and caught it adeptly with his free hand.

"Atlas Shrugg, one of the contestants in tomorrow night's contest," Bad Dog announced, "will join our house band, The Tiki Idols, for an Elvis song that's one of my favorites, and I'm sure it's one of *your* favorites too."

Temporarily supplanted as the band's frontman, Moby stood, his arms folded across his broad chest, looking faintly amused as "Blue Hawaii" blasted from giant speakers arranged around the stage, and Atlas lip-synched the words.

One of the dancers shimmied and shook up to Elvis with a gaudy pair of gold-rimmed sunglasses, and another helped him into a white-fringed, rhinestone jacket several sizes too big. Elvis slipped on the sunglasses and waved to the crowd, looking serenely content.

As the song wound down, Bad Dog walked over and stood beside Elvis again. "For the next four days and three nights, I proclaim you the Tahitian Princess's honorary Elvis Presley." There was another modest round of hooting and applause.

"For the next four days, I get to be Elvis Presley?"

"That's right."

"But I don't have to wear the jacket and sunglasses the entire time, do I?"

"No, not the whole time, I guess. So, what's your favorite Elvis tune?" he asked, trying to redirect the conversation back to the script.

"'Alison,'" he answered without hesitating.

"That's one of my favorites too."

Bad Dog stared at his notes, trying to remember that particular song. Another dancer hulaed over with the coconut full of quarters. Bad Dog grabbed a meaty paw of coins and spilled them back into the shell. "Do you like playing the slots?"

"Fifty pieces of silver?" Elvis asked.

Bad Dog glared at the marketing guy who had suggested the millionth-guest promotion. "I think there's actually more like a hundred. Not a hundred pieces of silver, a hundred dollars." Badoglio quickly did the math in his head. "That's like four hundred quarters."

Bad Dog plucked one from the coconut and set the coin in Elvis's palm. He stared at it for a moment before walking over to a progressive slot machine cordoned off with velvet ropes.

A frenetic swarm of Tahitian dancers surrounded him, working the crowd into a frenzy. The drumbeats swelled until the whole room seemed to shake and then, with a dramatic flurry, fell silent. Elvis held the quarter theatrically over his head, pinched between his thumb and index finger, and panned a slow three-sixty.

Morrison was herded by the crowd until he was standing within a few feet of the sumo wrestler from McDonald's. Before Morrison realized how close he was, he reached between his bodyguards and squeezed his arm like they were old friends.

"Oh, Mr. Morrison, this is rich. You have to appreciate the irony. The casino manager is convinced they have picked the only guy in Vegas with no idea who Elvis is."

Before Morrison could say anything, Elvis turned, dropped the quarter into the slot, and pulled the lever, setting the spinning reels in motion. The cheers and clapping of the assembled multitude grew steadily quieter as the slot wheels spun to a stop.

Jackpot.

Jackpot.

Jackpot.

Jackpot.

By the time the final wheel clicked into place, you could hear a pin drop.

Jackpot.

The cavernous room erupted in an explosion of lights and a deafening cacophony of bells, whistles, and sirens. To Morrison's left, the phalanx of bodyguards quickly closed around their charge and hustled him away. Distracted by the electronic fireworks, Morrison barely noticed as the neon crawl above the slot machine flashed dollar signs and a string of numbers.

Elvis had just won $26,126,810 and some change.

17

Deep in the bowels of the DOD labs, a half dozen floors beneath their feet, Lawless Childs was working around the clock on a special project the chairman of the Joint Chiefs and his aide had come to review personally.

"The situation with that guitar player's been a damn nightmare," McCullough grumbled. An unlit cigar jutted from his mouth like a bloated, chocolate toothpick.

Timkins stared straight ahead, avoiding eye contact. "Hendrix?"

"Right, Hendrix."

"It's been a difficult situation, sir."

"Difficult? Hell, until SEAL Team 13, he *was* the invisibility program." The general bit the cigar, trickling brown spittle down his chin. "And I mean to use them to get him back." McCullough pressed the elevator call button again. "Just when I thought the FBI couldn't find their dicks to take a leak, they stumbled across him. Looks like your hunch to check out the other two paid off. What were their names again?"

"Morrison and Presley, sir. It's in the report."

When the elevator doors slid open, they stepped inside. "I'm tired of rattling sabers at every loudmouthed towelhead screaming about his hotline to God on the evening news."

Timkins pushed the button for the subbasement. He'd heard the tirade before.

"Since Christ was a corporal, I've bailed presidents outta situations bad diplomacy got them into. Not *one* of those bumbling idiots could get outta their own way." McCullough yanked the cigar from his mouth and pointed it at his aide. "When did running the country become a knee-jerk reaction to opinion polls? Presidents aren't supposed to do what's popular or even what's right. They're supposed to do what's necessary. McDannold would wear a pink tutu and club baby seals on the Disney Channel if it would bump him a percent in the polls."

The elevator lurched to a stop. As the doors slid open, the space filled with the static hum of a Lockheed Martin jet engine venting a hundred million cubic feet of air per hour, but it wasn't enough to keep the subbasement from smelling like college dorms have since the Nixon administration.

"This is our floor, sir."

McCullough ignored him. "America's nuclear arsenal is rusting away because of a thaw in the Cold War. Détente's a damned waste of resources if you ask me. Trouble is, nobody's asking me."

Timkins coughed into his fist. "No, sir. Nobody's asking me either."

McCullough glared at the *No Smoking* sign over the lab door. His eyes narrowed. "But they will. And when they do, things are gonna be different."

He had brown-nosed his way up the ranks and was poised to make the transition from ass-kisser to baby-kisser. Though he wasn't carved-in-stone positive about the order of succession, McCullough was pretty sure the chairman of the Joint Chiefs came either right before or right after the VP. It would've been better if the vice president was leading the Jamaica mission, but the general was confident he could get the nosey, do-gooder out of the way when the time came.

"Well, let's get this over with." McCullough jammed the cigar back in his mouth and motioned for Timkins to follow.

At a glance, the lab looked like a morgue, which is what it was until late summer when the spongy, gray bodies recovered from the UFO crash site were packed in dry ice and shipped to Area 52. Along the far wall, SEAL Team 13 was sleeping in cadaver drawers made up as beds, surrounded by automated smokers hotboxing a particularly potent strain of OG Kush. The hybrid was originally developed by DARPA for enhanced interrogations and had been requisitioned from the country's strategic sinsemilla reserves.

195

Reggae covers of Led Zeppelin songs blasted from oversized speakers. The band, Dread Zeppelin, was fronted by a three-hundred-pound, Vegas-era Elvis impersonator. Being musically challenged, Lawless Childs, the MIT whiz kid McCullough recruited to run the program, relied on the recommendation of a stoner clerk at Hemp Records where he picked up the CDs.

Along the other wall was a row of arcade games like Mortal Kombat and Street Fighter II Turbo, euphemistically referred to as "training simulators" in accounting reports. Despite the astounding amount of money being spent on Twinkies, Snickers bars, and delivery pizza, the project was still under budget.

Childs was staring at nothing in particular when the general and his aide walked into his office. With his boyish features and unruly, dark hair, he looked like he was playing dress-up in his daddy's lab coat. Not predisposed to the rigors of military protocol, he didn't stand or salute and only begrudgingly glanced their direction.

"Dr. Childs, we're here so you can get us up to speed. Where are we on the invisibility project?"

Childs, owlish in his wire-rimmed glasses, blinked twice and grinned. "Let's just say if you guys were playing hide-and-seek, I'm pretty sure they'd kick your ass." His lack of deference made McCullough uncomfortable. The general glanced over his shoulder, reassuring himself the three of them were alone.

"There've been some new developments I'm not at liberty to discuss."

Childs leaned forward and rested his elbows on the desk. "All very hush, hush, I suppose."

McCullough nodded. "I knew you'd understand. It's imperative we move up our timetable." He assumed Child's bloodshot eyes were from nervous exhaustion, but the doctor had been smoking nearly as much dope as the SEALs. Partially transparent, Childs shimmered slightly in the fluorescent lighting.

McCullough didn't notice. "I've scheduled a training exercise. They're shipping out this afternoon."

"I'll see they're fired up."

McCullough jerked the cigar from his mouth and poked it at Childs. "Ground transport will be here at thirteen hundred hours."

"So, that's like one o'clock?"

The general nodded, gritting his teeth. "I'm keenly aware how hard you've been working on this project." He reached over and gave Childs a fatherly pat on the shoulder. "I want you to know, it's in the service of a grateful nation."

Childs recoiled slightly at his touch. "Just doing my part."

McCullough grinned broadly. He knew how much his little pep talks meant to the men in his command.

As soon as they were gone, Childs retrieved the bong he stashed when he heard them coming and fired it with his lighter. He took a deep drag, slipped on his headset, and adjusted the volume on the commlink. When they were sleeping, Childs fed the SEALs the subliminal messages McCullough had ordered as a fail-safe. It was bad science, but he understood the general's concerns. SEAL Team 13, the raw material for the project, was not exactly raw. Like the rest of McCullough's harebrained scheme, they were half-baked.

Two years ago, when McCullough testified before a congressional oversight committee, he argued striking terror in the hearts of America's enemies required more than the robotic efficiency of existing special ops units. He characterized the proposal as developing "guided misguided missiles."

"What's necessary," he insisted, "are frenzied fighters, the modern military equivalent of Viking berserkers." In hindsight, Childs would assess the guided part of McCullough's appraisal as overly optimistic.

When Congress tabled funding for his pet project, McCullough diverted money originally earmarked for overpriced toilet seats. Assembled from applicants culled from the regular special ops program, SEAL Team 13 was made up entirely of individuals deemed unsuitable during their psych evals. Rather than disciplined and mission-oriented, they resented authority, did everything by the seat of their pants, and generally couldn't color inside the lines.

They had been training together for more than a year and moved in the private shorthand of people so hardwired into each other's nuances every smile, or nod, or glance meant something. They even went to the bathroom in standard cover formation.

Childs charted early test subjects, including Jimi Hendrix, and came up with a profile for the optimum invisibility candidate. He ran his search parameters through the DOD database. The top twelve results were all members of SEAL Team 13. When he suggested assigning them to the project, McCullough enthusiastically greenlit his proposal. Every day since, Childs had grown more skeptical about the wisdom of his recommendation.

Unaccustomed to working with human subjects, he found the opinionated and often argumentative lab rats not just troublesome but scary. They had all the lethality of standard special ops units but none of the discipline.

Behind their backs, most folks in Washington referred to the president and Chairman of the Joint Chiefs as Big Mac and Little Mac, an insult that would have driven McCullough straight up a wall. That McDannold got top billing would have sent him into the stratosphere. Childs, who'd briefly met the president at a White House function, didn't care for either of them.

"Big Mac's a jerk-off," he mumbled into the mic. Childs failed to notice the commlink was still open. To the severely medicated SEAL Team 13, the doctor's snarky comment sounded like a priority-one command. Unduly influenced by the Jamaican context, the directive got further garbled in translation. The snoozing SEALs chanted in a groggy chorus: "Big Macs with jerk sauce. Big Macs with jerk sauce. Big Macs with jerk sauce."

Childs, who couldn't hear them over Dread Zeppelin, grabbed a couple of buds from the Ziploc in his drawer and packed himself another bowl.

Hennigan and his partner arrived a few minutes early and decided to wait in the car. Cheezesteak backed into a spot in front of the Dewdrop Inn with a clear view of the Circle K. The meeting place had been his suggestion. The FBI guys pulled in and parked across the lot, closer to the convenience store. After the Expedition was stolen, Orange had downsized to a black Explorer. He got out and shuffled toward the detectives.

"They've returned to the scene of the crime," Hennigan chuckled. "Probably here to stake out the bathroom."

Cheezesteak rolled down his window. "You look a little flush, Mr. FBI man."

"Can we talk?" Orange asked, nodding toward Hennigan. "Alone?"

The detective glanced at his partner. "If you'll excuse us."

Hennigan caught up with Orange on the far side of the lot, out of earshot of both cars. "It's *your* party," he said curtly. In pow-wows between law enforcement agencies, he'd learned he who did the most talking lost.

Orange didn't respond at first. He stood quietly fidgeting with a thin, manila envelope and didn't offer to shake hands. "Thanks for coming."

Hennigan's eyes narrowed. "You seem scratchy," he said, hoping the remark would keep the fed off balance.

"This morning, when I opened my file cabinet, I discovered somebody had stuffed it with toilet paper." Orange stared at his shoes. He was having a hard time making eye contact. "My career's pretty much down the toilet."

Hennigan shrugged. "Things will blow over in a year or two."

"Between now and then, I'm one smartass remark away from shooting somebody."

"Well, I'd appreciate it if you did it in somebody else's jurisdiction. My caseload's backed up already."

Newmeat got out and positioned himself behind the Explorer, using it for cover. His hands clasped together, he stretched his arms across the roof and sighted down the barrel of his index finger. The shiny sides of his crew cut gleamed in the moonlight. He had the practiced look of somebody who watched too much TV.

Orange glanced over his shoulder at his partner. "Still wet behind the ears."

"I hate breaking in new guys."

"Newmeat fits the classic mold of the crime-busting G-man, but once he's in, there's a lot of room left over." Orange pulled open his windbreaker, exposing a small microphone transmitter.

"So, we're on a party line?"

"Don't take it personally. Newmeat insisted. He quoted the FBI training manual." Hennigan started to walk away. "Wait. I brought something." When the detective turned around, he realized Orange was offering him the envelope. "Keep this between us. My partner doesn't approve, and I didn't exactly ask Washington for permission."

Hennigan assumed this was the FBI's version of good cop/bad cop. Senior agents didn't take a dump without filling out the paperwork first.

Orange glanced over his shoulder again at Newmeat. "I heard there's been a rash of Elvis sightings." His smile looked forced.

"Here and there." Hennigan's expression didn't change. "So, what's with the FBI's sudden fascination with Elvis Presley?"

"Read the file."

As Hennigan reached for the envelope, he leaned into Orange and pulled open his windbreaker. "I heard Amelia Earhart's working the swing shift at Caesars." Out of the corner of his eye, he saw Newmeat pull a pen and notebook from his jacket pocket and jot something down.

Orange shook his head. "I'm sure he'll check that out later."

Hennigan made no attempt to conceal his distaste. "Does the Academy still teach green peas local law enforcement's a good source of information?"

"Probably." Orange nodded toward the envelope in Hennigan's hand. "Take a look, please. I could use extra eyes on this."

"Taking your abduction personally?" Orange glanced at the red rings around his wrists but didn't answer.

Cheezesteak rolled his window down and cupped his hands around his mouth. "Dispatch radioed. Kids are setting off cherry bombs in the dumpsters around back. Costanza's en route but needs us to seal the other end."

Hennigan waved the envelope at Orange. "Duty calls. I'll get back to you on this."

He walked across the lot and slid into the car beside his partner. As Cheezesteak wheeled the car around, Hennigan tossed the envelope on the dash and fastened his seatbelt. On the hard turn into the alley, the envelope slid to Cheezesteak's side and landed in his lap. He picked it up and handed it to his partner. "Did he ask about Elvis?"

Hennigan tapped the tip of his nose with his index finger. "Given the FBI's fascination with paperwork, does this file seem suspiciously thin to you?"

He tore open the envelope and pulled out a grainy photograph of a man in a baseball cap and sunglasses taken at an ATM. Orange got proprietary about the ones he used to identify Elvis and Morrison and left them out. Hennigan held up the picture, trying to get better light when the radio crackled. It was Costanza. He was in position. The Crown Vic and the black-and-white rolled into opposite ends of the alley, boxing in a group of gawky teenagers who scrambled up a dumpster and were using it to scale the wall.

"Well, big fella, how do you feel about a little, old-fashioned police work?" Hennigan braced himself against the dash as his partner stomped the brakes.

Cheezesteak scowled. "I think I shoulda kept up my gym membership." He slammed the gearshift into park, shouldered open the door, and took off in hot pursuit.

Except when the SEALs commandeered the plane, the flight from Andrews was uneventful. As the Gulfstream V made the descent into Nellis, the passengers and crew were as high as ever. Cabin visibility was limited by the sticky, sweet clouds of marijuana hanging in the pressurized air. Lieutenant Commander Geronimo Nieto, commanding officer SEAL Team 13, banked to the left, checked his airspeed, and lined up the runway.

"Cannibal" Jane Hawkings, the unit's executive officer, slid into the copilot's seat beside him. She stared intently out the cockpit window, but Cannibal Jane, CJ for short, brought intensity to everything she did -- even sleeping. She had big, blue eyes and blonde hair cut in a short shag.

"They're taking things pretty much in stride except the captain," she said. "He's curled up in the last row shitting cookies."

"When I took the stick, I might've left him with the impression this was my first time in a real cockpit."

"Let me guess. You told him all your flight hours were in a simulator."

"You know me too well." Geronimo leveled the wings and lowered the landing gear. The original flight crew was arguing loud enough to be heard over Dread Zeppelin's funky, reggae cover of "Whole Lot of Love."

"What was I supposed to do?" the copilot very nearly shouted. "Talk about armed and dangerous. They're a SEAL Team, for Christ's sake."

Geronimo grabbed the intercom mike. "Don't make me pull over and come back there," he growled, and they immediately fell silent.

Raised on the Mescalero Reservation in New Mexico's Sacramento Mountains, Geronimo was admitted to the Naval Academy on the strength of his test scores and a growing attitude of political correctness. He graduated in the top five percent of his class, but instructors noted a tendency toward cockiness that bordered on insubordination. With a round, cherub face and mischievous brown eyes, he perpetually wore the expression of a precocious child testing boundaries.

When the Gulfstream touched down, Geronimo reversed the engines, and the tower directed them to a hangar on the far side of the field. With the area secured, Geronimo set about winning the hearts and minds, or more accurately, wooing the hearts and blowing the minds of the ground personnel. There was plenty of dope to go around.

CJ immediately set about organizing mission resources with objectives best described as life, liberty, and the pursuit of happy hour.

Oh, did I forget to mention Big Macs?

The ground team packed the base armory into three trucks, stowing enough weapons and ordnance to bomb England and Scotland south of Loch Ness back to the Stone Age. A grinning airman first class from Huntington, West Virginia and two of his friends volunteered to drive the support vehicles behind the Humvees Geronimo appropriated for the mission. The convoy formed quickly. Most of the column headed south on the 15 to establish a base camp closer to Vegas, but two Humvees peeled off for a Micky D's run.

"Lock and load, boys and girls." Geronimo's orders crackled through the comm-units.

"Fearless leader's putting on his war paint," CJ teased. Geronimo, who had smeared eye black on his cheeks, slipped on a pair of Oakley Heaters.

"This isn't combat," Geronimo reminded them. "We're here to grab some goodies and be gone. Holstered close-quarter weapons and aerosol sleep agents only. Stow serious hardware in transport."

When the golden arches came into view, CJ alerted the rest of the team. The Humvees took a U-turn at the back of the lot and parked by the entrance, facing the street, motors running. Exit strategy in place, Geronimo, CJ, and Trigger moved with surgical precision, hustling out of the Humvees, their backs against the wall.

"Heads on swivels," Geronimo reminded them. "Everybody frosty."

"Ladies first? I remember when sisterhood meant back of the line," CJ joked with a dry smile and no real rancor.

While Trigger took up a position on the exit, Geronimo and CJ waited inside. A few skittish customers looked over anxiously, but most of the diners took the heavily-armed guests in stride, assuming they were part of a publicity stunt or hungry actors on break from a movie shoot. When it was their turn, Geronimo heaved a khaki knapsack on the counter and pulled the mic on his commlink away from his mouth.

"Big Macs, please. Fill 'er up."

The girl at the register had braces and straw-colored hair in a ponytail. She was staring at the smudges of eye black on the SEAL commander's cheeks. "Would you like fries with that?"

Geronimo glanced over his shoulder at CJ then back to the menu board. "No, but do you have any jerk sauce?"

18

Early enough to still be light outside, a sliver of blue sky crept through the part in the curtains. Sparkle draped her arm across Morrison's chest and nibbled gently on his ear.

"You're a lot more manageable after sex," she teased.

"A small price to pay to make me fit for human companionship," Morrison chuckled softly. "Now that you've shamelessly slept with me on *several* occasions, I think it's time you opened up and shared a little."

"I talk about myself all the time. I just haven't gotten around to talking about myself with you."

"Well then, go ahead. I'm all ears."

Sparkle grinned wickedly and raked her nails along his inner thigh. "Now we both know that's *not* true," she whispered softly.

Morrison rolled onto his side. "Well, just for a moment, let's pretend I'm all ears. Here, I'll get you started. Where were you born?"

"Is this multiple choice?"

"Sparkle," he growled, trying to sound firm.

"Okay. Lynwood."

"In LA?"

Sparkle nodded. "My dad was working at an engineering company in Downey and finishing his Ph.D. at Cal Tech. When I was two, we moved to Castro Valley."

"The artichoke place?"

"No, that's Castro*ville*. Castro Valley is East Bay, south of Oakland. Castroville's down toward Santa Cruz and Monterey."

"Okay. Gotcha. So, why there?"

"He went to work with his brother at the Lawrence Radiation Lab."

"Wow, glow-in-the-dark stuff, huh?"

"If by that you mean thermonuclear weapons development, then yes."

"Is that how you wound up in Las Vegas, all the weapons testing in the desert?"

Sparkle shook her head. "No, it was more like the exact opposite. When I was seven or eight, Dad and his brother got into an argument at a backyard barbecue. They were always fighting about the moral implications of Uncle Sam using their research to kill people, at least that's how mom explained it later. Anyway, things got heated, and Newt stormed out before the steaks were done. They haven't talked since, not even Christmas cards."

"So, how *did* you wind up in Vegas?"

"I doubt Dad had a plan. He walked into the lab the next morning and gave his notice. Two days later, we were packed and on the road. We had this car --" Sparkle hesitated, "-- actually, we still have it, and Vegas is where the transmission died. I don't know if Dad saw the Citroën breaking down as a sign or if he ran out of options. He tinkered around doing odd jobs and eventually fell into the wedding thing."

"Seems like an odd career arc."

"He always liked to sing, and it's as far from building weapons of mass destruction as he could get. Remember *Gilligan's Island*?"

Morrison nodded.

"You know how the professor could build a nuclear reactor out of conch shells and coconut husks but couldn't figure how to lash an acre of bamboo into a raft?"

Morrison chuckled. "Sure."

"Well, Digby's like that."

"You know, you've barely mentioned your mom."

Sparkle stared at the ceiling for a moment, deciding what to say. "She was a drama queen. The night before Honey's fifth birthday, we were getting ready for the party. Apparently, she wasn't getting enough attention. She started bitching about the Winnie-the-Pooh decorations, threw a bunch of clothes in a suitcase, and stormed out the door. I think leaving was the only way she could make it about her."

"And you haven't seen her since?"

"Every year we get a card at Christmas. They're signed but no note or return address. The postmarks are mostly California." Sparkle pulled the top sheet around her shoulders and tucked the edge under her chin. "When I was a kid, I thought everybody's mom was like mine. I was in high school before I realized how much she drank." Her voice was barely a whisper. "Every morning, no matter how late she'd been drinking the night before, she took three beers into the shower. I asked her why once, and she told me because she expected to throw up the first two."

Morrison's brow furrowed. "Sounds like a hard way to go."

"I used to lie awake at night and wonder if she'd ever come out the other side."

"Sometimes, eventually, people do."

Sparkle's expression saddened. "But usually they don't."

Morrison brushed away a wisp of hair that had fallen across her face. "Raising Honey must have been that much harder after she left."

"Not really. Mom was never much help, and Dad was, well, Dad."

"You were so young. You and Honey kind of grew up together."

Sparkle grinned wide enough to show her dimples. "We took mother-daughter tea parties to a whole new level."

"Was her father much help?"

Sparkle smiled softly and shook her head. "No, he wasn't in the picture."

"She introduced herself to Elvis as Honey Maxwell. Is that her father's name?"

"Maxwell's Mom's maiden name. Working at a strip club requires anonymity. It makes it harder for creepy guys to look her up in the phone book."

Jaxx, who'd been sleeping quietly at the foot of the bed, pawed his way a few feet forward. Sparkle reached down and scratched him behind the ear. "I was barely nineteen when Honey was born. After high school, I ran off and did the hippy-dippy thing. When I got preggers, I came home to have the baby."

"So, running off's a family tradition?"

"You should be so lucky."

Morrison scratched the sandpaper stubble on his chin. "Ever married?"

Sparkle shook her head. "Teen pregnancies are socially awkward. I dated some, but when guys find out you have a kid, they lose interest. When Honey got old enough, I started taking college classes."

"Here in Vegas?"

"Yes, at UNLV. I wanted to get my credential."

Morrison smiled sheepishly. "I keep forgetting you're a teacher."

"Well, I am. I took a year off to finish my masters."

"So, Honey works at the club where Moby plays?"

"Tends bar. I'd rather she worked some place besides a strip joint, but she makes good money."

"Seems like she's doing okay."

"Without much help from Dad or me, she has her own place and is putting herself through college." Morrison was staring at the cluster of dried roses hanging on the wall. "Honey's father gave them to me."

"An incurable romantic?"

Sparkle shrugged. "Somebody gave them to him, and he just passed them along."

The roses looked like shriveled, shrunken heads. Finally, Morrison summoned the courage to ask the question he'd been working toward all evening. "So, what's Honey's father like?"

Sparkle took a deep breath and exhaled slowly. "I was a freckle-faced teenybopper, barely eighteen. I hitchhiked to LA with my best friend to see a band we liked."

Morrison laughed. "Renaissance girls aspired to be saints and martyrs. In the sixties, they wanted to be groupies."

"It was the seventies," she said, "even if only barely. Anyway, Christy worked one of the crew, and he snuck us in the back door while the band was doing some session work. We hung around the studio until they finished, and we all went clubbing. I hooked up with the lead singer and went with him to the Chateau Marmont, where he was staying."

Morrison's eyes narrowed. "When was that?"

"January 1971. Honey's last name's Morrison." Sparkle dropped her chin, dangling wisps of hair across her face. "I waited a long time to see you again."

"Damn. I'm a father," he muttered softly. "I mean, we're a father."

"No, I'm a mother, and you're *the* father."

Morrison took Sparkle in his arms, but before he could kiss her, the doorbell rang.

Sparkle sat up. "We've got company. I'll get the door. You put a kettle on the stove for tea."

Morrison arched his eyebrows. "How about I get the door, and you put on some panties?"

Sparkle blushed, realizing she was wearing only his flannel shirt. Morrison pulled on a pair of jeans and bounded downstairs, taking the steps two at a time. When he yanked open the door, everything he thought he knew dissolved into a confusing, new paradigm.

Five life-size action figures in black camouflage were standing on the porch.

Hennigan punched the brake pedal so hard, Cheezesteak spilled his coffee. "There's the guy we're looking for," he said excitedly. "Male Caucasian. Mid-twenties." He was pointing at a skinhead with inked-up arms standing in line at Mogi's Do-Nuts.

"Black T-shirt? Lots of tats?"

"That's the guy." Cheezesteak was unaware until that moment, they were looking for anyone. He leaned forward and sorted through the litter at his feet for napkins.

By the time they caught up with the guy on Hennigan's personal BOLO, he'd settled into a place at an empty concrete table and didn't realize he had company until the detectives sandwiched him from opposite ends of the bench.

"Cheezesteak, there's somebody I want you to meet. Virgil, this is Detective Chestakowski. Detective Chestakowski, this is Virgil the Scumbag."

Cheezesteak stuck out a paw still gummy with spilled coffee. "Pleased to make my acquaintance, I'm sure." He sounded winded. Virgil took his hand without much enthusiasm. "Virgil the Scumbag? My mom warned me to watch out for people with *the* as a middle name."

"Jack the Ripper," Hennigan suggested.

"Attila the Hun."

"Bozo the Clown."

Virgil scowled but didn't say anything. Cheezesteak licked his lips as he eyed the confectionery hoard.

"Bad cop," Virgil growled. "*No* doughnuts."

That was all the prompting Cheezesteak needed. He lunged at the box like a five-year-old on a sugar rush, grabbed a jelly doughnut, and savagely tore into it, dusting his jowls with powdered sugar.

"You can't do that!" Virgil screeched. "That's private property."

"Virgil, you look like a nineties kinda guy," Hennigan grinned. "Haven't you heard?"

"Sharing is caring." Cheezesteak finished, his lips smeared with strawberry filling.

"One of you is supposed to be nice and the other not nice," Virgil growled. "That's how the good-cop-bad-cop thing works."

"You mean we can't *both* be assholes?" Hennigan asked smugly. "Maybe you should call the police."

Cheezesteak licked powdered sugar from his fingers and smacked his lips. "I got what I came for. Let's get outta here." He stood and took a couple steps toward his partner like he was leaving.

Hennigan grabbed him by the arm. "Not so fast, big fella. We've still got business with our boy here."

"Oh, right." Cheezesteak eyed a frosted doughnut with chocolate jimmies. Virgil moved the box to his lap and scooted forward, sheltering it under the table.

Hennigan leaned forward and rested his weight on his elbows. "Among our cowboy's many divergent career paths, he mules dope into County for Benji Cienfuegos. A neat little trick, really. He rolls the tops of his socks down, tucks the drugs inside, then gets picked up for something minor."

"Like public urination."

"Always a popular choice. Virgil pulls his socks down from the top when he gets naked for the strip search, and the dope drops into the toe. An hour later, he's back on the street with extra spending money and Benji's good graces."

"If he's in a hurry, maybe we can help. Whatta you think, partner? Should we slap the cuffs on him?"

"You got nothing on me," Virgil growled, cutting Cheezesteak off before Hennigan could answer.

"Now, that's where you're wrong. You remember Officer Costanza? I believe he's had the pleasure of arresting you on several occasions." Virgil nodded without realizing it. "Costanza and a cadre of fellow officers raided a chop shop this morning. Half the cars there had your prints on 'em."

"That's bullshit. My attorney will have me out in an hour."

211

"Why does every lowlife have an attorney?" Cheezesteak growled.

Hennigan didn't answer. "Hey, I got an idea. How about we do a quick catch-and-release and get word back to Cienfuegos, you rolled over on him? Maybe he'll get you a Kevorkian gift certificate for Christmas."

"He wouldn't." Virgil's voice was quivering.

"Oh, he would. If Benji knew we were talking, he'd be deciding whether to have you shanked in the mess hall or the laundry room."

Three tables over, Hennigan recognized an elderly couple grazing on glazed twists. He was wearing a horned helmet and a purple bowling shirt. Too busy teasing each other to notice him, the wife poked her husband in the ribs, and they broke into giggles as Hennigan decided Virgil had stewed long enough.

"The good news is Virgil's lived life by one simple rule: why go to the pen when you can send a friend?"

Virgil stared glassy-eyed at his dirty fingernails. "I ain't no snitch."

Hennigan grinned. "I knew we could count on your complete cooperation."

Virgil nervously stroked his wispy goatee like he was thinking about bolting.

"Easy." Hennigan rested his hand on his shoulder. "Don't get your panties in a bunch. We're a little scratchy. We still gotta drive across town and chat up two more budding lowlifes, Frank and Joey Cozzaglio. Maybe you know 'em?"

Virgil shook his head.

"How about Bobby Ray Darling?"

He shook his head again.

"Maybe you should. It was his Grand Prix, you and Be-Bop jacked the other night."

Virgil's jaw clenched.

Cheezesteak leaned over until they were nose-to-nose, close enough to smell stale coffee on Virgil's breath. "How about Anthony Venetti, aka Fat Tony?"

"Big-time mobster, right? I've him on the news."

Hennigan nodded. "And Bobby Ray's his number one gun. The buzz around town is he and the Cozzaglios are looking for you, Be-Bop, and some girl. I'm guessing you're gonna tell me you've got no idea why."

Virgil swallowed hard, his Adam's apple bobbing up and down like a cork in storm surf.

Cheezesteak stole another glance at the box of doughnuts in Virgil's lap. "Maybe you should make sure your Blue Cross premiums are current just the same."

"We're looking for these guys." Hennigan slid copies of the photographs Orange had given him in front of Virgil. "This one goes by Elvis Presley." He pointed to the picture of Morrison.

"And the other one's Jim Morrison," Cheezesteak added, tapping his index finger on Elvis's picture. "*Maybe,* if you find them, we'll forget to tell the bad guys where to find you."

Hennigan stood to leave. "Oh, almost forgot. An Expedition boosted from the Circle K turned up at the chop shop with your prints." Again, without realizing it, Virgil nodded. "It's leased to an FBI Special Agent."

Virgil looked like he'd been sucker-punched in the gut.

"I *am* the good cop. I haven't told the feds *or* the hitman where to find you -- at least not yet." Hennigan handed him a business card with an embossed, gold shield. "I look forward to hearing from you."

Virgil didn't react when Cheezesteak helped himself to another doughnut. The detectives were almost to the car before he looked up from the card.

One of the figures in black camouflage held his finger to his lips as the five of them slipped inside, as silent as shadows, and fanned out in a defensive perimeter.

"Anyone else here?"

Morrison gestured over his shoulder toward Sparkle, who was frozen halfway down the stairs. "Just us and the dog." Jaxx was sitting beside her, rigidly at attention.

"Copy that," answered one of the shadows gliding past Sparkle. At the landing, they divided and disappeared down opposite ends of the hallway. "We're buttoned-up here. Area's secure."

"Permission to speak freely, sir." Morrison, surprised by his formality, nodded. "Geronimo Nieto, Lieutenant Commander, United States Navy, Commanding Officer, SEAL Team 13. My people and I are here to protect you."

"To protect us? From what?"

"An alphabet soup of government agencies you know by initials but mostly from Abrams McCullough."

"The general running the invisibility project? Jimi talked about him."

Geronimo glanced at the SEAL who had taken up a position beside him. "McCullough has a deep and abiding interest in Mr. Hendrix and everyone associated with him since his disappearance."

"And that's why you're here?"

"No, that's why we were sent. I swore an oath to serve and protect," Geronimo explained. "I'm acting on my conscience. Not my orders."

"Lucky for you, our boy has troubled relationships with authority figures," added the second SEAL. With her close-cropped hair and decidedly military swagger, Morrison hadn't realized she was a woman. She sensed his surprise. "That's right. There *are* girls in the SEALs. We're the new-and-improved, politically-correct Navy." Her voice was flat and monotone, without a hint of sarcasm.

"This *is* a Kodak moment," the SEAL beside her taunted. "Hey, CJ. How often do you get mistaken for a girl?"

"Not as often as you," she fired back.

Geronimo shot them a sideways glance. He'd heard the routine before. "This is my crew. The two merry pranksters are Cannibal Jane Hawkings, AKA CJ, and Pig Pen. The handsome rascal at the top of the stairs is Mink de Ville, and the girl by the back door's Trigger Peachfish." Trigger and Mink executed a two-fingered approximation of a salute. "The rest of the team's setting up base camp and grading a landing strip."

"I get this isn't a social call, but can you tell us what the hell's going on?"

"Our assignment is to tidy up this situation for the DOD."

"*This situation* being us?"

"Affirmative. Our orders are to bring you to Washington for debriefing and disposal."

Morrison glanced at Sparkle, his heart pounding in his chest. "Disposal? You mean, kill us?"

Geronimo nodded. "McCullough doesn't craft missions with tactical precision. He believes you find the proverbial needle by setting fire to the haystack and sifting through the ashes. We're supposed to be doing advanced recon, pinpointing mission targets, and finalizing plans for extraction. We'll feed them phony intel and stall for a couple days to buy some time."

"Time for what?"

"Any chance of understanding the what begins with the *why*."

Morrison blinked, and the room spun into soft focus. In Geronimo, he saw a younger version of the face from his dream. He'd almost forgotten about the old Indian. But now, standing in the foyer, images of that ancient face, rutted by countless cycles of sun and wind, came rushing back.

"I live in two worlds," Geronimo explained, "yours and the one of my birth. Like you, I was brought here by my grandfather's vision. I'm Mescalero Apache. You hold long, cherished beliefs about a dying shaman's soul leaping into your body, but my grandfather didn't die in a truck crash in New Mexico. He lived another forty-five years and died a week ago today."

"The night Elvis showed up."

Geronimo nodded. "When I was eight, my grandfather told me he knew when he would die because he lived his life backward."

Morrison shook his head. "I don't understand."

"Some things aren't meant to be understood."

"And that's the why?"

"Part of it. He told me the story of the day your family drove past him lying on the side of the road. He said your spirit and his danced like hawks on the back of the wind and that one day, you and I would take a great journey together."

"A great journey? Where?"

"I'm getting to that. Anything else I need to know?"

Morrison glanced at Sparkle. "We kinda ran into the FBI. They're looking for us and Elvis too."

"And they know about Jimi being invisible," Sparkle added. "He had to rescue us."

"Trigger," Geronimo called to the SEAL by the back door. "Set up scanners to monitor FBI and police bands for all four subject names, this address, and any keywords that come to you."

"I'm on it."

Geronimo turned back to Sparkle and Morrison. "Keep a low profile. Don't use your ATM or credit cards or anything that links back to you electronically. When the DOD realized you were in Vegas, they retasked satellites to keep tabs on you. Coverage is intermittent, but without a cell, it's the best they could do."

Morrison half shrugged defensively. "Until recently, I didn't have anybody to talk to."

"Well, that worked out. I'll get you a secure satellite phone in case we need to talk. In the meantime, keep your head down and be as inconspicuous as possible."

"Elvis might be a problem. He was the gazillionth guest at a casino."

"The Tahitian Princess," Sparkle reminded him.

"Right. He's supposed to judge an Elvis impersonator contest tomorrow night."

Geronimo's eyes narrowed. "It would probably draw more attention if he didn't show up. You should be there to keep an eye on things. How about Hendrix?"

"Jimi's more conspicuous in his absence than his presence."

"Because he's invisible?"

Morrison nodded.

"I can see how that could be a challenge. Where's he now?"

"Probably Sinderella's, a strip joint downtown."

"We'd better go find him. CJ can take the crew and one of the Hummers to base camp. We'll take the other and collect our wayward guitar player."

"I'll call Moby and have him meet you out front," Sparkle said.

"Moby?"

"One of the good guys," Morrison assured him. "I'll explain on the way."

"Good. Besides enough arms and equipment to take over a small country, we have forty pounds of OG Kush, prime bud, shrink-wrapped and vacuum sealed for shelf life."

"For invisibility?"

"The other reason to round up Hendrix. Being invisible would give us a strategic advantage."

"For whatever the hell you're planning?"

Geronimo nodded. "My grandfather's grandfather rode with Geronimo. I was raised in the old ways. The spiritual part, the medicine man, never took, but if you're outnumbered and surrounded, I'm your guy."

Morrison's brow furrowed.

"Think of him as your personal boy scout," CJ explained, "in case you need somebody to help a little old lady across the street or rub sticks together and start a fire."

Geronimo turned his cherub face toward Morrison. "Or thwart the invasion of an enchanted Caribbean isle."

19

Morrison waited with Moby and Ishmael in front of Sinderella's while Geronimo parked the Hummer. He appreciated the urgent need to find Jimi but was uncomfortable the SEAL commander kept referring to their strip-joint field trip as *our mission.*

The length of a '67 Coupe de Ville away, the bouncer slouched on a bar stool, pawing a zit-faced kid's ID. He was massive, nearly as wide as he was tall, with no forehead and a bulging brow ridge that protruded over his eyes and the bridge of his broad, flat nose. The Harley-Davidson T-shirt under his tux jacket was stretched across his chest as tautly as a drumhead. He looked more bored than satisfied as he handed the kid his license and waved him inside.

Morrison didn't realize Geronimo had joined them until the rest of the group started toward the club. The bouncer recognized Moby and Ishmael and held the door as they approached. Inside, Morrison handed the hostess the VIP passes Sparkle had given him for cover charges.

"There's a two-drink minimum," she explained. Morrison nodded he understood.

Though only a little after eight, the club was two-thirds full and reeked of spilled beer and cigarette smoke. "Welcome to the Jungle" was blasting from a wall of arena-sized speakers. Morrison worked the back of his neck with his fingertips, massaging the dull beginnings of a headache.

Their eyes were still adjusting to the strobing lights as they wound their way through the warren of tables and table dancers. Moby spotted an empty booth near the main stage where a leggy brunette was pole dancing four frat boys in USC sweatshirts. They were folding dollar bills lengthwise and tenting them end-to-end along the railing. Morrison could hear their drunken laughter above the music. Ishmael left an empty seat on the outside when they slid into the booth, assuming Jimi would be joining them.

Moby cupped his hands around his mouth. "Can't beat a titty bar for ambiance," he very nearly shouted over the music.

Morrison forced a smile. "I don't think I've ever tried this sober."

"There's a cure for that," Geronimo said as he flagged down the waitress. "Draft pitchers." He held up two fingers, then switched to five for glasses and sketched a small circle over the tabletop.

Three booths over, a platinum blonde was table dancing a group of men in business suits. Morrison recognized Miss Vikki and the man who called him "Mr. Morrison" just before Elvis won the progressive jackpot. He looked away from the stripper long enough to nod curtly their direction.

Morrison was still puzzling over how regularly their paths had crossed when the waitress brought the pitchers and dutifully filled each glass, including the one in front of Jimi's seat. Morrison gave her a twenty and a ten and waved her off. As she walked away, he realized he had no idea how much the beer was and what, if any tip, he'd given her.

"Put your hands together in a warm, Sinderella's welcome for Bambi," the DJ announced as a petite Asian woman in a plaid skirt, a white button-down shirt, and black, patent-leather shoes scampered up the stage steps.

"My girlfriend, Ruby," Ishmael said, "has a 1-900 phone-sex gig. It's like when we dress up as the love children of Carmen Miranda and Chiquita Banana and lip-synch Jimmy Buffet songs -- low-stress work that demands nothing but our dignity. When she gets home, she's so tired of talking about sex, she doesn't want to fool around. It doesn't help she talks dirty in her sleep."

"I can see how that would be a problem." Morrison tried to sound sympathetic. He could only hear bits and pieces of the table talk over "Tush" blasting from the speakers.

Geronimo was locked in a cobra-mongoose stare-down with Bambi who was sea-sawing a feather boa back and forth between her legs. As ZZ Top bled into "Dream Weaver" and a blonde in a red bikini took the stage, Geronimo grabbed the second pitcher and poured another round.

Bambi slipped back into her parochial-school look and circled the club, chatting with patrons and collecting tips. Their booth was her last stop. She leaned over and whispered something to Geronimo, who nodded, a beery grin slathered across his face.

"I'll be right back," she giggled and hurried off to the dressing room.

"Bambi's a sweet, young thing," said a disembodied voice. Jimi lit a joint and passed it to Ishmael. The pungent smell of smoldering ganja brought the waitress in a hurry.

"You're gonna get me fired," she pleaded. "I don't wanna give you guys a hard time, but we get hassled enough by the cops. Party outside and come back, just not in the club." Ishmael stared blankly her direction as he passed the joint to Moby.

"Who do we talk with to sort out this misunderstanding?" Geronimo was trying to sound diplomatic.

"That would be Floyd, the pretty boy in the Harley shirt." She pointed toward the bouncer who was talking with the hostess. "He's the complaint department."

Morrison grimaced. "Floyd? So, our boy has no neck *and* no last name." Geronimo started to protest, but Morrison cut him off. "We've got Jimi. Let's get outta here."

Bambi strutted out of the dressing room in a black-vinyl bodysuit, waving a riding crop as they stood to leave. Geronimo was handing her a ten-dollar bill when Morrison grabbed him by the arm.

"No time for long goodbyes."

Floyd was headed their direction at ramming speed, chin down, his stubby, tree-trunk arms pumping furiously across his massive torso.

Bobby Ray and Cleopatra were lying side-by-side on the heart-shaped bed. He was calculating how long he had to wait before jumping her again. Cleopatra's eyes were open just wide enough to see her reflection in the mirrored ceiling. She was pretending to be asleep.

After tying her up, Bobby Ray had ignored her strenuous objections and shaved off all her pubic hair. She ran her fingertips across the stubbly surface. Using her toes, Cleopatra reached for the comforter. It had bunched at the foot of the bed but slipped away and spilled onto the floor.

"You know, baby, it's getting to be that time again," he said, realizing she was awake.

Cleopatra was rubbed raw after several poorly prefaced sexual encounters. Bobby Ray, unaccustomed to physical activity, was so sore he couldn't lift his hands above his head. Earlier, after another round of drinks in the bar, they stopped at the gift shop pharmacy counter for K-Y Jelly and Ultra Strength Ben-Gay. Both were on her nightstand.

Cleopatra figured she could get by with a hand job and was reaching for the lubricant when an entirely different approach occurred to her. She squeezed a greasy wad of balm onto her palm and slipped her hand under his waistband. By the time Bobby Ray recognized the smell of camphor and menthol, it was too late. He jumped out of bed and ran screaming to the bathroom like his underwear was on fire.

Bobby Ray soaped and rinsed his chemically-torched genitals a dozen times until he finally accepted additional showering would hurt more than help. He wrapped himself in a towel, waddled across the tiles like they were hot coals, and squatted on the toilet without closing the door.

When he was finished, Bobby Ray studied the bowl's contents. His toilet ritual was a mixture of superstition and hypochondria. Like an ancient priest examining goat entrails, he tried to divine the future. The porcelain altar did not give up secrets easily, but the omens weren't promising. The Ben-Gay incident looked like the harbinger of bad juju to come.

He slipped into the robe hanging on the door hook, wrestled the childproof lid from the Vicodin on the counter, and dry-swallowed two before hobbling back to the bedroom. After deciding his tender man parts didn't require additional poaching, he sat beside the Jacuzzi and dangled his feet in the water. Cleopatra rolled over so her back was toward him and picked up the TV remote.

"It was an honest mistake," Bobby Ray mumbled. "Coulda happened to anybody."

Cleopatra flipped through the channels until she came to the Home Shopping Network. "It wasn't a mistake. I read about it in *Penthouse Forum*. Didn't it really get you off?"

"Sure. Yeah. I mean, forget about it," he stammered, already plotting make-up sex. He walked gingerly to the bed and slid in beside her without drying off his feet. "How's about a little kiss?"

She turned up the volume, ignoring his clumsy overture. Bobby Ray had watched enough afternoon talk shows to know women liked to chat and settled on an approach he'd seen on *Oprah*.

"I've been thinking about my dad. He died when I was four."

Cleopatra ignored him. A jocular host in a Cat-in-the-Hat hat was hawking Dr. Seuss-themed watches available in silver and gold finishes.

"He and a couple guys from the old neighborhood got arrested joyriding in a stolen Plymouth. The judge made them choose between enlisting and jail time."

"I'm guessing he picked prison."

Bobby Ray chuckled. "Not my old man. He joined the Marines and shipped off to Parris Island for basic training. That was the first time he'd been farther than Yankee Stadium."

"Wow, a regular globetrotting jetsetter." Cleopatra had decided against a watch and flipped through the channels again.

"He was stationed in Japan in the mid-fifties."

"Him and a hundred thousand other GIs." Cleopatra turned up the volume on the TV. She was past the point she wanted to play *let's get to know each other.* "In my country, we call that the Occupation."

Bobby Ray decided *occupation* must mean something in Japanese besides somebody's job. "Lucky for my dad, he was Don Bruno's cousin. You know Mafia?"

"I saw *The Godfather.*"

"Right, like Don Corleone. Anyway, Don Bruno got him transferred to the Supply Corps."

"Lucky him."

"Real lucky. Tokyo was the perfect place for a streetwise hustler like my old man. Japan's where he met my mom. She was a secretary in his office. He wooed her with cigarettes, chocolates, and silk stockings. You couldn't get stuff like that after the war."

"It was a hard time in Japan."

"Well, maybe you people shoulda thought twice before sinking Pearl Harbor." Cleopatra wrapped herself in the top sheet and scooted to the edge of the bed. Bobby Ray didn't notice. "Nympha told me those days were the happiest of his life."

"Nympha?"

"My aunt." Bobby Ray picked absentmindedly at a ragged nail. "She told me there was a rooftop garden on their building where they ate dinner sometimes and listened to the Winter Olympics on Armed Forces Radio."

"My mother loved her garden." Cleopatra stared sadly at the ceiling. "She died when I was twelve."

Bobby Ray sensed a thaw. "I was named for Buffalo Bob on *The Howdy Doody Show.* My last name's Darling on account of my aunt and her husband adopted me after my old man died. Did you know I was born there?"

"In Japan?"

Bobby Ray nodded. "Tokyo. When mom died, dad brought me to the states."

Cleopatra sat up. A nagging discomfort was eating at her. Parts of his story sounded uncomfortably familiar. She pulled the sheet tightly under her chin. "What was his name?"

"Whose name?"

"Your father. What was his name?"

"Aldo Dante."

Cleopatra leaped from the bed, but her feet tangled in the sheets, and she stumbled headfirst into the Jacuzzi.

Bobby Ray bolted upright. "What the hell?" he squealed.

Her hair plastered against her skull, she looked like a cornered animal. Her lips were trembling, and her whole body quivered. Cleopatra wrapped herself in the bed sheet that was nearly transparent as soon as it soaked through.

"Aldo Dante was my father," she shrieked, shaking her fist. "*Your* father was *my* father!"

His elbows buckled, and Bobby Ray collapsed into the pillow, too stunned to respond. Cleopatra slumped against the coping and buried her head in the crook of her arm. It was thirty minutes before she climbed out of the tub, crawled across the floor on her hands and knees, and pounced on Bobby Ray.

They made love in an extraordinarily brief encounter that built into a feral passion bordering on rage.

Hiroshi Shinozawa slipped off his shoes before entering the villa that served as his residence and command center during his frequent visits to Las Vegas. Koichi, his nephew and heir apparent, followed a few steps behind him. Hiro moved with the grace of a much smaller man, and tonight, there was a pronounced bounce in his step. When they reached the study, Hiro punched in the security code and motioned for Koichi to follow.

The room was dimly lit. Hiro's eyes were so sensitive he often wore dark glasses, even inside. Koichi waited until Hiro nodded toward the chair across the desk before sitting down. Unlike most of his generation, he understood respect. Hiro appreciated that. Western decadence had spread through the young people of Japan like a cancer.

When Koichi and his older brother were in grade school, they lived with their uncle, Tomio "Ice Pick Tommy" Nakanishi. One afternoon after class, Motojiro snuck into the study, borrowed his uncle's 14th century Masamune katana, and "beheaded" his bonsai collection. Koichi took the blame and the caning. Hiro often used the story to remind his nephew why one day, he'd be *oyabun* and his black-sheep brother would never be more than an errand boy.

Hiro patted his head dry with a silk handkerchief and tossed it on the desk. He wasn't just bald. He had no body hair at all, mute testimony to the August morning Hiroshima was reduced to ash and cinders. The guilt of living through that terrible day weighed on him. The name he chose for his Yakuza family honored those who died -- the *Hibakusha*, the bombed ones.

"My life is full of ghosts," Hiro mumbled softly. Koichi looked visibly unsettled but said nothing. Hiro fished two aspirin from the bottle on his desk and swallowed them dry. "The ramblings of an old man," he said, waving dismissively.

Koichi nodded, but his expression didn't change. Hiro was having a hard time bearing his discomfort. He'd worn the same pained expression all evening. "You seem troubled, nephew."

Koichi squirmed anxiously in his chair. "Behind your back, the American gangsters make fun of how you talk."

Hiro grinned. "The *gaijin* fail to find humor in their ignorance." He made a point of speaking English in Las Vegas. *Gaijin,* Japanese for foreigner, was one of the few words he allowed himself. He was proud of his fluency and found it condescending to talk to Americans in their native tongue. Though accented compared to the standardized flat, nasal twang of network TV, it was no more so than Fat Tony's, and his grammar was certainly better. That was the best part of the joke.

226

Hiro pulled a gold case from his jacket and offered his nephew a cigarette before choosing one for himself. Koichi lit his uncle's and then his own. Hiro took a long drag and exhaled a scratchy ribbon of blue-gray smoke.

"Winston tastes good..."

"...like a cigarette should," Koichi finished. It was one of their rituals.

Hiro snapped at a fly buzzing around his face, trapping it in the hammy folds of his fist. Koichi nodded, acknowledging his uncle's feat. When Hiro opened his hand, the fly buzzed away.

"With the *gaijin*, Uncle, we will not be so generous?"

"No, Koichi. We will not be so generous." Hiro closed his eyes, remembering his teenage, black-market days with his sister's boyfriend, Aldo Dante. "Crime's an incestuous business," he said softly, "and the wheel's come around again."

Hiro peered over the rim of his coffee cup and scowled at the cigarette butt he put out in the dregs before they left for the club. He had no respect for Americans, who he saw as a weak and mongrelized race, but prized much that was American, including cigarettes and coffee.

"Should I make a fresh pot, Uncle?"

Hiro retrieved two glasses and a bottle of single malt Yamazaki from his desk drawer and poured them each a drink. Koichi took that as a "no" and raised his glass with a curt nod. Neither felt the need to fill the space with noise, both content to enjoy each other's company and a glass of good whisky.

When the phone rang, Hiro picked up on the first ring. Most of his uncle's half of the conversation consisted of grunts and nods. Koichi assumed he was talking with Noguchi.

"Remember the puzzle box I gave you when you were a boy?" he asked after hanging up.

"Yes, Uncle."

"Plans within plans within plans," he said softly. Koichi nodded, even though he had no idea what his uncle meant.

Hiro rocked forward and picked up the closest thing to a personal item he had on his desk: a framed photograph of the Kagoshima Naval Air Group Monument. The memorial depicted a young airman ascending to Heaven. No family photographs survived the Hiroshima firestorm. Hiro liked to imagine the figure was the father he barely remembered.

Before the war, Takeo Shinozawa was a senior flight instructor at Tsuchiura Naval Air Base. Many of the pilots who attacked Pearl Harbor were former students. In 1945, he transferred to Kagoshima and trained cadets in the Kamikaze Special Attack Corps. When Americans were within striking distance of the home islands and there were no students left to teach, Takeo led the attack on the *USS Tatum*, a high-speed transport patrolling Okinawa's Hagushi beaches. He died ten weeks before the atomic bomb killed his wife and youngest daughter.

Hiro raised his glass. "God's blessing for our work here, my young sir." He finished his whisky and glanced at his watch. Fluent in the language of the unspoken, Koichi understood the gesture at once. Miss Vikki would be arriving soon, and his uncle needed time to get ready. Koichi stood and bowed before he and his uncle shook hands, another of their rituals.

As soon as his nephew had excused himself, Hiro retrieved the greasy, black pompadour wig from his closet and changed into a white silk kimono. The sequined pattern on the back suggested an erupting volcano or maybe fireworks. Batteries in the belt powered a string of LED lights that blinked in time with the music. Hiro poured another whisky, turned up "Jailhouse Rock," and did a slow pirouette like one of Fantasia's dancing hippos.

He shimmied and shook through "Teddy Bear," "Hound Dog," and "Return to Sender," then fished the karaoke mike from his desk drawer and joined Elvis for a soulful duet of "Love Me Tender." When the song ended, Hiro, his face filmed with sweat, plopped down in the chair.

"A million people through the door, and the casino manager thinks they picked the only guy who's never heard of Elvis Presley."

The more he considered the comic possibilities, the funnier they got. When security let him know Miss Vikki had arrived, he was laughing hard enough to cry.

20

Cleopatra waited until Bobby Ray started snoring before getting out of bed to dress. She stumbled to her suite in a fog, curled up in a corner chair, and fell asleep. When she awoke nearly ten hours later, it felt like she'd been trampled by stampeding bulls at Pamplona.

As she was rummaging through her purse for aspirin, Cleopatra realized she'd forgotten to turn the lock in the previous night's turmoil. She cracked the door just wide enough to hang the *Do Not Disturb* sign on the knob, slammed the door closed, and twisted the deadbolt so hard she broke a nail.

She crossed the room in three quick strides, heaved her travel bag onto the bed, and retrieved her .45s, a matched pair of M1911s. Cleopatra checked the magazines, slammed them back in place with the heel of her fist, and set the Colts on the bathroom counter. She turned the shower on full blast but left the lights and fan off. The room quickly filled with steam that beaded on the ceiling and fell to the tiled floor like rain.

She stripped off her clothes and dumped them in the wastebasket. Too ashamed to meet her stare in the mirror, Cleopatra grabbed a handful of soaps and shampoos from the counter and climbed into the shower. She flattened her palms against the wall on opposite sides of the showerhead, dropped her chin, and let the water beat against the back of her head and sheet across her cheeks. Half an hour later, she recovered enough to wash in a dozen furious cycles of soaping, scrubbing, and rinsing until her skin was raw and abraded.

As the water-soluble part of her guilt washed away, revenge fantasies took over. She imagined Bobby Ray on his knees, one of the Colts in his mouth, the barrel shoved between his teeth and tongue. Before she splattered One-Pump Bobby's brains all over the walls and carpet, she wanted him to understand who was really in charge -- who'd always been in charge. What would she say? What would be the last words he heard before she pulled the trigger? She imagined the debris field from his head wound splattered across the pastel pink backdrop of his room like a gruesome Rorschach test.

She shut the water off and glanced at the 45s, reassuring herself they were still side-by-side on the counter. Even in the steamy near darkness, she felt exposed and vulnerable. Cleopatra wrapped herself in a towel, picked up the hotel phone, and punched six.

"Concierge desk. How may I be of service?"

"I need the number of a company that rents high-end cars."

"Yes, ma'am. Exotica's just around the corner. Would you like me to arrange something?"

"No. Just the number, please." She called from her cell, asked for a car with smoke-black windows, and decided on the 911 Turbo S.

"I'm staying at the Tahitian Princess. How soon can you be here?"

"Thirty minutes."

She glanced at her watch. "Call when you're downstairs."

Cleopatra pulled on a pair of designer jeans, a white silk blouse, and the same powder-blue cowboy boots she wore to the airport. She upended her purse and dumped everything except her wallet on the bed to make room for the pair of Colts she retrieved from the bathroom counter.

While she waited for the car company to call, Cleopatra was flipping through the channels when a cosmetic case on the Home Shopping Network reminded her of the black lacquer box. She had to stand on her tiptoes to retrieve it from the top shelf of the armoire. She opened the lid and was cradling the snow globe in her hands when rage welled up inside her, and she hurled it against the wall. Cleopatra was grinding shards of glass and plastic into the carpeting with her bootheel when the phone rang: the Porsche was curbside. She unclenched her fists, grabbed her purse and a pair of Versace sunglasses, and stormed downstairs.

The red 911's windows were so darkly tinted she could barely make out the high-back seats through the windshield. Cleopatra nodded her approval and signed for the car. She would have preferred being invisible but would settle for anonymous.

She slid behind the wheel and rolled onto Las Vegas Boulevard, then west on the 15 with an eye on the rearview to make sure she wasn't followed. She hummed past a caravan of motorcycles on the high side of a hundred and was almost to the state line before the angry, judgmental chorus inside her head began to quiet. The Porsche kicked up dust clouds as she cut across the medium and drove back to Hiro's estate.

Cleopatra wound past the main house and parked by the long, narrow barracks beside the garage. Three stretch limos were parked in front, lined up end-to-end. The *shatei* her uncle called his "shock troops" were loading arms and equipment into the trunks. Koichi met her at the car and walked her to the door.

"Have I come at a bad time?"

Koichi didn't answer. He punched the security code into the keypad and motioned her inside. "Your uncle knows you are here. He is waiting in the study."

She found Hiro leaning against the desk. The blinds were drawn, and he wasn't wearing his sunglasses. "I was not expecting you," he said tersely.

"I was in the neighborhood."

Something flickered across his face – anger or at least impatience. Cleopatra regretted her flipness but couldn't explain why she'd come.

"You were careful?"

"I took every precaution. I would do nothing to jeopardize your work here."

Hiro nodded. "Good."

"You're busy?"

"Always."

"Can I be of help?"

"No. This is a matter without delicacy." He stepped forward, cradled her chin in the crook of his index finger, and lifted it until their eyes met. "We have American friends to save from themselves," he said softly. "Our task requires a sledgehammer, not a butterfly."

Cleopatra smiled. *Choo*, Japanese for butterfly, was her uncle's nickname for her when she was little. "Hiro-san."

"Yes, my child."

"What sort of man was my father?" She immediately regretted asking but couldn't take it back. Hiro leaned against the desk and folded his arms across his chest. Cleopatra stood rigidly at attention, her head slightly bowed, stoically bearing the weight of his stare. Several minutes passed before Hiro broke the silence.

"Your father treated your mother, my sister, like a whore. He stole your brother and disappeared without saying goodbye. Did you forget?"

It's true then. I have a brother. The revelation rattled Cleopatra, but she refused to let it show. "No, I did not forget. I only needed to hear it again."

Hiro nodded he understood. "That is what your father did. I leave it to you to judge what sort of man your father was."

"Thank you, Hiro-san."

Hiro appraised her for a moment before speaking. "We have things to talk about, but not now. You can wait if you like. What is it the Americans say?" His face brightened. "Chill."

The tension suddenly and unexpectedly broken, Cleopatra smiled. Hiro smiled back. "Now, please excuse me." Just as he reached the door, Hiro stopped and turned. "If you wait until I get back, we can talk then."

"Thank you for offering."

Hiro's eyes narrowed. "Your mother was not a mail-order bride. She loved you and, though I will never understand why, she loved your father too."

"Until the day she died."

Hiro nodded. "Even after, I think." Koichi appeared in the hallway, said something too softly for Cleopatra to hear, then bowed and excused himself. "When I return, we can talk about why you are here in Las Vegas. In the meantime, *chill*."

"Yes, Hiro-san." Cleopatra bowed curtly again as he turned and disappeared down the hallway.

She walked to the living room window, pulled back the draperies, and watched the limos roll to a stop in front of the villa. The first and last cars were riding visibly lower. Koichi and her uncle climbed into the one in the middle.

As Hiro and his entourage were driving through the gates, one of the landscapers, a wiry man with dark skin and long hair braided in soft, fuzzy curls, took at least a passing interest in their leaving. He leaned on his rake, pulled a cell phone from his pocket, and answered a call. It was probably nothing, but she would mention it to Hiro when he returned.

After watching *Goodfellas* in the theater room, Cleopatra played several games of 3-ball but had a hard time staying focused.

"I cannot kill my father," she mumbled as she missed an easy corner shot. "He is dead, but for the dishonor and shame he brought my mother, I will kill his son." Her hand was fisted so tightly around the cue, the fingernails carved crescent moons in the soft flesh of her palms. "And," she whispered through clenched teeth, "for reasons of my own."

Cleopatra was racking balls for another game when she remembered Hiro's tea garden, his "island in the storm." She took the short walk from the main house to the climate-controlled outbuilding, not sure if she remembered the code, but successfully disarmed the alarm on the first try. The transformation was instantaneous. Outside was Las Vegas, but beneath the *trompe l'oeil* ceiling painted by the same artists who did the skies over Caesar's Forum Shops, she was in the gardens of Hiro's mountain estate above Hiroshima.

She followed the flagstone path that wound through the stylized landscape of dwarf pine, willow, and cypress trees to a pond and sat lotus-style on a granite boulder. Clouds of mist hanging in the dense air collected in a cool film against her skin. She was watching koi circle in and out of patches of lotuses and water lilies when she realized this was the pond she dreamed about on her flight from Tokyo.

The dream was a warning, I heard too late.

Determined to put everything out of her mind, Cleopatra took a deep, cleansing breath and let it out slowly, repeating the exercise until the tension in her neck and shoulders slowly began to subside. An hour later, she was perched Zen-like on her rock when more than twenty tons of dry ice poured through the open skylight and buried her alive.

On his way to the trailer park, Bobby Ray stopped at a sporting goods store and bought a wooden bat like Primo's. Even family connections as tenuous as a Louisville Slugger seemed important since Cleopatra's "revelation."

"I look just like my dad," he muttered. "Everybody says so." While he waited for the light to change, Bobby Ray studied his reflection in the rearview mirror. It was a cruel trick, he'd decided. Women had disrespected him his whole life. This time was no different. When the light turned green, he punched the accelerator.

"I *can't* be half Japanese," he growled. "I don't even like rice."

He found an empty space in visitor parking, grabbed the bat from the passenger seat, and went looking for Frank's trailer. He'd left a dozen messages since breakfast but hadn't heard from either brother. If the Cozzaglios hadn't located the carjackers, Bobby Ray intended to vent his frustration on them until they did.

Trailer parks are magnets for natural disasters, and this one had been visited by at least three Horsemen of the Apocalypse. After the demolition derby, he stopped at Frank's just long enough to grab some sweats, and Bobby Ray wasn't sure he could find his way back. As he wandered up and down the rows of dilapidated double wides, Bobby Ray thought he recognized a bicycle sitting on two flats, leaning against a porch post. Halfway up the steps, he caught a whiff of wet dog, the one detail he remembered about Frank's trailer.

Bobby Ray yanked open the door and poked his head inside. The brothers were sitting side-by-side on the couch, drinking beer, and watching TV. Joey looked up from *Gunsmoke* long enough to wave.

"C-C-Come on in," he stuttered. "I'll grab you a beer." Joey stood and was headed for the kitchen when Bobby Ray confronted him, jabbing the bat in his sternum forcefully enough to make him lose his balance. Joey flopped on the sofa next to Frank. The mobster waved the Slugger menacingly at the brothers.

"You two are next," he growled as he turned and squared up on the TV. The bat careened off the screen, leaving a spiderweb crack radiating from the point of impact.

Joey slid onto the floor and curled up in a ball, his hands clasped over his head. Frank jumped up and was making a mad dash for the door when he glanced back at Bobby Ray, tripped over his brother, and crashed face-first into the wall.

Bobby Ray ignored them and set his feet for strike two. He swung like he was teeing off on a hanging slider, but the bat ricocheted off the TV and smacked him in the mouth, shearing off his bottom left incisor at the gumline. Bobby Ray stared at the broken tooth lying on the floor in disbelief.

"Son of a bitch," he growled as he cocked the bat and took another swing. This time the screen exploded like a giant light bulb. Bobby Ray pounded the TV until all that remained was a smoldering pile of rubble.

Frank, who had crawled behind the sofa, popped up like a prairie dog, a puffy, red mouse blooming around his eye. His mouth formed a perfect circle, but no words came out.

"W-w-we was watching *Gunsmoke*," Joey stuttered, pointing toward the ruins of the TV.

"Well, w-w-we was *supposed* to be looking for the assholes who stole my car!" Bobby Ray screamed, his face as red as a hooker's lipstick.

Joey covered his head with one arm, waving a wallet with the other like a white flag. "W-W-We got something for you. W-W-We went back to where they dropped you off in case they came back."

Bobby Ray snatched the wallet from his hand.

"W-W-We found it in the Circle K bathroom. Some FBI guy named Newman's MasterCard's inside." Frank had already stashed a Visa, a second MasterCard, and Newmeat's FBI credentials in his sock drawer.

Bobby Ray snapped open the billfold, stuffed the credit card in his pocket, and flicked the wallet frisbee-style, hitting Joey squarely between the eyes.

"Ow-w-w-w-w," Joey wailed as a red mark blossomed on his forehead. "Am I bleeding?"

"Not yet," Bobby Ray screamed. "Where are the assholes who jacked my car?" As he cocked the bat over his shoulder and was deciding what to demolish next, he glanced out the kitchen window.

A black, stretch Lincoln with Virginia plates was parked behind Frank's trailer. If he was ten feet closer, Bobby Ray might have recognized the .38-caliber hole in the dashboard as his handiwork, but he was focused on two guys with buzz cuts and inky arms working under the hood.

When they heard about Morrison's car troubles, the Hitler twins offered to replace the blown head gasket. While Be-Bop and the tow truck driver loaded the limo on the flatbed, Virgil pulled Sparkle aside and told her about his encounter with police detectives. She asked him to keep it quiet.

Honey observed the conversation from a distance. She was having a hard time wrapping her head around her mom dating Jim Morrison and was anxious about driving Elvis to her place. Her "uncle," as she'd decided to introduce him, told Morrison he felt like a third wheel and had volunteered to tag along.

Honey's trailer was four down from Virgil and Be-Bop's. She and Elvis stopped long enough to water the plants. On their way to check the twin's progress, they ran into another neighbor, Ida Mae Williams.

The elderly spinster's well-maintained double wide was the exception to the park's hodgepodge collection of mostly run-down trailers. Ida Mae was watching a black-chinned hummingbird sip sugar water from the feeder hanging from her awning. When she glanced in their direction and waved, Honey waved back.

"How you doing, Ida Mae?"

"To tell you the truth, I'm kinda achy. You wouldn't think with the weather this warm my joints would act up, but sometimes, they *just* do." Ida Mae appraised Elvis. "And who's this handsome rascal?" she asked, her blue eyes twinkling.

"This is my uncle. He's staying with mom."

Ida Mae looked skeptical. "That so?"

Elvis shook her hand. "Very nice to meet you." Ida Mae held his long enough to make Honey antsy.

"I just fixed a pitcher of lemonade. Why don't you two come in outta the heat and have some?"

Honey glanced anxiously at her uncle. "We'd love to," he said before she could answer.

Ida Mae led them up the steps, opened the door, and motioned them inside. The swamp cooler labored to keep the air in the high seventies but felt almost comfortable after the brutal heat outside. Ida Mae directed them to the living room before heading to the kitchen.

Honey was dumbstruck. The entire space was a shrine to the King. Meticulously hand-painted movie posters and album jackets covered every square inch of the walls and ceiling. Her uncle didn't seem to notice.

When Ida Mae walked in with lemonade, Honey was staring at the poster for *Kid Galahad.*

"They've been there so long," Ida Mae murmured self-consciously, "I barely see 'em anymore."

Honey nodded toward the pitcher of lemonade. "Would you like some help?" she offered, trying to diffuse the awkwardness.

"Land sakes, no." Ida Mae set the tray on the coffee table and handed a glass to Honey and another to her uncle.

Elvis sipped his thoughtfully. "You turn out a fine lemonade, Miss Williams."

"Please, call me Ida Mae."

"Yes, ma'am. I'll do that."

Ida Mae fidgeted with her napkin as she looked around the room. "I guess you're wondering about all this."

Honey forced a smile. "It's kinda hard to miss."

Ida Mae chuckled. "I reckon it'd be silly to think you wouldn't notice." She set her glass on the table, folded her hands in her lap, and took another look around. "I was president of the Elvis fan club in Paducah, Kentucky, where I grew up. I was older than the rest of the girls, and when I heard he was headlining at the New Frontier, I told my parents I was moving to Las Vegas."

"How'd they take it?"

"Pretty well, actually. Momma cried, but they were always supportive. That afternoon I packed everything I owned in an old DeSoto and started driving. I got a job with the phone company and bought the trailer with some help from my parents."

"And lived here ever since?"

Ida Mae nodded. "Even before my things were unpacked, I joined the local fan club." She looked around the room again. "We used to hold our meetings here. The girls helped with the painting, but I did the detail work after everybody left."

Elvis sipped his lemonade. "Well, you have a real gift, ma'am."

"The style's called photorealism. It's supposed to look like a photograph pasted on the wall."

"Or ceiling," Elvis added.

Ida Mae smiled. "Well, it's no Sistine Chapel, but it was a labor of love, I can tell you that. After a while, the other girls moved on, got married, and had families. Eventually, it was just me." Her face brightened. "I nearly got to shake his hand once."

Elvis set down his lemonade. "Really?"

Ida Mae nodded. "I was waiting in front of The International when he walked by and started saying 'hello' to everybody. But one of his boys, the Memphis Mafia, we called them, grabbed him by the arm before he got to me, and they took off in his Cadillac."

"I'm sure they were just watching out for him."

"I suppose, but I truly wish I'd got to shake his hand. It would have meant the world to me." Ida Mae sipped her lemonade, studying Honey's uncle over the rim of her glass. "A year later, he was gone. When he passed, it didn't feel right painting over everything."

Elvis patted her hand. "I guess that would've seemed disrespectful."

"That's exactly how I felt. I never got around to finding the right time. To tell you the truth, I don't think about it anymore. It's like white noise." Ida Mae pressed her fingers to her lips. "Oh, listen to me prattle on. Would you care for more lemonade?"

Elvis nodded. "Yes, ma'am, I'd like that."

Ida Mae refilled his glass. "There was this time, about eight years ago. I had posies on the windowsill in a Jiffy jar. Their shadow made the perfect silhouette of Elvis on the refrigerator. I called every newspaper, TV, and radio station in a hundred miles. They were all too busy to come out right away. By the time somebody from the *Sun* finally showed up, the flowers were wilted, and the shadow looked like, well, like wilted posies in a Jiffy jar."

Not sure what to say, Honey gulped down the last of her lemonade. "Would it be okay if I used your bathroom?"

"Surely, child."

As she stood, Honey leaned over and squeezed Elvis's shoulder. "I'll be right back." She closed and locked the bathroom door and leaned against the counter, facing the mirror. Honey was staring at the fan-magazine photo, dried flowers, and votive candle arranged in a shrine beside the sink when she heard the Hitler twins squabbling outside.

She peeked through the curtains and saw Virgil and Be-Bop working on the limo. Three men were approaching them from behind. One was her neighbor Frank and a man who looked enough like him to be his brother. The third was the guy they carjacked and left nearly naked at the diner. He was waving a long-barreled gun directing the other two as they got closer. Virgil and Be-Bop were waist-deep under the hood and didn't see or hear them coming.

Honey dropped to her knees and flattened herself against the wall beneath the sill. There were muffled shouts and somebody barking orders, then gravel footfalls and an agonizing silence. When she collected enough courage to peek outside, the twins were being marched at gunpoint up the stairs to Frank's trailer. She slumped against the wall and cradled her face in her hands.

She and Elvis were trapped. Anyone in Frank's living room had a clear view of Ida Mae's front door. Honey couldn't call the police after the Hitler twins carjacked the Grand Prix. She didn't think cops would buy the class-project angle. After assessing her options, she did the only thing she could think of -- Sparkle picked up on the second ring.

"Mom, I need your help. The guys next door took Virgil and Be-Bop."

"Took them? I don't understand." Sparkle squeezed the phone, trying not to panic. "Honey, you have to call the police."

"I can't. I was with Virgil and Be-Bop when they stole this guy's car. I can't really explain right now."

"What the hell were you thinking?"

"Mom, this *really* isn't the time. If the guy doesn't kill me, you can put me in time-out for the rest of my life, but right now, I need help, and I need it fast."

"Okay. Hold on. I'll think of something."

"I'm next door at a neighbor's. You gotta hurry. They've got guns."

After she hung up, Honey stole another peek out the window. Frank's curtains were drawn. She knew it wouldn't take the Hitler twins long to give her up. Honey checked herself in the mirror, convinced there was nothing to do but hunker down and wait. She took a deep breath and headed for the living room. Ida Mae was sitting alone on the sofa, sipping lemonade.

Elvis had left the building.

21

The Cozzaglios trussed the Hitler twins with so much silver duct tape, they looked like foil-wrapped mummies. Bobby Ray waved the *Dirty Harry* hand cannon in Virgil's face, emptied six .44 magnum hollow points into his hand, and reloaded them one by one. Blood was seeping along the gumline of his sheared incisor, and his lips throbbed like they'd been slammed in a car door.

"You're gonna give me the girl and my money," he growled, "or I'm gonna paint the wall with your brains." Bobby Ray pressed the muzzle against Virgil's forehead. His muffled squeal sounded like a terrified hamster. As Bobby Ray cocked the hammer, he glanced at his watch.

"Shit. I gotta pick up Carmine. We're gonna be late for Tony's party."

"How come *we're* not going?" Joey whined.

"On account of it being invitation-only," Bobby Ray snapped, "and *you* not getting invited. Besides, you and your brother gotta stay here and babysit these two."

Frank glanced Bobby Ray's direction with his one good eye and nodded. He was duct-taping a bag of frozen Tater Tots over the other, which had completely swollen shut.

Joey held up his hands. "Okay. Okay. I didn't mean nothing."

Bobby Ray poked him in the chest with the .44. "While I'm gone, see they stay put and figure out a place to take 'em where we *won't* be interrupted." He glanced over his shoulder at Frank. "You know where they live?"

"Sure, I guess."

"Well, guess your ass over there and find my money."

Bobby Ray checked his watch again. His visit to the trailer park had been productive but dragged on longer than expected. He didn't need to worry about Verduci. He caught a cab rather than risk antagonizing their host by being late.

As things worked out, Bobby Ray would be otherwise occupied and miss Fat Tony's soiree altogether.

Morrison was thinking his new life had all the elements of a Disney story: a beautiful girl, an absentee mom, and a scatterbrained inventor dad when the phone rang. Sparkle picked up on the second ring. He could tell she was talking with Honey but wasn't paying any particular attention until he saw the terrified look on her face.

"What's going on?" he asked as soon as she hung up.

Sparkle cupped her hand over her mouth, trying to compose herself. "Three guys took the Hitler twins at gunpoint and Honey's afraid she's next."

"Jeez. Is she okay?"

Sparkle nodded in a quick, up-and-down motion. "She's hiding out with Elvis at a neighbor's place."

"We have to call the police."

"We *can't* call the police. Honey said something about stealing a car."

"Whose car?"

"One of the guys who have the twins."

The phone rang again, and they both jumped. Sparkle pounced on the phone but when she realized it was Moby, handed it to Morrison, who quickly explained the situation.

"Sit tight," Moby told him. "We'll be right over."

While they were waiting, Honey called several times with more details, including the space numbers for Frank's and Ida Mae's trailers. Sparkle jotted down the addresses. Morrison stuffed her note in his pocket. He was trying to figure out how to contact the SEALs when Moby's Econoline van arrived, and they hurried to the curb.

"Got here as quickly as we could. We had to grab party favors." Moby twisted sideways to reach the cargo door's inside handle. As it slid open, a sticky, sweet cloud of smoke billowed up from the back seat where Jimi and Ishmael were sitting. On the floor was a cardboard box with handguns, machine pistols, and boxes of ammunition.

"You brought *Uzis*?"

"No sense showing up to a gunfight empty-handed. They're noisy and will encourage nosey neighbors to mind their own business." Morrison pulled a Sig from the box, the same 9mm model as his. "You're a scary boy."

Sparkle stood on her tiptoes and stole a peek over Morrison's shoulder. "Where'd you get all these?"

"My stockpile for the zombie apocalypse," Moby answered, grinning.

Ishmael exhaled a scratchy ribbon of blue-gray smoke. "I'm not sure about this hero stuff. My idea of risky behavior is a rowdy evening with double-jointed cheerleaders."

Moby shot Ishmael a sideways glance. "Ignore him. He's been whining since we picked him up."

"Please be careful," Sparkle reminded Morrison as he opened the passenger door and climbed into the van. "You have a reputation for recklessness."

"Ancient history."

"That will be easier to believe if everybody comes back in one piece, including the Hitler twins, if it's not too much trouble."

Morrison arched his eyebrows. "What could possibly go wrong?"

"I'm trying not to think about it." Sparkle clasped her hands together and tried not to fidget. "Please let me know when everybody's okay. Okay?"

"Will do. Can you keep an eye on the mutt?" He stopped short of saying *in case something happens* but knew that's how she heard it. Morrison watched Sparkle through the window until the van turned the corner. "Ready to rock?"

Ishmael pulled the slide back on a Glock 17 and chambered a round. "As ready as action movies have prepared me for a vigilante commando raid."

Jimi fired another bowl. "How about some tunes?"

Ishmael slid a box of eight tracks out from under the seat.

"Where'd you get those relics?" Morrison asked.

"Garage sales and swap meets mostly. I've been collecting since I was a kid." He sorted through the tapes until he found Edwin Starr. Morrison slotted it in the deck and cranked up the volume. "War" exploded from the speakers. The song finished for the third time as Moby pulled in and parked beside a black Grand Prix.

After memorizing the addresses, Morrison stuffed the note in his pocket and looked around, trying to get his bearings. The park looked deserted. If anybody was home, they were holed up inside, taking refuge from the midday heat.

"I think they're over that way," he said and started walking toward the center of the park. Sweat beaded on his forehead and trickled down his cheeks as he counted down the addresses. Ida Mae's place was down a narrow corridor of single wides. Before he could motion the others to spread out, Moby tugged his sleeve.

"The bad guys," he whispered, pointing toward a turd-brown trailer.

Morrison jerked a thumb over his shoulder. "Elvis and Honey are in the one behind us."

They took cover behind a Cadillac convertible with a tangle of scratches on the trunk and a chunk of Styrofoam insulation wedged inside the bumper.

"...too many war toys during your formative years," Ishmael grumbled as he tucked his braids into a brightly striped tam.

Moby rolled his eyes. "Do you need to wait in the car?"

Jimi covered Ishmael's hand with his. "All for one..." he whispered, just loud enough for the others to hear.

Morrison covered Jimi's hand with his. "And one for all."

Moby added his to the pile. "God save the Queen," he grunted, and they all laughed.

Morrison was squatting behind a swamp cooler with a clear line-of-sight to the porch and front door when a white limousine lumbered down the gravel road toward them. Elvis slid in beside him, and he nearly jumped out of his skin.

Presley tapped his wrist where a watch would be if he was wearing one. "Here come reinforcements, right on time."

"Jeez, you startled me! Aren't you supposed to be watching Honey?"

"Just checked. She's on the phone with her mom. Ida Mae was watching *Oprah*, and Cosmo suggested I keep an eye on things."

Moby was crouching close enough to overhear the remark. "Who's Cosmo?"

"My cat."

Morrison held up his hand before he could ask. "It's a long story."

"His friend Flynn's worried things might not go as planned. Cosmo said we should sit tight until everything's sorted out."

Before Morrison could ask *what things*, the limo rolled to a stop in front of Frank's, and four men in white HazMat suits jumped out and charged the trailer. The lead man bulled open the door, and the other three stormed in behind him without breaking stride as two more limos pulled in and parked behind the first. Heavily armed men in black suits and wraparound sunglasses fanned out in an arc in front of the trailer.

The single wide erupted with the shouts of men barking orders. Through the ruined door, Morrison could see the Hitler twins wrapped in silver duct tape. Two other men were sitting beside them on the sofa, their hands clasped over their heads.

"Deal's soured, man." Ishmael's face was shiny with sweat and nervous energy. "Time to beat feet."

247

Elvis squeezed his arm. "Relax. We're just holding down the peanut gallery."

Ishmael's face flushed with anger. "You knew all along?"

Morrison shook his head. "Really? Now, you're whining because you're *not* going to get killed?"

"No, but..."

Elvis grinned. "That's what happens when you miss staff meetings. We've got floor seats, front and center."

"*Five* seats," Jimi reminded him. "Just 'cause I'm invisible doesn't mean you can talk about me like I'm not here."

"Right, five." Elvis stood and started toward Frank's trailer. When Morrison hesitated, he motioned him to follow. "It's okay. We're expected."

They stopped a few steps short of the porch. The faces of the men on the door were so impassive, Morrison wasn't sure they'd seen them. One of the men in a HazMat suit stepped outside to greet him. When he raised his filter mask, Morrison recognized him from Sinderella's.

"Mr. Morrison, if you and the others could wait here, I will be right with you. The men you came for are safe, and they will be released as soon as the medical staff has examined them. Now, if you will excuse me, I have business to attend to inside."

"Who *are* these guys?" Moby whispered.

Morrison shrugged. "I'm not really sure."

"Well, I have *no* idea. So, take your best guess."

Elvis chuckled softly. "For now, let's be glad they're here to help." Moby made a face but didn't say anything.

Morrison watched the scene in the living room through the busted door. The duct tape around the twins had been unwrapped, and a man was hunched over Virgil with a stethoscope. The hostage-takers were still sitting on the sofa. One was staring at the ceiling. The other buried his face in his hands and looked like he was crying. Morrison didn't see Hiro exit the second limo and didn't realize he

248

was there until he was standing beside them, holding his hand up like a traffic cop.

"You gentlemen should wait outside. My people are wearing hermetically sealed suits and shoe covers to minimize trace evidence." Hiro was impeccably dressed and spoke in a clear, steady voice.

"So, what's all this?"

"In good time, Mr. Morrison. We have not been properly introduced. My name is Hiroshi Shinozawa."

"Mr. Shinozawa."

He shook Morrison's hand and then Elvis's. "Mr. Presley, I cannot tell you what a great pleasure it is to meet you."

Elvis bowed curtly. "Shinozawa-san."

Hiro glanced over Morrison's shoulder. "And these gentlemen would be Mr. Dix and Mr. Ahab."

Ishmael looked leery. "I got your name, but who are you?"

"In the vernacular of your movie culture, I am the proverbial cavalry."

"No, I mean..." Ishmael halted mid-sentence, realizing he had no idea what he meant.

"Let us say for the moment our mutual interests coincide. Which reminds me, is Mr. Hendrix present?" Morrison looked surprised. "*Information age* is not just a figure of speech," Hiro chuckled. "I am anxious we talk. I understand he is the next step in technology worth pursuing."

"He's around. He's hard to find sometimes."

"But worth looking for, or so I am led to believe. I would appreciate it if you made introductions when we have a moment."

Hiro nodded toward the twins. "Your two associates were darted with succinylcholine, sea snake venom, and a mild psychotic, sort of a synthetic curare that disrupts neural transmissions. In several hours they will wake up with flu-like symptoms, no clear recollection of what happened, and a craving for Strawberry-Kiwi Jell-O shots, a side effect we have been unable to account for."

249

Morrison nodded toward the two men on the couch. "And what about them?"

Hiro glanced at the Sig tucked in Morrison's jeans. "To what lengths would you have gone to protect your daughter?" he asked gruffly.

"Whatever was necessary," Morrison answered softly, his voice almost a whisper.

Hiro's eyes narrowed. "As will I." He glanced over his shoulder at the Cozzaglios and barked orders to his men in Japanese. "Do not trouble yourself, Mr. Morrison. Those two are tools and rather dull and useless tools at that."

Moby leaned closer. "What did he mean by *your daughter*?"

"Another long story."

Moby started to say something, but Morrison hushed him as two men in HAZMAT suits helped the Hitler twins down the porch steps.

"Take them home and tuck them into bed," Hiro said.

Out of the corner of his eye, Morrison saw Honey standing in Ida Mae's doorway. "Are you all right?"

"Sure, I guess."

"Good. Please call your mom and let her know everybody's okay."

"*Is* everybody okay?" Honey asked. All eyes were on Shinozawa.

"Nearly everybody," Morrison said. "We're still negotiating a few sticking points."

Hiro grinned. "My father told me the sharpest sword is of no use to a man with no arms. I would think that would be truer still for a man with no head." He glanced over his shoulder at the Cozzaglios. "The fate of these two is of no consequence. Some of my men can wait here until our work in Las Vegas is done -- sort of a catch-and-release program. If we throw these little ones back, would that be acceptable?"

Morrison nodded.

Hiro's eyes narrowed again. "But I will have something in return. You will arrange lunch between Mr. Hendrix and some of my people."

"You'll have to ask him."

"Mr. Hendrix, would you be so kind as to make yourself available? Say Tuesday?"

"Sure," came the disembodied reply.

"Excellent. My car will pick you up at Mr. Dix's at 12:30." Hiro glanced at his watch. "Mr. Dix, Mr. Ahab, Mr. Hendrix, while I am delighted to have made your acquaintance, there's a pressing matter that demands our attention." As his driver opened the limo door, Hiro gestured for Morrison and Elvis to join him.

"Gentlemen, let us go cut off that head."

22

After checking to make sure Honey was okay, Moby, Ishmael, and Jimi piled into the band's Econoline van and headed for the Strip. It was nearly time for Ishmael's shift, and Moby was dropping him at work. Ishmael rummaged through the box of eight tracks until found a Marley tape and slotted in in the tape deck.

"I hope Jim and Elvis are all right," Jimi mumbled, barely audible above "Get Up, Stand Up" blasting from the speakers.

Traffic moved at a snail's pace, and "Small Axe" was playing by the time Moby dropped them at the Tahitian Princess and drove off down Tropicana.

"Okay if I hang a while?" Jimi asked.

Ishmael patted his pockets and grinned. "We can probably find a way to entertain ourselves."

They walked across the gaming floor, through an Employees Only door, and down a wide hallway to the locker area. Ishmael hung his street clothes on a hook, moved his pipe, a lighter, and a small bag of dope to a pair of clean coveralls, and tugged the zipper closed. As he was slotting his time card, he saw Ernie Badoglio, the casino GM, jabbing a pudgy finger his direction.

"You work here, right?"

Ishmael tapped the Tahitian Princes logo patch on his coveralls.

"Good. I gotta job for you." Bad Dog retrieved a roll of antacids from his coat pocket, thumbed two into his mouth, and ground them between his back teeth. "Gonzo the Great's opening's been pushed back again on account of construction delays, but none of the geniuses who work for me canceled the dry ice deliveries for his smoke machines."

Ishmael glanced at his supervisor who was standing beside Badoglio. His shirt looked like he'd dressed straight out of a sauna without toweling off. "Nobody told *me* the magic guy wasn't doing tricks," he whined.

"Oh, he's doing tricks, all right," Bad Dog growled. "He's hanging out in the bar, disappearing his Johnson into cocktail waitresses two at a time."

"I shoulda gone to magic school," Ishmael joked.

"Don't crack wise with me," Bad Dog snapped as he reached into his pocket for more antacids. "We're outta freezer space, and the weekend groceries are gonna be here in an hour. You're gonna drive the ice out to the desert and dump it. Grab a couple guys from the delivery dock to help and make sure the wrappers get tossed *before* they're loaded on the truck. I don't want a bunch of tree huggers whining about how we littered their friggin' sand dunes."

Ishmael had already started toward the door when Bad Dog called after him. "And use a truck with a lift bed so you can dump it by yourself." Ishmael waved he'd heard him without breaking stride.

Loading the truck turned out to be a major operation. Even with a forklift and two more guys, it took three hours. The thirty-pound blocks were too cold to handle without gloves, and since there weren't enough to go around, they had to take turns. Two guys loaded the truck while the other one drove the forklift and picked up discarded wrappers. Jimi waited in the cab and tried to stay out of the way. When all the blocks were loaded, Ishmael climbed in beside him, and they headed out of town.

As the truck lumbered down the ramp to I-15 North, Ishmael remembered something he meant to tell Jimi earlier. "You know how you asked me to find out where Vikki took off to the other night?"

Jimi nodded.

"Floyd drove her to a private party in Summerlin. I found this in his locker." Ishmael offered him a crumpled piece of paper.

253

Jimi snatched it from his hand and read the address out loud. "Where's Summerlin?"

Ishmael rocked forward and pointed out the window. "Over that way, northeast of downtown. It's where the rich people live. Wait, I know that address. I worked there with my brothers. What's today?"

"Friday, I think."

Ishmael glanced at his watch. "They might be there now." He grabbed his cell, punched a number from his contacts, and put the phone on speaker.

"Waddup?"

"Where you at?"

"Ishmael?"

"Your brudda like no other. You at the Jap guy's house?"

"We're at Mr. Shinozawa's."

"I worked there once, right?"

"You leaned on a rake and complained about how hot it was *once*."

Ishmael gave Jimi a thumbs-up. "Perfect. I'm on my way."

"Unnecessary. We'll be home right after work."

"Jimi's with me and wants to see the place."

A moment of dead air followed. "Well, I guess you can swing by. There's nobody here but us."

Ishmael snapped his phone shut. "Whatta you got in mind?"

"No idea. But we have twenty tons of dry ice and half an ounce of inspiration. Confidence is high we can come up with something."

Ishmael waved at his brothers, who were trimming the boxwoods and privets along the street, and parked behind the house. Jimi climbed on top of the cab and was looking for a place to dump the ice when he spotted an out-building half-buried in a hill.

"Is that the guest house?"

Ishmael cupped his hands over his eyes and squinted. "No, a tea garden with plants and a fish pond."

"Why's it dug into the ground like that?"

"Makes it easier to keep cool. The building's climate-controlled."

"Isolated and quiet?"

Ishmael smiled sheepishly. "Really quiet. I snuck in there and took a nap."

"That'll work. Park on the far side by the skylight."

Ishmael moved the truck, and Jimi hoisted himself onto the roof, pried open the skylight, and peered inside. He couldn't see Cleopatra because she was sitting under a rock overhang. Jimi arranged the dovetails so the ice would funnel down the chute into the garden when Ishmael raised the truck bed.

By the time Cleopatra realized what was happening, it was too late. Protected from falling blocks by the overhang, she was immediately trapped in an igloo-like hollow with dry ice walls six feet thick.

Fat Tony's palatial estate had been remodeled to look like his favorite local haunt, Caesar's Palace. He added several personal flourishes, including a gauntlet of faux marble nymphs that lined the cobbled driveway and a garden fountain with live flamingos.

Three sentries were sitting in a Mark VIII just outside the gate, listening to the radio. The motor was running, and the air conditioner turned up full blast. The guy in the driver's seat put out his cigarette when he saw Hiro and his entourage approaching.

"Looks like the Jappers are finally here."

His buddies were still snickering when the limousines rolled to a stop, and he slid out of the car. He aimed the remote at the control box and stepped back as the massive, wrought iron gates swung open. Hiro's driver, a wiry guy in a black chauffeur's uniform, emerged stiffly from the limo.

"We are expected," he said gruffly as he turned and opened the rear door.

A squat, square-shouldered man in sunglasses and a dark suit got out of the car. In the heartbeat the chauffeur screened the sentry's line-of-sight, the suit in the sunglasses drew a machine pistol. He stepped to his left to clear the chauffeur and fired a short burst into Fat Tony's man, who staggered backward and collapsed. Two more shooters appeared on the opposite side of the limo and shot dead the guys in the Lincoln before they could react.

Fat Tony's spacious pool was in the glass-roofed atrium in the middle of the villa. Verduci was sprawled on a lounge-style beach chair beside a row of gilded swans spewing water from their beaks. He plucked the olive from his Tanqueray martini, munched it anxiously, and looked around again. Bobby Ray was supposed to be his ride to the party. When he was a no-show, Verduci took a taxi rather than risk being late.

Verduci lived in mortal fear of his cousin. When they were kids, Fat Tony buried him to his chin in the schoolyard sandbox. Only seven years old, the boy who would one day head New York's most notorious crime family, was already hiding bodies in construction projects.

Fat Tony was holding court on the far side of the pool. He had the displacement and tan lines of an albino hippopotamus. Surrounded by tough guys in shiny suits and young men in togas serving drinks and *hors d'oeuvres*, he was waist-deep, finishing a story about his brother and a hooker.

"So, he *trained* her three afternoons a week at the Venus de Milo Arms. That's how Santino got a special citation from the Mayor himself for his work-release program." Fat Tony snorted uproariously. His audience joined him in a chorus of nervous laughter. "I need another drink," he bellowed.

Venetti had been drinking steadily since breakfast and looked like his face was sliding off. He rolled slug-like up the pool steps, wrapped himself in a towel the size of a bedsheet, and trudged across

256

the marble deck to the bar. A woman in a bikini with teased-out hair and unnaturally firm breasts handed him a cola-colored drink. He raised his glass, and the crowd around the pool fell silent.

"Here's to honor," Fat Tony grunted as he leered at the woman behind the bar. "Once you get on her, stay on her."

There was another round of nervous laughter. The guests had heard the toast before.

Verduci laughed longer and louder than most, gulped the last of his martini, and handed the glass to the effeminate young man attending him. "Thank you, Frederico," he said as the boy exchanged it for a fresh drink. His nametag read Carlos, but Verduci had decided to call him Frederico. "Breakfast of champions." The boy gave him a small smile and nodded politely.

"Fetch a tray of these and meet me by the Jacuzzi." Verduci was using his puffed-up, confidant-of-the-President voice, hoping to lure him into one of the two dozen bedrooms before drinking himself into a stupor.

As he was watching Frederico walk to the bar, he caught Fat Tony's disapproving stare out of the corner of his eye. With some difficultly and very little grace, Verduci extricated himself from the lounge chair and toddled unsteadily to the far end of the pool. He kicked off his flip-flops, stripped down to his swim trunks, and piled his robe and sunglasses on a towel.

When Frederico arrived with a fresh tray of drinks, he was floundering in the Jacuzzi like a drunken manatee. Verduci took a huge gulp of air and disappeared beneath the frothy surface. He was trying to impress Frederico with how long he could hold his breath. Verduci didn't stay under very long, but his timing was impeccable.

The Venetti's travel agent booked nonrefundable round trip tickets. As things worked out, the plane would be flying back from Las Vegas with lots of empty seats.

Morrison and Hiro had a clear view of Fat Tony's estate from the grassy knoll by the gate. Except for a few bodyguards, most of Hiro's men were by the limos that had looped around the driveway and were idling by the bullet-riddled Mark VIII.

Hiro took off his sunglasses and polished the lenses with a silk handkerchief. "You're wondering why we're here."

"My guess is you're banking social debt though I don't know why."

"I have no immediate purpose, but I find it useful to have people indebted to me."

"So, you're going to kick down the door and shoot up the place in case you need a favor someday?"

Hiro chuckled. "You watch too much TV."

Morrison nodded toward Elvis, who was sitting cross-legged a few feet away, reading something on his computer. "Then why are *we* here?"

"The man hunting your daughter is inside. And though we both have something personal at stake, today is a sales demonstration."

"A dog-and-pony show for the merchants of death?"

"Overly poetic, Mr. Morrison, but a reasonably accurate assessment. Killing is big business, but the real money is in selling the means."

"By supplying both sides?"

"Only if both sides have money," Hiro answered dryly. "Your government lives in mortal fear of new weapons falling into the wrong hands, *wrong hands* being a euphemism for anybody's but theirs. I leave it to them to infer there are other interested parties."

"That's all it takes?"

"That's all it takes. I *always* sell to the Americans. You have the deepest pockets. If I knew how well the invisibility protocols worked, I would have sold them more dearly."

Morrison's brow furrowed. "If you developed them, how could you not know?"

258

"Our field tests were only modestly successful. When my people reviewed the Pentagon results, they realized Japanese newborns develop neural pathways that bypass certain receptors. Because our culture is so rigid, we lack the neuroplasticity to achieve the same success as Mr. Hendrix."

One of Hiro's men hurried over, bowed, and said something too softly for Morrison to hear. Hiro answered in Japanese. The man bowed again and excused himself.

"Thermal scans indicate we have a full house. Tora 1 has been cleared to engage." An F-16 skimmed the rooftop of the neighboring estate and fired a missile that exploded through Fat Tony's picture window. As the plane banked hard right and disappeared into the clouds, the house erupted in a blue fireball so intense the villa seemed to flicker and roll up at the edges like a dry leaf. A moment later, it appeared, except for the shattered window, as if nothing had happened.

"Sweet Jesus," Morrison stammered. "What the hell was that?"

"Cryogenic napalm. A chemical cold fire that burns everything organic, leather, paper, wood, to a fine, gray ash."

"And people?"

"Yes, Mr. Morrison, and people."

Morrison hunched over his knees like he'd been sucker-punched in the gut.

Hiro scowled. "The man hunting your daughter was inside? She would never be safe as long as he was alive."

Morrison shifted his weight uneasily from side to side but didn't say anything.

"Do I need to remind you, yours is the only country to use nuclear weapons on other human beings?"

"That was barbaric, but at least that was war."

The guttural sound escaping Hiro was close to a growl. "No, Mr. Morrison, at *most* that was war, and you no longer have the luxury of pretending it was not."

"Yes, but..."

Hiro held up his hand to cut him off. "I have a story, one best not shared with children." He squeezed his eyes shut, taking refuge in the darkness behind the lids. When he opened them, he spoke slowly, his words slow and measured.

"I was born sixty-two years ago in Hiroshima. I remember the day the bomb came in terrible detail. I was playing with friends along the railroad tracks on the edge of town. I can still feel the shock wave slamming into me and the withering heat of the firestorm that followed.

"I picked my way through charred stumps of camphor and willow to my home. In the rubble, I found a tin of tangerines my mother was saving for a special occasion but nothing identifiably human. The ashes I interred on Mt. Ida a decade later were pebbles I collected along the river.

"I spent a year recovering from burns and the next two in an orphanage. My older sister was out of town on a field trip and was spared the horror of that day. It took three years for her to find me. We barely recognized each other.

"We lived with her boyfriend in the Tokyo garment district. The difficulties of war had been replaced by several orders of magnitude the difficulties of peace. Times were tough. I was tougher. In the long shadow of that terrible day, I was reborn. That day was your country's gift to me. Today, Mr. Morrison, is my gift to you."

Hiro stood stoically, staring at a patch of clear, blue sky along the horizon line. "Our work here is complete." As his driver opened the door, Hiro stepped aside and made a sweeping gesture. Elvis ducked his head and slid inside. Morrison looked over his shoulder at Fat Tony's villa.

"So, what now?"

"Mr. Presley is due at the Tahitian Princess Event Center. As the winner of their one-millionth guest promotion, he has an Itty Bitty Elvis Contest to judge. Can I give you a lift?"

When Verduci resurfaced through the roil of bubbles, he realized he was alone. He clambered out of the Jacuzzi in a panic and onto an overturned drink tray in a debris field of glass and spilled martinis. He bent down, brushed aside a toga clasp, and plucked a set of keys from a chalky pile of gray ash. As he was scuttling past an unusually large mound of cinders, he felt a jabbing pain in the arch of his foot. When Verduci glanced down, he realized he was standing on Fat Tony's pinky ring.

Hiro watched a nearly naked man scurry across the lawn to a row of parked cars, frantically checking locks until the door on a rust-bucket Chevy Nova popped open.

God spared him for a reason, Hiro decided and chose not to second-guess His judgment. He waited until the Nova disappeared around the corner before telling his driver it was time to go.

23

The driver parked at the curb in front of the Tahitian Princess Event Center. As Morrison, Elvis, and Hiro got out of the limo, the *oyabun*'s men enveloped them in a human shield. Morrison marveled again at how well-choreographed their movements were.

"Will you be joining us?" Hiro's face was impassive behind his Wayfarers.

Morrison shook his head. "No, but thanks."

Hiro nodded curtly, and he and his entourage swarmed up the steps. Morrison was deciding what to do next when he saw Helmut Schmidt waddling toward them in a purple, crushed-velvet tuxedo. With his pear-shaped body, he looked like a giant, bow-legged eggplant. Even with lifts, the porcupine-quill tips of his spiky, crew cut barely came to Morrison's eye level.

"I'm Helmut Schmidt, Special Events Director," he reminded them. He wore the peevish expression of a child bullied into an unsavory task. Helmut pursed his lips and pointed a glitter-green nail at Elvis. "I'm sorry. I didn't get your name."

"Elvis Presley," Elvis answered with a hip swivel and a sneer.

Helmut rolled his eyes. "Don't bury yourself in the roll, sweetheart." He drummed his pudgy fingers against his cheek and studied Elvis down the bridge of his nose. "We need to get you into hair and makeup. The girls have a *lot* of work to do." Before he could herd him up the steps, a stretch limo with the resort's garish, hula-girl logo pulled up to the curb. A vacuous-looking man in a white dinner jacket emerged from the car.

Helmut leaned into Morrison as if confiding some great secret. "Mr. Debonair hosts *Movie Theater Classics* on KVIG weekday afternoons. He's our master of ceremonies."

Morrison forced a smile. When Debonair was a game-show host in the seventies, he appeared regularly in tabloid stories about cocaine and underage girls. He still looked like he spent two hours every morning getting his tan on straight.

"Oh, Dirk," Helmut cooed as Debonair, smiling a big, toothy grin, turned a slow hundred and eighty-degree arc, waving at nobody in particular.

"So *wonderful* to see you again!" Helmut gushed.

When Debonair realized who was calling him, his grin faded abruptly. After dropping a bundle on a pony with the dubious moniker Sir Alpo, he was given a choice between emceeing and getting knee-capped. Hosting won in a photo finish. Terrified of sexually transmitted diseases, he tucked his hand in his pocket, ignoring the chubby paw Helmut offered.

"Chop-chop everybody," Helmut chirped, ignoring the rebuke. "It's almost showtime." While he ushered Elvis and Debonair up the steps and backstage for makeup and publicity shots, Morrison snuck off long enough to find a payphone. He called Sparkle and let her know everything was okay.

When the house lights flickered, Morrison poked his head through the curtains. The orchestra pit was empty except for a man in headphones monitoring a playlist of Elvis hits. The audience was seated dinner-theater style at tables arranged in tiers. The Littles were toward the center, four rows back. Elmo was hard to miss in his horned helmet. Gladys spotted Morrison and motioned for him to join them. Relieved to see a pair of friendly faces, Morrison made his way to their box.

"Come sit with us," Gladys said, patting the empty chair beside her.

"We left a ticket for Dickie in will-call," Elmo explained, "but I doubt he's gonna show."

Morrison glanced at Elvis, who was sitting at the judges' table, staring serenely at the crowd. The smallest traces of a smile were visible in the corners of his mouth.

Gladys reached over and squeezed Morrison's hand. "Please join us."

"Thanks," he said as he pulled out a chair and sat down.

"The Happy Hobo arranged for a loaner RV," Elmo said as he slipped off his helmet and set it on the table. "They're writing off the Winnebago as a total loss."

Before Morrison could say anything, the lights dimmed, and an instrumental cover of "Hound Dog" built from white noise to a bone-rattling crescendo. Dirk Debonair strolled onto the stage to a synthesized drum roll, waving and smiling his game-show-host smile. The audience broke out in alcohol-tinged applause.

"Ladies and gentlemen, I'm Dirk Debonair and have the very great pleasure of being your host this evening. On behalf of the Tahitian Princess Resort and Casino, I would like to welcome you to the first annual Itty Bitty Elvis Contest."

The DJ segued to "Blue Suede Shoes" as more than a dozen contestants shuffled on stage for introductions. Morrison craned his neck, sizing up the field.

Elmo pointed to a diminutive entrant with a particularly tall pompadour. "See that fella over there? That's Atlas Shrugg." Morrison recognized him from the One Millionth Guest promotion.

Gladys stood and applauded as Shrugg was introduced. "He's an honorary Viking," she reminded him.

"Most of those fellas worked the pro-wrestling circuit." Elmo winked slyly. "There's a *lotta* bad blood up there."

Morrison turned as a platinum blonde strolled past on the arm of a rail-thin octogenarian in a bolo tie and black Stetson. Most of her face was hidden beneath a pair of oversized sunglasses and a wide-brimmed hat. Morrison thought she looked familiar and was trying to place her when he realized it was Miss Vikki, the dancer from Sinderella's.

Because his back was to the stage, Morrison didn't see how the melee started, but when he heard shouting, he turned in time to see Atlas piledrive a black-leather Elvis into the floor. In an instant, the fracas divided into two camps: motorcycle-jacketed, rebel Elvises on one side and bloated, Vegas-headliner Elvises on the other.

"Jailhouse Rock" blasted from the speakers as the audience surged forward, straining for a better look.

Debonair staggered backward, trying to extricate himself from the brawl, but his escape was blocked by a thigh-high Elvis with bushy, black sideburns, twirling a microphone by the cord like a lariat. When Dirk turned to run, he flung it bola-style, ensnaring the emcee around the ankles. Debonair belly-flopped onto the stage. The diminutive Elvis jumped on his back, snatched his toupee, and Frisbeed it into the audience. It landed on a woman in the third row.

"Kill it! Kill it!" she screamed hysterically. A red-faced man with a bulbous nose threw it on the floor and stomped it furiously.

A group in black leather hoisted a fallen comrade like a battering ram and drove him, headfirst, into a stampeding wedge of sequined Elvises, scattering them like bowling pins. The white-fringed Elvises launched a furious counterattack, wielding French bread hoagies from the Green Room buffet. They club-sandwiched the young Elvises with such ferocity, the first three rows of the audience were showered with turkey, ham, and shredded lettuce.

The dividing line between factions quickly blurred, and the fracas devolved into a free-for-all. As the theater began to empty, Hiro's bodyguards hurried him up the steps, the prow of their formation parting the crowd like the Red Sea.

Gladys climbed onto her chair and pumped a greasy pompadour "scalped" from one of the contestants in the air. Elmo clambered onto the chair beside her, waving his horned helmet in big loopy swings over his head.

As Morrison elbowed his way to Elvis, Helmut Schmidt hurried past him, headed the opposite direction. His spiky crew cut had begun to wilt. He screeched something incomprehensible and disappeared in the huddled masses streaming toward the exits.

Dancers from a local strip club were supposed to swarm the stage spinning flaming baton-torches for the big finale — a *Blue Hawaii* booty shake. As Morrison and Elvis were heading out the door, one of the girls backstage accidentally set her grass skirt on fire stoking her bong. Except for a scorched patch of pubic hair, she was unharmed, but the smoke triggered the building's sprinkler system. It malfunctioned and dumped hundreds of gallons of water into the orchestra pit and flooded the first row to the seatbacks.

The Bureau spent a decade trying to build a case against the Venettis, but after ten years of surveillance and phone taps, hadn't collected enough evidence for a jaywalking indictment. By mid-August, the Deputy Director was ready to pull the plug when another low-level informant was found floating in the East River, strangled with his FBI wire.

But over Labor Day weekend, a rookie cop out of the 111th busted a hooker named Cherri Polachowski in the Little Neck section of Queens. He found enough coke in her handbag for a second strike. After hastily considering her options, Cherri rolled over like a dead fish.

When she was still Charles, before reassignment surgery and a career move to prostitution, Cherri worked three years as a court stenographer. Names, dates, and places spilled out of her like a slot machine jackpot. When Santino Venetti's name came up, the officer, angling for a transfer to the FBI, turned her over to the feds.

Fat Tony's older brother's principal interest in the family business was training working girls in the art of fellatio and was devoted to the task with a fervor that bordered on maniacal, "training" six to eight women a day. He was partial to short, fat ones with bad teeth. Having a flat head did not, as far as the FBI had been able to determine, appear to be a prerequisite.

For a cozy WITSEC deal, the FBI got enough for a warrant and wired Santino's suite at the Venus de Milo Arms, where he and Cherri met three times a week for sound and video. At Bureau headquarters, the "evidence" developed a cult following. Trench-coated agents packed the screening room for each new episode. Vending machine popcorn sales skyrocketed.

But their liaisons had not produced anything for a grand jury until a phone conversation between Santino and his brother was caught on tape. Fat Tony had decided killing a congressman on the take would be more cost-effective than keeping him on the payroll. He called as Cherri was leaving and gave his brother the details. The FBI filmed the murder from three different angles and never considered intervening.

The Bureau has well-ordered priorities.

Special Agents Orange and Newmeat walked briskly out of the FBI's Las Vegas headquarters. The night was electric, and Orange was glowing like neon on the Strip. The federal grand jury in lower Manhattan had issued warrants for sixteen members of the Venetti crime family, seven of whom, including Fat Tony, were in Nevada. Anxious men with automatic weapons swarmed everywhere. A black van with SWAT painted on the side screeched to a halt and disgorged more men. The parking lot looked like the staging area for extras in a Rambo movie.

Orange climbed onto the hood of their black Explorer, and Newmeat handed him a bullhorn. More than two dozen FBI agents, plus a like number from the Las Vegas Police Department's SWAT unit, gathered around. Orange cleared his throat and waited for everyone to settle down.

"For those of you who haven't had the pleasure of meeting me, I'm Senior Special Agent Spencer Orange, head of the Nevada Division of the FBI's Special Task Force on Organized Crime." Newmeat clapped enthusiastically.

"The Task Force is an integrated, multi-jurisdictional effort involving federal, state, and local law enforcement agencies." There was a chorus of jeers from the back where most of Las Vegas's finest had clustered. The cops knew what that meant: the FBI felt free to commandeer whatever state and local resources they deemed necessary for their dog-and-pony show.

Orange tugged at his tie. His face flushed. "Our ongoing mission is the investigation, indictment, and prosecution of members of organized crime."

There was another wave of snickering. Orange was gripping the bullhorn so tightly, his fingers turned white. "It says so in our mandate," he whined. Somebody toward the back shouted something he didn't hear, and the last few rows erupted in laughter and catcalls.

This is the thanks we get for bringing in the locals, he muttered to himself.

Orange coughed into his fist, trying to regain his composure. "Because of the extreme secrecy of our mission, our targets will not be identified until we're en route, but I can tell you this: today we strike a death blow at the very heart of organized crime."

A low murmur greeted his final remark. Cynicism had given way to apathy. Orange took it as a sign he was winning them over. "And try not to get yourself killed unless it's absolutely necessary."

"What's the matter?" somebody shouted. "Afraid you'll get stuck with the paperwork?" Even Orange couldn't help but smile. The Bureau certainly loved reports.

"Let's roll!" he shouted and pumped his fist in the air. Newmeat helped him down. All around them, men scrambled into waiting vehicles.

"We should synchronize our watches," Newmeat suggested as he slid into the passenger seat. Orange gritted his teeth, ignoring him. When he decided everybody was ready, he led the caravan out of the parking lot.

Newmeat looked anxiously out the window. "I stopped at Caesar's yesterday and checked out the Amelia Earhart lead. Nothing so far. It might be a dead end."

It took Orange a moment to recall Hennigan's comment about the missing aviator dealing blackjack. "I'll expect a full report."

"Yes, sir. It'll be on your desk in the morning."

"Great." Apparently, the FBI taught typing and good manners at the academy but not sarcasm. Newmeat was breathing so hard, he looked like he was about to hyperventilate. His eyes had glazed over, and his face was the color of guacamole. At a red light, Orange dug through the take-out litter at his feet for a paper bag.

And then my partner fainted would not look good in his report.

"Here, breathe into this." Newmeat clamped the bag over his nose and mouth. Orange had watched lesser agents win recognition and promotion on the coattails of major arrests his whole career. Now it was his turn. He stole another glance at his partner.

That is if I can keep J. Edgar, Jr. in line.

Orange checked his look in the rearview, readying himself to deliver the speech he'd been fine-tuning since joining the Bureau. He picked up the handset and cleared his throat.

"Gentlemen, today we're going to arrest seven members of America's most notorious crime family, including Anthony Venetti." A wave of *Fat Tony* murmurs washed over the caravan. Orange gave the mic a white-knuckle squeeze. "This is one small step for law enforcement and one giant leap for justice."

Orange grinned, smugly confident he'd perfectly delivered the line he'd rehearsed for over an hour in front of the bathroom mirror.

"Tomorrow morning, that will be the headline of every paper in the country." Newmeat's voice was barely audible through the bag.

"Considering the FBI's policy on major arrests, I should've said *one giant leap for just us*," Orange whispered to his partner. He was too busy preening to realize the commlink was still open and broadcasting. A low rumble rolled through the rest of the convoy.

Orange could have said *for just me*. He patted his pocket to make sure he had breath mints and a comb. He "leaked" the pending arrests over dinner and drinks to Diana Woo, a local affiliate reporter. The KVIG news van joined the caravan a couple blocks from the mobster's villa.

The raid was being executed during a pool party so all the principals could be collared at once. The first indication everything might not go as diagrammed in the ready room immediately became apparent. The Mark VIII parked just outside the open gates had been shot to hell.

All that was visible of the driver was the sole of his shoe on the window ledge. Beside him, the passenger was propped against the far door, his head rocked back like he was staring at the roof. The guy behind him was slumped forward, his face buried in the front seat headrest.

Newmeat craned his neck, trying to get a better view. "Are they dead?"

"You better check to make sure."

While the FBI was sorting out what to do next, the KVIG news crew bolted from their van and set up for a remote broadcast. Diana Woo checked her makeup in the visor mirror and added fresh lip-gloss, scrubbing a red smudge from her teeth with the tip of her finger. She positioned herself so the Lincoln would be in the frame behind her. Woo tugged at the hem of her blazer that had bunched around her shoulders and signaled the cameraman she was ready. When he nodded, she counted down from three, introduced herself, and started narrating the live broadcast.

The shot widened to include Newmeat as he unlocked the door after several failed attempts and slid out of the Explorer. An arc of agents formed behind him. His left foot forward, his Glock pointed at the body slumped in the front seat, he scooted toward the Mark VIII half a step at a time. The air was still except for Diana Woo's running commentary and the crunch of Newmeat's wingtips on the gravel.

Even ventilated with bullet holes, the temperature inside the Lincoln had climbed to a hundred and thirty degrees. As Newmeat yanked open the door, the pungent bouquet of death assaulted him. He staggered two steps backward and threw up on his shoes.

A few harried refugees from the Itty Bitty Elvis Contest hurried past, but nobody paid them any particular attention. Morrison's plan was to drop Elvis at the elevator to his suite, cut across the gaming floor, and grab a cab out front. They were in the parking garage, nearly to the Tahitian Princess, when Elvis stopped in his tracks. The hair had worked loose from his ponytail and radiated out in a fuzzy, white corona. He looked like an Old Testament prophet back from a chat with God.

"He's here," he croaked softly.

"Who's here?"

"The guy after Honey."

"You saw him?"

Elvis nodded. "He's two rows over."

Morrison pointed toward a short, round guy in a Hawaiian print shirt rifling through the trunk of a black Grand Prix. "You mean *him*?"

Elvis nodded again. Morrison checked to make sure the Sig was still in his waistband, and they walked over, stopping ten feet short of the Pontiac.

"Excuse me, sir." No response. "Excuse me," Morrison repeated, a little louder this time.

"Get lost, asshole." Bobby Ray's words were muffled. His head was still inside the trunk.

"May I have a word with you."

Bobby Ray stood up and glared at Morrison. "Jesus. What the hell's your problem?"

Morrison tucked his right arm behind his back and wrapped his hand around the Sig's grip. "My problem is you're looking for my daughter."

"Your daughter?"

"I understand she borrowed your car without your permission."

"That was your kid?"

"I arranged for two of your associates, Frank and Joey something, to be released unharmed."

Bobby Ray shook his head. "Released? Christ. I left 'em watching your kid's a-hole friends. How'd they screw *that* up?"

"It's not important. Let's just agree her debt's been settled and leave it at that."

"I got a better idea. How 'bout I stuff you in the trunk, and we drive around town until we find her?" Bobby Ray reached down and grabbed the tire iron before realizing Morrison was pointing a 9mm at his chest.

"I was hoping it wouldn't come to this." Morrison glanced at Elvis then back to the mobster. "Maybe Hiro was right."

Bobby Ray scowled. "You ain't no hero. You're just an asshole with a gun."

Morrison raised the Sig to a point dead center between Bobby Ray's eyes.

"Great. So, now what?"

"Start by losing the tire iron."

Bobby Ray relaxed his fist, and the tire iron clattered to the pavement.

"Now, take off your shoes."

"They're Bruno Maglis," he whined. "Three-hundred bucks a pair *wholesale*. I just bought 'em to replace the ones your daughter and her friends stole."

"That's unfortunate." Morrison stepped forward and pressed the gun against Bobby Ray's forehead. "Most people find loaded firearms persuasive. It probably has something to do with the immediate threat of getting shot."

"Sure. No problem. The shoes are off, see? Just take it easy."

"Put them in the trunk along with your pants."

The mobster glared at him. "What *is* it about you people and my underwear?" Morrison pushed the Sig hard enough against his forehead that a red mark mushroomed around the muzzle.

"I don't think you got the stones to pull the trigger."

Morrison's eyes narrowed. "Willing to bet your life on it?"

Bobby Ray was so angry his hands were shaking. As he slid out of his trousers, Morrison stepped back and motioned toward the trunk.

"Nothing inspires cooperation like a loaded gun. I bet you'd hop on one foot and howl at the moon if I asked."

"That's me," Bobby Ray growled. "A regular Fred Astaire."

As he was adding his slacks and loafers to the trunk, Bobby Ray spotted the snub-nosed .38 he was looking for when Morrison interrupted him. The tip of the barrel was poking out from under the spare tire. He grabbed the gun but banged his head on the trunk lid as he straightened up and spun around.

Morrison took a quick step forward and stuck the Sig in his ear. Bobby Ray panicked, squeezed the trigger, and shot off the tip of his big toe. The recoil, coupled with an exquisite bolt of pain, knocked the gun from his hand. The revolver clanked against the pavement and spun to a stop at Elvis's feet.

His toe spurting blood, Bobby Ray hopped around on his good foot howling. Inside the parking garage, they couldn't see the moon, but, as things turned out, on the whole Fred Astaire hopping-and-howling thing, Morrison didn't even have to ask.

Elvis picked up the gun by the skull-and-crossbones grip and sprinted with Morrison past the double doors to the gaming floor toward a wall of service entrances. Morrison spotted one ajar and yanked it open. Inside was a windowless room with chimps and monkeys in cages. The door on the far side was propped open with a mop bucket. As they hurried down the gauntlet of outstretched hands, Elvis slid Bobby Ray's .38 through the bars of one of the cages where it disappeared in the straw and rotting fruit at the bottom.

Elvis tugged Morrison's sleeve. "How about my place till things cool off?" Morrison nodded, and they beelined to the penthouse elevators.

24

Red-hot meteors of pain were exploding like fireworks in Bobby Ray's brain. He propped himself against the Grand Prix and tried not to stare at the blood from his ruined toe puddling on the pavement. A visit to the emergency room would mean a police report, so he stripped to his tank top and wrapped the blood-soaked sock in his shirt.

As he limped awkwardly across the parking garage, he caught the attention of two busboys who had snuck outside for cigarettes. Bobby Ray dragged himself into a service elevator and was punching the fourth-floor button when he saw one of them scurrying in circles like a bow-legged crab with hemorrhoids.

"Not funny," the mobster growled. Their high-pitched giggles faded as the doors wheezed shut. Bobby Ray leaned against the railing and tried to keep the weight off his crudely bandaged foot.

The elevator lurched to a stop on the second floor, and a maid backed in with a cart of linens and toiletries. When she glanced down and noticed the bloody shirt wrapped around Bobby Ray's foot, her face turned as white as her freshly-starched uniform. She frantically punched the door open button, but it was too late. With one hand on the cart, the other clutching the gold cross around her neck, she got off on the next floor without turning around.

When the elevator opened on four, Bobby Ray hobbled to his suite, grabbed two Stolis from the mini bar, and sat down on the toilet. He twisted the lid off the Vicodin on the counter, gobbled a handful like they were M&Ms, and washed them down with vodka.

Bobby Ray grimaced as he wrestled off the bloody shirt and sock, wrapped a hand towel around his foot, and tied the ends together. The stump of his big toe bled steadily into the towel bandage until it looked like a red-faced bunny slipper. He stashed the

Vicodin in his pocket, grabbed the last two Stolis from the mini-fridge, and collapsed on the heart-shaped bed.

Half an hour later, staring at the ceiling in a drug-addled stupor, Bobby Ray heard someone knocking. He covered his face with a pillow, but the knocking got more insistent.

"Commming." Bobby Ray washed down two more Vicodin with Stoli and staggered unsteadily to the door. When he opened it, a tall, platinum blonde chewing an enormous wad of gum was waiting in the hallway. Bobby Ray was staring at her chest, which, with her spiky heels and the difference in their heights, was conveniently at eye level.

She decided the window-shopping segment of their meet-and-greet was over and blew a giant bubble that popped, startling him. "Remember me? Vikki?"

Bobby Ray looked bewildered.

"We met the other day at brunch."

Nothing.

"Bad Dog introduced us."

Still nothing.

"So, we gonna party or what?"

Bobby Ray stared blankly as she strutted across the room and dropped her purse and a nylon gym bag on the nightstand.

"Yeah, s-u-u-ure. Come in, I guess."

"I got here as quickly as I could. I was already in the neighborhood, and the guy downstairs didn't take his full half-hour." She waggled her cell phone at Bobby Ray. "My service called. Floyd said it was an emergency. Sorry about the whole brown-sugar mix-up. Most guys get off on her looking like Whitney Houston." Vikki popped her gum again and looked around. "The honeymoon suite, huh? How romantic."

She sat on the bed, patted the comforter, and motioned for Bobby Ray to join her. As he limped across the room, she glanced at the trail of bloody footprints with casual interest.

"Hangnail," he explained.

275

Not being the curious type, Vikki shrugged. "Well, you got thirty minutes, Sugar. Time's money, and my meter's running."

"Thirty minutes?" Bobby Ray held his watch to his face. "I'm still on New York time."

"Really? You're from New York? I just moved here from Long Island myself." Vikki leaned in and lowered her voice. "I had to relocate on account of having to testify in front of the grand jury. It's worked out great, though. The rooms are first class, and I've met the nicest people." She left out the part about being born Charles Polachowski and that she worked as Cherri after sexual reassignment surgery but before joining WITSEC.

"Speaking of which, we should get down to business." Vikki patted the bed again, and Bobby Ray sat down beside her. She took his glazed expression as an indication she should take charge. "Well, Sugar, you wanted the special, right?" All Bobby Ray could muster was a sloppy grin. "Floyd, my agent, said to give you a discount because of the misunderstanding, not including my gratuity, of course."

Bobby Ray stared blankly in her direction through a thick fog of painkillers.

"You wanted a number eight, right?"

"A number eight?"

"That's the special. I brought the toys." She patted the nylon sports bag.

"Sure. An eight would be great." He managed another sloppy grin.

"Will this be cash, check, or money order? All major credit cards accepted."

Bobby Ray pulled a MasterCard from his wallet and handed it to Vikki, not realizing it was the one Joey found at the Circle K.

"Take off everything but your underwear and lie down on the bed. I'm gonna change in the other room and call my service," she said, waving the credit card.

Bobby Ray undressed and stretched out on the bologna-colored comforter. Vikki emerged a minute later in knee-high boots and a fishnet teddy. She tightly cinched his wrists and the ankle of his good foot to the bedposts with leather belts and strapped a ball gag in his mouth. As soon as he was properly immobilized, she popped a mixtape in a portable boom box and started a slow bump and grind.

Even though Bobby Jr. wasn't showing any interest in joining the party, she slid his underwear around his ankles, reached into her bag, and pulled out a giant, chocolate-colored dildo.

His eyes wide with terror, Bobby Ray twisted his wrists first one way then the other, trying to break free, when a furious pounding on the door interrupted their conjugal visit.

Maimed by trigger-happy lunatics, stoked to the gills on Vicodin, bound to a heart-shaped bed wearing only the boxers around his ankles, and straddled by a half-naked woman waving an enormous dildo, Bobby Ray didn't realize somebody was at the door until after Vikki's dismount. She was halfway across the room, holding the dildo upright like a lit candle before he heard the knocking.

Vikki pressed her eye against the peephole. "Oh, shit. It's my manager."

She opened the door, and a muscle-bound guy the size of a left tackle stormed inside. He crossed the room in three quick strides, shoved aside a pillow, and sat down on the bed. All Bobby Ray could see was his giant, pitted face hovering over him, waving a credit card slip. Floyd leaned over and pulled the gag down around his chin with his index finger.

"We have a problem with your account, Mr. Newman."

"Newman?" Bobby Ray whimpered.

"Mr. MasterCard says thanks, but no thanks."

"There's gotta be a mistake."

The massive figure looming over him nodded. "The mistake is, you're over your limit." He stroked Bobby Ray's cheek with the credit slip as if shaving him with a straight razor, then slid it down to his neck and ripped it across his throat, leaving a paper cut just above his Adam's apple.

Bobby Ray howled and retreated as deeply as he could into his pillow. *I gave her that little prick FBI guy's card,* he realized. "I-I-I can explain."

The pimp pressed his index finger against Bobby Ray's lips. "This is the painful, awkward part of our getting to know each other. I'll tell you what we're gonna do. We're gonna play *Let's Make A Deal*. I'll be Monty Hall, and you'll be some low-life from Iowa."

"New York," Bobby Ray croaked weakly. "I'm from Brooklyn."

"Right. Like I give a shit. Here's the deal. Either you pay this young lady for her time, or you're gonna get what's behind door number one. And, there will be an additional administrative fee because I had to make a service call." He leaned forward until their noses were almost touching. All Bobby Ray could see was his pitted moon face.

The mobster was about to explain how this was a simple misunderstanding when Floyd slapped him hard across the face.

"Go fuck yourself," he growled, forgetting he was bound spread-eagle across the bed with leather bindings.

"Judges, can we have a decision?" The pimp glanced at Vikki, who looked up from the nail she was manicuring and shook her head. "No, I'm sorry. That answer's unacceptable."

Before Bobby Ray could say anything, Floyd yanked the gag over his mouth and popped him hard on the chin with a short jab.

"Wanna go to *Double Jeopardy,* where the money doubles and the scores can really change?"

Bobby Ray tried to answer but, snared in the gag, his lips wouldn't work. *He switched shows*, he was thinking before Floyd punched him again, and he passed out.

Ernie Badoglio was at the desk in his downstairs office. The Itty, Bitty Elvis Contest had been his excuse for missing Fat Tony's party, then he skipped the contest too. He hadn't heard about the midget free-for-all or the damage caused by the fire and flood. If he had any idea how things turned out at Fat Tony's and the Event Center, he would've been drinking a lot faster.

Bad Dog was pouring himself another scotch when he sensed something brush past him. The lingering smell of dope smoke and patchouli oil evoked memories of raked leaves burning as a kid in Flatbush. He pulled open the top drawer of his desk, fished out a dime bag of coke, and slipped it into his jacket pocket. He'd already finished half a bottle of Black Label and didn't realize Jimi had boosted his keys.

Badoglio rarely worked himself into a down-on-his-knees, toilet-hugging drunk but was thinking about grabbing a couple Keno girls and tying one on. Free liquor and cocktail waitresses were his two favorite job perks.

Down the hall, the tiger roared, startling the monkeys and sending them into a screeching panic. The racket went on so long, Bad Dog considered asking security to check on them. But, as a career criminal, his distaste for law enforcement, even in its most insipid form, was too well-developed. It was bad enough he paid rent-a-cops to play grab-ass with the waitresses without having them babysit Fat Tony's pets.

Despite his impressive name, Samson was scrawny and ill-tempered. Months in a cage barely wide enough to turn around had not improved his disposition. Bad Dog wanted to compete with animal acts at other casinos and had orchestrated the tiger's *rescue* after seeing a Diana Woo piece on KVIG. Samson had to be relocated from the single wide in Henderson he shared with his oddball owner after the director of the preschool next door complained.

Fat Tony, who ate a box of Frosted Flakes every morning, wanted to rename the tiger, but the family's lawyers convinced him

Samson looked better on the marquee and would keep the casino out of a lawsuit with Kellogg's.

Since acquiring the tiger, a dozen mangy chimps and monkeys had been scrounged from surplus zoo populations. They were being kept down the hall while their permanent enclosures were completed, but the project kept running into delays. The Venettis always had one more stiff to hide in the concrete footings. Enough bodies had been buried in the foundation to affect structural integrity. Sometimes Bad Dog wondered if he was managing a hotel-casino or a zoo-cemetery.

He was standing to leave when he heard a loud pop that sounded like a gunshot. Samson roared again, sending the primates into another agitated chorus. Bad Dog considered checking himself but decided not investigating meant plausible deniability. He patted his pocket to make sure the coke was still there, switched off the lights, and headed out the door to collect a couple of Keno girls.

25

When he opened his good eye, Bobby Ray was lying face-up on a room service cart, sprawled across a half-eaten pancake breakfast. His other eye, still stinging from a short jab, had swollen shut. He was naked except for his underwear and a blood-soaked towel wrapped around his foot. A massive human being was hovering over him, drizzling maple syrup up and down his body in long, looping swings. It took a moment for his head to clear enough to remember the trouble with the hooker and the FBI guy's credit card.

He tried to sit up, but Floyd pinned him in place with one enormous paw. Barely able to turn his head, Bobby Ray stared helplessly at the ceiling as the pimp rolled the cart to the end of the hallway and unlocked the laundry chute with a maid's key.

"*Bon Voyage*," he crooned sweetly, his cratered face inches above Bobby Ray's.

Vikki leaned over and gave him a peck on the cheek. "Drop us a postcard."

Floyd wedged the cart against the wall, rocked it onto the front wheels with one hand, and dumped Bobby Ray in a harrowing, three-flight freefall into an oversized hamper of pillows. Several exploded on impact, burying him in a swarm of faux feathers that clung to the maple syrup. A maid, who was in the laundry room folding sheets, stood on her tiptoes and peered into the bin.

"*¡Ay Dios mio!*" She clutched the gold crucifix around her neck and pressed it to her lips as she turned and scuttled out the door.

Bobby Ray heard something careening down the chute and looked up as his wallet came hurtling out and hit him squarely between the eyes. It had been turned inside out, and everything was gone, even his Dunkin' Donuts punch card.

"Great. Just great," he grumbled as he swung his legs over the hamper rim and lowered himself to the floor. If he strolled through the casino in his underwear and a downy coat of polyester fiberfill, he would attract unwanted attention, so he wrapped himself sarong-style in a freshly-folded sheet and belted it at the waist with a pillowcase. He grabbed clean towels for bandages and hobbled out the door opposite the maid's exit like a short, round Dorothy Lamour in molt.

The door slammed shut and locked behind him before Bobby Ray realized it led to the parking garage. A steady stream of Itty, Bitty Elvis refugees was trudging past, and he nearly ran into an elderly couple and a thigh-high impersonator in a sequined, white jumpsuit. The woman stopped and stared at Bobby Ray.

"Whaddya looking at, lady?" he growled. Before she could answer, he stormed off along the wall of service entrances, leaving a contrail of shed plumage in his wake.

On the third try, he found an unlocked door and limped into a room with monkeys in wheeled cages arranged in narrow rows. A howler stuck his hand through the bars, begging for food. When none was forthcoming, the monkey tried to urinate on him. Bobby Ray barely had time to sidestep the acrid, yellow stream in time.

"You peeing on *me*?" he snarled. The monkey made a face and hooted softly. "Then who the hell else you peeing on? I'm the only one here." Bobby Ray held his hand like a gun and aimed his index finger at the howler.

In a classic bit of monkey-see-monkey-do, the howler rooted through the debris at the bottom of his cage and recovered the gun Elvis had hidden there. He pointed the .38 at the gangster, who recognized the skull-and-crossbones tape on the grip.

Before he had a chance to wonder how a monkey got his gun, the howler pulled the trigger and shot off the big toe of his good foot. Ripped away by the recoil, the pistol banged loudly through the bars and clattered to the floor. The gunshot, Bobby Ray's scream, and a roaring tiger set off every primate in the place. In a bizarrely choreographed dance, the mobster and the monkeys jumped up and down, shrieking and flailing their arms.

His teeth clenched in pain, Bobby Ray crawled under the baboon's cage and retrieved the revolver, took dead aim, and shot the howler in the chest. The tiger roared, setting off another round of monkey howls. He tucked the gun in his pillowcase belt, squatted on the floor, and wrapped his freshly wounded foot in a towel. Blood soaked through the terry cloth even before Bobby Ray could drag himself to the service elevator.

When the lift stopped on three and the doors slid open, he recognized the maid from the laundry room. She stood frozen, clutching her crucifix, and made no attempt to get in before the doors closed.

Bobby Ray got out on four and was hobbling to his room when he ran into Harper Valentine, the Hitler twins accomplice at the rental car agency. He was leaving the escort service another message. It had been thirty minutes since they sent a black woman by mistake, and a different girl was supposed to be over right away. He didn't care who thought she looked like Whitney Houston. He needed his pipes cleaned, not his room. When Valentine looked up and saw Bobby Ray wrapped in a bedsheet, covered head-to-toe with white feathers, wearing red bunny slippers, he burst out laughing.

In no mood to see the humor in the situation, Bobby Ray yanked the .38 from the pillowcase belted around his waist and fired twice. The first bullet burrowed into the wall at the far end of the hallway. The second pierced the cartoon heart on Valentine's *I Love Las Vegas* T-shirt, nicked the pulmonary artery underneath, and severed his aorta.

After they got back from dumping dry ice in the tea garden, Jimi decided to hang out with the animals while Ishmael finished his shift. He had the GM's keys and was working on a plan to liberate the monkeys when Bobby Ray showed up. When the mobster shot the howler, he was standing close enough to be splattered with blood and bits of fur.

Jimi followed Bobby Ray to the service elevator and watched the blinking light on the overhead panel stop, start, and then stop again. "Three or four," he muttered softly.

He pushed the call button and, after the elevator headed back down, retraced his steps and unlocked the monkey cages one by one. The troupe gathered around the dead howler, hooting mournfully. They reached through the bars to stroke his fur, then linked arms, including Jimi's, and formed a circle.

With Samson facing forward like the dragon prow on a Viking ship, Jimi and the primate posse used the tow bar to steer the cage through the door, down the hallway, and into the elevator. Jimi decided on the fourth floor after he saw the red smudge on the button.

When the doors opened on four, he followed the trail of bloody footprints and felt, as much as heard, Samson's low, guttural growl as the cage rolled past Valentine's body. The monkeys pressed themselves against the wall and slipped by, hooting softly.

The bloody trackway led to the Honeymoon Suite. Jimi maneuvered Samson's cage until it aligned with the door, wedged it against the jambs, and set the hand brake. As he unlocked the safety bar and raised the gate, the monkeys crowded around him. Jimi knocked but got no response and knocked louder a second time until he heard footsteps on the other side. Samson crouched low on his haunches like a tightly wound spring.

As the door opened and he saw the expression on Bobby Ray's face, Jimi was wishing he had a camera. It was definitely a Kodak moment.

Bobby Ray squatted beside the heart-shaped Jacuzzi, floundering in a cocktail of Stoli and Vicodin. His face contorted with pain, he wrestled the bandages from his feet. Blood oozed from the mangled stubs of his big toes and pooled in the channels between the tiles. He needed something more absorbent than a hotel towel, so he hobbled to the phone and called room service. The kid who answered sounded sixteen.

"Gimme a box of Super Maxi Pads."

"Yes, sir. Your room number, please?"

"Four-Twenty."

"I'll run them right up." He heard snickering in the kid's voice and knew what he was thinking: *they're in a Honeymoon Suite, and she's on the rag.*

Bobby Ray retrieved the Vicodin from the robe he'd left crumpled on the floor and washed down another handful with the last of the vodka. He didn't realize there was someone at the door until they knocked again. As he limped across the room, Bobby Ray sidestepped the ball gag the hooker had left accidentally. By the time he got to the door, he was hoping it was Vikki, back to make amends and not the kid with the Maxi Pads.

She reminded him of Julie Newmar. In high school, Bobby Ray fixated on the actress. When Aunt Nympha got home with weekend groceries and the *TV Guide*, he always checked if Catwoman was the coming week's *Batman* villain and never missed her episodes. As he twisted the knob, Bobby Ray caught a whiff of singed cat fur, another staple of his teenage years.

"Here kitty, kitty," he mumbled woozily under his breath.

26

When he got the call about the Tahitian Princess homicides, Hennigan cut his workout short, showered and changed into street clothes, and drove straight from the gym. As he was getting off the elevator, he nearly ran into Officer Martinez, who was interviewing a freckle-faced kid in a hotel tunic. The boy was clutching a box of Maxi Pads so tightly against his chest, he'd crushed the packaging. The Littles were several doors down, waiting their turn. Gladys waved as soon as she saw him.

"Hello, Detective," she cooed.

"Good evening, Mrs. Little."

"We're having quite the visit."

"Yes, ma'am, I'd say you are." Hennigan glanced over his shoulder. "If you'll excuse me, I think Officer Martinez is ready for your statements."

Down the hallway, Costanza knelt beside a body draped in a bedsheet. "I believe you know the Littles," he said without looking up. "They found the body."

"Yes, we've met."

"The kid's with room service. He came along right after they did."

Hennigan peeled back the bedsheet. "So, whatta we got here?"

"Harper Valentine. His driver's license has a Henderson address. The front desk confirmed that's his room." Costanza jerked his thumb toward the open door behind him. "Judging by the hole in his chest, I'm guessing a .38. There's two hundred bucks in his wallet, so we're probably not looking at a robbery."

"Harper Valentine? Why's that name sound familiar?"

"Ran his record. When you were in uniform, you busted him twice – solicitation and a DUI."

"Local boy makes good or at least the coroner's log. Speaking of which, are they here yet?"

"Wexler told me to take a number and stand in line. Apparently, you've been keeping him extra busy." Costanza stood up and scribbled something in his notes. "You okay? You seem grumpier than usual."

"Sorry. I was supposed to have Amanda this weekend. Her mom called last minute and left a message not to pick her up."

"What's her excuse this time?"

"She didn't leave one and isn't returning my calls. For now, let's just focus on the homicides."

"Sure. Follow me. You're gonna wanna see this." Costanza started down the hallway, showing no particular concern about treading on the bloody trackway, and stopped in front of the Honeymoon suite.

"Fugitive monkeys," he said cryptically, pointing to the red footprints congregating in front of the door.

"Fugitive monkeys?

Costanza nodded. "They followed the second victim here. The lines are from the wheels."

Hennigan poked his head inside the door. "The wheels on *that*?" he asked, pointing at the cage beside the heart-shaped bed, Inside, a tiger was lying on his back, snoring loudly.

"He was asleep on the bed when Martinez and I got here. Since we were absent the day they taught tiger wrangling at the academy, we waited outside until the handler arrived. He darted him and, with help from some *very* anxious maintenance guys, used the comforter like a sling and slid him into the cage."

There were more gunshots upstairs, and they both flinched.

"What the…"

"I'm getting to that part. There's a hostage situation one floor up. The FBI was already setting up a command post in the stairwell when we got here."

"We can worry about upstairs later. For now, that's the fed's problem."

"You're the detective." Costanza fished his notepad from his pocket. "I already talked to NYPD. The vic's a greaseball named Bobby Ray Darling, an enforcer for the Venettis. He's got a police file as thick as a five-borough phone book. He did two years in Attica for loan sharking and four more at Lompoc for racketeering."

"Sounds like a model citizen."

Costanza flipped the page in his notes. "The suspect's a 600-pound Bengal tiger named Samson. Judging by the blood evidence, he jumped Darling by the door and dragged him poolside for a midnight snack."

Hennigan glanced at a lumpy pile of blood-soaked sheets by the Jacuzzi. "How thoughtful. Getting blood stains outta shag's a real bitch." Samson stirred and made a noise between a snore and a growl.

"The third homicide's a monkey shot dead downstairs."

"The same shooter as the guy in the hallway?"

"We won't know for sure if the slug in the howler matches Valentine's until we hear back from ballistics, but that would be my guess."

"Have you checked the tapes?"

Costanza pointed to the eye-in-the-sky about halfway to the elevator. "Except for the gaming floor, most of the cameras are just for show. There's a working one in the room with the monkeys. Dad ran the video and thinks whatever happened started off-camera."

"And the monkey got caught in the crossfire?"

Costanza shook his head. "Near as dad could tell, there was nobody but Darling and the howler."

"He thinks the vic got into an argument with the monkey and shot him?"

"Actually, it looks like the monkey shot Darling first, probably in the foot or lower leg. He's limping in the video. The blood in the elevator and most of the blood in the hallway is his."

"So, Darling shot the monkey then made good his escape with a caged tiger in hot pursuit?"

"That's the story the blood trail tells." Hennigan started to say something, but Costanza held up his hands. "Just following the evidence."

Hennigan bent down and studied the bloody footprints clustered outside the suite. "And you think monkeys fed the mobster to a tiger?"

"Until you come up with a better story, I'm going with vigilante justice monkey-style."

"Have suspects been rounded up and hauled downtown for questioning?"

Costanza shook his head. "They're upstairs, holding hostages at gunpoint." He aimed an index finger at the ceiling and grinned.

"The FBI standoff? You're *not* serious."

"Just the facts, ma'am. Nothing but the facts." Costanza held up his hand, palm forward like he was getting ready to testify.

There was another round of gunfire and dull footfalls of men running upstairs. Hennigan stared at the ceiling and imagined the Wicked Witch's henchmen from the *Wizard of Oz* with automatic weapons.

Life was imitating art again.

Verduci went straight from Fat Tony's party to the Gulfstream IV waiting at McCarran. While the crew readied for takeoff, he called the Tahitian Princess and told housekeeping to ship his things to DC. By the time they landed at Dulles, he was so drunk he had to be carried off the plane.

It was nearly noon by the time Verduci showered and dressed. He was slumped over the desk, his head cradled in his hands, mustering the strength to listen to his intern. Jaysen was getting him up to speed on White House gossip. His rant about the president wasn't helping Verduci's hangover.

"My God, you know how the man is. You can't say 'good morning' and get a straight answer." When Jaysen laughed, it sounded like he was snorting coke. "And the country practically worships the guy. You gotta wonder if the rumor party hacks are putting something in the water's true."

Verduci washed down another handful of aspirin with two fingers of Chivas and waggled his empty glass. "Be a good boy and fix me another, would you?"

Jaysen grabbed fresh ice and poured two more fingers of scotch. Verduci stared suspiciously at the drink.

I wonder how long it will take whatever's in the water to worm its way into my system if I only drink single malt? He scooped the ice cubes out with his fingers and tossed them in the wastebasket.

Jaysen pretended not to notice. "The president's taken a personal interest in the Jamaica mission."

Verduci upended his glass, drained the scotch in one gulp, and coughed into his fist. "All right, I'm fortified. Give it to me."

"He suggested we beam in, said it would give us *the element of surprise*."

"He's been watching *Star Trek* again, hasn't he?"

"Judging by the conversation we had yesterday, I'd guess the entire weekend marathon."

Verduci buried his face in his hands again. "Maybe he should go, and I'll stay here and watch TV."

Jaysen poured him another two fingers of scotch. "I could come with you."

"To watch *Star Trek*?"

"No, silly. Jamaica." Jaysen balanced himself on the arm of the chair, pointed his chin toward the crown molding, and shook out his hair.

Verduci sat up a little straighter. Images of his intern in cammies made his pulse quicken. "You've been there, right?"

290

"Yes, when I was nine. I went with daddy dearest and stepmom number three."

"Your firsthand experience would be invaluable, but you'd have to be suitably attired, of course."

"I'll see the White House tailor this afternoon and get fitted. Where are your back issues of *Soldier of Fortune*?"

"There's one on the nightstand and a stack on the floor in the closet." Verduci glanced at his watch. "We'd better get ready. I'm supposed to brief the Cabinet in a few minutes."

"Can't we just cozy up in front of a warm fire? Hanging out with those guys is like getting drunk with derelict alumni during homecoming week."

Verduci managed a lop-sided grin. "But they're the president's *trusted* advisors, selfless patriots who've dedicated their lives to public service. It says so in the White House tour brochure." Jaysen scowled but didn't say anything. "The vice president's still outta the country, right?"

"At a trade conference in Jakarta."

"Good. Meetings are more cordial without that wet blanket."

"Sugarman won't be there either."

"The Interior Secretary?"

Jaysen nodded. "He was indicted. Oil lease kickbacks."

Verduci slid his empty glass on the desk and stared at it glumly. "Anybody won your frat house pool yet?"

"You mean Indictment Bingo?"

Verduci nodded.

"Not yet. But some of us are *really* close." He smoothed Verduci's collar and straightened his tie. "So, what are you gonna to say?"

"Same as always: something vague about grave consequences and national security, then open things up for bickering." He dragged himself to the bar, filled his glass with the last of the Chivas, and motioned for Jaysen to follow. In the Cabinet Room, Verduci took his place at the table. While everybody settled in, he fortified himself with more scotch.

"The president sends his regrets for not being here personally." Verduci neglected to mention McDannold was in the theater room watching *Star Trek*.

"Gentlemen." The word hung in the air. He always started that way, believing it gave meetings a sense of shared purpose.

"We have a situation." He always said that next. He thought that gave things a sense of urgency. After a suitable pause, he leaned forward and tapped his index finger on the table like a revivalist preacher thumping a Bible. "And I'm confident we have a solution."

The few cabinet members paying attention looked up, surprised. Wallace Hartley, the Attorney General, who was playing a handheld, video poker game, gasped. He couldn't have been more startled if Verduci had announced he was feeding the multitudes with a tin of sardines and a loaf of Wonder Bread.

"This is going to require all of our special skills."

"You mean besides being able to make a passable martini?" Hayden Price, the Defense Secretary, quipped.

Verduci glanced at his nearly empty glass. "Capital idea, Mr. Secretary." He pushed his chair back and rubbed his palms together. "Before going any further, I propose we whip up a batch or two. Anyone else like a martini?"

"I second the motion," Price said as he led the stampede to the wet bar. Verduci shook the shaker until everyone had filled, emptied, and refilled their glasses.

"Recent developments too sensitive to discuss here have made Jamaica strategically critical." Verduci paused long enough to sip his cocktail. "In consultation with the Chairman of the Joint Chiefs, the president has authorized a plan to invade Jamaica and annex the island as the fifty-first state."

A low murmur rumbled around the room. "Exactly what sort of government's down there now?" asked the HEW Secretary. He was black, and the chief of staff hadn't bothered learning his name.

Verduci shook his head. "No idea. I don't like getting bogged down in details."

Defense Secretary Price pinched the toothpick between his thumb and forefinger and raked the olives off with his teeth. "There is a plan, though, *right*?"

Verduci nodded. "Our departure point's an airbase in south Florida. We'll establish a beachhead on the south side of the island and secure a base of operations within striking distance of Kingston. From there, under cover of darkness, we'll target key military and government installations and overwhelm opposition forces."

"That's it? That's your entire half-assed strategy?" Rowland Talmage, the Secretary of State, grumbled. "Our boys stumbling around in the dark with their dicks in their hands isn't much of a plan."

Verduci clenched his teeth so tightly, his cheeks puckered. "I want our field commanders to have operational flexibility," he said as calmly as he could manage.

Hands on his hips, Jaysen fired an incendiary scowl in the Secretary's direction. "Besides, *we're* going to be there personally to oversee the mission."

The Defense Secretary drained his glass. "Well, Carmine, if your mastery of a cocktail shaker's an indication of your skills, I have every faith in our success."

"Thanks, Hayden." Verduci packed the shaker with fresh ice, gin, and dry vermouth, shook it vigorously and refilled the Secretary's glass. After a few more rounds, the mood in the meeting room grew noticeably more relaxed.

Hartley produced a black lacquered humidor from under the bar and raised the lid. "Cohiba Espléndido, anyone?"

Verduci peered into the open box. "Cubans?"

The Attorney General grinned. "No, Carmine, evidence. Customs seized them from a Dominican ballplayer at Miami International."

Verduci plucked one from the box and slid it back and forth under his nose. "I'd hate to have you smoke alone." Most of the Cabinet members joined him, except the Secretary of State, who had dozed off and was snoring loudly. Verduci bent over and blew a cloud of smoke his direction. "But he didn't inhale," he chuckled.

Hartley wiped a dribble of brown spittle from his chin. "The gentleman who brought us these fine cigars had a bottle of mud-colored potion in his bag. When the customs agent opened it and took a sniff, the guy started shouting he needed it to be *strong like bull*. It took six guys to wrestle it away from him."

Verduci vigorously shook another batch of martinis. "Like a testosterone-Viagra cocktail?"

"Hell, it could be sheep jizz for all I know, but the customs agent's sprouting man-boobs." Hartley took another puff on his Cohiba. "We should swing by my office. His supervisor sent pictures."

Hayden drained the last of his martini and grinned like a sushi chef's cat. "Lead on, my good man."

"And while we're there, the Coast Guard boarded a sloop yesterday and confiscated two tons of Haitian Chronic." Hartley winked slyly. "I saved a couple bricks in the evidence locker."

"That reminds me," Verduci said as he emptied his glass, "the code name for the Jamaica mission is Operation Cannabis."

There were more gunshots upstairs. Hennigan instinctively reached for his sidearm.

"Two for flinching," Costanza teased.

A little self-consciously, Hennigan straightened up again. "I'm guessing the feds are treating this like every other hostage situation?"

Costanza nodded. "Right outta their playbook. They've isolated the abductors and are waiting for demands. Oh, and one more thing, the new guy's in charge."

"Newmeat?"

"He was jogging when he got the call. You know how FBI guys *love* to exercise." He made a face when he said "exercise" like it left a bitter aftertaste. "A horny but nearsighted baboon mistook Newmeat's red shorts as a sign of his amorous availability. It took three burly agents to pry them apart. It probably didn't help they were laughing their asses off. The whole thing would be hysterical if not for the hostages.

"How the hell did monkeys get guns?"

"While Samson was turning the late, great Mafioso into a bedtime snack, the monkeys raided his personal armory. He packed enough firepower to start a war. One of the spotters told me a trigger happy chimp blew a hole in the door the size of a basketball with a 12-gauge." There was more muffled shouting and Newmeat's high-pitched squeals on a bullhorn.

Hennigan glanced at the ceiling again. "Anything on the hostages?"

"The room's registered to Richard Little, a hotshot Beverly Hills plastic surgeon."

Hennigan massaged his temples between his thumb and forefinger. "Any relation to Gladys and Elmo?"

"Their son. I interviewed him at the demolition derby."

"Right. I remember now. Somebody should say something before they leave."

"Be my guest, but I'm pretty sure the doctor's lady friend's a hooker. One of the bellboys told me her name's Vikki. Apparently, she's a regular around here."

The ME's guys had bagged Valentine's body and were loading it onto a gurney. "Any idea how a two-bit hustler got himself gunned down by a mobbed-up greaseball?"

"Not really. I'm guessing he was just in the proverbial wrong place at the wrong time."

Hennigan quickly did the math in his head: a really bad guy killed a sort of bad guy, then a tiger ate the really bad guy. He didn't know about the stolen Grand Prix and the *almost* instant karma part. Getting shot dead for grand theft auto might have been a knee-jerk overreaction, but for a lapsed Catholic, Hennigan was a quick study.

27

Morrison phoned Sparkle as soon as he and Elvis got to the penthouse suite. She seemed anxious when he told her about the near-riot at the Itty Bitty Elvis Contest, so he decided not to mention the shooting in the parking garage. By the time they hung up, Elvis had stretched out on the living room floor and fallen asleep.

Morrison ordered a club sandwich from the room service menu and ate it watching *Saturday Night Live*. By the closing credits, he'd decided the coast was as clear as it was going to get and called Sparkle to let her know he was on his way. He grabbed a taxi in front of the casino, completely unaware police were investigating two homicides, one tiger-involved, or that the FBI was in a hostage situation with armed and dangerous monkeys.

It was already mid-morning when Sparkle and Morrison trudged downstairs. They stopped in the kitchen long enough to start water for tea and say hello to Moby and the Ahabs who were making coffee. From the living room, they could see the Littles and a dozen Viking couples through the chapel doors. They were clustered around boxes of doughnuts, chatting with Digby and Itty Bitty Elvis contestants.

Elvis was watching the news with Jimi, or so Morrison assumed from the sag in the sofa beside him. Before he could ask what was going on, the door banged open, and Jaxx bounded in with Honey in tow and the Hitler twins close behind.

"We took your dog for a walk. I hope you don't mind." She unhooked the leash and was handing it to Morrison when her hand brushed against his.

He glanced at Sparkle and wondered how much she'd told her. "Not at all. I'm sure he was happy to get out."

She wrapped her arms around Morrison and gave him a hug. "Thanks for coming to our rescue."

"I'm not sure how much I helped, but I'm glad everything turned out okay."

"Handsome *and* modest, Mom. This one might be a keeper."

Sparkle cupped her hand over her mouth, hiding a smile. "Well, he's too big to throw back."

Elvis yawned and stretched, pretending to notice Sparkle and Morrison for the first time. "Well, good afternoon. Nice of you to join us." She smiled sheepishly and raked her hair back with her fingers.

Morrison jerked his chin toward the congregation milling around the Chapel d'Love. "So, what's all this?"

"The great gathering of the tribe," Elvis answered, grinning.

Before Morrison could ask what he meant, he recognized Helmut Schmidt on TV. He had on the same crushed-velvet tuxedo he was wearing at the midget Elvis free-for-all. His eyes were bloodshot, and his crewcut had wilted. He was trying to spin a news story about gun-toting monkeys as a wacky publicity stunt and didn't mention a tiger had eaten a guest.

Morrison was picturing a swarm of chimps with automatic weapons terrorizing the casino when the station broke for a commercial. After the local Ford dealer finished hawking cars, the morning anchor told viewers a local man had been shot dead outside his room at the Tahitian Princess.

Gladys, who had joined them with her husband and several Viking wives, clapped her hands with excitement. "Elmo and I found the body," she said, pointing at the TV.

"The two policemen and the nice detective from the Circle K were there too," Elmo added. "They took our statements and everything. Third time this week."

Sparkle chuckled softly. "This has certainly been a memorable visit."

"That's what the detective said. We were going to see Dickie but got off on the wrong floor." Gladys squeezed her husband's hand. "Elmo meant to push five but pushed four instead."

One of the wives took Gladys by the arm and pulled her toward their circle. "You just *have* to tell us everything."

Sparkle nodded. "It's okay. I have hostess duties. We can catch up later." She heard the kettle whistling and was headed to the kitchen when there was a sharp rap of knuckles on the door. When she opened it, half a dozen grim but determined Navy SEALs were standing on the porch.

Morrison motioned Geronimo and the rest of the team inside. "I'm guessing this isn't a social call."

"Roger, that. Things in Washington are ramping up faster than expected." The SEAL commander looked around the living room at the eclectic assortment of people gathered there. "You need to get to high ground as quickly as possible. Everyone here is either at risk or crucial to the mission."

"The *mission*?"

"Uncle Sam's proprietary about what's his, and sooner than later, he's gonna want his invisible man back." Geronimo glanced at the patchouli-scented sag in the sofa. "But we have a more pressing problem: the White House is planning to invade Jamaica and annex the island as the fifty-first state."

There was an audible gasp, then everyone started talking at once. Morrison held his hands up until things quieted down, then turned back to Geronimo. "Why the sudden interest in Jamaica?"

The couch cushions sighed softly as Jimi stood up. "McCullough wants Jamaica for his invisible army. He has research that suggests invisibility works best on Rastafarians who play video games."

"We're invading Jamaica so he can draft stoners hunched over *Pac Man* with Bob Marley leaking from their headphones?"

Jimi chuckled. "*Pac Man*? Dude, you *are* old."

"All I meant was—"

Geronimo cut him off. "Like any strategic resource, the government wants control." He motioned to CJ, who handed him a map. He unfolded it on the coffee table and pointed to a spot east of town. "We're bivouacked about twenty clicks up the road." He turned toward Sparkle. "You know where Sleeping Indian Mesa is?"

She nodded. "I hike there sometimes when it's not too hot."

"You need to get everybody there now."

"How will we find you?"

"Don't worry. Once you're close, we'll find you."

Morrison leaned over to get a better view of the map. "So, what's the plan?"

"Operational details haven't been fleshed out, but in broad strokes, we're gonna requisition a plane from Nellis, fly to Jamaica, and thwart an invasion by the most powerful military force on the planet."

Moby stepped forward. "Sounds like a hoot. Where do we sign up?"

He and Geronimo shook hands. "Appreciate you volunteering. With Jamaican nationals in command positions, the rest of us can be there in a strictly *advisory* role."

Elmo shuffled toward the SEAL commander. "Count me in too. I swore an oath to uphold the constitution, and after teaching high school civics for forty-three years, I'm pretty sure I've read the fine print."

A slightly stooped man a little taller than Elmo stepped up and stood beside him. "I don't care how tightly they wrap themselves in the flag, what those Washington boys are fixin' to do is just not right."

Elmo nodded in agreement. "Everybody's gonna have to speak for themselves, but I'll do what I've always done: size up the situation and choose sides."

Geronimo started to object, but Elmo interrupted him. "The Monday after Pearl Harbor, I lied about my age, joined the Marines, and spent the next three and a half years in the backseat of a dive bomber, dodging flak and Zeros and sending as many Jap ships as I could to the bottom of the sea." He gestured toward the man beside him. "Tom Martin here skippered a Higgins boat on every major landing in the Pacific."

"Beached some of the first Marines on Iwo Jima," Martin added, "and spent three days before that helping UDT teams clear the way."

Elmo nodded toward a tall, thin man standing beside the couch. "Before Doc Jensen was an orthodontist, he was a second lieutenant and bombardier in the Army Air Corps. The war ended the week his B-29 squadron left for Tinian in the Marianas. They were gonna soften things up for the invasion of the Japanese home islands."

Elmo glanced around the room until his eyes settled on a burly, dark-haired guy fiddling with the horned helmet squeezed between his hands. He looked a few years younger than the other Vikings. "Magnus, no time for false modesty. Hike up your shirt and turn around." He flashed a grizzled smile and did as he was asked. "See the nickel-sized scar halfway down the left side of his rib cage? That's a souvenir from a Russian burp gun he picked up at the Chosin Reservoir when ten Chinese divisions came a-calling. Magnus was a platoon leader in Recon Company, First Marine Division. When his unit pulled back, he dressed the wound in the least muddy T-shirt he could find and hiked out under his own power. There's another dozen stories here. I can keep going if you like."

"I meant no disrespect," Geronimo said. "I just figured you've earned the right to sit one out."

Elmo's flinty blue eyes narrowed. "Commander Nieto, this country was not built by men who *sat one out*. Every man here is a caretaker of that legacy."

"Well then, welcome aboard." Geronimo gave him a crisp salute. One of the Vikings toward the back raised his hand. "Maybe we should nuke the place first to soften things up?"

Geronimo shook his head. "No unnecessary collateral damage. We want to *save* Jamaica, not bomb the country back to the Stone Age. We're going in strictly small arms, just a simple insertion and extraction."

Morrison's brow furrowed. "What exactly are we extracting?"

"The head of the United States invasion forces or a reasonable facsimile thereof." Geronimo glanced toward Honey.

"Need a war correspondent?" she asked.

Geronimo grinned. "Rumor has it, you've done some work in front of the camera."

"Just stuff for class at the college TV station."

"Bring your makeup bag and something nice to wear. You're gonna be the *very* pretty face of our adventure." Honey was blushing as Virgil grabbed Be-Bop by the collar and yanked him out of his chair. "Our camera gear's in the car. We can be her film crew."

"Perfect," Geronimo said as they shook hands.

Atlas burrowed through the sea of legs and tugged on the SEAL's shirtsleeve to get his attention. "Got room for us?" he asked hopefully.

Geronimo knelt so they could be eye to eye. "God made big men, and God made little men, then Colt made the .45, and they're all the same size." He unholstered his sidearm and handed it to Atlas. "It's a 9mm, but you can trade it for the 1911 I have at camp."

Atlas raised the pistol over his head and wheeled around as the little Elvises stood as one and pumped their fists in the air.

Sparkle and Elvis were inside with Digby marrying a middle-aged couple from Frognot, Texas. Morrison was anxious to get everyone else to the SEAL camp and had made a command decision: the others shouldn't wait. He tugged on the brim of his baseball cap as

Honey, Jaxx, and the Hitler twins pulled away from the curb. They'd commandeered Sparkle's pickup, piling clothes and audio-video equipment in the back.

Jimi, Moby, and the Ahabs were right behind them in the band's Econoline van. Moby clutched the steering wheel in one hand and a huge, smoldering spliff in the other. Morrison tugged his cap again as Elmo rolled past, hooting and waving his horned helmet out the window. The rest of the Viking RVs and the little Elvises fell in behind them.

As the tightly-grouped caravan wound around the corner and disappeared, Morrison hurried up the sidewalk. He waited anxiously on the porch until Digby, still dressed as Reverend Elvis, emerged behind the newlyweds in matching powder-blue tuxes and white cowboy hats. Inside, Morrison found Sparkle frantically rifling through her purse.

"I can't find Honey's keys anywhere."

"We have to find them. The limo's dead."

Sparkle bit her lip and took a deep breath. "It's okay. We can take Dad's car."

They collected their bags and hurried down the garden path toward the garage. Morrison grabbed the handle with both hands and heaved open the door. It swung up in a wide arc and banged heavily against the frame.

Inside, covered with dust and cobwebs, was a Citroën 2CV. Morrison recognized the make and model from his time in Paris. The car resembled a squared-up VW's ugly stepsister. Built right after the war, the paint had faded to jaundiced shades of mustard. He shaded his eyes and peered in the window. The seats looked like old lawn chairs: simple metal frames with taut strips of canvas woven between coiled springs.

"I know what you're thinking, but it runs better than it looks," Sparkle reassured him.

Morrison forced a smile. "If we make it to the end of the driveway, it runs better than it looks."

Sparkle rolled her eyes. "While you pack our things in the trunk, I'm going to light a fire under Dad and Elvis." Morrison snapped to attention and saluted. Hands on her hips, Sparkle scowled in mock anger. "When we get back, remind me to have you court-martialed."

"Yes, ma'am," Morrison grinned. He watched until she turned the corner then rearranged the tiny trunk's contents to make room for their bags.

Elvis arrived first and squeezed into the rear seat with his computer and backpack. Digby was right behind him. He'd unbuttoned his cleric collar but was still wearing the pompadour. Morrison crammed his things into what little space was left and slammed the trunk.

Sparkle materialized behind them. "Did you pack extra socks and underwear?" Digby shook his head. "We'll make do somehow." As he was sorting through his keys, she plucked them from his hand. "I'll drive," she said firmly.

"This car has *lots* of idiosyncrasies."

"It's okay. I'll manage."

Digby reluctantly wedged himself beside Elvis as Sparkle slid behind the wheel. To her visible relief, the car started on the first try. She released the hand brake, shifted into reverse, and eased the Citroën down the driveway.

Morrison slammed the garage shut and hurried to join them. His senses were under assault as soon as he opened the door. The Citroën smelled like somebody had killed a walrus and left it to ripen through the long, hot summer. As he slid inside, there was another nasty surprise: the seat-pad felt like it had been upholstered with the beast's warty hide. It was bristly enough to cause abrasions. He rolled down the window and gasped for air. Digby had retrofitted the car with air conditioning, which Morrison cranked up full blast but left the window open.

The drive through town was a white-knuckle ride. Sparkle drove with minimal regard for stop signs, speed limits, traffic lights, pedestrians, or other cars. They were nearly to the freeway when she stopped for traffic across the median from a Ford Explorer headed the opposite direction. Sparkle and Morrison spotted Orange and Newmeat the same time Orange spotted them.

"Uh-oh…" Morrison pointed out the window. "We've got company."

"Hang on," Sparkle warned unnecessarily. She squeezed the Citroën between a minivan and the curb, ran a red light, and accelerated onto the freeway.

As soon as there was a break in traffic, the Explorer clambered over the median and chased the Citroën down the on-ramp.

28

The hostage situation at the Tahitian Princess was resolved without further loss of life because of Orange's expert negotiating skills. At least that's how he planned to spin it in his report. He was also going to say Newmeat was wounded in the line of duty, which was mostly true. After all the monkeys were rounded up and disarmed, he accidentally shot himself in the foot. His wound was nearly identical to the one inflicted on Bobby Ray by the howler.

When the hospital released him nearly ten hours later, Orange loaded his partner into the Explorer like an unwieldy sack of potatoes and belted him into his seat. Newmeat was so doped up on oxycodone, he could barely hold up his head.

"We're gonna be stuck in Montana keeping tabs on white supremacists the rest of our careers," Orange groaned as they slowed for a light.

"Are there monkeys in Montana?" Newmeat's eyelids ratcheted slowly shut and then open again.

"Mostly cows, I think."

"Good. Cows are better." Newmeat fumbled with the lid on the painkillers but lacked the dexterity to pry it open. Foiled by the childproof packaging, he stared at his bandaged foot until his eyes rolled back and only the whites showed. A thin ribbon of drool ran from the corner of his mouth and pooled on his shirt.

"At least we didn't get handcuffed to a toilet," Orange muttered. That morning an envelope of "crime scene" photos was delivered to his office. He propped his glasses on his forehead and pinched the bridge of his nose between his thumb and index finger.

The news guys are gonna have a field day with trigger-happy monkeys. God help us if they get ahold of those pictures.

"I hate the First Amendment," he grumbled under his breath.

Orange was contemplating early retirement when he glanced across the median at a rusted, yellow Citroën idling at the light. He immediately recognized the two suspects from the Circle K sitting in the car, their female accomplice, and an as-of-yet unidentified man in a black pompadour and cleric's collar.

Sparkle's eyes darted back and forth between the road and the Explorer she was tracking in the rearview mirror. Less than a quarter mile back, the FBI guys were closing fast. As she was checking the speedometer, she realized the gas gauge was nearly on empty.

"Daddy," she pleaded, "please tell me the gas gauge is broken."

"No, Sweetheart. It's working just fine."

"You told me you filled the tank the last time you drove the car." She was trying to sound calm, but the alarm was evident in her voice.

"I did. A whole gallon."

"A whole gallon! When we run out of gas, the people behind us are going to make things *very* unpleasant."

"We *won't* run out of gas," Digby answered peevishly this time.

Sparkle glared at him in the mirror. "We're running on fumes. We're sure as hell going to run out of gas!"

"We *won't* run out of gas," he repeated firmly. "And don't curse." He rested his forehead on the window glass. "Isn't the desert lovely this time of year?"

Sparkle checked the rearview again. The Explorer was less than a hundred yards back. "We're ten miles from the SEAL camp. We'll never make it."

"Of course, we will. I fixed the engine."

"Daddy, what did you do?"

"You know how I hate stopping for gas now that all the stations are self-serve?"

"Yes, right, self-serve." Sparkle glanced in the rearview mirror. The hundred-yard gap had been halved.

"I fixed the engine so we'll get a thousand miles to a gallon. The tank's smaller, and a gallon's all it will hold, but we don't have to stop as often. I can explain how it works if you like, but if you're in a hurry, throw that switch by your right knee."

The FBI car was less than twenty-five yards back. "This one, by the ignition?"

Digby rocked forward so he could see over Morrison's shoulder. "Right. If you pull it toward you, it will open the valve on the nitrous tank."

Sparkle met her father's eyes in the mirror and smiled. The Explorer was within a couple of car lengths. "I love you," she mouthed softly.

"I love you too. Also, it'd be a good idea if everybody grabbed something to hold onto."

Not waiting for permission, Morrison reached across Sparkle's knee and snapped the switch open. This time when she floored the gas pedal, the Citroën surged forward, hurtling furiously down the desert highway like a pop bottle rocket. Knobs shook off the radio and jitterbugged around the floor. The car was shaking violently enough to rattle loose fillings.

Sparkle gripped the wheel tightly with both hands as she slalomed through traffic, including a column of RVs. She kept the pedal to the metal until the Explorer had all but disappeared behind them. As she eased off the accelerator, the Citroën filled with the acrid stench of hot oil.

The walrus got deep-fried, Morrison thought, as he righted himself.

Sparkle was so focused on what was behind her, she nearly rear-ended the Little's Winnebago. She stomped the brakes and wrestled the car under control with all the adrenalin-spiked strength she could muster.

A flatbed loaded with scrap metal was chugging slowly uphill beside the motorhome, blocking their escape on the narrow, four-lane highway. Sparkle nimbly whipped the Citroën from side to side, probing for a way around the lumbering behemoths. When she tried passing on the right, the passenger-side tires spun sluggishly on the unpaved shoulder. She cranked the wheel hard and jerked the car behind the RV.

Morrison leaned over and frantically pounded the horn. When Elmo realized they were behind him, he waved his helmet out the window and bounced up and down on his seat, grinning. Sparkle stole another glance in the rearview mirror. The Explorer was back and closing fast.

As they crested the grade, RV inched slowly past the truck. Morrison leaned out the window and waved his arms, trying to get Elmo to pull over. That set off another round of helmet waving and sloppy grins. Sparkle tucked in as tightly as she could behind the Winnebago, slipped through the narrow crease between the Littles and the flatbed, and goosed the accelerator.

Morrison was reaching for the nitrous again when he spotted the SEAL camp. He pointed frantically toward a dirt road that split off from the highway. Humvee and heavy truck tracks wound around a dry wash and up a mesa.

"Turn here," he very nearly shouted.

Morrison might have smelled the camp first if not for the overwhelming stench of dead and now deep-fried walrus. A billowy haze of cannabis smoke hung over the bivouac in the cup-shaped formation of a rocky escarpment. A small inversion layer had formed over the tents like a smoggy day in the LA basin.

The SEALs were giving the expression *holding the high ground* an entirely new meaning.

Geronimo steadied the rocket launcher on his shoulder and fired a warning shot that exploded twenty yards in front of the FBI car. The Explorer was showered with debris as it swerved to avoid the crater but stayed hot on the heels of the Citroën.

"Some people just can't take a hint," he grumbled dryly.

CJ was stretched out on the ground beside him, tracking the feds through the sniper rifle's telescopic sight. "I wonder if large-caliber bullet holes are covered under their tire warranty," she wondered out loud as she squeezed off the perfect shot.

The Explorer was closing on the Citroën as it slowed behind a motorhome and a flatbed truck. As the car crested the hill, it slipped past the RV and accelerated again. Orange maneuvered through the rolling roadblock in time to see the suspect vehicle veer off the highway and onto a dirt road that wound around a mesa.

"We've got 'em now," Newmeat squealed. The rush of adrenaline had momentarily cleared his head. Before Orange could say anything, a section of road in front of them disappeared in a cloud of dust and debris. The shock wave from the blast concussed the car so badly, Orange nearly lost control.

"What the hell was that?" he shrieked. Newmeat didn't answer. His face was the color of curdled milk.

Orange glimpsed a muzzle flash high on the mesa an instant before the right front tire exploded. The Explorer careened off the highway and tore through scraggly stands of yucca and white bursage before plowing to a halt. Newmeat dug his nails so deeply into the upholstery, they gouged holes in the faux leather.

The agents shouldered their doors open, scrambled up a small embankment, and took cover behind a rocky outcrop.

"They're trying to kill us," Newmeat shrieked. He looked like he was calculating a graceful way to check his pants for skitters.

Orange was pretty sure the shooter only intended to disable the car, but before he could prepare his rebuttal, a Javelin missile hissed past them, definitively settling the argument.

As soon as the FBI agents were safely clear of the blast radius, Geronimo steadied the launcher and pressed the trigger.

"Now you see 'em," he said softly, as the missile roared out of the launch tube. There was a high-pitched whine as the motors ignited, and the rocket screamed toward the target. An instant later, the Explorer disappeared in a pillar of fire.

"...and now you don't."

Between the dead lady in the tea garden and whatever happened at the mob boss's villa, Hennigan and most of Metro Homicide had been out all night. Elizabeth was not pleased when he canceled dinner plans, and his it-comes-with-the-shield excuse did not appease her.

Hennigan found out he and Cheezesteak were part of the Multi-Jurisdictional Task Force on Organized Crime when he read it in the *Review-Journal*. Cheezesteak read the same article and phoned twice while Hennigan was in the shower. When he called back, Hennigan asked him to swing by the morgue on his way to the office.

It didn't take a detective to know what "multi-jurisdictional" meant. If anything went right, the FBI would take credit. When everything went wrong, the police department would get blamed.

Hennigan was nearly to Metro Homicide when the lieutenant called. His meeting with the mayor and the undersheriff had wrapped up, and he wanted to be briefed. Hennigan was getting coffee when Dougherty poked his head in the breakroom.

"My office, please." Hennigan followed the lieutenant through the bullpen and sat down across the desk from him. He looked as tired as Hennigan felt.

"Where are we on the Fat Tony investigation? Wild stories are bouncing off the walls, and I'd appreciate having some idea what the hell's going on."

"You and me both." Dougherty's brow furrowed, but he didn't say anything. "We found three dead guys in a car by the gate. Tight clusters head and center mass, typical mob overkill, and the shooters picked up their brass. Whatever happened happened during a pool party, but besides the stiffs in the car, we didn't find any bodies. Soto and Tomlinson are working up a list of possible victims: hookers, the catering staff, Fat Tony, and, we're guessing, a dozen business associates, none of whom are present *or* accounted for."

"So, what the hell happened?"

"I've got no idea. There's no blood evidence or any sign of foul play, nothing but little piles of dental work, belt buckles, lace eyelets, keys, toga clasps, and powdery, gray ash. There's a trail of footprints from the Jacuzzi to the front door and the impression of a Birkenstock sandal, size 11, from a vantage point with a clear view of the villa."

"That doesn't sound like the work of a guy wearing Birkenstocks."

"Probably not, but maybe he saw something."

"Cheeze and I interviewed the housekeeper. She was off yesterday. Oriental rugs from the den, living room, and upstairs bedrooms are missing along with the furniture except for the hardware, a Van Gogh, two Monets, a Picasso, and three paintings on loan from the Vatican."

"Do you think it was some kinda robbery?"

"To tell you the truth, I don't know what to think."

Dougherty rocked forward and rested his elbows on the desk. "The mayor asked if the feds have a secret new weapon for the war on crime. The FBI's been uncharacteristically silent on the matter. I can't tell if they're involved or trying to garner street cred."

His phone rang, and he scowled as he read the caller ID. "Christ, I gotta take this. It's the undersheriff again. I know you've got a lot on your plate but keep me in the loop."

Hennigan nodded as he excused himself and closed the door behind him.

29

Dr. Franklin Wexler, the Clark County coroner, wasn't good with people, at least living ones, but attempted to be cordial whenever he had company. When he saw Cheezesteak walking toward him, he snapped off a latex glove to shake hands. A gaunt, cadaverous man, Wexler was two or three inches taller than the detective with prematurely gray hair, coke-bottle glasses, and a pronounced stoop.

"Hennigan called an hour ago. I'm guessing you're here for an update." He jerked his thumb toward the refrigerated room where bodies were kept. "I'm still catching up. Apparently, it escaped his attention murder's a growth industry around these parts."

Cheezesteak folded his dimpled arms across his chest and leaned against the autopsy table, savoring the coolness of the morgue. "In our line of work, homicides are job security."

Wexler's face was flat and expressionless. He'd developed a high degree of detachment and was immune to the nervous twitter of Las Vegas's finest. To a man, they found the county morgue the perfect stage for their sophomoric humor.

"You want the CliffsNotes or not?"

The detective nodded contritely. He'd come for a favor and had managed to ruffle the odd duck's feathers. Cheezesteak brushed against a furry, black paw poking out of a body bag as he braced himself to stand up.

"Jeez, Doc," he screeched, "you doing chimp autopsies now?"
Wexler's eyes narrowed. "It's a monkey, actually, a black howler, *Alouatta caraya*, and I'm not doing a necropsy. Hennigan asked me to retrieve a bullet."

Wexler tucked the paw inside the bag and jerked the zipper closed. He picked up the x-ray lying on the table and slid it into the lightbox. "The bullet entered here on his right side between the third and fourth ribs and lodged in the muscle beside the left clavicle." He traced the bullet's path to a white, mushroom-shaped object in the monkey's shoulder with his index finger. "Except for grazing costal cartilage, the slug hit soft tissue and appears relatively pristine. I already bagged Mr. Valentine's. If you wait a couple minutes, you can take them both with you."

Cheezesteak hesitated, then nodded. "Sure. I'll run 'em over to ballistics, but first, how about the morning highlights."

"Of course." In his experience, police rarely showed interest in the minutiae of his work. Wexler picked up his clipboard and thumbed through the paperwork until he came to his notes for the tiger mauled body from the Tahitian Princess. Comparing Samson's dental impressions to the victim's bite marks would only confirm the obvious: the tiger killed Mr. Darling and disposed of his body, or at least most of it. The torso was severed mid-thorax, and the right arm chewed off above the elbow, exposing denuded bone. The phrase "massive tissue loss" appeared several times in the findings, which concluded with the cryptic notation "this was no boating accident."

Cheezesteak coughed into his fist. Wexler looked up, owlish behind his thick glasses. "Where to begin," he mumbled softly. He laid out his findings over the next twenty minutes while the detective scribbled notes in his scratchy, cop shorthand.

"So, that's what it's gonna say in your report?" Cheezesteak asked when he finished.

Wexler nodded. "Except for the part about jerky dust. I'm going to play that close to the vest."

Morrison watched as the taxi slowed, veered onto the shoulder, and rolled to a stop. The driver leaned out the window, transfixed by the charred remains of the Explorer. He sank deeper and deeper into the seat until the top of his head was barely visible over the steering wheel.

The younger agent, using his crutch for balance, bunny-hopped to the cab. The older agent held the door while he flopped awkwardly onto the seat, then walked around to the other side and got in. The taxi spewed a cloud of dust as it roared across the median and headed back toward Las Vegas.

Geronimo lowered his binoculars. "They won't be back without serious reinforcements."

"*Serious* reinforcements?" Concern was evident on Morrison's face.

"See the crates under the camouflage netting? It would take an airstrike to root us out, and those are *Star-Trek: The Next Generation* SAMs, enough tactical firepower to turn a few billion dollars of the Air Force's finest into spam in a can. McCullough won't risk a debacle like that on national TV. Besides, while he's focused on Jamaica, we're the least of his concerns."

Morrison's brow furrowed. His only firsthand Washington experience was with the resourceful and determined bunch at the Agency.

The Nellis crew had bulldozed and paved an airfield on the north side of the mesa. The Hitler twins were loading film gear onto the Gulfstream V the SEALs had commandeered along with tanker trucks of fuel. Behind them, the Winnebago caravan rumbled up the dirt road toward camp.

"CJ, radio Mink and tell him to make sure the RVs park in the designated parking area."

"Roger, that."

"And let 'em know the midget contingent will be bunking with them. After they've settled in, have 'em meet us at the range. Speaking of which," he said as he turned toward Morrison, "it's gonna be dark in a couple hours. Ever fire a weapon?"

"I took a basic firearms class at Langley."

Geronimo motioned for him to follow. They walked across camp toward a group of SEALs who had set up a shooting range with paper targets pinned to yuccas. Geronimo unholstered his sidearm and handed it to Morrison. "Let's see what you can do."

315

His HK was smaller and lighter than the Sig Morrison was used to. The bullet ricocheted off a rock a foot wide of the target.

"You shoot like a girl," Geronimo teased. "Bend your knees a little and rotate your front shoulder toward the target. CJ, how about showing him how it's done?"

Cannibal Jane walked to the firing line and squeezed off two quick shots, bulls-eyeing targets on opposite ends of the lineup.

Geronimo grinned. "Regular Annie frigging Oakley, right?"

"Nice shooting," Morrison agreed.

"Trigger, get your ass over here."

She scowled. "Really? I hate doing stupid human tricks."

Geronimo grabbed one of the hand towels he brought to wipe gun oil off the new assault rifles, blindfolded Trigger, and spun her around three times. "Here's a little something we like to call *Pin the Tail on the Peachfish.*"

Trigger slid into a crouch, lower and tighter than CJ's, and pivoted on the balls of her feet. She rotated nearly a full 360 degrees before slowing to a stop with the gun pointed at Geronimo's chest.

"Very funny," he growled.

Trigger nodded curtly, the gesture nearly lost beneath the towel blindfold, wheeled, and put three in the black in three different targets in rapid succession.

"Jeez!" Morrison screeched. "How'd she do that?"

Geronimo shrugged. "Nobody's figured it out, but you can bet she walks point on night ops."

When he saw the Vikings and little Elvises headed toward the makeshift range, Geronimo pried the lid off a crate of M4A1s and started passing them out. Most of the Vikings had traded their usual caps for ones with stitching like *The Chosin Few* and *Pearl Harbor Survivor.*

The Higgins boat driver walked to the firing line, wearing a dark blue cap with *USS Waters* in gold letters. He banged home a magazine with the heel of his fist and squeezed off eight or ten rounds, hitting the target with nearly every shot. The succession of Vikings that followed showed similar skills.

"They'll do fine," Geronimo assured Morrison. "Besides being combat trained, most of them hunt."

"I know. I just wish they weren't going to be in harm's way."

"You wanna tell 'em they can't go?"

"Point taken."

Geronimo pulled Morrison aside and left CJ and Trigger to run the live-fire drill. "We're gonna be in the crosshairs. A Quapaw friend of mine told me not to worry about a bullet with my name on it but said I should watch out for the millions addressed '*To Whom It May Concern.*'"

"Wise words."

"He spent two tours in-country and didn't come home in a body bag. There's wisdom in that."

Morrison started to say something, but CJ interrupted him. "While you boys are sucking face, I'm gonna check on things at base camp. The natives are getting restless."

As she was walking away, Geronimo leaned in close so only Morrison could hear. "I'll leave a couple of my people and you'll have the Nellis crew, but if this goes south, find some big-mouthed media type, make as much noise as you can, and become a very public figure *very* fast.

"Understood."

"Is there somebody you trust?"

"I guess I'll take my best guess if it comes to that."

"Let's hope it doesn't."

There was a faint humming. Geronimo pulled his phone from his pocket and held it to his ear. "Commander Nieto." He listened intently for a moment then snapped the phone shut. "We have an update. Washington's sending weekend warriors, not regular military units."

"Weekend warriors?"

"Reservists. Accountants and barbers on holiday. The bad news is, they've moved the launch window. If we're gonna have boots on the ground when they get to Jamaica, we gotta be wheels-up first thing in the morning. Trigger, get me a forecast."

She retrieved a laptop from her backpack and logged onto an uplink that immediately started streaming data.

"Weather satellite, low earth orbit," Geronimo explained.

Trigger gave him a thumbs up. "Except for a cloudy patch over east Texas, we've got clear skies all the way to Jamaica."

Before Geronimo could raise CJ to let her know they were leaving at o'dark hundred, her voice crackled in his ear. "Commander, we have a situation."

"What's the big emergency?" He could practically hear her grinning through the headset.

"There's a live chicken running around camp. Ishmael told one of the little Elvises, he's gonna chop off its head and drain the blood into a bowl with pennies, cat bones, and a turtle shell. He says it's *very* powerful mojo."

"Where the hell did he get a live chicken?"

"Damned if I know, but the last time I saw him, he was headed to the mess tent for a cleaver."

"Great. I'll be right there. Sounds like we need a sit-down with the GLA high command."

Morrison looked puzzled. "The GLA?"

"The Ganja Liberation Army. Moby's idea. Now, if you'll excuse me, I gotta see a man about a chicken."

Exhausted and struggling to stay focused, Hennigan flipped through Takahara's file, puzzling over how whatever happened to her and whatever happened at Fat Tony's might be related. The more he thought about it, the crazier the scenarios got. He was hip-deep in weirder and weirder possibilities when the phone rang.

"Hennigan, Homicide."

"Cheezesteak, Multi-Jurisdictional Task Force on Organized Crime."

"Funny. So, what'd you find out at the morgue?"

"Harper Valentine, the guy shot dead in the 'I Love Las Vegas' T-shirt, took one through the heart from about eight feet. His bullet matches the ones from the wall and the monkey."

"So, ballistics confirmed what we already suspected."

"Roger, that. Freakenstein's still working on the stiff from the tea garden, but you're not gonna like what he's found so far."

Hennigan sighed. "Let's hear it anyway."

"The bruises on her palms and knuckles are perimortem but don't appear to be defensive. Her ears, nose, and the fingertips on her right hand were gnawed off by scavengers, probably rats. Freakenstein got prints from her left because it was tucked under her body. No hits in AFIS, but she's in Interpol's database. Apparently, her uncle's a major Japanese gangster."

"So, she's Yakuza. Is that her connection to Fat Tony?"

Cheezesteak chuckled. "Spoiler alert. If you skip ahead, you're gonna miss the *good* part."

"Okay, so what's the cause of death?"

"Hypothermia. She froze to death. There's evidence of frostbite on the stubs of her ears, fingers, and nose. Petechial hemorrhaging suggests asphyxiation."

"So, she was choked, alive when she was iced in a freezer, then dumped in the hothouse?"

"Doubtful. There are no indications of manual strangulation. Freakenstein can tell from lividity she died where we found her. Her liver temp was the same as the hothouse's, which doesn't make sense if she died mid-afternoon or later, and she was alive enough early afternoon to rent a car. There's zero decomp, which doesn't fit with liver temp or anything else he used to calculate the time of death."

Hennigan grabbed the Excedrin bottle from his desk drawer, wrestled off the lid, and washed down four caplets with the last of his coffee. "At least some of the other stuff's starting to make sense. Plants in the hothouse showed signs of distress caused by a severe drop in temperature. The heaters kicked on right after the mercury dipped and ran full blast until everything finally warmed up sixteen hours later.

"The building's climate-controlled and a computer logs every time the system cycles on or off. The heaters started huffing hot air at 4:20 yesterday afternoon. The tea garden's metered separately, and the spike in usage matches the log. The only other thing CSI came up with is a jump in CO_2 levels, but they have no idea why. They said there's an internal consistency in the data, whatever that means. Do you think her uncle had something to do with it?"

"Doubtful. When I gave him the we'll-do-everything-we-can-to-bring-the-killer-to-justice speech, he growled only if we found him first."

"Maybe he already did."

"How's that?"

"Her homicide might be related to the one at the Tahitian Princess."

"The guy shot dead in the hallway?"

"No, the tiger snack by the Jacuzzi. The lab says the female DNA on Darling's sheets is Takahara's."

"So, the Yakuza and the Mafia were in bed together."

"And, that's not the twisted part. They're siblings."

"You gotta be kidding me."

"Not just this once. Darling and Takahara were brother and sister." Hennigan massaged his temples between his thumb and forefingers. His headache was getting worse. "How about Fat Tony's place? Does Freakenstein have any idea what happened?"

Cheezesteak chuckled. "There's a reason I saved the best for last. May I have a drum roll, please?"

Hennigan put his feet up on the desk. His partner was having way too much fun.

"His report won't identify the gray ash, but, off the record, Freakenstein compared the residue to freeze-dried jerky dust."

"Freeze-dried jerky dust?"

"*Off the record.* I could smell bologna sandwich on his breath when he leaned in and whispered, I didn't hear it from him."

Hennigan puzzled over that for a moment. "You thinking what I'm thinking?"

"That the gray powder's Fat Tony and friends?"

"That's real *National Enquirer* stuff."

"Well, you didn't hear it from me." Cheezesteak was still chuckling when he hung up the phone.

Hennigan shook the last two Excedrin out of the bottle, swallowed them dry, and wondered how the DA would explain freeze-dried jerky dust to a grand jury. Silver fillings, a partial bridge, and a crown swept up in a dustpan would be a new twist on identifying somebody from their dental records.

If Fat Tony got that literal about the dust-to-dust thing, he probably had help. Hennigan flipped through the file again, pausing at the photograph of the Birkenstock shoe print. Maybe if Elvis had worn blue-suede shoes, it would have been a better clue.

As Morrison and Sparkle crossed the open space between the mess tent and theirs, he took her hand. They'd stayed after dinner to review operational details with the SEALs. The moon wasn't up yet, and this far from the city lights, the night sky looked like a velvety blanket of stars.

"You have to admire Geronimo's willingness to refer to a Jamaican steel drum band, a senior citizen RV club, and a dozen midget Elvises as *our men* with a straight face."

Sparkle shrugged. "He's just working with what he's got."

"I guess, but do you think they could stop calling me, *sir*?"

"What I think is, you've milked the reluctant hero thing dry. What did Elmo say about right's right and wrong's wrong and all we have to do is choose sides? It's *always* simple. It's just not easy."

"Right from wrong? I love that old coot, but I'm not sure he can tell right from left." Morrison hesitated when he heard footsteps shuffling along the gravel path toward them.

"That's me, sharp as a marble," Elmo said, grinning. He was wearing a Kevlar vest and his Viking helmet.

"No, offense," Morrison stammered. "It's just that..."

Elmo held up his hand, palm forward. "None taken. The good news is if I'm captured and tortured, bamboo stakes under the fingernails and all that, I'd be hard-pressed to remember my name, much less rank and serial number."

"Let's hope it doesn't come to that." Morrison sighed. "I feel badly dragging you into this."

"Don't. None of us are conscripts. We're volunteers, perfectly capable of making our own mistakes." Elmo sensed Morrison was on the verge of a 'yes, but.' "Every man who stepped forward loves this country and has always done what needed to be done. Nobody comes home from war as good as they left, and some don't come home at all. We learned that lesson a long time ago. None of us were raised on movie wars. We don't talk about it much, even amongst ourselves, but we've seen war up close and personal." Elmo grinned. "Besides, this is the most excitement I've had in years."

Sparkle gave him a hug. "You do seem a little more on your game."

Elmo chuckled. "Gingerly put. Apparently, it hasn't occurred to either of you after being happily married for fifty years, a little senility might be a survival skill." Morrison and Sparkle looked at each other and laughed. "Well, I'd better be going before Mother sends out a search party."

As he turned to walk away, Morrison remembered something Elmo had said earlier. "You told Geronimo you flew a Hellcat."

Elmo shook his head. "Helldiver, a two-man plane. I was a radio

operator and gunner. Ace of Spades squadron. Hellcats are fighters."
Elmo stared absentmindedly at nothing in particular. "That's the
funny thing about getting old. I remember stuff that happened half a
century ago like it was yesterday, but stuff that happened yesterday,
I can't remember worth a damn. I really am as sharp as a marble."

"I think my dad flew a Hellcat."

Elmo grinned. "Yes, I know, son. He was one helluva pilot.
Now, if you'll excuse me, I gotta get some rest. Big day tomorrow."

30

Verduci mustered all the tactical acumen he'd accumulated during late-night games of Risk with the president and spent nearly an hour planning the Jamaica mission. He used intelligence sourced from travel brochures and a well-thumbed issue of *National Geographic*.

The biggest logistical challenge turned out to be getting Reserve and National Guard units onto the island. Constrained by time and McCullough's dictate not to use regular military resources, he scrapped his original plan to bring two Pacific Fleet carrier groups through the Panama Canal to rendezvous with one from the Mediterranean and one from the Persian Gulf. McCullough suggested such a maneuver would be "too high profile."

Undeterred, Verduci re-envisioned the landing as a two-pronged naval assault that would launch simultaneously from Guantanamo Bay and Port-au-Prince before coming together in a massive jet-ski flotilla. As wave after wave came ashore, combat photographers could record the moment in images as iconic as the flag-raising on Iwo Jima. Verduci pictured himself straddling a Sea-Doo on the front page of every paper in the country until Jaysen pointed out a three-hundred-mile trek across open ocean exceeded the range of personal watercraft.

Verduci reluctantly settled on a plan with less dramatic flair. He called Kitty Sheehan, White House travel director, and had her book commercial flights for the bulk of the expeditionary force. Arrivals were spread over the island's three international airports. Unwilling to give up the idea of a Sea-Doo photo op entirely, Verduci had her arrange for buses to shuttle troops to tourist beaches where they could rent jet-skis for the final leg to the rendezvous point.

The launching pad for "the tip of the spear," as Verduci referred to the advance team in briefings, was a remote hanger at Homestead Air Reserve Base near Miami. He and Jaysen arrived at the staging area two hours late after stuffing themselves with jerk squab and pigeon pea risotto at a James Beard nominee's Palm Beach bistro. They fortified their resolve on the drive over with a second bottle of Cristal and had to be loaded into one of the waiting helicopters like cheap Louis Vuitton knock-offs.

Oblivious to the grumbling around them, Verduci and Jaysen slumped in side-by-side seats, belted into place by a gruff sergeant major in the North Dakota Army National Guard for the six-hundred-mile flight. Three dozen weekend warriors from Petaluma, the mission photographers, and a mountain of equipment, including eight camouflaged coolers of Bud Light, squeezed into the other five Black Hawks.

The advance team's objective was to establish a base of operations along an undeveloped stretch of beach near Portmore, but they couldn't stick the landing without a casualty. PFC Ogden Stash, a stoner in the California National Guard, was surfing the helicopter door just before touchdown when the pilot, bucking a slight headwind, banked hard right as he was circling to land. "Cowabunga," as Stash was known to family and friends, pitched forward, fell twenty feet, and snapped his right tibia.

While the field hospital and command tents were erected and medics tended Private Stash, Verduci insisted on being photographed slogging ashore wearing aviator sunglasses and smoking a corncob pipe. Pummeled by waves, he lost his balance and fell backward. If the photographer hadn't grabbed him by the ankle, Verduci would have been swept out to sea and drowned.

Other phases of the invasion plan were going badly as well. Officers and NCOs were supposed to arrive early on an Air Jamaica flight forced to land in Key West. The closest they got to Kingston was lounging in the airport bar while the ground crew replaced a cockpit window cracked in a collision with a particularly hardheaded brown pelican. Leaderless groups of men were left to wander around the Jamaican airports. A few exchanged their tickets for earlier returns and found a quiet place to nap until their flights were called.

Others loitered on the curb, waiting for a shuttle. The few buses that actually showed up left less than a third full. Many of the men who made it to a beach shifted their primary mission objective to finding a shady spot to hydrate at one of the palm-thatched bars.

The few soldiers sober and resourceful enough to rent jet skis either ran out of gas or suffered mechanical breakdowns before they got very far. Two Kansas National Guardsmen suffered mild concussions when a drunken game of Waverunner chicken went horribly wrong.

A group of Georgia reservists had to be rescued by the Jamaican Defense Force Coast Guard. They were found with their jet skis lashed together, passing a bottle of Bacardi 151 and drifting steadily northward toward Cuba. When one of the Jamaican crew asked where they were going, a drunken lance corporal from Attapulgus pumped his fist in the air like a Super Bowl winning quarterback and shouted, "I'm going to *Disneyworld!*"

He roared off on a lemon-yellow Sea-Doo with the throttle wide open, spraying a foamy rooster tail in his wake. The *Manatee Bay* captain watched from the pilothouse as the trooper carved manic figure eights a hundred yards off the stern until he ran out of gas.

At the staging area near Portmore, the point of the spear was playing beach volleyball and frolicking in the surf while "awaiting further orders." Jaysen's official designation was mission observer, but the only thing he'd observed was the back of his eyelids. After consuming several canteens of a Meyer's and tropical fruit juice concoction, he passed out in a camouflage netting hammock stretched between two palm trees.

The Ganja Liberation Army met zero resistance. The guardsmen, appearing more bored than defeated, were quietly rounded up and disarmed without incident. Trigger and Elmo and the Vikings guarded the POWs while the rest of the GLA advanced on the command tent.

Being useless, there was nothing for Verduci to do. Stoked to the gills on Dramamine and scotch, he was strutting stiffly back and forth like a plump turkey the week before Thanksgiving. The dry cleaners put too much starch in his fatigues and his thighs were starting to chafe. The only US personnel in shouting distance were two half-brothers from Rabbit Hash, Kentucky posted outside. Mindful of fragging stories he heard in Vietnam, Verduci had confiscated their weapons.

Oblivious to the sudden turn of events, he was pouring himself another drink when Cannibal Jane and the Hitler twins barged in and started setting up lights. CJ pressed a finger to her lips, signaling him to hush. Verduci was shaking so badly, he spilled most of his scotch. When the twins finished with the lighting, Virgil grabbed the camera and Be-Bop the boom mic and signaled they were ready.

Moby made a dramatic entrance looking like he was dressed for a reggae *Sgt. Pepper's* album cover shoot. He was wearing a green silk tunic with a yellow sash and gold epaulets, a red cape, and baggy, purple parachute pants. He closed the distance between himself and Verduci in three quick strides, tucked his swagger stick under his arm, and snapped off a crisp salute.

"General Dix, Ganja Liberation Army, and this is my staff." Moby made a sweeping gesture toward the Ahab brothers, the little Elvises, and Geronimo, who had filed in behind him.

"W-w-what do you want?" Verduci stammered, trying to recall his rank and serial number. He was staring at the midgets who were holding automatic weapons taller than they were when he caught a whiff of patchouli oil and felt an invisible finger poke him in the chest. He nearly jumped out of his camouflaged skivvies.

"I bet you're surprised to see me again," said a disembodied voice. Too terrified to answer, Verduci stood frozen in place. He was staring at a wiry black man with a smoldering wreath encircling his head. Ishmael had woven black-tar wicks into his dreadlocks and set them on fire.

Moby tapped Verduci's chin with his swagger stick. Fixated on Ishmael, Verduci waved his hand dismissively as if shooing a pesky fly. Moby swatted him, this time on the cheek, to get his attention.

"That hurt," Verduci whimpered softly. His eyes were wet with tears.

"This is Pilot-Liaison Nieto," Moby said, introducing the SEAL commander. "He'll be supervising your interview." Geronimo rested his .45 on the bridge of Verduci's nose.

He swallowed hard. "But, but…"

"No, this is the barrel, and that's the butt." Geronimo angled his sidearm so Verduci could see the grip. When Verduci opened his mouth to say something, Geronimo shoved the muzzle in deep enough to gag Linda Lovelace. The chatter of his teeth against the barrel was audible. "Are we ready to move on from basic firearms?"

Verduci nodded, trying not to gag again.

"Good. A word of warning, I'm structured and inflexible. Comes from being toilet trained at gunpoint, a lesson you may have to relearn." Verduci was standing in a puddle of his own urine. One of the midgets said something, and a chorus of snickers erupted behind Geronimo. "This test will not be graded on a curve. No points will be awarded for partially correct answers. Get one wrong, and you won't be moving on to the bonus round. Are we clear?"

Verduci nodded again.

"Do you swear to tell the truth, the whole truth, and nothing but the truth, so help you Smith and Wesson?"

"I do," Verduci croaked weakly.

Geronimo stepped aside, his aim centered on a spot between Verduci's eyes. His arm and the .45 would not have been steadier if they were carved from a single block of stone. Honey stepped forward and nodded to Virgil she was ready as he counted down to zero.

Verduci droned on longer than an Academy Awards acceptance speech. He was rambling and incoherent, and she made him backtrack several times. She dogged him with questions and made sure he included details about the president and McCullough. Piece-by-piece, he spilled the plan to draft dope-smoking Rastafarians into an invisible army. After thirty minutes, he started to repeat himself.

When Honey decided he'd given up everything he had to give, she looked at Virgil, who flashed a thumbs up.

"Don't think of this as retreating," Geronimo said as he turned Verduci by the shoulders and pointed him toward the tent flap. "If anybody asks, you're attacking at a hundred and eighty-degree angle." Another chorus of snickers erupted behind him.

Verduci didn't have to be told twice. He scurried out of the tent and sprinted two hundred yards to the Black Hawks as fast as his chubby legs would carry him. Trigger released the captured reservists who joined him in a sprint up the beach. Moby and the GLA high command took up a position on a sandy hillock and watched the frantic crush of men piling into helicopters.

Morrison was with Elvis in the mess tent watching *I Love Lucy* and trying not to fidget. Geronimo had called to say the Jamaica leg went down by the numbers, but he was still as skittish as a bowl of ice in a microwave.

"Any idea where Digby might be?" he asked when the station broke for a commercial.

"He overheard CJ say how cool it would be to fly around in Wonder Woman's invisible jet and asked to borrow my computer. I think he's in the Littles' RV designing a cloaking device."

Elvis picked up the remote and switched to CNN as regular programming was interrupted for a Special Report. The screen filled with images of the packed White House pressroom as President McDannold stepped to the microphone.

"My fellow Americans. Today US forces undertook a top-secret mission to the critically strategic island of Jamaica, a crucial first line of defense for the precious freedoms we hold so dear." The president paused to make eye contact with a few of the more sympathetic members of the White House press corps.

"The scope and objectives of the mission are classified, and, as a matter of national security, I cannot discuss them without putting those in the service of our great and grateful nation at risk. But I can tell you, I have personally talked with the mission commander, and he told me our heroes are coming home after accomplishing all of our objectives without any civilian casualties or the loss of a single American life."

The president grinned his toothy smile, clasped his hands together, and shook them triumphantly over his head. There was a smattering of applause from a few shills in the audience. The rest of the White House press corps just sat there looking bored.

"God bless the United States of America," he shouted as he pumped his fist in the air.

A horde of secret service agents swarmed in and hustled him off the podium, suggesting the briefing was over and that the president would not be taking any questions.

Geronimo skimmed the Gulfstream along Florida's Atlantic coast all the way to Georgia. Honey and the Hitler twins set up a workspace in the back where they feverishly edited the Verduci footage into a tight news piece. The rest of the Ganja Liberation Army was huddled around the cabin TV, watching the president's press briefing when Geronimo's voice boomed over the intercom.

"Ladies and Gentlemen, this is your captain. We're on final approach. Please fasten your seatbelts and return your stewardesses to the upright and locked position. And thank you for flying Ganja Airlines."

Verduci leaned into the mirror and admired the puffy, red mouse under his eye. He got it heaving into his helmet when the chopper hit a patch of turbulence. Jaysen also made the casualty list. He chipped a nail climbing into the helicopter during their extraction. By the time they got home, Jaysen was in such a snit, he shut himself in the closet and threatened to stay there until the nail grew back.

Verduci poured another scotch and sat down to watch the news. He wrote the president's brief before leaving for Jamaica and was confident it would play well in Peoria. McDannold looked presidential. If nothing else, he was well cast.

Like any cornered animal, Verduci continued to calculate his options. With his keen grasp of the obvious, he knew to shift blame, dodge responsibility, and identify a fall guy in case the whole enchilada unraveled. He settled on Abrams McCullough.

Verduci switched off the TV before the Ganja News Network segment and had no idea how far behind the power curve he really was. The McDannold presidency was hurtling toward Earth at terminal velocity and, unless the political equivalent of Newton's Law of Gravity was repealed, was going to Humpty Dumpty all over Main Street. He poured himself another scotch, still spinning contingency plans for poking pudgy fingers in a dike that was already gushing torrents.

The president watched Verduci's Jamaica interview alone in bed. He finished his hot chocolate and Oreos before turning off the TV. The bulb had burned out in the Snow White lamp on his nightstand. Backlit by the nightlight, the Dwarves looked sad and tired. The president patted Dopey on the head. It certainly had been that kind of evening. He punched the pillow twice to get it just right, rolled over on his side, and closed his eyes. Five minutes later, when the cat jumped on the bed and curled up beside him, McDannold was already fast asleep.

If you were one of the millions of Americans watching CNN the next morning when the second Ganja News segment aired, you'd have seen a squat, middle-aged man in spiky, high-heels and too much lipstick, handcuffed to a four-poster bed. Wiry tufts of salt-and-pepper hair poked out around the edges of his black teddy. The leather-clad dominatrix sitting beside him was smoking a cigarette and waving a leather cat-o-nines as if fanning herself.

McCullough was screaming into the phone. You could tell he hated it when Verduci whined.

"You and McDannold screwed the pooch on this one, and you're *not* dragging me down with you. You two could mess up a wet dream."

McCullough had prospered because he lived by one simple rule: don't be the only one without a chair when the music stopped. But this time, when the fat lady quit singing, there would be a chronic shortage of everything except standing room only.

31

An hour after the Ganja News Network segment aired, a nondescript man walked into the mess tent and delivered a package to Morrison. His name was printed on the outside in black copperplate. Morrison recognized Hawkings' handwriting and his handiwork. He watched a few minutes of McCullough with the dominatrix, slid the video back in the envelope, and met the Gulfstream when it landed. As soon as the tanks were full, the flight and film crews were airborne again, headed back to Atlanta.

At home in Falls Church, Carver Hawkings glanced out the window at his wife's Volvo. *It's a really safe car,* she was fond of saying. He knew what that meant. Saying a car was safe was like saying a blind date had a great personality.

Hawkings had been in the spook business a long time. In his fifty-odd years with military intelligence and the CIA, he'd worked for a lot of weird birds, but the current bunch was the most peculiar. McCullough's behavior was particularly baffling. If his intention was plausible deniability, cross-dressing with a hooker seemed like an odd alibi.

He grabbed the remote and switched off the TV. The second Ganja News piece turned out even better than expected. The boys had done a great job editing, and the girl was a natural-born anchorwoman. Hawkings checked the time. It was getting late. He was thinking about taking the rest of the night off.

The feds stopped at Hennigan's desk on their way to the lieutenant's office. Newmeat balanced precariously on his crutches so he and the detective could shake hands. Doped up on painkillers, his grip felt like overcooked linguini.

Dougherty shut and locked the door behind them and closed the blinds. Hennigan could still hear bits and pieces of the conversation. They were tossing the Cleopatra hot potato back and forth. If she was alive, everybody would've screamed for jurisdiction. Since she was dead, nobody wanted her. Hennigan was mulling over the irony when the phone rang.

"Metro Homicide."

"You have to find my son," a woman shrieked.

Hennigan sat up straighter in his chair. "How old is he?"

"Thirty-three."

Hennigan stopped rummaging through his desk clutter for a pen and paper. The call should have been routed to Missing Persons anyway, not that they'd drop everything to look for a guy too busy with slots or strippers to call his mom.

"When did you last hear from him?"

"Yesterday. He's staying downtown but isn't answering his phone. When I called the hotel, nobody would tell me anything."

Hennigan was flipping through his Rolodex when a darker possibility occurred to him. "What's your son's name?" She must have heard something in his voice because she hesitated. "Ma'am?" he asked, not sure she was still on the line.

"Valentine. Harper Simpson Valentine."

Hennigan took a deep breath, steeling the resolve he'd called on too often during his years in Metro Homicide. "Mrs. Valentine, I'm afraid I have some terrible news for you."

Early the next morning, the Littles stopped by the Chapel d'Love. Sparkle and Morrison met them curbside for a last round of hugs. Gladys climbed the steps to the RV, settled into the passenger seat, and strapped on her seatbelt. As she was waving goodbye, she dabbed her eyes with a tissue. Elmo rolled down his window and adjusted the rearview mirror.

"We got a great grandbaby due next week, so Mother and I are gonna skedaddle before the blubbering starts."

Morrison reached up and shook his hand. "Thanks for everything."

"Wouldn't have missed it for the world." With one last wave of his horned helmet, Elmo pulled away from the curb.

By the time the Disneyland-bound caravan assembled in front of the Chapel d'Love, it was already mid-afternoon. Sparkle and Morrison used volunteering to stay and run the business as an excuse to beg off the Magic Kingdom trip. Morrison wasn't anxious to rediscover his celebrity status as a wedding mill minister and was relieved when Atlas agreed to perform the ceremonies. Besides having the schtick down, it was a big plus he came with his own outfits.

The Hitler twins were already in the back seat when Elvis stowed his bag in the Citroën's trunk. "I've given some thought to what you said about my second coming inspiring religious fervor," he told Morrison. "The problem is, people resist change, and we have a long and troubling history of shooting the messenger."

"Or nailing them to a cross."

"Not an attractive alternative. For now, I'm happy just being a face in the crowd."

"…at Disneyland," Morrison teased. Their handshake dissolved into a hug. "Next time you plan a middle-aged children's crusade, count me in."

"You're at the top of my shortlist," Elvis grinned. They shook hands again, and he climbed into the passenger seat beside Digby.

By the time Morrison caught up with Sparkle, she and Honey were hugging goodbye. He stood behind them looking uncomfortable.

"How about if you two just ease into things?" Sparkle suggested.

Morrison looked at Honey and smiled. "How about we give that a try that when you get back?"

"I'd like that." When she hugged him, Honey kissed him on the cheek, then climbed into the first Hummer.

As Morrison glanced over his shoulder at the Citroën, Sparkle squeezed his hand. "Apparently, you haven't noticed the growing mutual attraction between the SEAL commander and our daughter."

Before Morrison could say anything, Geronimo appeared beside him, snapped to attention, and saluted. "I meant what I said, sir, about kicking down the gates of Hell and warring on the Devil with sticks and stones for you."

Morrison smiled. "Glad it didn't come to that. In the meantime, you can ease off the *sir* stuff. The militia's disbanded, and I'm a private citizen again."

"Gonna be one of those old soldiers who just fades away?"

"Hopefully." Morrison appraised him for a moment. "Your grandfather would be proud of you."

"He *is* proud -- of both of us."

CJ leaned out the driver's side window of the second Hummer. "If you boys are done sucking face, we're burning daylight."

Geronimo jerked his thumb her direction. "Duty calls."

Her chin resting on his shoulder, Sparkle and Morrison watched the caravan disappear around the corner. Morrison took her hand, and they strolled up the sidewalk, following Jaxx through the big, double doors of the Chapel d'Love.

That night, the old shaman came to Morrison in a dream, thanked him, and told him *goodbye*.

Epilogue

Ronald McDannold skipped the news frenzy prompted by his resignation and was watching cartoons in the Oval Office when he was served divorce papers. Six and a half months later when their divorce was final, his ex-wife eloped with Emmett Washburn, one of the secret service agents on her protection detail. They were married in Vegas by a midget Elvis impersonator.

The morning after the Ganja News Network tapes aired, attorneys for Abrams McCullough released a brief statement saying he was "a simple soldier who did his duty to God and country" without acknowledging he sometimes did his duty in lady's lingerie. A few days after Thanksgiving, McCullough turned in his stars and accepted a position with Weldon-Crapper, a Flushing, Ohio manufacturer developing waterless toilets for the space program. In April, he died in what *The Washington Post* characterized as "a tragic plumbing accident." While demonstrating a prototype for members of the House Appropriations Committee, he dropped his drawers in an over-the-top display of salesmanship. His flabby butt, honed by decades of sitting behind a desk, made a perfect seal. The toilet's vacuum pump ruptured his hemorrhoids and sucked out a gallon of blood. He was buried at Arlington with full military honors.

Carmine Verduci pleaded *nolo contendere* to bribery and tax evasion charges and was sentenced to six years in federal prison. He's writing a thinly-veiled fictional account about the perils of power in the Oval Office with his cellmate, Leon "Oz Dog" Willis, a twenty-two-year-old from Compton doing a stretch for bank robbery and a drive-by shooting. A film crew for a proposed documentary, *Behind Bars*, shot a series of interviews with the aspiring authors. The project was scrapped when the footage developed an out-of-sync feel after the editor voiced over Oz Dog's repeated references to Carmine as "my wife."

Jaysen Rush cashed the winning card in his fraternity's Bingo pool the afternoon Verduci was indicted. He splurged on twenty-two pairs of red-soled stilettos at Louboutin's Paris shoe salon and used the rest to underwrite a Milan showing for his new love interest, designer Ecco Puzzi. The line, featuring puffy silk shirts and quilted parachute pants, was inspired by a *Seinfeld* episode.

Bobby Ray Darling's tiger-gnawed remains were interred at Brooklyn's Our Lady of the Immaculate Conception Cemetery in an open-casket service during a light but persistent drizzle. FBI surveillance teams outnumbered mourners by more than three to one.

The coroner's office cremated Cleopatra Takahara's remains per her uncle's request. That she was still wearing her ben-wa balls was not disclosed to the funeral director. Clark County and the mortuary are in litigation over *alleged* damages to the crematorium.

Cosmo, the prodigal cat, cut short his *Endless Summer* tour through French Polynesia to manage Elvis's progressive-jackpot winnings. Sometimes his directions are vague. That's the problem with burning bushes and their ilk -- they can be maddeningly fuzzy about details. A cynic might argue it has something to do with free will.

Made in the USA
Las Vegas, NV
26 April 2022

48052019R00187